PUSHKIN

'From the tenements of London's Jewish East End, to the lush costumes of the slowly declining Ottoman Empire, Goldin brings a long-lost era to life in vivid, evocative detail'
Financial Times

'A zip-along plot, packed full of political machinations, strange deaths and ruinous romance'
Daily Mail

'Entertaining... the writing is as colourful and bouncy as Ben's character'
Literary Review

A.E. GOLDIN is a British writer and musician. He read English at Trinity College, Cambridge and studied classical piano at the Royal Academy of Music. He works as a screenwriter for television companies in London and Los Angeles. *Murder in Constantinople* is his debut novel. He lives in London.

MURDER IN CONSTANTINOPLE

A.E. GOLDIN

PUSHKIN VERTIGO

Pushkin Press
Somerset House, Strand
London WC2R 1LA

Copyright © Aron Eliezer Goldin 2024

Murder in Constantinople was first published by Pushkin Vertigo in 2024
This paperback edition published in 2025

The right of A.E. Goldin to be identified as the author of this Work has been asserted by him in accordance with the Copyright, Designs & Patents Act 1988

ISBN 13: 978-1-78227-919-8

All rights reserved. No part of this publication may be reproduced, stored in a retrieval system or transmitted in any form or by any means, electronic, mechanical, photocopying, recording or otherwise, or for the purpose of training artificial intelligence technologies or systems without prior permission in writing from Pushkin Press

A CIP catalogue record for this title is available from the British Library

The authorised representative in the EEA is
eucomply OÜ, Pärnu mnt. 139b-14, 11317, Tallinn, Estonia,
hello@eucompliancepartner.com, +33757690241

Designed and typeset by Tetragon, London
Printed and bound in the United Kingdom by Clays Ltd, Elcograf S.p.A.

Pushkin Press is committed to a sustainable future for our business, our readers and our planet. This book is made from paper from forests that support responsible forestry.

www.pushkinpress.com

1 3 5 7 9 8 6 4 2

Contents

Map		viii
Prologue		1
1	Canaan & Sons	3
2	An Incident at Claridge's	13
3	Two Daguerreotypes	33
4	The Girl from Paris	44
5	Fugitive from the Law	54
6	Lennie and the Dogs	67
7	The HMS *Midas*	78
8	Shabbat at the Ahrida	91
9	The Interrogation	106
10	The Greek Prince	120
11	Rendezvous at the Morgue	129
12	The White Death	137
13	A Risky Game	145
14	The Madwoman in the Mountain	158
15	The Sultan's Harem	171
16	Portrait of a Chameleon	187
17	Needle in a Haystack	203
18	The Scorpion's Kiss	214
19	The Lost Queen of Poland	227

20	Baccarat at the Pierrot	236
21	An Immodest Proposal	246
22	The Tannhaüser Overture	259
23	Death at Dolmabahçe	275
24	Ms Nightingale's Patient	286
25	The British Ambassador	299
26	The Third Section	309
27	A Brush with History	316
28	An Interview at No. 10	326

Epilogue 335

Not I, not any one else can travel that road for you,
You must travel it for yourself.

— WALT WHITMAN, *Leaves of Grass* (1855)

Dolmabahçe Palace

PERA

Hôtel Pierrot

Mavros Estate

Kuzguncuk

SCUTARI

BOSPORUS

Selimiye Barracks

TOPKAPI PALACE

HAGIA SOPHIA

Belgrad Forest

BEYKOZ

Carmino Estate

New Crimea

SEA of MARMARA

Büyükada

Prologue

As soon as she saw him, she knew that she was going to die.

She had not noticed him at first. She was too focused on getting away. It was only once she had stepped from the jetty onto the sailboat and cast off that she caught sight of his face.

He was sitting beneath the boom, wrapped in a cloak, hands gloved – staring at her in the darkness that shrouded the waterfront.

Her heart jabbed in her chest. She knew that look.

'Go on,' he said, in a gentle voice. 'Don't let me interrupt you.'

She scanned the waterfront one last time. They were alone. Moored *kayiks* and cutters creaked in the tide. Firelight smouldered on the skyline across the Strait, tracing the contours of rutted rooftops and towering spires. She tasted the air: burnt dust, salt, softened by a cool night-breeze.

'How did you know?' she asked.

He shook his head. 'Don't make this harder than it has to be.'

He took the tiller from her and guided the boat onto the open waters of the Bosporus. The lights of Constantinople drifted away. Now the moon was their only beacon, shining through a thin sheen of cloud-cover.

'It's a nice boat,' he said, patting the deck. 'You could have sailed far.'

'Why don't we sail together? We can disappear.'

He raised a hand to silence her. 'I have no choice. The decision was unanimous. You knew what you were doing when you went to Heathcote.'

He was right. The die had been cast. Tears formed in her eyes.

'Give me a moment, please.'

She listened to the faint ticking of his pocket-watch. She took a deep breath, trying to remember every sensation: the churning waters, the crisp air, the singing of the nightjars. Then a sinking feeling – the life ahead of her that she had wanted to live, that she would never live.

'I'm sorry,' he finally said. 'There's never enough time to say goodbye.'

He donned the mask, obscuring all but his grey eyes. It suddenly struck her that she had never considered what it felt like. Was it painful? Or was it as peaceful as falling asleep? She closed her eyes and a murmured name escaped her lips—

'Ben—'

It was the last thing she said.

1
Canaan & Sons

It was Friday night in London's Jewish East End. Across four miles, from Cheapside to Blackwall, the bells of St Mary-le-Bow were ringing. As the city sweltered in the evening smog of high summer, the East End began to close up shop.

Young *yeshiva bochers* migrated to synagogue in black-clothed droves, released from rabbinical study to bring in the Sabbath. A frenzied whistle stabbed the air as the last omnibus left Whitechapel. Fruit-hawkers and florists loaded up donkey-drawn wagons with pears and peonies and the market squares gradually emptied. Meanwhile, the pubs were filling up with day-labourers, chimneysweeps and men of the docks, knocking back the first of many pints as twilight congealed in a thick haze at the window.

Teetering over Whitechapel Road – that squalid thoroughfare of jewellers, sponging houses and struggling artisans – was a narrow three-storey house. It perched precariously above a tailor's, where a sign was hanging: *Canaan & Sons*.

From the outside, it looked unremarkable. Just another worse-for-wear abode belonging to some humble craftsman and his small family enterprise. But inside was a different story: a home bursting with the benign chaos peculiar to Jewish households on the Sabbath eve.

Tonight, one question was on everyone's lips. A familiar question, but no less urgent: *Where's Benjy?*

It echoed up and down the house. From the dusty workshop in the basement – cluttered with half-made suits, mottled mirrors, treadles and needles, bobbins and fabrics – up to the shuttered shop on the ground floor. Through the kitchen swirling with steam and the scent of chicken broth, where the matriarch Ruth was cooking up a storm. Then up the rickety stairs lined with miniature watercolours from the Bethnal Green flea market. And finally, to the very top of the house: that mysterious attic-room which nobody but the absent Benjy was permitted to enter.

Grandfather Tuvia sat in a leather armchair in the living room: his fireside throne. He was an odd-looking fellow – short and stooped, with an unusually full head of white hair. Strangest of all was the pinkish scar that ran along his chin, just under his lower lip, which was curled into a smile as he sucked on a pipe and squinted at the *Jewish Chronicle* through thick spectacles. Next to him was his wife of fifty years: Hesya, deftly knitting a scarf without so much as looking at her fingers.

'That boy will be the death of us, lovie,' she intoned mournfully, in Yiddish.

'Speaking of death,' Tuvia replied, 'guess who's pushing up daisies.'

'Who?'

'Rudolph Zemmler.'

Hesya set down her knitting. '*Rudolph Zemmler?* But he was in such good health! He swam fifty laps of the baths at Goulston Square every Sunday. How did he die?'

'Heart attack,' Tuvia tutted. 'Forty-ninth lap.'

'What a brilliant man!' Hesya sighed dreamily. 'And a *mensch* to boot. He looked after himself. Not like you with your smoking.'

'"He looked after himself"? He's dead!' Tuvia barked – then, in an apologetic undertone, 'May God rest his soul.'

'You're just jealous because he was tailoring for Cabinet ministers while you were out hawking *schmutters* to *yidden* fresh off the boats!'

Tuvia shook his head. 'Rudolph Zemmler was like all those Viennese types: looking down his nose at us Litvaks. What's more, he was a chancer. Like when he never showed up for my seventieth – "sick with scarlet fever" – but was sitting on his *tokhes* at the races the very next day!' Tuvia puffed on his pipe in indignation, then convulsed in a fit of coughing. He was feeling a little sorry for himself. 'Pah! Next it will be me.'

Hesya took her husband by the hand. 'May you live to a hundred and twenty, my love,' she said, pecking him on the lips.

'Bobba! Zeyde! You'll get the flu!' A waif of a girl, no more than six, was standing in the doorway, hands on her cheeks in an expression of utter shock.

'Nonsense, Golda,' Tuvia said merrily. 'Kissing is the cure!'

Golda took a few cautious steps towards her grandparents, twirling her black locks. 'Mama's asking if you've seen Benjy…'

'Benjy, Benjy!' Tuvia cried, 'How could I see Benjy when I'm marinating like a pickled onion in this *farshtinkener* chair?'

Ruth appeared behind Golda, red-cheeked and flustered, wiping chicken fat onto her apron. 'Papa, have you seen Benjy?'

'Why would you send the child if you were going to ask me yourself?!'

'Why do you always answer a question with a question?'

'*I haven't seen Benjy!* Now leave me alone! Can a man not read his newspaper, *Erev Shabbos*, without interruption?'

Ruth retreated to the kitchen to finish dinner before her father launched into another one of his tirades. A bespectacled eleven-year-old boy was sitting at the kitchen table, sipping chicken broth as he pored over a notebook filled with numerical scribblings.

'Max!' she shouted, and the boy jumped out of his skin, 'I told you to go find your brother!'

'But Mama, I'm looking for a way to help Papa reduce his expenditure! Anyway, Benjy is always late and evidently not home.'

'Don't give me lip. "Evidently"! For all we know he's already snuck in and is hiding in that den upstairs. Why don't you make yourself useful and go check?'

Max traipsed off. Benjy causing problems again! Did they not realise that Max was cracking something infinitely more important than his delinquent older brother? Nobody dared talk openly about it, but the business was in dire straits: running at a loss, with expenses mounting and turnover dwindling. For the past week, Max had devoted himself to tallying up the costs of fabrics – cashmere, cotton and crêpe, tweed, twill and toile – and coming up with a plan to economise.

His theory went like this. Currently, his father was buying overpriced muslin and fine calico by the pound from those miserly Ganguly brothers in Spitalfields. Max calculated that it would be more efficient to buy cheaper fabric in bulk from the wholesalers up in Dalston. His father objected that this would compromise the quality of their garments.

But Max had seen the kind of business those slopsellers were attracting – the ones making enough money to leave

Whitechapel for Kensington and Islington – and it was not because of their superior craftsmanship. It was because they had the one thing that all the retail bigshots at synagogue murmured about: *scale*. If his father hired junior tailors with his disposable income (plus a bank loan for short-term capital if needed), he could create more product and give the shop real volume—

'Haven't you heard of knocking, you nosy thing?'

Max came to his senses. His older sister Judit, with her bright crop of ginger hair, was lying on her bed, clutching a sheet of paper to her chest.

He could tell from her blush that the letter was to Jack Hauser: their father's apprentice – a prattling *langer loksh* who could juggle five apples in one go and took her to the music hall most Saturday nights.

'Is Benjy in here?' he asked.

Judit's cheeks were burning. 'Hmm, let me check…' She looked under the pillow. 'Not here.' She opened the drawer next to her bed. 'Not here either.' She peeked down her blouse. 'And not here. I guess that means that Benjy must be elsewhere! Maybe you should check the races, the boxing club – or Newgate Prison!'

Max rolled his eyes. 'Now, now, there's no need to be facetious.'

Judit flared up – 'What did you call me?!'

'It means "to treat a serious issue with flippancy"! I read it in the dictionary.'

'Never mind! Listen, I need you to do something for me.' She folded the letter and offered it to Max. 'The next time Jack Hauser comes round to run his errands, you are to give this to him. Got it?'

Max's hand was hovering over the letter. 'Oh really? And what's in it for me?'

'The good fortune of not having your backside whipped!'

Max was still sceptical.

'And a block of Mr Benady's toffee,' Judit added.

'Done!' Max snatched the letter, stuffed it in his pocket and scampered out.

No sooner was he gone than Judit let out a happy sigh and fell back on her bed. For two months now, practically from the day that Jack had loped through their front door, he and Judit had carried out a covert courtship right under her family's nose. Normally she was indifferent to romance. In her mind, boys were half-formed men, and men were half-formed creatures – so at best boys were a fraction-formed and not a worthwhile investment.

But... Jack Hauser! 'Hurricane Hauser', he called himself. The fastest talker in Whitechapel, rattling off hare-brained schemes to get rich. 'Piccadilly rich!' he would boast – with dreams of becoming an impresario in the West End, joining the ranks of those well-to-do Sephardim in Belgravia, the pinnacle of the Jewish bourgeoisie.

Just the thought of it drove her mad with joy. She leapt out of bed and ran downstairs to join her mother and Golda, who were setting out warm plates, candlesticks and silver cups for Friday night *Kiddush*.

'Mama,' Judit entreated, 'would it so terrible to invite that Hauser boy for Friday night sometime?'

'Why are you so concerned all of a sudden with dinner invitations?'

'Mama,' Golda piped up, 'you know he can juggle *five* apples in one go!'

'He's a nice boy,' Judit said, 'and he works very hard for Papa. If you want my opinion, he'd make a fine match for some lucky woman.'

Judit should have known better. A runaway train of worries left the station in Ruth's feverish mind. *What does she mean, 'match'? Hauser's father was in Marshalsea for defaulting on his debts! God knows we have troubles of our own! If only she showed the same interest in Geoffrey Lovat, whose father runs the grocery shop next door – such a lovely boy…*

Ruth turned to Judit decisively. 'We can talk about Jack Hauser with your father. More importantly, where is Benjy—'

As she spoke, they heard the sound of the front door opening. Max sprinted downstairs. 'Speak of the devil and he shall appear!'

But when he reached the entrance hallway, Max was greeted not by Benjy, but by his father: Solomon Canaan.

As ever, Solly's face revealed next to nothing – outwardly neutral, inwardly always thinking, observing. He was dressed in his trademark grey suit: understated and businesslike. The aloof sobriety of a man forged by decades of diligent service. Whose feelings were placed second to duty. Whose pleasures were small. Who stood upright even as the burdens of life weighed on his shoulders.

Next to Solly stood his cousin Herschel, plump and dishevelled, with the air of an extraordinary gentleman fallen on hard times. His clothes were hand-me-downs: a wilting red boutonnière, a discoloured silk cravat, oversized loafers. As the resident gopher of the Canaan clan, Herschel was always playing some unspecified role in Solly's workshop. In exchange, he had food, a bed in the back room, money for gambling and brandy, plus the security of never having to look after himself.

Solly picked Max up and kissed him on the cheeks. 'Good *Shabbos*, young man.'

'Papa, I have amazing news!' Max babbled excitedly, 'I've formulated a business model based on a *discrepancy* in the shop's outgoings…'

'Max,' Solly cut him off. 'There's a time for business, and a time for rest. It's Friday night… It can wait.'

Solly trudged up to the living room to find his parents-in-law seated by the fireplace. '*Shabbat Shalom*,' he said with a respectful bow.

'Good *Shabbos*,' Tuvia croaked, 'and if you ask me where Benjy is, I'll bludgeon you.'

Solly's features sank. He had sent his eldest son on a ninety-minute round trip to Chelsea to deliver three exquisite dinner suits to an esteemed client. Suits that had taken him the better part of two months to complete – a crucial sale in the doldrums of summer. But that was five hours ago…

The boy was up to something. Solly could feel it in his bones.

As Ruth emerged from the dining room, Herschel whipped a bouquet of flowers from behind his back: 'For the most beautiful woman in Whitechapel!'

'Where'd you get the dosh for that, you silly goat?' Tuvia laughed.

Herschel embraced him. 'Nicked it, old man. I had practice you know – a spell as a pickpocket in Tangiers many moons ago—'

'Not now, Herschel!' Solly snapped, 'Tell your stories later!' He let out a sigh. The whole room seemed to breathe it in. 'We'll have to start without Benjy.'

Before dinner, Ruth took Solly to one side, away from the prying eyes of her parents and their precocious children. 'I made do with what we had,' she said, 'but the chicken is our last meat – there's only one challah – I had to shave mould off the potatoes…'

'Times are tough for everyone,' Solly said with a wave of the hand. 'There's a war on.'

'It's not just that. You know how it is with my father and his gallstones… He's been in such pain, but we have nothing for him aside from cheap cognac!' Ruth broke off for a moment. 'And, well… I spoke to Rabbi Frankel, and he said – he was *very* clear – that there are ways for us to get help. The programme at Bevis Marks, or a West London synagogue if you don't want to be seen—'

Solly folded his arms across his chest and narrowed his eyes. 'Are you suggesting that I go out and ask for *relief?*'

'It's *something*. We can get fresh food – oil for the lamps – medicine. This is worth more than your pride, Solly.'

But Solly was unmoved. 'Ruth, I was not born a *schnorrer* and I do not appreciate you trying to turn me into one. Besides, these "programmes" don't help poor Jews – they just help rich Jews feel better about themselves. The last thing we need is to give ammunition to those who claim that we Litvaks are a burden on the community. The belt is tight, but we will make it through. I will turn the shop around…'

'With whose help?' Ruth whispered. 'Your eldest son?'

Solly darkened. He had no response.

'Let's eat,' he finally said. 'The children must be hungry.'

He smoothed his wife's hair affectionately and walked slowly back into the living room, assuming his position at the head of a dining table where the family had assembled. The Canaans welcomed the Sabbath angels with a hearty *Shalom Aleichem*, followed by a blessing for the brave boys who had gone to fight in Crimea.

Solly put on a cheerful smile for his children's sake. Despite these pressures, he told himself that he had much to be thankful for: his steadfast wife, his precious children, his health, his community. But behind that smile, an infuriating question was irking him:

Where the hell is that no-goodnik?

2

An Incident at Claridge's

As the Canaan family sat down to give thanks to the Almighty and Her Majesty the Queen, three boys were striding through Mayfair, decked out in exquisite woollen suits, with tailcoats and white bowties.

On the left, Leo Pereira: the only undefeated prize-fighter at Houndsditch boxing club. He was a bruiser through and through, as broad as he was tall and bursting out of his clothes like a gorilla, with a lazy eye and a gravelly Portuguese-inflected drawl to boot. A few too many knocks to the head had left Leo slower than the average East End scamp. But where words failed him, his fists did ample talking.

On the right, 'Hurricane' Jack Hauser: a gangly six-footer with a shock of curly hair that bobbed up and down as he deftly shuffled a pack of cards. Jack made up for Leo's doziness and then some, chattering at full tilt about anything and everything – from the muggins he had scammed that morning, to his latest idea for a madcap farce that would take the West End by storm.

And in the middle, one step ahead, was a boyishly handsome young man sporting a red carnation, top hat tucked under his arm, his hair slick with Macassar oil in the style of a Docklands gangster. He was tanned olive and clean-shaven. Yet behind his eyes simmered something darker: a pinch of mischief, a dash of melancholy, a glint of intelligence, and a generous helping of restlessness. In a word: *trouble*.

This was 'Benjy'. But only his family called him that. Out here, he was Ben Canaan. And together, these three were the 'Good-for-Nothings'.

The East End was their stomping ground. Tonight, however, they were shot of the ghetto and deep in enemy territory. This was a world of gentlemen's clubs, grand red-brick apartments and leafy squares, where a dress worn by an heiress cost more than five years' income for the most successful Whitechapel businessman. The only Jews who could afford to live here were prominent banking families from the Continent: Rothschilds, Spielmans, Sassoons. Not quite Ben's crowd – but, thanks to the outfits so assiduously crafted by his father, he and the Good-for-Nothings blended right in.

Their destination was Claridge's – formerly Mivart's, lately come under new ownership and catering exclusively to the upper crust. An invitation ball was being held for its wealthy clientele: a perfect opportunity for the Good-for-Nothings to snag a free meal, flirt with a few birds and filch a few bob.

The trio huddled in a circle beneath a gaslight on the corner of Brook Street and Davies Street, opposite the façade of Claridge's.

'Right, lads,' Ben said. 'Technically, we're not invited. But breaking in is always more fun!'

'What's happenin'?' Leo asked.

'I'm playing the bigwig, so I'll behave like a right knob. Jack: you're the good guy – so keep it nice and friendly.'

'Easy-peasy,' Jack scoffed. 'Bit of the old Hurricane Hauser charm and they'll be eating out my hand.'

'And if things go south,' Ben turned to Leo, 'I'll need you to *do your thing.*'

'Smash their 'eads in,' Leo grunted, cracking his knuckles.

'When we're done, we take the staff door through the kitchens. Out the south wing onto Brooks Mews, down Avery Row, and hotfoot it back to Whitechapel before the bobbies get wise. And just in case…'

Ben reached into his pocket and pulled out a polished silver revolver.

'Webley Longspur,' Ben whispered. 'Best five-shot on the market.'

'What a beauty!' Jack reached for it. 'Bet I could sell her at a fine—'

'Hands off!' Ben snatched it away. 'It's not mine. It belongs to Lennie Glass.'

'The opium smuggler?' Jack gulped. 'So you *do* know him!'

'Lennie and I do the odd bit of business together. He's asked me to look after this unlicensed firearm. Hand-over's next week in the Docklands. Meantime, it's ours. If we get rumbled, I'll fire off a warning shot – create a little disturbance so we can make a break for it.'

'Are you mad?' Jack exclaimed. 'That'll get us a year in the nick!'

Leo was grinning fiendishly. 'Chuffin' hell! Lennie's gonna kill you.'

'Long as nobody gets hurt, he'll be none the wiser,' Ben said. 'Now let's go. No time like the present.'

They marched up to the door of Claridge's. Ben donned the

top hat and slotted a rimless monocle over his right eye – Pallow's signature look, word had it.

As they entered the grand hotel, a doorman stepped in their way. 'Invitations, gentlemen.'

Ben straightened up and put on his finest Etonian sneer. 'I am late enough as it is. Out of my way.'

But the doorman did not budge. 'Sir, I will have to take your name.'

'For God's sake, my dear fellow – keep your voice down!'

Jack stepped in with a charming smile. 'You must not have recognised my friend – an innocent mistake, I'm sure! This is Sebastian Pallow: son of the Earl of Northbridge.'

'Tell the whole world, why don't you?!' Ben fumed, whipping out a calling card, 'Yes, it's true. I am Pallow, and Pallow is I. And I've come here *specifically* from my father's country house in Hampstead, to indulge in some revelry!'

'And these gentlemen?' The doorman gestured to Jack and Leo.

'Reginald Arthur Penrose-Forsyth Esquire,' Jack said, producing his own card.

Leo said nothing. He simply squared up to the doorman and puffed out his chest.

'Protection,' Ben said. 'Where I go, he goes. Now let's be done with this dithering! My company is waiting for me, and if you embarrass me any further, my papa the earl shall have your guts for garters.'

The doorman gave a resigned shrug. It was only when the Good-for-Nothings had crossed the marble lobby and were proceeding down a carpeted corridor to the ballroom that Ben dropped the act.

'Slick job, lads. When does the actual Pallow get here?'

'My guy on the inside told me nine-thirty,' Jack replied.

'Can we trust that estimate?'

'He's a hand in Pallow's stable – they know when the carriages come and go.'

'Alright then,' Ben said, 'two hours. Let's make hay.'

They followed the sound of music to a ballroom, where the pampered progeny of lords and ladies were gliding to a waltz that swelled from a small orchestra. Tables were laden with roast hog and decanters of wine. Older aristocrats rubbernecked from their seats, eyes peeled for the latest debutante swanning in.

Jack schmoozed his way into the circle of a recently ennobled shipping merchant and finagled a steady supply of port. Leo, like a shark trailing blood, sniffed out partygoers too wrapped up in caviar and canoodling to mind their wallets. Cash, jewellery, watches, family heirlooms – nothing was safe from his nimble fingers.

Ben, meanwhile, had his eye on something different. From the moment he walked in, his interest had been aroused by an entourage in a corner of the ballroom, seated before a red velvet arras. A group of military men: decrepit generals with wine-flushed cheeks, medallions and signet rings – products of Sandhurst and a lifetime of venal office. And hovering at the margins, like lovely flowers on a stagnant pond, were three arrestingly beautiful young ladies.

The clothes told Ben everything he needed to know. Their ruby brooches, spotless-white kidskin opera gloves and gowns with low bertha necklines screamed *money*. But not just any kind of money. There was something antiquated about them: lace ribbon engageantes, pleats round the shoulders that he would have expected from a ballgown made half a decade ago. And none of London's latest crazes: no crinolines, flounces, passementerie trims or broderies anglaises.

Of course: this was *old money*. Out-of-towners – heiresses down from the family seat somewhere up north where the vogues took longer to reach. Provincial scions of a bygone Tudor dynasty, drawn to the big city and the allure of the bourgeoisie like moths to a flame.

They were sisters. The eldest in her late twenties, already taken – arm in arm with a strapping squire twice Ben's size. The youngest in her teens, barely fifteen.

And lastly, the middle one: a warm, trusting face – bright locks tumbling in corkscrew curls – looking around expectantly for a dashing beau to sweep her off her feet.

But the old military men were protecting the fort. Ben would have to pick his moment wisely. And so, for fifteen minutes, he lingered by the dancefloor, sipping champagne and waiting for an opening.

'Ben Canaan?'

A voice just to his left. Ben flinched and pretended not to hear. If someone had indeed recognised him, he would need to hold his bluff.

'Ben! I know it's you! I'd recognise that mug anywhere!' Ben felt an index finger gently prod him in the ribs.

There was no getting out of it now. He turned to face a young moustachioed gent in a fine black dress-coat, wearing white gloves and a gold pince-nez. He had a strong, confident profile and his eyes glowed earnestly.

'Sandy Rosen!' Ben cried, shaking the young man's hand. 'What are you doing here?'

'I should be asking you the same thing on a Friday night,' Sandy replied with a wink. 'I thought your old man was a stickler for tradition.'

'Not like the Rosens these days, so I've heard.'

Sandy seemed embarrassed. 'Well, since my father sold the business and we moved to Mayfair, we've reformed our ways. He goes to the opera on Shabbat, can you believe!'

Ben's smile faltered and he let go of Sandy's hand. The last time he had seen Sandy, the young man was a weedy thing routinely pelted with apple cores by roaming schoolboys from the nearby Catholic school. Now he seemed effortlessly upper-class and debonair – easy enough to mistake for the very man that Ben was impersonating.

'But in all seriousness, what *are* you doing here?' Sandy said.

Ben hesitated and waved away Sandy's question. 'Oh… We do the suits for Mr Claridge.'

'Still in the family business, then! Good for you.' Sandy gave a self-satisfied smile. 'As for me, I was called to the Bar last week by Inner Temple. I know: *me*, of all people!'

Ben said nothing. His free hand clenched in his pocket.

'And do you know the funniest thing?' Sandy said, coming in close and linking his arm with Ben's. 'As I fitted on my wig and gown, I was thinking about you. The old days at the Jewish Free School. How we were joined at the hip, sneaking into the British Museum to read books that our parents would *never* have let us read – Hume, Descartes, those dodgy Schopenhauer translations, remember?! They were good times.'

'They were,' Ben said wistfully.

'I was heartbroken when my father packed me off to St Paul's. It worked out for me in the end – the virtues of a bona fide education, I suppose! But my heart broke even more for you, Benjy. Taken out at fifteen… Headmaster Angel, I heard, begged and pleaded with your father not to do it. Is that true?'

Sandy was right. Ben could remember the conversation as if it were yesterday. The headmaster's musty office giving onto the courtyard at JFS where his classmates were playing hopscotch. The piquant smell of Angel's cologne and the bowl of candied lemons on the mantelpiece. His father's hand heavy on his shoulder, Angel behind the desk, silhouetted by shafts of light from the noonday sun. The testy exchange between father and mentor: the battle between aspiration and duty, talent and obedience. That slow, sinking feeling in Ben's chest, as the realisation dawned that the dream which gave him solace had already slipped away.

'Yes. It's true.'

Sandy tutted in disappointment. 'For the dolts it's one thing. But you were the brightest star by a country mile and then some. I was in awe of you, Benjy. You were so much smarter than me. You had an utterly forensic eye. In the time it took me to read one book and clumsily parrot its meaning, you could read five and have a catalogue of insuperable arguments at your disposal. Those are the skills they teach at Oxford and half the students can't even begin to master it. *But you had it.* Like breathing.'

Ben looked away. Sandy was well-intentioned. But his slightly gloating tone made Ben's stomach tighten.

'I should get going, Sandy,' Ben said. 'There are a couple of people I need to talk to before the night's out.'

'Wait, one moment, please,' Sandy said. 'Everything happens for a reason. To think that after not seeing you for six years, I might find you just one week after my call, in Claridge's of all places! Here's what I propose: *come work for me.* I'm building a practice and I'll need a legal assistant. Someone with a big brain who knows their way around a library.'

'But... Sandy, I don't even have a degree...'

'Oh, please,' Sandy chuckled. 'Your education can be the field. There are a few Silks who I'm sure will vouch for you once they see your mettle. I won't mince my words: it's relentless work and the pay is non-existent for the first few years. But...' He pinched Ben's cheek. 'Who knows where it might lead? You always wanted to be a barrister. And when I was called to the Bar, I knew in my heart that you should have been there with me. So, how about it, Benjy? I can have a word with your old man if need be.'

Ben looked at Sandy with momentary affection. But the longer they stood there, and the longer the music went on, the more Ben felt the passage of time. The untraversable road between now and then.

His gaze flitted back to the girls. That middle one was still waiting expectantly for someone just like him – or, at least, the man he was pretending to be.

'Thanks, Sandy,' Ben said, shaking his hand. 'Let me have a think about it.'

'Of course,' Sandy replied, sliding his card into Ben's pocket. 'But don't stand around thinking for too long! I'll need to fill the post sooner or later. Write to me.'

Ben drifted across the dancefloor. By the time he had crossed the parquet and was in the eyeline of the middle sister, he had already decided that he would not be writing to Sandy.

As the dancers struck up a lively gavotte, he gave the girl a chivalrous bow: 'My lady. Might I tempt you to a dance?'

She opened her mouth to speak but was cut short by a bark from one of the geriatric generals: '*And who might you be?*'

Ben gave him a quick once-over. He was eighty if he was a day, with medals from another era and no wedding band. A sozzled uncle, no doubt – there to 'chaperone'.

'Sebastian Pallow,' Ben said confidently. 'Son of Earl Northbridge.'

'Earl Northbridge! Goodness! You don't look a bit like him. I heard he was pursuing a venture in…' he narrowed his eyes at Ben, '*Ceylon.*'

'Madagascar,' Ben corrected him. 'It proved profitable. I cannot say more.'

The old dodderer seemed satisfied with Ben's response and splayed a palm to the young lady, as if to say: *you may continue.* The young lady accepted Ben's offer without a moment's hesitation.

'My name,' she said, 'is Catherine Arbuthnot. Who was that you were talking to?'

'Oh, my legal counsel. Jewish, you know. They're very bright – if somewhat loquacious.'

He took Catherine's hand and led her to the dancefloor. A first dance became a second, then a third. Soon an hour had passed and, as the clock struck eight-thirty, Ben and Catherine nestled into an alcove for champagne and ices.

Ben regaled her with tales of his illustrious family history: how his father had risen through the ranks of the East India Company and bought large tracts of land in Tasmania. 'Papa hates fanfare,' he said, adjusting his carnation.

'But surely,' Catherine said, 'those who *are* aware of his immense wealth are clamouring for your attention?'

'If only you knew, my dear,' Ben said. 'I am quite alone. And there comes a time when a man craves nothing more than a companion. Someone to love and cherish every day.'

'I think I should very much like to be that someone.'

'Then I propose, Catherine, that you and I share one more dance. This tempo is decidedly more intimate.'

Catherine leant in close. For a moment, their noses brushed. 'That sounds *scrummy*.'

As they waltzed chest to chest, Ben spoke of his plans to emigrate to Tasmania. 'My only worry,' he said, 'is the wombats.'

'*Wombats?*'

'Oh, yes. Vicious creatures. They can tear one limb from limb. But I shall brave them. Family duty comes before all. Then again... Who said I must travel alone?'

Catherine laughed and fell into his arms. 'You are so silly, Sebastian!'

'You're right,' Ben said, chiding himself. 'To hell with tomorrow! Let's live for the moment – it's all one has to call one's own!'

She turned her face longingly to meet his. Ben considered going in for the kiss, right then and there.

But he never got the chance. He felt a hand grip his shoulder and he was unceremoniously spun round – coming face to face with a plump, snub-nosed, double-chinned fellow wearing an identical monocle and top hat, who snarled: 'Dastardly mongrel!'

Two footmen swooped in and pinned Ben's arms behind his back.

'Gentlemen!' Ben barked. 'What is the meaning of this? Who are you?'

'I'm Sebastian Pallow,' the homunculus spat, 'and this is a gift from the House of Northbridge!'

Pallow decked Ben and sent him sprawling. For a pint-sized toff, it was a surprisingly powerful punch.

'Fools!' Catherine shrieked. 'Don't you know his father owns half of Tasmania?!'

Pallow went to kick Ben in the gut. But Ben caught his leg and rolled, dragging Pallow to the floor where the two scuffled and writhed about. The music broke off, the other dancers retreated and the footmen leapt in to separate the pair.

As Ben was being hauled off the dancefloor, Pallow turned to Catherine: 'My lady, I fear you have been duped. *I* am the real Sebastian Pallow. That boy is but an imposter – an *actor*.'

Catherine went pale: betrayal turned to shock, then shock to fury. She dashed over to Ben and slapped him square in the face: 'Monstrous cad!'

But Ben was more concerned with finding his crew. 'LADS!' he yelled. 'A hand please?'

Leo burst from the throng and barrelled into the footmen, unleashing a cyclone of hooks and uppercuts. Ben was sent sliding across the dancefloor. The Webley Longspur flew from his jacket pocket, bounced across the varnished parquet, and went off with a deafening *bang!*

Pallow jumped up and down with a porcine squeal, clutching his left leg as blood ran down to drench his dress shoes. 'God in heaven! I've been shot!' he cried, before promptly fainting.

Claridge's descended into chaos. Guests flooded out of the ballroom. The orchestra scattered, holding their violins aloft in the crush. An unconscious Pallow was dragged to safety by his footmen. Ben scooped up the revolver before it was lost in the stampede of pumps and Derbies.

Jack appeared at his side, pointing to the service door. 'Time to get the pistons firing, mate.'

Ben did not need to be told twice. He caught a final glimpse of Catherine as she was bundled away by her chaperone, and he waved his top hat to her, shouting over the melee: 'See you in Tasmania, Ms Arbuthnot!'

And with that, the Good-for-Nothings scarpered.

Claridge's was in such a state that they were able to slip out unnoticed via the service door, through the kitchens, and out onto Brooks Mews. As Oxford Circus filled with the screech of bobbies' whistles, they darted off, keeping to the back-alleys of Mayfair en route to the East End.

'Nine-thirty?' Ben shouted to Jack as they ran.

'That's what I was told! So what?! I'm not a nanny for these inbred toffs.'

It took a full hour and a half to get back to Whitechapel. The streets were mostly empty now – just a gaggle of fleet-footed pickpockets loitering by the Aldgate Pump and a few dishevelled drunkards slumped on the kerb.

They took refuge at the Hoop & Grapes. The place was packed to the rafters and bobbies would not venture here tonight. At a corner table, shielded from prying eyes, they totted up their winnings in a haze of tobacco-smoke. Some banknotes and loose change – a signet ring – a glass eye – an ivory snuff box – and a penknife with a mother-of-pearl handle.

'Not bad for an evening's work!' Ben grinned.

'What was it you said,' Jack teased, 'about nobody getting shot?!'

Ben waved his hand dismissively: 'So he won't play polo for a few weeks! Bring out the violins.'

'It's not Pallow I'm worried about, Ben. Lennie Glass puts men face-down in the Thames for a lot less.'

'How we splittin' this?' Leo grunted.

Ben divvied up the cash three ways and each boy took a piece of jewellery. 'Who said there was no honour among thieves?' He slipped the penknife into his back pocket. 'Plus a little bonus for me – seeing as I laid on the threads. Fair's fair.'

Ben bought another round and they went their separate ways. 'I need those suits back by Monday!' he called out as Jack headed north to his digs in Spitalfields. *'Dry-cleaned!* Or I'm a dead man!'

Ben strolled down the high street, back to Whitechapel. The first drops of summer rain pattered the cobblestones – a chorus of whispers guiding him home. He breathed in the dewy aroma and lifted his face to the night sky to let the rain cool his flushed cheeks.

For a moment, as the adrenaline subsided, Ben felt free. He forgot where he was and what was waiting for him around the corner. He was simply alive – thanks to nothing but his quick feet and his even quicker wit. Nobody was telling him what to do or how to be: he was his own man.

Then the downpour got going, just as the lights of the Canaan family home came into view, studding the muggy black like nuggets of gold in the dirt. All at once his happiness drained away. No matter how far he ran, he was always reeled back here, like a fish with a hook in its cheek: to the ramshackle buildings hemming him in, to the stench of carbolic soap and white onions, to the smog and miasma of human filth wafting from the Thames.

Ben's smile faded and he trudged homewards.

He climbed over the fence and let himself in through the back door, into Solly's office behind the shop. He glimpsed the clock on the wall: nearly eleven. The house upstairs was silent. Friday night dinner had long since finished and the little ones were likely in bed.

Ben crept upstairs, onto the landing. From the living room on the other side of the thin wall, he could hear voices: his father, Herschel and his grandparents chatting. Judit and Ruth were in the kitchen, stacking plates and wringing water from hand towels into a wash-bucket.

He tiptoed to the stairwell leading to the upper floors. If he could get to his bedroom without being detected, he could change clothes and concoct a hasty alibi—

'Benjy?'

Standing at the top of the stairs was Golda, in her pyjamas, staring at him in wide-eyed wonder. He put his finger to his lips, but it was too late. The conversation in the living room ground to a halt. Slow, measured footsteps creaked across the landing below him – and Ben turned to see his father, one hand resting on the banister.

'Good evening, Benjamin.'

Ben knew that look and tone: disappointment, tinged with relief. It was an expression that put the lid on all feeling, yet it still made his blood boil. He tramped down, avoiding Solly's gaze. Solly stopped him with a firm hand to the chest, the other turning Ben's cheek to the flickering lamplight: 'Are you alright?' Solly said. 'You're not hurt?'

'Just a shiner. Adds character, I think!' Ben said – then, under his breath, 'It's my business anyway.'

Solly took in Ben's attire. The torn collar. The stains on the lapels. The cuffs dappled with cigarette ash. The sodden top hat. His expression soured as he joined the dots. 'Why don't we have a chat in the living room, Benjamin?'

Ben pushed past his father without a word, gearing up for the hiding of a lifetime. He slouched into the living room to find Herschel and Tuvia swirling their habitual after-dinner cognacs. Hesya was fast asleep, passed out in her rocking chair.

'*Shalom*, Benjeleh,' Herschel said. 'Nice of you to join us. It's a wonder you didn't come crashing through the roof.'

'You look like you've been in a brawl,' Tuvia croaked.

Ben could not contain a mischievous grin. 'You should see the other guys!'

Ruth burst in from the kitchen and examined Ben fretfully. 'What happened now, Benjy? Where were you? What have you done? Have you eaten?! I saved some food for you – I kept it warm especially…'

She bustled Ben into his seat at the dinner table and heaped food onto his plate: challah smeared with chicken schmaltz, a drumstick with roasted potatoes, along with a bowl of hot broth and a *Kiddush* cup which she filled with the last of the sweet wine. Solly pulled up a chair and studied the enigma that was his eldest son. As Ben inhaled his food, Solly folded and re-folded a napkin.

'Where are the other suits?' Solly said quietly.

Ben took a bite of his drumstick. 'Is that all you care about? *The suits?*'

'You know that's not true.'

'The suits will be fine and dandy. Come Monday.'

'That's not the point, Benjy. The suits should have been with Mr Golowitz in Chelsea this afternoon. He paid me good money to—'

Ben snorted. Solly bristled.

'He paid me,' Solly continued, 'to provide a service. And part of that service was delivering the suits by a particular date and time. I shouldn't have to explain that to you at the age of twenty-one.'

'Just tell him that you found a way to bring the trousers in even better than before and that you needed the weekend. He can't tell the difference either way.'

Solly shook his head in disbelief. 'I've lost count of the number of times you've acted out, and yet still you manage to leave me speechless.'

'If you're speechless,' Ben said, 'why are you still talking?'

Ruth opened her mouth to reason with Ben – to persuade him to show some contrition. But Solly got there first.

'There are two more suits missing. Who did you go out with tonight?'

Ben polished off the last of his potatoes. 'Nice try. I'm no rat!'

'But you *are* a rat. You're a gangster, a thug, a good-for-nothing. I've heard the rumours – that you're running around Limehouse and the Isle of Dogs with those racketeers that give us Jews a bad name. Where does this end, Benjy? Prison? The gallows?'

'And where does *this* end, exactly?' Ben said, spreading his arms wide in a gesture of frustration and futility. 'How is this any less of a prison?'

Anger flared in Solly's eyes. 'This life that you so clearly disdain is an honest one – clean-cut – reputable. It's a family business that you, as my eldest son, have a responsibility to take on.'

'It's a sinking ship in a stinking ghetto!' Ben bubbled over. 'And I can't stand it. Stale challah, cheap oil, windows that rattle in the wind, debt, destitution, the unbearable smell... I could have been anything, Papa. I could have gone to university like I dreamed of doing – become a learned, well-to-do man – used my mind – made something of myself! *But you took that from me.* You just couldn't stand the idea of me spreading my wings wider than you ever could, so you clipped them and shoved me in a basement where I spend my days squinting at hemlines and stitches, slowly becoming a half-blind consumptive just like you—'

That final insult pushed Solly over the edge. He slammed the table, sending Ben's *Kiddush* cup toppling over. '*Enough!*' he seethed. 'You resent me for trusting you with my life's work? For giving you a structure that you never could have built yourself? How dare you belittle what I've done for you, after the sacrifices your mother and I have made!'

'You're an idiot,' Ben shot back. 'I was your way out of this hellhole! If you had trusted me to be my own man instead of some knock-off *schmutter* merchant, I could have fixed your problems, we could have left Whitechapel like Sandy Rosen and his old man—'

'Maybe I don't *want* to leave!' Solly said for all to hear. He paused for a moment, breathing hard, and straightened his tie. 'Maybe I don't want to abandon my faith and my people like every other Jew seems all too eager to do these days! How do you think Sandy got into Oxford? They had him *baptised*! And when was the last time the Rosens wrote to us since they made a bit of money and started hobnobbing with gentiles? I'll give you a clue: NOT. BLOODY. ONCE. Is that what you want? To trade in your family and community for a fantasy?'

'*You never gave me the choice!*' Ben roared. 'You call me a good-for-nothing, but you destroyed the one thing I was good for! And you expect me to be grateful?'

'I expect you to be a man and face up to your responsibilities—'

They were cut short by the shrill iron doorbell. Ben froze. No Jew would ring the doorbell at this hour on a Friday night. And who else would be roaming around Whitechapel after dark? It could only be a bobby – or, worse still, had Lennie Glass already found out about Ben's exploits and sent a man to take care of him?

Solly headed downstairs to the front door. Ben remained seated, looking nervously between his mother and Tuvia, who was quietly observing from his armchair by the embers.

Solly opened up to find a diminutive courier standing before him, in a uniform and patrol cap wet from the summer shower.

'Is this,' the courier squeaked, 'the home of Solomon Canaan, tailor?'

Solly looked perplexed. Another one of Ben's hijinks? 'This is he.'

The courier produced a letter from his breast pocket.

'Pardon the late hour, sir, I got lost! Letter for you. More than my life's worth if you don't read it tonight. Have a good evening.'

Solly took the letter. The courier leapt onto a post chariot and bolted off at speed. Solly returned to the dining room table, opened the envelope and scanned the contents.

'It's from the Home Department,' he murmured, holding up the letter. Sure enough, printed at the top of the letter was the seal of the United Kingdom, along with the insignia of the Home Office.

'But what does it say?!' Herschel exclaimed.

'Are we in some kind of trouble?' Ruth asked.

'Wait!' Solly adjusted his spectacles and read the letter aloud: 'Dear Mr Canaan. We are writing to you from the office of Viscount Palmerston, Home Secretary of the United Kingdom. The Home Secretary is in urgent need of a bespoke suit. However, our regular tailor, Mr Rudolph Zemmler, has latterly become *indisposed*. A conversation with your client Sir David Salomons has brought your work to the Home Secretary's attention. On Sir David's recommendation, the Home Secretary requests your presence for a first fitting at his residence at Cambridge House, 94 Piccadilly, on Monday morning at the hour of ten o'clock. Anticipating a response in the affirmative, a carriage has been arranged to transport you directly to Cambridge House. Yours et cetera…'

Solly's fingers trembled over the bottom of the page, where Palmerston's spidery signature was scrawled. Ben expected him to start jumping for joy – to bustle downstairs to his workshop to set up his tools well in advance – to wave the letter in his son's face as if to say, 'You see? *You see?*'

But Solly did nothing of the sort. The reality of the letter was almost too much to comprehend. He seemed oddly cowed by the magnitude of the opportunity. He let the paper drop to the tabletop and removed his spectacles to rub his eyes.

'Change your clothes, boychik,' he whispered. 'We need… I need to…'

There was something about Solly that made Ben swallow his anger. As he slunk upstairs, he caught sight of Tuvia on his fireside throne. His grandfather raised his cognac in the air:

'Rest in peace, Rudolph Zemmler!'

And he knocked it back with a show of great reverence.

3

Two Daguerreotypes

Ben rose at dawn on Monday morning. Jack Hauser was waiting for him in the back-alley behind the White Hart in Mile End. 'Good as new!' Jack said proudly, producing the suits from Friday's shenanigans, now pressed and dry-cleaned. 'How are you going to explain this?'

Ben shrugged him off. 'Leave it with me.'

He went straight back home and ambled down to the basement workshop where his father was kitting out a large canvas tool-bag for their session with the Home Secretary. He placed the suits on a rack: '*Et voilà.*'

Ben made to leave just as quickly as he arrived. But before he had one foot out the door, Solly cleared his throat: 'How did you get them back?'

'How doesn't matter. I got them back, like I said I would.'

Again, Ben tried to escape. But again, Solly interrupted him – this time with the scrape of his chair as he got to his feet.

'Look at me, boychik.'

Ben bit his lip. He was anticipating another lecture: more of the finger-wagging and scathing disapproval to which he had become so accustomed. Against his better judgement, he turned around. Solly was supporting himself with one hand on the worktable – he looked weary, even a little frail. But he spoke with calm resolution: the fixity of a man who believed deep down that he knew best.

'I am not going to feed the conflict between us, Benjy. Certainly not on a day like today. Do you understand?'

Ben nodded.

'I will give you one more chance, not least because this is a valuable opportunity for you to see the potential of our business. But I expect you to behave. If you want to go out and sully your reputation, do it on your own steam. When *I* am standing before the Home Secretary, and *I* am the one bearing the burden of his approval or opprobrium, then you have a duty that extends beyond yourself.'

Ben ached with the things that he could have said. That this 'opportunity' did not mean half as much as Solly had convinced himself. That 'one more chance' was precisely what he did *not* want. But at least Solly was not looking for an argument, and Ben knew better than to pass up that lifeline.

Jack arrived an hour later and did a fine job of feigning ignorance about the suits. They had a breakfast of millet porridge and tea. All the while, Max pestered Ben to ask the Home Secretary about the war in Crimea – the young boy's latest obsession – though Solly insisted that they would do nothing of the sort.

A sleek black carriage arrived, the gold insignia of Her Majesty's government emblazoned on its doors. Ben, Solly and Jack mounted the carriage and the driver set off at a clip, bound for Piccadilly.

For much of the ride, they sat in silence: Jack with a toolbag jammed between his knees, Solly geeing himself up, Ben staring out the window as London flashed by like a zoetrope at full tilt.

Sunlight flashing across the Thames, where skippers on Brixham trawlers doffed their caps. Navvies at the water's edge, knee-deep in mud as they built the foundation of the Victoria Embankment. Then onto the Strand, where pasty stalls and candied-peanut vendors crowded the street corners. A demonstration underway in Trafalgar Square – radicals taking to the podium to whip up a crowd against the war in Crimea. Grenadiers marching up the Mall to Buckingham Palace. Fashionable demoiselles with parasols in St James's Park, watching pelicans strut at the edge of the Duck Island.

And finally, Cambridge House: a Palladian-style villa with a sweeping view of Green Park. The iron gates opened and they rolled up to the portico, where a tall man with hawk-like features, not much older than Ben, was waiting to greet them.

'Solomon Canaan, I presume,' he said as the new arrivals dismounted.

'That is correct,' Solly said with a servile bow, 'along with my son Benjamin and my apprentice Jacob Hauser.'

'My name is Charles Barrington – I am Viscount Palmerston's private secretary. I will accompany you through Cambridge House and will supervise the session.'

Ben sized the place up. It was more imposing than anything he had ever seen up close: a classical splendour that put the townhouses and crumbling shopfronts of the East End to shame. Strange to think this place was as ordinary for the man whom they were about to meet as 82 Whitechapel Road was for Ben.

'This is the kind of place I'll buy when I've conquered the West End!' Jack whispered in Ben's ear.

'And he'd be happy to sell it to you, would he?'

'I'll be so full of bread 'n' honey, he'll *have* to say yes.'

Ben picked up the tool-bag – 'You're full of something, alright!'

They approached the main entrance. But Barrington blocked their path.

'This way, gentlemen,' he said, pointing to an altogether less glamorous side entrance. Ben was in half a mind to object, but Solly obeyed without a second's protest, so he followed his father's lead. The route was circuitous, taking them through the servants' quarters, only to end up back in the parlour of the main house. No doubt they would have arrived there in half the time, Ben thought to himself, had they been given the dignity of a proper entrance.

Barrington disappeared to fetch Palmerston, leaving a butler at the door. As Jack unpacked the tool-bag, Ben noticed a copy of *The Times* lying on an oak roundtable in the middle of the room. He scanned the headline:

> WAR IN CRIMEA! FIRST TROOPS
> DEPLOYED TO SIEGE
> Ottoman Sultan welcomes British,
> French soldiers to Constantinople

Palmerston arrived thirty minutes late, bursting through the double doors in a huff. His hair was wild, a shock of grey swept into the air like a breaking wave, mutton chops down to the collar. Ben imagined him popping right out of the womb with that stormy profile, indignant at the midwife's ineptitude and his mother's histrionics. Were it not for the setting, the British Home Secretary might have been mistaken for a short-tempered butcher at Smithfield Market.

Behind him trailed Barrington, carrying a black double-breasted dress coat folded over his arm. Palmerston nodded to his aide, who stepped forward and declared: 'Gentlemen, the Home Secretary thanks you for accepting the invitation. Unfortunately, we have only fifteen minutes for the first fitting instead of the allotted hour. We hope that this shall not be a problem.'

Solly bowed stiffly. 'An honour, your lordship.'

Barrington unfurled the dress coat and hung it on a rack by the chaise longue: 'This is a typical jacket worn by the Home Secretary. Please use this as a model for your design. Once the initial measurements are complete, you may take it back to your workshop.'

Solly bowed a second time, even more obsequiously. 'Most grateful, your lordship.'

Palmerston's gaze passed over the ensemble with the cold indifference of a lunar eclipse. The head tailor, with his slavish air. His preposterously tall assistant in dire need of a haircut. But it was Ben who caught Palmerston's attention: the only one to look back at him directly instead of deferentially at the floor – and with a conspicuously swollen black eye.

Ben raised an eyebrow and smiled. The tiniest twitch of reciprocation flickered in the corner of Palmerston's lip.

The Home Secretary removed his dress coat and the butler

stepped in to hang it on the rack, alongside the identical double-breasted garment left there by Barrington.

'Hebrew tailors are reputed to the finest in their craft,' Palmerston said, with a silver sonority forged at Harrow and polished every day in Parliament. 'Best not disappoint.'

Then he launched into a lengthy monologue setting out in detail his preferences for the new suit, rattling off instructions as though he were proposing a bill at the despatch box. It was to be a double-breasted jacket of merino wool, fully lined, with a shawl lapel, precisely twelve ounces in weight, and no more than two millimetres thick. An Italian shoulder was out of the question – only a Neapolitan would suffice.

When Palmerston had given his instructions, Solly set about measuring him: starting at the neck, across his chest, at several points along the arms and his belly, hips and fleshy thighs. There were about thirty-five measurements all told, but still Solly was able to finish with a minute to spare.

'Thank you, sir,' Solly said to Barrington, not daring to address Palmerston to his face. 'We shall proceed with the initial work immediately.'

'Excellent,' Barrington said. 'Here is the dress coat for your design…'

He went over to the rack, where the two identical jackets were hanging. For the briefest moment, his hand hovered over the jackets, unsure of which one to select.

'Come on!' Palmerston barked. Barrington jolted – grabbed the jacket to his right – and handed it to Ben. Palmerston slipped on the other dress coat and, without a word of thanks or even a glance at the tailor and his assistants, he swept out.

The fitting had ended in the blink of an eye. It felt anticlimactic:

an abrupt visit to a pompous lord fortunate that his father had been born before him. Barrington seemed in a great hurry to eject them from the premises.

In the courtyard, Solly had one foot inside the carriage when he stopped and turned to Barrington. 'One last thing, sir – if you will permit.'

'What is it?'

Solly reached into his pocket and produced a business card. 'Should you – or your family – require a suit, sir, we would be honoured to provide a discount, given our relationship.'

Barrington soured, as though Solly had just handed him a dead fish. He took the card before causing any further embarrassment and waved the carriage away in haste.

Just before they turned a corner and the courtyard of Cambridge House vanished from view, Ben caught sight of Barrington tossing Solly's card to a footman with disdain.

He glanced at his father. The man was grinning as he cleaned his spectacles – an expression of unbridled joy.

On their return, the Canaan household was flooded with excitement. Solly regaled the family with his impressions of their momentous encounter. He was overwhelmed with the conviction that, from the jaws of failure, their fortunes were about to take a dramatic turn for the better. Soon the Canaans would be the talk of the East End: their humble family business, wedged in between Mrs Adler's bakery and Mr Lovat's grocery store, in bed with the Home Secretary himself! Max grilled Solly as to whether he had picked up any gossip about the war in Crimea – but Solly fobbed him off: 'It doesn't work like that, Max. We discussed business and sartorial matters. It would not have been appropriate for his tailor to bring up foreign policy!'

Ben sat at one remove from the celebrations. There was something spectacularly naive about all this self-congratulation. The notion that an English aristocrat would engage with a clan of lowly Litvaks other than to extract a menial service from them! Solly was acting as though he had just been granted a Royal Warrant. If there had not been an insult at the root of it all, he would have found it laughable.

On his father's orders, Ben holed up in the workshop and got started on Palmerston's suit. As the Canaans nattered away upstairs, he sat in the dusty squalor, sketching Palmerston's measurements on tracing paper, then cutting it into distinct pieces. Even this mechanical drudgery was preferable to being party to his family's grand delusions.

Evening fell across Whitechapel and the light began to fade at the tiny latticed window. Ben turned his attention to Palmerston's dress coat, which had been left hanging by the door. He removed it from the hanger and laid it on the worktable to inspect it.

It was a fine suit. The kind that, in another life, he might have worn beneath a gown at the Royal Courts of Justice.

He laid a hand on the double-breasted lapel. That was odd. There was something rigid in the inside pocket. He reached in and removed an envelope. It was frayed and already open – the side-fold stained with an inky thumbprint. The letter was addressed to Palmerston himself.

Ben thought about opening it, but hesitated. There was no way on God's green earth that Barrington had intended to give them a dress coat containing Palmerston's private correspondence. He must have mistakenly handed over the dress coat that Palmerston had been wearing when he entered the parlour, instead of the display garment. For all Ben knew, the contents were classified information, and reading this letter would be an offence against the state.

But it was not every day that he had a window into the life of the upper echelons of society. And given Palmerston's haughty manner, he was inclined to a little nosing around. He adjusted the light of the kerosene lamp and glanced around the workshop. Just the tailor's dummies lurking in the shadows.

He opened the envelope with great care, to reveal a letter and a metal card: a daguerreotype on silver-plated copper. He laid them on the dark cloth of the suit.

He peered at the image first: a beautiful woman on the prow of a ship. Wind had blown her hair to one side and she was squinting at the camera through sunlight. One hand cupped her chin and a playful smile was discernible in the cracked black and white. At the bottom of the image, beneath her flowing dress, was a date: JUNE 1854.

He held the daguerreotype to the light. His breath caught. It was as though the air had been sucked from the room. Deaf to the voices upstairs and oblivious to the work that had consumed him for the past two hours, he traced the image with his fingers.

Her face was unmistakeable.

He looked again at the date. Impossible. It had to be some cruel joke. But faces do not lie, and this one was etched on his memory. It followed him wherever he went, haunting him like a ghost that refused to be banished.

He turned the letter over. A single sentence:

<u>The White Death</u> – *more to come – trust no one*
– Heathcote

Ben was brought back to his senses. Footsteps descending the stairs to the workshop. Then his father's voice: 'How are you getting on, boychik?'

He stuffed the letter and daguerreotype into his pocket and headed for the door. 'Just finishing up!' he said. 'I left Palmerston's suit out for you to look over.'

Before Solly could process his son's strange demeanour, Ben was leaping two steps at a time up to his attic-room. He slammed his bedroom door shut behind him and leant against it. He tried to steady himself with a deep breath, but in vain: his cheeks were burning and his heart was thumping.

He pried open one of the floorboards under his bed and removed a tin box. He blew off a film of dust and tipped out the contents: a bundle of letters – a few faded sketches – a lock of blonde hair – and a second daguerreotype, of a woman sitting on the edge of a bed in a hotel room.

He went to the window. The chimneys grimaced back at him like a set of crooked teeth in the smog-tinted air of the East End, beneath a sky streaked with charcoal-smoke. He held the two images side by side in the dying light, comparing every minute detail: Palmerston's daguerreotype of the woman on the boat – his own daguerreotype of the woman on the bed.

The proportions of her face. That familiar gesture – her right hand cupping her chin. That look in her eyes: beguiling and sad and unreachable. It was surely her.

Ben set the images down on the windowsill. He felt as though he had surfaced from a great depth and he took another deep breath, murmuring a name that he had not spoken for three years:

'Elizabeth.'

4

The Girl from Paris

It was the summer of 1851. Three years before war, before the Good-for-Nothings, before Ben fell in with Lennie Glass and got into the habit of carrying unlicensed handguns. Three years after Ben's education was brought to an untimely end – when the run-down workshop of Canaan & Sons replaced the British Museum and the evening sessions with Headmaster Angel studying Montesquieu and Spinoza. Ben's adolescent fantasy of wandering Oxford's hallowed quadrangles had been well and truly put to bed.

Trinity term was over, and come Michaelmas those lucky few from Ben's former cohort would go to university. That very day – Saturday the 5th of July – there was a lunch at the Rosens' newly refurbished Grosvenor Square apartment, to celebrate Sandy's acceptance to the ranks of the great and the good at Oxford. Ben had been invited, but he had made his excuses.

Instead, Ben walked from 82 Whitechapel Road all the way to Hyde Park. He had a single shilling in his pocket, but it was enough for a ticket to the summer event that had quickly become the most talked-about affair in London: the Great Exhibition. He had heard descriptions of the Crystal Palace built just south of the Serpentine, but nothing could have prepared him for the sight. It was half a kilometre of sheet-glass held together by cast-iron girders: an enormous jewel sparkling in the sunshine.

There were thousands of inventions on display. Some were newfangled – an automatised cigar-maker by Señor Adorno of Mexico, a waterproof pistol, a 'tempest prognosticator' to predict oncoming storms. Others were built for the mundane: toilet brushes, razor-guards, self-adjusting buttons, coffee urns. It was a monument to the relentless innovation of the modern industrial age.

At midday, after a cheese sandwich and a ginger ale, Ben visited the astronomy section. In the shadow of a ten-foot telescope, he studied a display-case containing images of outer space – moons, stars and galaxies swirling vividly on silver photographic plates.

A strange feeling welled up in him. The same as when he saw a carriage pass by, belonging to some gentleman about town, or when he saw postcards of exotic cities in the window of the local newsagents. A longing for the unknown and a desire to go to faraway places, even though he knew it was just another phantom he was chasing.

'Wondering what's out there?'

He heard her voice before he saw her. At first, he thought he was imagining it. He turned. A young woman had appeared next to him. She was wearing baggy trousers in the Turkish *salvar* style, with a short skirt falling a couple of inches below the knee and a long-sleeved vest up to a high neckline. She wore no hat, and her chestnut-brown locks flowed freely to her shoulders. Her attire was drawing stares from the prim and proper crowd.

Ben was too taken aback to speak.

'What's the matter?' she said, cocking her head, 'Cat got your tongue?'

Only then did Ben come to his senses. 'I heard you. I've just never seen a woman in trousers before!'

'It's all the rage these days,' she replied. 'Blame those Bloomers across the pond. They've thrown off the despotism of long skirts and whalebone corsets. It's both a utilitarian choice and an overt political statement.'

Ben's interest was piqued. *Overt political statement!*

He gave a wry smile. 'So what's the utilitarian rationale behind baggy trousers?'

'Watch.' She knelt down, undid the buckles on her shoes and fastened them up again. 'Five seconds. Try doing that in a crinoline!'

'Well,' Ben laughed. 'The next time you're out and about, and you need to unbuckle and rebuckle your shoes in five seconds, you'll be ready.'

'You horrid cynic. If you had to spend all day in a bodice, ankle-length skirt and three layers of petticoats, you wouldn't be so snide.'

'Don't take it personally,' Ben replied, 'I'm a tailor's son. I've handled more frivolous items of clothing than you can possibly imagine. So, of all people, I should know: fashion is designed to be useless. It's an exercise in futility.'

She screwed up her eyes. 'So you're dedicating your life to something futile?'

'We have to pick our poison, don't we? Besides, isn't everything futile in the end?' He pointed to the images of outer space. 'All these grand celestial bodies. They'll disappear one day too. That's life: a constant process of dying.'

The young woman drew closer: 'Schopenhauer – *The World as Will and Representation*.'

Ben did a double-take. 'You know Schopenhauer?'

'Shocking, I know: I'm an educated woman!' she smirked. 'Ever met one of *those* before? But you never answered my first question. Do you wonder what's out there?'

'I wonder all the time,' he said. 'I wonder if there are people just like us, looking at the same pictures and asking the same questions. I wonder if everyone everywhere is just trying to escape.'

The young woman grew serious. 'You suffer from a terrible condition.'

'Namely?'

'*Restlessness*. Everyone has it. Most tame it with duties and distractions. They derive comfort from reducing the universe to the mundane, one foot in front of the other. But some poor souls are unable to do that. Too easily bored, too self-aware, too curious. They spend their lives striving for a deeper purpose, only to be disappointed when no such purpose takes shape. Caught between the search for what lies ahead, and the longing for what was left behind.'

She spoke with affection. Ben was entranced. It was as though she was giving voice to a taboo. Some part of him wanted to politely cut her off and walk away.

But something beyond his control compelled him to stay.

'Is that your diagnosis?' he asked.

'I *am* a doctor's daughter…'

'And what's the cure?'

'*Companionship!*'

For as long as Ben could remember, his mother had impressed on him that, in social situations, men approached women. Or was that just how it worked on Whitechapel Road?

'Why did you come over to talk to me?' he asked.

'Maybe I suffer from the same disease. Birds of a feather,

wouldn't you agree?' She turned to face him. 'Or maybe I just like the way you look.'

'You could tell that at a glance?'

'More than a glance.' She reached out a hand. 'Elizabeth de Varney. But my friends call me Lise.'

Ben took her hand. Her skin was cold and soft, but her grip was strong.

'Ben Canaan.'

'Well, Ben Canaan, were you planning to head off anytime soon?'

'As it happens, I have the afternoon to myself…'

'Then how about you and I explore this place together? It's always more fun in pairs!'

She gave him a sweet smile. At once, all Ben's preoccupations – the celebrations at the Rosens' Grosvenor Square apartment, the evening of stitching and mending that lay ahead – took flight like the turtledoves scattering from the roof of the Crystal Palace.

'Where shall we start?' he said.

They spent the afternoon roving around the Exhibition. Craftsmen from far-flung places showed off their wares: Maoris with pouwhenua totem poles, the Swiss watchmakers Patek and Philippe, American hydrographers with models of the ocean floor. People queued to view artefacts encased in glass – a block of stone from the Alhambra, the Koh-i-Noor diamond from India, bronzes from Ancient Greek temples. But Ben hardly noticed the exhibits. He was only interested in her.

Elizabeth was from Paris: the melting pot of art and revolution that had birthed modern democracy, a city that Ben had only read about in the library at the British Museum. By day, she went by *Mademoiselle de Varney*: assistant in the medical practice of her father, respected physician Dr George de Varney. While the doctor treated patients in his surgery, she balanced the books, ensuring that he was always well-supplied, that the rent was paid, that invoices were dispatched, that coffee was on tap. And when his practice took him abroad, she accompanied him – hence their summer-long sojourn in London.

But when work ended, she fraternised with a gang of louche bohemians, radicals and feminists that gathered on Friday nights in the Place des Vosges to drink, debate aesthetics and rail against the tyranny of the state.

Ben was embarrassed to tell her about his own parochial background. His Friday nights were spent with his father in the back row of the synagogue. Weeknights were confined to the workshop, squinting for the chalk lines on a pair of tweed trousers – or sitting by the fireside to keep his grandparents company, listening to the same old stories in Yiddish of the Old World, of the *shtetl*. He was expecting Elizabeth to be put off by how unremarkable he was. But she listened to his awkward anecdotes so attentively, as though his ordinariness was the very thing that made him fascinating.

By the end of the afternoon, Ben and Elizabeth were sitting on the lawn outside the Crystal Palace, sharing a tin cup of sorbet. The Serpentine soaked up the sun's dying rays. A travelling band from the United States stood at the water's edge playing 'Joe Bowers' and other tunes from the frontier-land, where so many thousands were flocking these days in search of gold. Crowds were gathering: tired parents with over-excited children in tow, hailing hansom cabs and heading on home.

They polished off their ice and lay on their backs, staring up at the canopy of a sycamore tree, birdsong in its branches.

Despite the band and the people milling about, it felt like it was just the two of them, alone in the world for that moment.

Their hands touched. At first, it could have been accidental. But then her hand pressed firmly against his own. He could feel her slow, steady pulse.

He glanced down to check that this was really happening. Lo and behold, her long slender fingers were gently interlocking with his. As he watched this miracle unfold, a blemish caught his trained tailor's eye. It looked like a tattoo on the inside of the middle finger of her left hand. Two tiny letters, slightly smudged: *T O*.

Elizabeth was staring into his eyes. She withdrew her hand and yawned. 'I should go,' she murmured. 'It's getting late. And you have family business to attend to.'

Ben collected himself. So, the magical afternoon had come to an end. He got up to brush himself off. 'Yes. I should be on my way…'

They stood facing one another. Elizabeth had her hands on her hips and was smiling suggestively, as if daring him to speak.

'Will I see you again?' Ben stuttered.

He braced himself for rejection. But to his astonishment, Elizabeth planted a soft kiss on his cheek.

'The Old Mo music hall on Drury Lane,' she said, 'Monday, seven o'clock.'

Ben was thrown by her closeness, the warmth in her voice, the scent of her perfume. Before he could respond, she was already striding away, towards the Serpentine. He watched her disappear into the milling crowds.

'I'll be there…' he whispered to himself.

*

It began like most first love does. It was silly and spontaneous and it could easily have never happened. But it did happen – not just on that Thursday afternoon at the Great Exhibition, but the following Monday at the Old Mo, where they danced the two-step and discussed philosophy over whisky. Then in Regent's Park, where they lunched under the gazebo and poked fun at the fashions of the nouveau-riche. Then the roof of Southwark Cathedral – where, at Elizabeth's instigation, they climbed under cover of darkness, to stargaze above the coal smoke that obscured the night sky. And then Burlington Arcade, where Elizabeth taught Ben how to pickpocket.

But the times that Ben remembered most vividly were in the run-down hotel room in Soho, which Elizabeth had rented for them. That was where they closed themselves off from the world, shared their innermost feelings, and, for the very first time, made love.

It had never occurred to Ben to ask Elizabeth why she had approached him that day – the affair was simply too thrilling. For a time, he had been granted a new lease of life: no duties, no shackles binding him to his father's calling. The wide world and all its possibilities were at his fingertips. With her, he could do anything and be anyone.

It lasted three months. Then, one September evening, in that familiar hotel room, the inevitable happened. As usual, Ben sneaked out through the window of his attic-room and took the omnibus from Whitechapel to Soho. As usual, he and Elizabeth had dinner sitting cross-legged by the heat of the stove. But later, as they lay in bed, just before Ben drifted off, he turned to look at her. She was awake and staring at the lace curtain billowing in the window. Maybe it was the way the moonlight dappled her face, but Ben could have sworn that he saw tears in her eyes.

He had never seen her cry. He was tempted to say something – to ask what was wrong – but he refrained, and soon he was fast asleep.

When he woke up, she was gone. Ben assumed that she had headed home without waking him. But a week passed without word from her, then another week. Soon a month had gone by and still Elizabeth de Varney had not materialised. Ben decided to pay a visit to the Baker Street apartment which she had told him was her father's summertime residence, but the place was untenanted. The landlord gave him a forwarding address in the 3rd arrondissement of Paris, but when he made enquiries at the Post Office, he was told that such an address did not exist. With nothing else to go on, he would linger in the long Sunday hours at their old haunts around London, scanning the crowds for her face – but Elizabeth was nowhere to be seen. She had vanished without trace or explanation.

Six months later, in March 1852, Ben's questions were finally answered. A letter arrived at 82 Whitechapel Road, addressed to him:

Dear Mr Canaan,

I trust this letter finds you in good health. It has come to my attention that you were acquainted with my daughter Elizabeth last summer, and that the two of you shared an affection for one another. Whilst I shall not address the circumstances of our departure from London, as it concerns matters of a commercial nature, I nevertheless believe that you deserve to be informed of recent developments.

Last week, at the close of February, Elizabeth passed away after a short but unforgiving battle with smallpox. She had otherwise been in rude health, but the onset was sudden and, despite my expertise, there was little that I could do to save her.

I can only apologise for the shock that you will surely feel hearing this news. But if it brings any consolation, know that she died comfortably, free of pain, with me at her side. She was dignified to the end.

Elizabeth mentioned you on a handful of occasions, and spoke of you only with affection. I am sorry that the matter has had to end this way. I wish you all the best in your future endeavours.

Yours sincerely,
Dr George de Varney

And now, at his window on this balmy summer evening, two years later, Ben read that same letter which he had kept in the tin box under his bed.

He placed it next to the daguerreotype that he had found in Palmerston's jacket. A letter dated March 1852, declaring her death. A photograph dated June 1854, clearly showing her alive and well – together with a cryptic note from one 'Heathcote': 'The White Death – *more to come – trust no one.*'

He turned over the envelope, looking for any further clues. There was a nondescript scribble on the rear side, just about legible. The slenderest of threads: a return address.

Lynton Arabin Heathcote
15 Nakkaş Haydar Sk.
CONSTANTINOPLE

5

Fugitive from the Law

The first thing Ben did was collar Max and drag him upstairs to the attic-room for a private chat. For once, that obnoxious know-it-all perpetually armed with an answer for everything might come in handy. Ben shut the door behind them.

'I will not be roped into your *chicanery*,' Max growled, folding his arms across his chest.

'No chicanery on the menu,' Ben said. 'I'd just like to pick your brain.'

'About what?'

Ben brought Max in close and whispered: 'This war that's afoot in Crimea.'

Max screwed up his face. 'Why?! And what's the matter with you anyway? You're acting weird.'

Ben tapped his nose. 'Ask me no questions and I'll tell you no lies. And if you cooperate, I can get you a block of Mr Benady's—'

'Already got toffee from Judit,' Max said nonchalantly. 'It'll have to be one of your special cigars, thank you very much!'

Ben was in half a mind to clap Max on the back of the head for trying to fleece his own flesh and blood. But he could not face negotiating with this bull-headed child. 'Fine. Now spill the beans: what do you think is going on out there?'

'Simply put,' Max said with relish, 'it's a clash of empires! On one side, you have the *Ottomans*: Islamic Turks whose reign sweeps from the Balkans, across Asia Minor, the Holy Lands, Egypt, Arabia and North Africa. Pretty big, wouldn't you say? But nowhere near as big as their enemy: *the Russian Empire*. Nine million square miles big – or thereabouts. Now lately, Russia has been expanding her sphere of influence into Ottoman territory.'

'Why's that?'

'For reasons longer than the *Thousand and One Nights*,' Max snorted. 'I'll give you the abridged version. The Russians would have you believe it's to protect the millions of Orthodox Christians living under Ottoman rule. But I think it's a power grab. The Ottomans act as a buffer between Russia and the Mediterranean. Taking Turkey out gives the Russians hegemony over much of Europe *and* Asia. Last year the Russians swept into the Balkans and have been skirmishing with the Ottomans ever since. And now Britain and France have stepped in to help the Turks.'

'But we're not exactly friends with the Ottomans,' Ben mulled. 'Why allow ourselves to be pulled into *their* war?'

'What do you think I was pestering you to ask the Home Secretary about?' Max snapped. 'That's the mystery of it. My guess is that it comes down to this: *my enemy's enemy is my friend*. Britain and France are afraid that Russian expansion will upset the global balance of power – which, of course, threatens everyone. Us included.'

Ben sat on the edge of his bed, trying to wrap his head around this great geopolitical scramble. 'Where is the battleground now?'

'The Crimean Peninsula. That's where the Russians have retreated – their main naval base is in Sevastopol, on the north coast of the Black Sea. And a good three hundred miles away, at the other end of the Black Sea, is Constantinople – the Ottoman capital on the Bosporus Strait, which provides the only viable passage by water to Crimea.'

'So Constantinople has become an outpost for the armies of Western Europe!' Ben said.

'That's right. And not only that: if Crimea falls to Russia and the Black Sea falls with it, Constantinople – and the Ottoman Empire itself – will be the first domino in the chain to tumble.'

Ben began pacing about his attic-room. Even Max, usually unfazed by his brother's antics, was unnerved.

'Are we finished? Can I have my cigar please?'

Ben reached under his bed. Tucked away next to the Webley Longspur was a cigar case with five golden-brown Cubans that he and Elizabeth had lifted from a dispensary on Burlington Arcade.

'Tell Papa and you'll be in a heap of trouble,' Ben cautioned, handing one to Max.

'Obviously not.' He ran the cigar beneath his nose, savouring the aroma. 'A lifelong collection begins here!'

Max sauntered off, satisfied with his haul. As he left, Ben called after him: 'One more thing!'

'What now, Benjy?'

'In your reading on this topic,' Ben said, 'have you ever come across the name "the White Death"?'

Max shook his head. 'Never. But it doesn't sound very pleasant. Why do you ask?'

'...Off you go, Max.'

Max shrugged, pocketed the cigar and went downstairs.

Ben's next step was his old haunt, the British Museum. He had not set foot here in six years. Teenage *yidden* were not welcome in the museum libraries, but Ben had struck up a rapport with a senior librarian, Miss Alma Hewitt, a kindly spinster who had taken a shine to him. They had developed a well-worn routine: Ben would tuck himself away in an unobtrusive corner of the library and Alma would ferry him Enlightenment-era pamphlets from the King's Library and books on natural history from the Cottonian.

And now, just like old times, Alma would be his way in. The old bird was delighted to see Ben appear at her desk after such a long absence. By lunchtime, she had installed him at a desk behind the stacks of the Harleian.

He started by rooting around for information on 'the White Death'. He searched medical textbooks, military annals and folk tale compendiums – but found nothing. The phrase, whatever it meant, remained a mystery.

Next he found a reference copy of a history of Constantinople. It was thirty years out of date, but it described the city in great detail. One of its many illustrations was of the Hagia Sophia – the city's most famous mosque, overlooking the Bosporus Strait where it met the Sea of Marmara.

Ben squinted. Something about it seemed strangely familiar.

He pulled out the June 1854 daguerreotype of Elizabeth, taken from Palmerston's jacket. In the background, over Elizabeth's right shoulder, was a dome encircled by four tall minarets, rising above the skyline at the summit of a huge hill – *identical to the Hagia Sophia*. Even the size and placement of the surrounding trees on the hill matched the illustration in the tome.

If this daguerreotype was a true likeness, it was not just 'Heathcote' in Constantinople – Elizabeth had been there too, and might still be. Perhaps Heathcote's return address could lead him directly back to her?

He kicked himself. And what then, exactly? Writing to Heathcote was not an option. If Heathcote was feeding information to Palmerston, then Palmerston would surely find out that Ben had gone through his correspondence. And travelling to Constantinople was sheer madness, not to mention impossible. From what he knew, it was a good twenty pounds for a steamer across the Mediterranean – well beyond his budget – and what few commercial rail services there were had been suspended because of the war. And on top of that, Ben would need a Foreign Office passport verified by the Turkish Consul, which he would never be granted.

There was something else bothering Ben. What if the woman in the daguerreotype was not Elizabeth? What if he was just seeing her face because he longed to see it? Was he just a deluded fool, unable to admit that the first girl he ever loved had abandoned him, died from illness and was never coming back? Her father had written to him about it. Would he really lie about his own daughter's death? And even if it *was* her in the daguerreotype, that raised an even more troubling question: what interest could Palmerston, the Home Secretary of the United Kingdom, possibly have in Lise de Varney – a twenty-year-old doctor's secretary from Paris?

A week passed with Ben stuck in limbo: taunted by the prospect of Elizabeth being, after so long, within touching distance, yet without the means to find her. He was trapped in a state of inaction – hardly sleeping, distracted at work, avoiding Jack and Leo, overcome with a disabling sense of unease.

On the Saturday following his discovery, the Canaan family had gathered in the living room for their noontime ritual of tea and cakes. Tuvia and Hesya in their customary armchairs. Herschel poring over his newspaper. Golda nestled on Ben's lap. Max on the floor reading the final chapter of *Hard Times* published in *Household Words* the previous day. Judit fixing her hair in a compact mirror. Ruth busying herself with various chores, stoking the hearth, refilling teacups.

A guest was round that day: Archie Greenbaum – a slopseller with intellectual pretensions and a small amount of knowledge about a great many things.

'Emancipation? I have very little to say on the matter,' Greenbaum declared – which usually meant that he had a great deal to say on the matter. 'Emancipation will do us Jews a world of good. Only when we have the rights and freedoms of a natural-born citizen of Great Britain, will we be *viewed*, *seen* and *perceived* as equals to the gentiles!'

'Benjy,' Golda said, prodding Ben's arm. 'What's he talking about?'

'Well, Golda, us Jews can't do important jobs, or go to the best schools, or be in the government. But non-Jews can. Emancipation means we will be allowed to do what everyone else can, even though we're different. It's like when Mama says you can't have a chocolate biscuit before bed because you're only six, but Judit can because she's seventeen. If you were emancipated, you could have as many chocolate biscuits as you want!'

Golda rubbed her hands together with glee. 'Mama, can I be emancipated?'

'Stop putting funny ideas in her head, Benjy!' Ruth scolded. 'Jewish emancipation and chocolate biscuits! Honestly!'

'*I'll tell you what it is!*' Tuvia roared, waving a teaspoon in the air. His sudden explosion caught everyone off-guard.

'I'm going to excuse myself so that I can focus on my Dickens,' Max muttered, sulking out with the serial tucked under his arm. 'It's the last chapter!'

'Pah!' Tuvia spat. 'Nobody interested in what an old man has to say anymore?!'

'We are interested, Papa,' Ruth placated. 'Tell us. And put that spoon down before you injure someone.'

'Emancipation,' Tuvia declared, 'is a sham! A plot to turn every Jew into an Englishman, teach him to be ashamed of his roots and erase his identity.'

Greenbaum nearly choked on his tea. 'But we *are* Englishmen!' He turned to Solly for solidarity. 'Solly, you were born here. Are you not an Englishman?'

Solly made a noncommittal gesture. 'On a technicality, I suppose.'

Greenbaum was incredulous. 'I can't believe what I'm hearing! Everyone here shelters under a British flag. Where's the shame in that?'

'Because it is not *our* flag!' Tuvia replied. 'I wouldn't expect you to understand, Greenbaum: you wouldn't know the Old Country if it pished in your teacup. But Jews like me, who fled here on boats, most of us didn't have the faintest clue where we were headed. We could have been sailing to Cape Town or Buenos Aires for all we knew. We ended up in England by chance and so by chance we shuffle around under the Union Jack. But we are a *wandering people* – and if you don't believe me, go ask the

English! To them, an English Jew is like a monkey in a redcoat. They treat us like beggars, shove us in ghettos and spit in our faces. They want nothing to do with us.'

'But they didn't turn you away at Southampton!' Greenbaum said indignantly. 'They took countless of us in, even when the Continent hoofed us out. If they hate us, they're not exactly doing a slap-up job of showing it.'

'The English don't hate us,' Tuvia said. 'They just *dislike* us, in that mild English manner we've all come to know and love. Their antipathy is unthinking – a habit like picking your nose, or lifting your little pinkie when you drink your tea, Greenbaum…'

Greenbaum self-consciously set down his teacup. 'I'm no fool, Tuvia. I understand full well that there are some people in this country who look at us with prejudice. But when they see Jews doing all the things that Christians do, you can be sure that perceptions will alter. When there are Jews in the Houses of Parliament, in the Royal Courts of Justice, in every Royal Academy from London to Edinburgh, when we become landowners…'

'And *which* Jews exactly are set to benefit?' Tuvia interrupted him bitterly. 'Me? You? Anyone in this room?'

Nobody dared say a word.

'Or is it just for Baron Rothschild? What do I care if Baron Rothschild sits in the House of Commons? I don't recall a Rothschild or their ilk deigning to buy my *schmutters*, or coming to my aid when the English schoolboys burnt my petticoats and slashed up my face…' He pointed to the scar under his lip. 'But when Baron Rothschild wishes to acquire the status of the very men who hold us down, now I must commit myself to his cause or be cast as a traitor!'

The old man was purple in the face. 'Nobody called you a traitor, Tuvia,' Solly said gently.

'It was implied. Go out on the street and ask any working Jew – the hawkers, the craftsmen, the grocers, the gangsters – ask any one of them what he thinks of Baron Rothschild and emancipation. What will he give you? *A shrug*. The only Jews who are *kibbitzing* on about emancipation are rich Jews – Jews desperate to assimilate. They buy country estates and fill them with Constables. They go horse-riding and shooting. They send their children to Eton and Oxford, where they can be taught gentile manners.'

'What's the answer then?' Greenbaum joked. 'Go back to the *shtetl*?'

Ben was expecting Tuvia to annihilate Greenbaum. But instead, he sighed softly and spoke as though from another time and place.

'I was fourteen when I fled the *shtetl*. Virny, it was called: a beautiful place on the Black Sea, surrounded by wonderful green lagoons. Then, in the course of one night...' He clicked his fingers. '*Gone*. Burned to the ground. It was a massacre. They came to kill us with knives, guns, flaming torches. But I learned, and so did every one of those six hundred souls who escaped on the boat with me, that you cannot kill the Jewish people that way. It only strengthens our resolve to survive. The only way you can kill the Jews is by convincing them to give up their Jewishness. Emancipation is a contract with the devil – he gives us luxury, and we give him our identity. That is a price no Jew can afford to pay. Unless...' He was looking directly at Ben as he spoke. 'Unless he wants to stop being a Jew altogether. Which he is free to do if he so wishes. But he will spend his life running from himself, in pursuit of the thing that he is not.'

Greenbaum had long since climbed down from his soapbox. Solly was not about to contradict his father-in-law. Herschel was still reading *News of the World*. Golda had fallen asleep in Ben's lap.

Ben looked at Greenbaum with a modicum of sympathy. There was something about the dream that this windbag clung to that touched Ben: not so different from the dream that he had once believed in.

'What are "gentile manners", *Zeyde*?' Ben said suddenly.

For the first time since he began his invective, Tuvia was stumped.

'Is it speaking the language eloquently?' Ben continued. 'Is it being clean and presentable? Is it standing upright, rather than kneeling? Is it owning a home and staying there, rather than constantly being exiled? Is it having means like the Rosens, or keeping up with the latest fashions like Uncle Herschy?'

'Amen!' Herschel intoned from behind his newspaper.

'Is it having friends who think differently to you, who believe in a different God? Is it having a job with prestige and status? Is it having the ability to do and say as you please, instead of serving someone else's whims?'

Ben paused. The room sank into silence.

'That's not "gentile", Grandad. That's *dignity*. Having dignity doesn't make you less of a Jew. And being an outcast, being downtrodden and marginalised, doesn't make you more of a Jew. I think that's just what they've told us to keep us out. Maybe we can be part of this new world without losing our identity. Maybe I'm a Jew because of something in my heart that no amount of

Earl Grey can ever extinguish. Maybe I can be a Jew and… go my own way. Do it myself.'

Solly's hand came to rest on his shoulder. His grip was not tight, but Ben could feel its weight. He looked around at his family, who did not seem to understand what he was saying – or why he was saying it.

There came a knock at the front door downstairs: three loud thuds. Solly got to his feet and strode off to answer it, while the conversation drifted to other inanities.

'In other news,' Herschel suddenly piped up, 'one Mrs O'Neill of Clacton-on-Sea was eaten by her own dog – a Skye Terrier!'

'What are you talking about, you *schmendrick*?' Tuvia croaked.

Herschel waved the paper in his face: '*News of the World*, old man! You blind?'

'I wish I was,' Tuvia said. 'Wouldn't have to look at your ugly mug all day.'

But Ben was not listening to their bickering. He was thinking about those knocks. It was the tell-tale sound of a policeman's truncheon: a thick wooden billy club pounding on their front door. He had heard it before, on raids to catch pickpockets at the Houndsditch boxing club, or to shut down a storehouse where the dockland gangsters had hidden fenced goods.

He slipped out onto the hallway and peeked downstairs as Solly opened the front door. Sure enough, standing before his father was a bobby from the Metropolitan Police, brandishing his truncheon. He had a striped armband on his left sleeve, which meant he was on duty – definitely not stopping by for a cup of tea or to debate the merits of emancipation.

'Can I help you?' Solly said timidly.

'Sergeant O'Connor of the Metropolitan Police,' the bobby said, 'H division – Whitechapel. Is this the abode of one Benjamin E. Canaan?'

Ben's heart leapt to his throat.

'It is…' Solly replied.

'May I have a word with him?'

'What on earth for?'

'We received a tip-off yesterday. A witness came forward claiming that last Friday week your son impersonated a well-known gentleman for fraudulent purposes, infiltrated a private function at Claridge's Hotel, besmirched the honour of a young lady, and shot a man in the leg. Quite the charge sheet, isn't it?'

Solly cast his mind back to Ben's hijinks the previous Friday night. The ruined suit and the boy's evasive manner. He had wondered what Ben had been hiding, even feared the worst – but he could never have imagined that it would be this serious.

'Who was your witness, might I ask?'

The bobby consulted his notebook. 'One Alexander Rosen – you might know him as "Sandy". He was present at Claridge's and even spoke to your son before the incident.'

Sandy bloody Rosen, Ben thought to himself. Safe to say that his job offer as a legal assistant had gone up in smoke. But now he was concerned with more pressing matters – namely, how to escape before he was unceremoniously banged up.

Solly turned to call after Ben and saw his son standing at the top of the stairs. 'Benjamin!' Solly shouted. *'What have you done?!'*

Sergeant O'Connor stuck his head in, clocked Ben, and shoved past Solly. Ben cast one last frantic look back at his family, who had rushed to the door of the living room. He bolted upstairs.

'BENJAMIN E. CANAAN, YOU'RE UNDER ARREST!' Sergeant O'Connor yelled in pursuit.

Ben burst into his attic-room and locked the door behind him. That would buy him a few precious seconds. While O'Connor got to work beating down the door, Ben grabbed the daguerreotype of Elizabeth, Heathcote's letter to Palmerston, the mother-of-pearl penknife, the Webley Longspur, and his savings – exactly one pound, five shillings and fivepence – and shoved it all into a canvas knapsack.

By the time O'Connor kicked the door in, Ben had thrown open his window and leapt out, sliding down a drainpipe to street-level. The rest was a blur: sprinting at full pelt down Whitechapel Road – the shriek of O'Connor's whistle – the startled faces of bystanders stepping aside as this breathless fugitive shot past them.

As Ben disappeared into the Saturday afternoon crowds of Aldgate, leaving everything he had known behind him in the dust, he knew that there was only one place he could go and one man who could help him.

6

Lennie and the Dogs

A mist was setting in as Ben slunk through the Isle of Dogs. Coal-smoke, sulphur and blasts of hot steam suffocated the canals and dry-docks. Sparks flashed like fireflies in the grey gloom as shipbuilders hammered into the husks of half-built brigs, slumped in the brackish waters like sacked temples. Packhorses strained under the weight of carbon-steel rebar, their whinnies bouncing off the windowless brick buildings that walled in the barren docklands of London's shadowy underworld.

Back in the day this place had been nothing more than a dismal marsh dotted with gibbets where unlucky pirates were left to hang – watched through telescopes on the other side of the river by any Tom, Dick and Harry for a penny a pop.

But this was Lennie Glass' neighbourhood now. His crew, known to all as 'The Dogs', took their name both from the locale and from Lennie's fabled first scalp aged just fourteen: slicing the pinkie off a gentile who called him a '*yiddisher* dog'. Legend had it that Lennie kept the digit preserved in formaldehyde as a keepsake – and a warning.

The Dogs' fingers, meanwhile, were in every pie. Pickpocketing rings, counterfeiting, loan sharking, bootleg moonshine, contract killing – not to mention the most lucrative market of all: *opium*. Ironically enough, this was Lennie's only racket that was strictly speaking legal. But Lennie was not interested in providing the fine people of London with a magical elixir for diarrhoea, whooping cough or jaundice. His angle was recreational, luring punters into his dens, where they could spend their hard-earned coin on his midnight oil and disappear into delirium.

And now Ben was about to come to eyeball to eyeball with the big man himself.

He crossed the West India Docks, ducking past stevedores as they reeled in a huge merchant barque. Then down Limehouse Causeway, into a dingy alleyway littered with old newspapers and rat carcasses that not even the stray cats dared eat. A single spectral lantern pulsed through the thickening fog, faintly illuminating a faded red sign: *Ah Jiang's* – London's most notorious opium den.

Three men loitered at the entrance, leaning against a brick wall, their murky silhouettes traced by the orange smoulder of their cigarettes. They saw Ben approach and stalked over to him. It was a posse of goons: Lennie's middlemen. The ringleader of the trio was Yanky – a Litvak card shark and burglar whom Lennie had dredged up at the turn of the decade from a prison on the outskirts of Vilna, with a gap-toothed snarl and a fondness for flipping his switchblade as he spoke.

'Look who's decided to show his rotten face,' Yanky drawled. 'You've been keeping Mr Glass waiting. He's not happy.'

'Well, I'm here now,' Ben said as he caught his breath, opening his knapsack to reveal the Webley Longspur, 'and I come bearing an early Hanukkah present.'

Yanky stubbed his cigarette under his boot and nodded to his henchmen. They grabbed Ben, one on each arm. 'Do us a favour,' Yanky said as he pocketed his blade. *'Try not to drop it this time, Mr Butterfingers.'*

They dragged Ben into Ah Jiang's. The first thing to hit him was the smell. Bitter ammonia, cheap incense, kerosene fumes – a mixture so pungent that it made his eyes water. The clientele came from every walk of life: a tramp with a cleft lip struggling to smoke from his pipe – a sailor in rumpled uniform, muttering frantically to a cat stretched out on his chest – a well-to-do young woman in a fine silk dress, staring sadly into the light of a sputtering spirit lamp as she heated a nugget of opium paste over the flame. Yet they were all equalised by the drug – sprawled on moth-eaten mattresses in low-ceilinged smoking salons, enveloped in an oppressive dark-brown haze of opium smoke, glazed eyes following Ben as he passed them. It may have been the middle of the day, but in Ah Jiang's it was perpetually midnight.

Ben was taken up a flight of stairs, onto a corridor lined with private bedrooms, where opium-eaters slept off the effects of the drug, played *khanhoo* with colourful Chinese cards, or drank absinthe in bathtubs. At the end of the corridor was a gold-plated door, guarded by two heavies in blue long-tailed *changshan*.

'For Lennie,' Yanky whispered, jerking his head in Ben's direction.

One of the heavies nodded and knocked on the door. Then came a muffled voice on the other side: 'Come in!'

Lennie Glass was sitting at his partners' desk. His office was a gaudy mishmash of oriental knickknacks, from statues of South Asian deities to Japanese woodblock prints and arabesques yellowed from smoke. On his desk was a silver tray with all the paraphernalia for an opium smoke: a stained bamboo pipe affixed to a metal bowl, a spirit lamp, scales, a sheet-copper casket, a needle, and a hop for the ashes. Behind him was a wall-sized map of London, the arc of the Thames forming a blue halo around his head. An elderly Chinese lady clad in an elegant red *qipao* sat on a chaise longue in the corner of the room.

And sure enough, taking pride of place on a nearby mantelpiece was a glass jar, and floating inside was the famed pickled pinkie.

Lennie had a clean-shaven babyface and was wearing a crisp maroon suit – but this soft, respectable veneer was betrayed by a nasty glint in his dull blue eyes. He spread his arms wide and gave Ben a compassionless grin. 'Benjamin E. Canaan. How considerate of you to stop by. I was starting to think I might have to send Yanky round your ends for a little talking to.' He motioned to the chair on the other side of his desk. 'Don't stand there like a mug – siddown.'

Ben hesitantly took a seat, knapsack on his lap. Lennie opened the sheet-copper casket and removed a glistening ball of black opium paste, pinched between finger and thumb. 'Have you ever seen such exquisite opium in yer life?'

'No, sir,' Ben said politely.

'Y'know what they said in Parliament the other day? Some posh *momser* dribbling about "the evils of opium". Load of sob stuff about how it corrupts the morals of good folk, promotes indolence and depravity.' Lennie smirked to himself. 'Don't hear 'em talkin' a blue streak about the gin they go back home to every night. Convenient, ain't it? They call me a merchant of death, but really I'm a… I'm a…'

'You're a purveyor of joy,' Ben said with a nervy smile.

'*Ex-actly!* A purveyor of joy. Old John Bull sends young men to die in foreign lands for reasons best known to himself, leaves the rest of us to wallow in filth and disease – but *I'm* evil for wanting to give people a moment of respite from their misery? Go to church and they'll tell you that you've gotta hand over yer life, yer every waking moment, to get a spot in heaven. But I'm liberal-hearted, y'see, so I give it to folks for a shilling. Ain't that right, Granny?'

He looked at the old Chinese woman sitting in the corner. She said nothing – just nodded sagely.

'That's Granny Ah Jiang,' Lennie said to Ben. 'I own the place, but the recipe is hers – and that's what keeps 'em comin' back! Anyway. Enough how-dee-dos. You've got something of mine.'

Ben reached into his knapsack and produced the Webley Longspur. Lennie inspected it, peered inside the chamber... and turned the barrel square on Ben.

'Would you look at that!' Lennie exclaimed. 'There's a bullet missing. Supposed to be fully loaded. I don't suppose there was some... *incident* earlier this week involving an accidental discharge?'

Ben's heart was doing the can-can, but he just about held his own. 'Had to check it was still working.'

'Mmm, so I heard. Got Johnny Hopper crawling all over me 'cos of your antics. Now I'm stressed, Benjamin E. Canaan! And you know what I'm like when I'm stressed. Trigger finger gets all shaky...'

'In fairness,' Ben said, raising his hands apologetically, 'the gun kind of fired itself.'

Lennie laughed and looked over at Yanky. 'Looks like we got a clown in town!'

He cocked the hammer.

'Look,' Ben said, 'I'm really sorry, Mr Glass. It wasn't part of the script—'

Lennie cut him off. 'Well, your performance certainly brought the house down. Got me wondering how you're gonna... bow out.'

Ben glanced at the door, wondering whether he could make a bolt for it. But Yanky and the two henchmen were standing in his path.

Suddenly Lennie dropped the gun and threw his head back, cackling like a maniac. Ben's shoulders sagged and he let out an audible sigh of relief. Yanky and the Litvaks shifted uncomfortably on their feet.

'Don't all wet yerselves at once!' Lennie roared. 'And don't you worry, Mr Canaan. I was never gonna make a mess on that armchair. Besides, there is one silver lining: at least nobody knows who you are.'

Ben winced. Time to face the music. 'About that... There's another reason I came. I was recognised at Claridge's. Police tracked me down, raided my house this afternoon. I barely got out. So they know it was me – my family does too. Soon everyone in town will be wise to it.'

The temperature in the room plummeted. Lennie's grin vanished and for the first time he looked deadly serious. Ben held his tongue – worried that if he broke the silence, whatever he said, Lennie would have him beaten to a pulp.

Lennie snapped his fingers. Granny Ah Jiang hobbled over to him and set about preparing his opium. First she struck a match and lit the spirit lamp, then took a pinch of opium paste from the casket and measured it out in the scales, rolling it into a ball. She pierced the ball with the end of the needle and held it over the flame of the spirit lamp, until it started to bubble and turn from deep black to gold – all the while stretching the paste into strings to cook it.

Lennie took up the pipe and she pressed the opium into the metal bowl. He took a long drag, held the smoke in his mouth, and exhaled slowly. Granny Ah Jiang returned to her chaise longue and Lennie slumped in his chair.

'What a cock-up…' Lennie mused. 'And you, of all people! When Yanky picked you up at the boxing club last year, he said you had yer wits about ya.'

'It won't happen next time, Mr Glass.'

'Let's sort this mess out and *then* we can worry about "next time", sonny.'

Lennie took another puff and stared at the ceiling, mulling his options. Finally, he sucked through his teeth and looked Ben dead in the eye.

'Time for the Disappearing Act,' he said.

Ben's heart sank. He had been afraid Lennie would say that. He had heard about Lennie's famed 'Disappearing Act': underlings with too much heat around them packed off to godforsaken parts of the country, forced to lie low under a false alias until things blew over and the law moved on. One fellow, Ossy Ringwald, had a dangerous liaison with a bobby's wife. He was sent to Ireland and had not been seen since. Rumour had it he was working the fishing trawlers off Ballinskelligs and drowned in a storm.

'Is that… really necessary, Mr Glass?' Ben protested.

Lennie chuckled. 'What did you think I'd say? *Zei gezunt?* Let you head back home to sew undies in yer old man's workshop, when the police have their elephant ears to the wall, shakin' doors east and west?'

He had a point. Going back home was not an option – not for now, at least. And even if the police were not scouring Whitechapel for his whereabouts, his parents might well turn him in, to avoid a collusion charge that would implicate the whole family and bring Canaan & Sons into disrepute.

'What if I worked out of Limehouse or the Docklands?' Ben asked. 'I can keep my head down, do good work for you…'

'You out of your tiny, shiny mind?' Lennie scoffed. 'The whole point of the Disappearing Act is that it puts a wall between you and me. I need deniability while the Met's sniffing around you.'

Ben was about to protest, but Lennie cut him off with a raised finger.

'Careful, Benjy boy. I'm the only one who's gonna help you and this is the best you're gonna get. So the next words out yer gob better be "Thank you, Mr Glass" – or I'll have to find a better use for yer tongue.'

'…Thank you, Mr Glass.'

'Good lad. Yanky: talk to Alf and see what's ticking. We're gonna need airtight cover for him. Granny Ah Jiang: find the lad a room, will ya? Nothin' fancy.'

Before Ben could say another word, he was whisked out by Granny Ah Jiang. His last glimpse of Lennie before the Chinese bodyguards closed the gold-plated door was of the crime boss taking another hit on his opium pipe, calling after Ben with a manic laugh: 'A purveyor of joy! I'm gonna use that!'

*

Later that afternoon, Ben was taken to see Alf, Lennie's counterfeiter extraordinaire – a 'varnisher', or *shoful-pitcher* as the Jews called him, specialising in forged banknotes and coinage. But he had also perfected the art of crafting fake identification for Lennie's Disappearing Acts. Now Alf had been tasked with doing just that for Ben, and pronto.

They found him in an office above the West India Docks, handsomely supplied by Lennie with looms, printers, inkpots and an impressive collection of calligraphy pens. Alf was unsure when he first met Ben what alias might suit him best. He inspected the boy's face: a Black Country miner might do the trick – some impoverished manual labourer hacking away at a coal seam in the Midlands. But he would need the night to figure it out.

Granny Ah Jiang offered Ben a straw bed in the brick-walled basement beneath the opium den, with only a spirit lamp to light up the dingy cellar crawling with cockroaches. The ceiling was porous and opium smoke drifted down to him all night, making him woozy. At midnight, Granny Ah Jiang stuck her head in with dinner – *hong shao rou*, pork belly on rice, served with a side of opium – neither of which Ben could bring himself to touch. Upstairs, he could hear the incessant twanging of *guzheng* zithers and the melancholy wailing of a Chinese soprano.

In the sleepless fog, his thoughts ran wild. Where was Lennie going to send him? To see out the rest of the year down a mine shaft, breathing in enough coal dust to put him in an early grave? Or to freeze to death on a fishing boat off the coast of Shetland, with only lobsters and scallops for company?

Just before dawn, the revelry upstairs began to wind down as the clientele slipped into unconsciousness. Ben removed the daguerreotype from his knapsack. Inky shadows played across the woman's face in the flickering lamplight. It had to be Elizabeth. Even though they were worlds and years apart, and the lifeless object in his hands was all he had left of her, it felt as though she was looking back at him with the same immediacy, the same love, as she had in the summer of 1851. Inviting him, daring him, as she had done in all their adventures.

Ben tried to remember the last time he had felt truly alive. It was not at Claridge's, or at Houndsditch boxing club. It was not at Bevis Marks, or the billiards tables and pubs of the East End with the Good-for-Nothings. It was certainly not at 82 Whitechapel Road: not in the attic, at the dinner table, or in the workshop.

The truth was, that the last time he felt as though the world was his, and his alone, was with her. His first love. A love that he believed to have died and that had somehow been resurrected.

An idea was taking shape in the haze of second-hand opium. At first he thought it was a product of his anxiety and fatigue. But it persisted, and he continued to circle it until it felt more and more real. An irresistible urge to follow this clue leading back to Elizabeth, wherever it went – even if it was into the unknown. Isn't that what she had taught him all those years ago? To go beyond the confines of the life that had been chosen for him?

The bells of London struck six. No sooner had their echoes died across the city's rooftops, than Ben was running out of Ah Jiang's and down to the West India Docks like a man possessed.

He found Alf exactly where he had left him, stooped over a worktable inspecting a set of birth certificates with a loupe. 'Hop it, Canaan!' Alf snarled. 'I work fast but I'm not a magician!'

'I have a question,' Ben said, 'and it might add some spice to the job.'

Alf turned around in his chair and set down his magnifying glass – a tell-tale sign that at the very least, Ben had his attention. 'Careful now,' he grinned. 'Too much spice and I'll get a runny tummy.'

Ben slapped Heathcote's return address down on the worktable: *15 Nakkaş Haydar Sk.*

'Tell me, Alf: have you ever sent a man to Constantinople?'

7
The HMS *Midas*

It took the rest of the week for Alf to finish Ben's documentation. In the meantime, Ben stayed put in the cellar under Ah Jiang's, eventually succumbing to the daily ration of pork belly on rice. It was eat or starve – and besides, as he chewed the hot, tender meat and washed it down with lapsang tea, he could not help but wonder what all the fuss was about. During his sojourn at the opium den, he was only allowed to venture out for fresh air in the early hours of morning, before dawn, when the clientele was catatonic and Limehouse was quiet. The incident at Claridge's had ruffled feathers and the police, as he had been reliably informed, were on the lookout.

There were moments – usually in the evening, when loneliness, boredom and the stench of opium were at their most oppressive – when Ben considered giving up the game and returning home, even if it meant being banged up by the Met. But he would quickly dispel the notion. Lennie would not permit it. He considered sending his family a note to reassure them that he was alive and would return soon. But that too was wishful thinking: he had no earthly idea how long he would be gone, and he did not want to make promises that he could not keep.

The following Sunday evening, Lennie summoned Ben back to his office above Ah Jiang's and revealed his new identity.

Rupert Rogers: twenty-three years old, born 6th of January 1831 in Wakefield, in the West Riding of Yorkshire, to Rupert Sr and Ethel Rogers, née Parry – with a birth certificate and verified passport bearing the British consul's stamp of approval. No schooling – Rupert started out in the mines at the age of thirteen, before training as a deckhand aboard a series of military steamers: the *Argo*, PS *Anglia*, RMS *Amazon* and SS *Great Western*.

As they spoke, half a dozen military steamships in Southampton were being loaded with supplies for the British and French troops recently sent to Crimea. The plan was for Ben to board the HMS *Midas* – the largest steamer of the fleet, with nearly a hundred crew to handle its goods. The *Midas* was bound for Yevpatoria, a coastal stronghold on Kalamita Bay on Crimea's eastern coast. But since the only point of access to the Black Sea was via the Bosporus Strait, the ship's route would take it through Constantinople.

Ben's way in would be the chief mate, Edwin Marshall, widely known as Captain Eddie. Ten years previously, Captain Eddie was a mid-ranking 'able seaman', when he had the good fortune to stumble across an opium stash which a group of engineers was smuggling into England on Lennie's dime. Eddie, partial to the occasional bribe, had found himself a lucrative sideline. When needed, a couple of guineas was enough to buy his loyalty.

One of Lennie's men had been sent down to Southampton ahead of time to obtain confirmation from Captain Eddie that he would help to stow Ben away as a member of crew. Eddie agreed, but given the risk involved, he doubled his rate. And so Ben was to travel to Southampton by train on Monday morning, meet with Captain Eddie on land that afternoon, and by dawn on Tuesday, he would be aboard the HMS *Midas*, with a chief mate to vouch for him as they set sail for Crimea.

Lennie was delighted with this turn of events. He did not say it to Ben directly, but sending the Canaan boy off to Constantinople was preferable to any destination closer to home. The Black Sea, where war had been raging for well over a year now, was considerably more dangerous than Gainsborough or Dudley. If Ben was to meet an untimely end out there, Lennie's hands would be washed clean of him. He slipped Ben a single gold sovereign before sending the boy packing: a lucky reward for whoever found his corpse.

Ben spent one final night at Ah Jiang's. Since they knew that he was heading off, potentially for good, he was allowed upstairs that night, to while away the hours drinking with the Dogs and laughing at opium-eaters unable to handle their narcotics, left to puke their guts out on the Causeway.

Early the next morning, Ben was escorted by Yanky to Waterloo Station and dumped on a packed London and South Western train bound for Southampton. He kept to himself for the entirety of the three-hour journey. He was paranoid that he might be spotted, even in this carriage of perfect strangers more concerned with the contents of the back pages and the view out the window than with a pasty young deckhand clutching a knapsack.

Just after lunchtime, the train terminated at Southampton's Blechynden Station. The town was unusually quiet despite having become a glorified outpost of the British Army. People went about their business in humdrum fashion: pharmacists doled out dried stramonium for asthmatics to burn and inhale – milliners flogged wide-brimmed leghorn sunhats – drayman lugged coffers of beer into the pubs along the high street.

Among these was the Red Lion Inn, a five-minute walk from Victoria Pier. It was marked out from the buildings around it by an elaborate Tudor design and a sign at its entrance dating it to the late 1400s. It was desolate inside – a deadpan fellow working the bar, a few sullen sailors nursing their ales. A distinguished older gentleman smoked a cigarette in a long jade holder, with a noble face that looked as though it had been carved from mahogany.

A red-headed sailor waved Ben over to the bar. He had an unruly beard, with a navy-blue tunic over a grimy undershirt and a seafarer's pipe in the corner of his mouth.

Ben took a steeling breath.

'Captain Eddie, I presume?' Ben asked.

He nodded. 'You presume right. Lennie's gettin' 'em younger and younger these days, I see.'

'How'd you know it was me?'

'You stick out like a sore thumb, mate. Pale little Jew-boy walkin' in lookin' like you've just discovered yer first stiffy. What's yer name again?'

'Benjamin E.—'

'Not yer *real name*, you dozy twit,' Captain Eddie cut Ben off. 'I couldn't give a monkey's bollock who you really are. All's I need to know is yer "stage name".'

'Oh… Rupert Rogers.'

Captain Eddie snorted. 'You got the loot?'

Ben produced three guineas, as promised. Captain Eddie pocketed the coins and gestured to the door. 'Off we go then, Rupert!'

On their way out, Captain Eddie tipped his hat to the gentleman with the jade cigarette holder: *'Está disfrutando de su almuerzo, señor?'*

The gentleman barely reacted, grunting a somewhat irritated *'Si!'* Captain Eddie nudged Ben as they exited the Red Lion: 'That chap's an Argentine. Juan Manuel de Rosas is his name – used to be the governor of Buenos Aires, till the Brazilians hoofed him out. Now he sups on jellied eel and still refuses to speak a lick of English.'

Captain Eddie walked Ben down to Victoria Pier. Six hulking steamers had taken anchor, connected to the pier by a series of ramps and wooden bridges, and the swampy banks of the Southampton Water estuary were heaving with stevedores and caulkers. Muscular shire horses and livestock were being loaded onto the ships, together with crates of every description: hardtack biscuits, lard and salted beef; muskets and rifles; bundles of winter coats and tattered leather boots; reams of paper for the men to write back home.

At the end of Victoria Pier was the HMS *Midas*. It was three hundred feet in length, with an iron hull, a towering funnel in the middle, and schooner-rigged masts for additional sail-power. Ropes and pulleys were slung down its massive broadsides, used by the seamen to haul the cargo onto deck.

'I have to admit,' Ben murmured as they crossed the bridge. 'She's pretty impressive.'

'Don't get yer hopes up. Like a Drury Lane whore, she's pretty on the outside – but you might find some crabs in her drawers.'

Captain Eddie was not lying. When Ben was taken below deck to the berths where the crew slept, he gagged at the smell. It was a sickening cocktail of gunpowder, body odour, and faeces that seemed to ebb and flow as the ship pitched in the water.

'Oh, you'll get used to it,' Captain Eddie laughed, clapping Ben on the back. 'It's how you'll smell in a couple of days!'

A few deckhands were laying out their belongings next to their hammocks. They shot Ben foul glares as he walked past. One of them, a burly Scot riddled with acne scars, gobbed on the floor: 'Look at this scrub!'

Ben kept his head down. This was no time for heroics – least of all with a man twice his size, who would have no qualms about snapping him in half.

Captain Eddie gave Ben a whistlestop tour of the ship, from the galley staffed by just three cooks for the hundred-strong crew to the storage compartments on the lowest level, down where the spur-and-pinion engines for the propellers were being fired up for the long journey ahead. They ended up back in the berths, where Ben was shown to his hammock.

'Tight squeeze,' Captain Eddie said. 'Then again, you won't be bringin' over any birds!'

Ben settled in for a quick nap, but Captain Eddie lifted the hammock and sent him tumbling to the floor.

'You're a deckhand, "Rupert Rogers" – start actin' like one. You know what we do to unauthorised persons out at sea?' Captain Eddie blew smoke in Ben's face. '*We throw 'em overboard.* And uncle Lennie ain't here to protect you. So make yerself useful before I turn you into fish-bait.' Captain Eddie had his money and he was determined to get his pound of flesh too. Ben had no choice but to comply.

It was a mad rush to get the ship ready for its departure at dawn. The *Midas* was mainly carrying ammunition – among the heaviest crates of all the supplies – and by sunset Ben's legs had given way. They had just fifteen minutes for dinner, which consisted of a tin cup of tepid coffee and a handful of hardtacks. After dinner, they worked through the night, to the sound of the crashing surf and the boom of departing ships.

By the time the sun rose over the placid waters to the cries of seagulls, the cargo had been loaded, the engines were in full gear, and the *Midas* was ready to set sail. Captain Eddie rang the bell port-side and the crew gathered at the gunwale to bid farewell to England.

As they chugged down the estuary, Southampton, with its curious blend of picturesque seaside streets and bleak industrial docks, faded away. The Solent, soughing with a north-west wind, took them past the rocky outlines of the Isle of Wight and into the Channel, where the waves were heavier and the air sent a chill down their spines. Soon the shores of England were just a green smudge on the silver blade of the horizon.

The ship had begun its journey into the unknown. And Ben, one of many faces in a throng of exhausted seafarers, was well and truly alone.

The *Midas*, as Ben soon discovered, was a special kind of hell. The food was enough to break a man's spirit. Bread so mouldy that he had to use his pocketknife to shave off the fungus. Hardtacks crawling with worms and cabbage soup infested with half-drowned woodlice. Filthy water, bitter coffee, everything liquid or solid tainted by brine and heavy fuel oil.

Then there was the seasickness. For the first week, Ben was violently ill – made worse by daily storms on the Atlantic that caused the *Midas* to list and sway. And since the men were not allowed on deck at night, they had to vomit into buckets by their hammocks, which left the berths reeking of fermented bile.

Just when Ben became accustomed to the ever-present nausea, disease began to spread amongst the crew. First came a general fever – sleepless nights tossing and turning, men muttering breathlessly and hot with sweat. Then came dysentery, typhus, and finally, the first case of cholera. Soon the berths were like the corridors of a madhouse, filled with deckhands shivering from the cold and struggling to hold down every crude remedy.

As the days wore on, the men became acquainted, jostling for status in the hierarchy of maritime life. Out here, names did not matter. Instead, a man was known by the worn-out look on his face, any weakness betrayed by his posture, the blisters on his hands from slinging rope, weeping lesions and impetigo pockmarking his skin, the hollow cadence of tiredness and despair in his voice. Some, like the giant Scot who had greeted Ben so fulsomely, asserted themselves at every opportunity, intimidating deckhands into handing over their rum rations and turning the mess hall into their own private fiefdom. Others were happy to follow, like the youngest crew-member – a fifteen-year-old orphan in the throes of puberty – adopted as a local dogsbody by the Scot and his thuggish entourage. As for Ben, he was happy just to survive – avoiding dysentery, brawling and excess talking at all costs.

Every man aboard this floating prison was impoverished. But money, which meant so much on land, had little value and even less purpose at sea. Instead, the men bartered their way up the greasy pole, trading in an improvised currency of rations, razorblades, clothing and deck duties. After all, you could not eat a sovereign – but a hardtack dipped in coffee might see you through the morning. A shilling would not keep you warm, but a strip of leather could be used to mend your rain-soaked boots. The most valuable denomination was the fifty-gram portion of salted beef doled out to each crew-member on Mondays, which Ben would trade for his scrubbing-duty on deck whenever there was a storm.

Their only escape from the drudgery of life aboard the *Midas* was gambling, booze and banter. The men would sit in circles in the mess hall and play endless rounds of poker, smoking roll-ups and taking guarded sips of their rum in fear that at any moment a neighbour might snatch it from them. During these nightly gatherings, they would often talk about the war – though few had any idea what it was over, when it would end, or who was their enemy. Most assumed that it would be finished by Christmas – that the boys in red would savour their victory over the 'Slav mongrels' with a mince pie and a yule log. But if one of the younger chaps were to ask how many men had died so far, the conversation would lull and the subject would quickly change.

Only one man seemed to think that the war was a fool's errand: the head cook, Jasper Johns. Jasper was a shrewd, laconic fellow from Cornwall who was rumoured to have done a stint in prison: for debts or murder, nobody quite knew. In any case, he took a shine to Ben – or at least, tolerated him when Ben was tasked with taking dirty dishes back to the galley after lunch and dinner. Ben came to suspect that Jasper had figured out that he was a stowaway under a fake alias, but had chosen not to upset the apple cart.

One night after dinner, Ben found Jasper starboard-side, having a smoke on deck. There was no moon and the ocean was a great wall of impenetrable black. One would not have known it was even there, were it not for the sea-spray and the sound of waves crashing against the hull of the *Midas*.

'History repeats itself,' Jasper told him, tipping ash into the void. 'I served in Afghanistan in '39 and it was the same old story. Some Whig aristo decides we need to go to war in the back of beyond and thousands of boys throw their lives away, never believing for a second that it could be them. But what it's all about – why they're shooting at people with whom they have no quarrel – what, in the end, it all amounts to… *that*, they could never tell you.'

Jasper lifted his shirt: a raised purple scar ran across the width of his chest, above the abdomen.

'I took four bullets at the Battle of Ghazni. Surgeon had to pry me open to fish 'em out. They didn't have ether in them days. Just a dram o' whisky and a slap on the cheek. And I was lucky. I got to go home. Still have nightmares about it – lyin' on that slab, strapped down and screamin', feelin' him rootin' around in my chest, powerless to stop any of it. I can only speak for myself when I say that I know history very well, 'cos I had to live it. Ain't it funny, what people choose to forget?'

Ben never mentioned the war again.

From the deck of the *Midas*, he watched half the world pass him by. The violent sea-storms that swept through the Bay of Biscay, off the coast of France. The Rock of Gibraltar at the mouth of the Mediterranean, where Spain met Africa. The *ancien port* of French-occupied Algiers, filled with Moorish madrasas and caravanserais. Fishermen off the coast of Syracuse in bright patterned gandouras, reeling in nets that teemed with sardines. The crumbling coastal fortifications of sun-baked Tunis and Tripoli, once used as slave markets, now a forum for jewellers and goldsmiths to flog their goods. Meadows on the hills of Malta, brimming with corn, oranges, figs and cotton. Glimpses of Greek isles across the Aegean: a tentacle of smoke trailing from Thera's volcano, a cluster of colourful huts on Samos, the sloping plains of Ithaca.

And then, late one September afternoon, after three interminable weeks of travel, a bell summoned the men to the bow of the *Midas*. The ship had crossed the Sea of Marmara and was approaching Constantinople.

The city sprawled along the shores of the Bosporus Strait, a majestic waterway with Europe on one side and Asia on the other. To the west as they sailed in was Seraglio Point – a lofty promontory on the outermost tip of the historical peninsula, where the minarets and domes of great mosques protruded from the skyline. On the Anatolian shore to the east was Scutari, where white Palladian mansions rose in tiers up the verdant slopes, giving way to cypress groves and secluded cemeteries. From the *Midas*, Ben could see for miles up the Bosporus, the landscape dotted with opulent estates, ornate domed *dargahs* and the towers of naval and military barracks.

The steamer looped round Seraglio Point and entered the Golden Horn, an inlet of the Bosporus where vessels large and small – from massive ironclad steamers and ships of the line, to one-man feluccas, merchant coasters and fishermen's *kayiks* – competed for space on the water. Here the western half of Constantinople was split in two. To the south, spread across the peninsula, was the old walled city of Stamboul; to the north, the commercial heartland of Galata and the more cosmopolitan district of Pera.

The *Midas* docked at a quay on the north shore of the Golden Horn, outside a munitions factory, to restock ahead of the final leg of its voyage to Crimea. Captain Eddie addressed his men:

'Right-ee-ho!' he roared. 'It's the twenty-sixth of September! Word from Crimea. Our boys have landed, and just last week they had their first big roll in the hay with the Russkies at Alma! Now, those vodka-soaked yahoos beat a retreat, but we've lost five thousand men in the process. So we can't hang around: three hours to resupply. Move it!'

The crew roared back, 'Yes, Captain!' and threw ramps down to the quay.

Ben had his knapsack slung over his shoulder and was ready to go. But before he got to the ramp, Captain Eddie laid a hand on his shoulder. 'A word, sonny.'

He handed Ben a red book. On the cover, in gold letters, it read: *MURRAY'S HANDBOOK FOR TRAVELLERS IN TURKEY*.

'You'll be needing this. And if you get in a spot of trouble, remember Cap'n Eddie's magic word: *baksheesh*. Ottoman coppers are always open to a bit of grease, if you know what I mean. It might just save your arse. Happy camping.'

Ben reached out to shake Captain Eddie's hand. But Eddie just laughed and hopped down the stairs below deck, humming a shanty.

Ben cast his eye across the quay, where wagon-drivers delivering wooden crates, disembarking seamen and reporters with cameras on tripods had amassed at the water's edge.

The crew of the *Midas* were distracted with their work. This was his chance.

He hurried down the ramp, passing a group of six deckhands as they brought a crate of thick winter coats on board. He slipped away from them, edged past a photographer taking snaps of the *Midas*, and disappeared into the heaving crowd on the waterfront. He picked up pace and soon the *Midas* was well behind him, merely another ship in the melee of the Golden Horn.

And just like that, the city of Constantinople swallowed Ben whole.

8
Shabbat at the Ahrida

Yanni Tokatlia was a hole-in-the-wall café overlooking the esplanade on the waterfront. It was a popular spot for the soldiers: injured redcoats on crutches, bronze-skinned French *zouaves* fresh from Algeria, moustachioed Ottoman infantrymen in fezzes and white sashes – chatting to each other between mouthfuls of dipping tobacco.

Ben found a quiet table where he could pore undisturbed over Murray's map of Constantinople and plot his next steps. While he read, Yanni brought him tea and flour biscuits known to the locals as *un kurabiyesi*, and helped him change his money. Two liras, comprising ten mejidîehs and twenty silver piastres: Yanni's best rate.

His finger alighted on Heathcote's address: *Nakkaş Haydar Sk.* – a thin, crooked line in Stamboul's Balat district, on the western side of the city.

He cast an eye out the window, across the Golden Horn. The sun was setting and the last dregs of daylight were draining away in the west, draping the minarets and domes of the peninsula's skyline in shadow. There was no chance of getting to Heathcote's before dark.

Ben did not fancy his luck out on the streets. According to Murray's, he was liable to be robbed, beaten and left for dead if he stumbled into the wrong neighbourhood. He needed a roof over his head.

But who would take him in? He had stowed away on a military supply ship and was completely alone in a foreign land, with no contacts, no friends and no family connections. If the British were alerted to his presence, they would court-martial him. Only Lennie Glass and the Dogs had any idea where he was. Nobody was coming to help him. And, to top it off, he did not speak a lick of Turkish.

His index finger tapped restlessly on the map. He peered closely at it. Hidden away in the tangled web of streets around Nakkaş Haydar was a red hexagram – a Star of David. And just below that was a name: AHRIDA SYNAGOGUE.

'Not *completely* alone,' he whispered.

He left two piastres for his tea and biscuits, gave Yanni a friendly nod and marched out, heading for the nearest bridge across the Golden Horn to Stamboul.

Even at the day's end, the waterfront was busy. Vagrants were washing their feet on stone steps leading down to the water, pleading for spare change with cries of 'Hey, English Johnny!' and 'Frenchman, Dis-Donc!' A couple of stevedores had stripped down to their breeches under a date palm tree, where barbers trimmed their beards in the dying light.

Ben crossed Galata Bridge, known as the Cisr-i-Cedid. Here, he was greeted by the many faces of the Ottoman Empire. Bulgarian fishermen in flared white kilts hoisted nets hanging in the waters of the Golden Horn from a grid of tall spars, teeming with herring and smelt. Syrian merchants in embroidered *keffiyeh* haggled in Arabic, while their slaves – young men in dark shawls and turbans, snatched from Turco-Egyptian Sudan – watched quietly. On the other side, at the entrance to Stamboul, was an Italian fish-market, where the last swordfish, bonita and sun-dried pilchard were being flogged before nightfall.

As Ben ventured deeper into the old city, the tumult around the Golden Horn faded far behind him. The streets became narrower and steeper – a labyrinth of cobbled alleys with the occasional Byzantine church. The broad French windows of a stately townhouse had been thrown open to release a rich dinnertime aroma of grilled lamb and fried cheese. Stray cats fought in the halo of gas lamps, scavenging for morsels before being shooed off by the maid of some well-to-do family. An elderly zither player plucked a plaintive tune at the gate of an overgrown cemetery, his lonely lament mingling with the adhan summoning the devout to pray the Maghrib.

Within the hour, Ben had reached a viewing post at the summit of Balat. The peninsula lay before him. A skein of plovers circled the rising moon, before descending to the terracotta rooftops. The peace and quiet felt sacred up here – as though Ben had wandered into another world, unchanged since ancient times.

He checked the map. Ahrida Synagogue should be around the corner. He came into a square with a fountain at its centre, ornamented with gilt arabesques, where a vagabond was scooping handfuls of water. On the near side of the square was an Eastern Orthodox Church, where supplicants had gathered before an icon of the Virgin Mary. Echoing from the far side was a chorus of voices, singing in a language that Ben recognised at once: *Hebrew.*

He crossed the square like a sailor drawn to a siren-song, up to the doors of the synagogue. Emblazoned in gold letters beneath a stained-glass Star of David was its name in Hebrew script: 'Ahrida'.

Ben entered to find a small congregation praying by candle-light. A few dozen men were ranged in wooden pews around the bema – drowsy octogenarians next to youngsters fervently rocking back and forth in white *tallit*. The women of the congregation sat on the balcony – wives, sisters and daughters keeping a close eye on the men below. A bearded rabbi was seated by an ark of green marble, the *atarah* of his *tallit* threaded with gold. A cantor led the service with an eight-part boys' choir, the congregation ending each blessing with an emphatic: '*Amen!*'

Ben found a spot near the entrance, watching the service unfold at one remove. He did not recognise the tunes, which were in the Sephardic tradition, but one word leapt out at him: *Shabbat*. So, he had travelled by sea for weeks on the *Midas*, only to arrive in Constantinople, fifteen hundred miles from home, right on time for Kabbalat Shabbat! The Friday evening prayers that, once upon a time, he had been forced to attend every week with his father.

He glanced up at the balcony. A young woman in the front row caught his attention. She stood out from the others on account of the vivid red of her dress, the elegant ribbon tied through her ebony locks, her undeniable beauty. She was staring into space, lost in her own world.

For a passing breath, her gaze flitted to Ben. She snapped from her trance and her features hardened. She whispered something to a woman on her left, who was wrapped in a black mantilla, face half-hidden by a thin veil. The woman glanced in his direction and laid her alabaster hands on the balustrade.

At the end of the service, the rabbi took to the podium and addressed the congregation in a foreign tongue. It was not Hebrew, Yiddish or Turkish – if anything, it sounded like an ancient dialect of Spanish. Ben gleaned something of the sermon from the rabbi's solemnity, the hush that descended over the congregation, and the grave expressions on the faces of the congregants. The rabbi made a deferential gesture to the young woman in red and her companion. For a second, all eyes were on them, but they remained inscrutable.

When the rabbi finished his sermon, the congregation murmured a subdued '*Bien hecho*' and filtered out of the hall with the customary embraces and glad-handing.

Ben kept his head down and waited. When the synagogue was almost empty, the rabbi came over and addressed him in a gentle voice, his words chosen with care like handpicked flowers: 'Are you lost, Englishman?'

The rabbi's brown eyes were twinkling with curiosity in the candlelight.

Ben stood to shake his hand. '*Shabbat Shalom*,' he said cautiously. 'How did you know I was English?'

The rabbi chuckled. 'The English have a special way of standing out – especially an Ashkenazi boy like yourself! My name is Shabtai Akbar. This is my synagogue.'

'Pleased to meet you, Rabbi Akbar. I'm…' Ben hesitated, 'Rupert Rogers.'

'And what brings you to Constantinople, Mr Rogers?'

'I arrived here today by sea, after a long and tiring journey.' Something caught in Ben's throat as he spoke – behind the charade, trepidation. 'I have nowhere to stay. This is the only place I thought someone might help me.'

Shabtai did not miss a beat. 'I live in the apartment upstairs with my family – why don't you join us for dinner? You must be hungry. Like Abraham, my tent is open on all sides.'

'It's not an imposition?'

'*¡Bavajadas!* Nonsense! We have a few guests dining with us – what's one more? Never mind how you look. I am always delighted to see a new face in our *minyan*.'

Shabtai ushered Ben upstairs and introduced him to the Akbar clan: his genial wife Perla, his two sons Hiram, the cantor, and Ishak, director of a seminary in Stamboul, along with their wives and a gaggle of grandchildren.

Shabtai's four guests were already seated at the dinner table. Among them was none other than the young woman in red whom he had spotted during the service. She pretended not to recognise him and gave him a frosty smile.

Next to her was the woman in the black mantilla. Her veil had been removed. She was in her early fifties, with an air of dignity and refinement, but her cheeks and brow were pinched with worry.

And on either side of the women, acting almost as a protective barrier, were two middle-aged men with long, dour faces, grey beards, a guarded manner and deep-set eyes that closely resembled those of the lady in the black mantilla.

The two men rose to their feet as Ben entered. The women remained seated.

'*Buena tadrada*,' Shabtai said. 'I hope you don't mind if we speak in English tonight – for the benefit of our new friend!' He laid a hand on Ben's shoulder. 'This is Mr Rupert Rogers. Mr

Rogers, these two gentlemen are Messieurs Gavriel and Shmuel Rafaeli – the Rafaeli Twins, as we call them.'

Gavriel and Shmuel said nothing, shocked by Ben's filthy appearance.

Shabtai brushed over the awkwardness with a gesture to the woman in the mantilla: 'Their sister, Lady Leonora Carmino.' Then to the young woman in red: 'And Lady Carmino's daughter, Mademoiselle Shoshanna.'

Ben gave a courteous bow. Up close, he could not help but notice the rich silk brocade and fine silver stitching of Shoshanna's dress – the kind only worn by the wealthiest aristocrats. She had the attitude to go with it. The firm unapproachability of an upper-class woman who knew that she was a cut above.

After the blessings over wine and challah, Perla brought in the food: rosemary and garlic flatbread, roast shoulder of lamb on a bed of fluffy couscous, grilled zucchini soaked in lemon and a steaming aubergine pie. Ben ate voraciously. His stint on the *Midas* had left him ravenous.

Shoshanna was looking at him with intense curiosity.

'You are from London, Mr Rogers?' she asked. Her English accent and pronunciation were tutored to perfection.

Ben nodded, swallowing a mouthful of couscous.

'Did they not have food on the boat?'

'Well, not food cooked by the blessed hands of Rebbetzin Akbar!' Ben grinned.

Perla beamed at the compliment. But Shoshanna was not amused.

'And why did you decide to come all the way to Constantinople?'

Ben flashed his copy of Murray's travel guide. 'Sight-seeing! A friend gave this to me as a gift and I was inspired to pay a visit.'

Shoshanna set her cutlery down. 'How peculiar.'

'In what way?' Ben asked with a frown.

'Well, you are paying a visit to a nation at war – a mere few days' sailing from the battlefield! Commercial steamers, as I understand it, have largely been grounded, and those that are running are prohibitively expensive. So you must be a man, at the very least, of reasonable means. And yet… You are wearing the clothes of a lowly deckhand. You do not appear to have eaten a full meal for quite some time. And please, pardon me for saying so, you carry a rather… striking odour. On top of all of that, you have clearly refrained from organising accommodation on your arrival.' She gave a casual shrug. *'Peculiar.'*

The silence around the table after that last word was palpable. Shoshanna had the air of a sly child taking some small pleasure in watching a spider trapped under a glass.

Ben cut another piece of aubergine pie. 'I apologise for my bedraggled state – there was a frightful mix-up with my luggage. Or would you rather I concocted an intriguing story for you? That I'm a fugitive from the law – a stowaway on a military ship, perhaps? Or that I was sent here by a criminal kingpin of some unsavoury description? That Rupert Rogers is a fiction cooked up to hide my real identity? That would be a ripping yarn, wouldn't it, Mademoiselle Carmino?'

Shoshanna's smile gradually faded as Ben spoke.

'Life is far more mundane than we give it credit,' Ben continued. 'Maybe I am just a young man with too little sense in his noggin, as we English call it, who believes that the best adventures are those sprinkled with… *peculiarity.*'

For a moment, both Ben and Shoshanna were deadly serious as they studied each other. Then Shoshanna looked at her mother with a mirthless chuckle: 'The English have the most delightful sense of humour!'

The rest of dinner passed uneventfully. The conversation moved from synagogue gossip, to the latest on the war's progress in Crimea and rumours of a Russian attack on Constantinople. A demonstration was being planned for the following day: disgruntled members of Ottoman society taking to the streets in protest at inaction on the part of the Sublime Porte. The Rafaeli Twins did most of the talking on Shoshanna and Leonora's behalf, but they avoided any meaningful discussion of the Carminos themselves: their work, their background, the goings-on in their lives.

Soon after a dessert of fresh baklava with toasted pistachios, nougat, honeycomb and fresh mint tea, Shoshanna, Leonora and the Rafaeli Twins hastily departed. Perla began clearing away the plates and ferrying them to the kitchen. Shabtai's sons took the grandchildren to bed. Ben was left alone with the rabbi, sitting in thoughtful silence.

'What did you think of our esteemed guests?' Shabtai asked.

'They seemed preoccupied.'

'The Carminos have much to ponder.'

Ben looked at Shabtai questioningly. The rabbi traced the rim of his empty teacup.

'The patriarch of their dynasty was Abraham Carmino: Leonora's husband, Shoshanna's father. An orphan who rose from obscurity to establish the Carmino Family Bank and, in the process, become one of the wealthiest, most powerful men in the Empire. The first Jew to join the Imperial Council and receive the title *Effendi*, an honour reserved for the highest nobles. There he worked hand-in-glove with both the Sultan's father and the current Sultan himself, in their efforts to modernise the

Empire's politics, infrastructure, economy and social mores. This process, which we call *Tanzimat*, would not have been possible without Abraham Carmino's influence and support.'

'You use the past tense when you speak about him,' Ben said pointedly.

Shabtai looked around for a moment and lowered his voice: 'In May of this year, Abraham Carmino was found dead. Floating in the Bosporus. An investigation was opened. What it uncovered ruined his reputation. Abraham, so it was claimed, had been selling gold bullion to the Ottomans *and* the Russians – funding both sides of the war effort at the very same time. An act of treason. The circumstances of his death remain murky, but the official story goes that Abraham was in over his head – did something to fall foul of the wrong people – and paid for it with his life.'

'Do you believe that story?'

Shabtai hesitated. 'I have no other story to believe. Whatever the truth may be, the scandal spelled the Carminos' ruin. The Sultan came down heavily on them: shutting down the Carmino Family Bank, seizing much of its capital and assets, forcing the Carminos to leave Constantinople and relocate to their estate in Beykoz on the outskirts of the city. About three hours away – hence their hurry to leave after dinner.'

Ben thought back to the lonely image of Shoshanna on the balcony of Ahrida, that melancholy look on her face, how she buried any hint of feeling as soon as she realised that she was being watched. A cool façade chiselled away by uncertainty and grief.

'What remained of the estate fell to Lady Leonora and her brothers – the Rafaeli Twins,' Shabtai added. 'But since they have no means of generating income, it is being rapidly dissipated. And without the protection of the Sultan, the Jewish community in Constantinople has never been more vulnerable. Now the principal financier of the Ottomans is a Greek royal – Prince Mavros is his name. Curious, how happy they were to replace Abraham with a non-Jewish counterpart. Just another way in which our people continue to be, as we have always been, *dispossessed*.' Shabtai gave a stoic shrug and rose to his feet. 'This subject does not befit the sanctity of Shabbat. Come.'

The rabbi led Ben to a spare room in the apartment. It was modest: a small bed, a change of clothing, a washbasin and a candle on a writing desk, with a view of orange trees in the tranquil courtyard below.

'It's not much,' Shabtai said, 'but hopefully it will do for a few nights until you find your feet.'

'I can't tell you how much I appreciate your kindness,' Ben said, taking the Rabbi's hand. 'I'll find some way to repay you – I promise.'

'No Jew owes another Jew anything. We are family – one that extends beyond nationality, language, style and status. And that family comes before everything.'

Shabtai left Ben to his own devices. Ben lay down on the bed, flooded with exhaustion. The Carminos, the *Midas*, Heathcote and Elizabeth were soon forgotten. All he could think about was his family. Max wandering in, rattling off a new theory. His mother smelling of chicken broth, smothering him with loving kisses. Tuvia cracking another joke at Herschel's expense. The sober voice of his father – 'Hand me another pin, boychik!'

As these ghostly echoes rattled about in his memory, Ben closed his eyes and fell into a deep sleep.

Early the next morning, Ben set off for Nakkaş Haydar, ten minutes by foot from Ahrida. It was a run-down street of terraced houses climbing at a steep angle. Ben stopped outside number 15 – Heathcote's return address. The cottage was overgrown with ivy and adjoined a walled garden. It had latticed windows behind metal bars and the curtains were drawn. A sign was hanging on the rusted iron gate: *Entrée interdite, ne frappez pas.*

'Probably not a welcome sign…' Ben muttered, already sweating from the early morning sun.

He looked up and down the street. Nobody in sight.

He pushed the gate open and darted into the garden – a *potager* in disrepair. Tomatoes, artichokes, asparagus and squash had been left to fester in the soil. Mottled leaves were falling from the branches of an olive tree. A mound of compost left to dry in the sun at the far end of the garden gave off a sickly smell. If Heathcote was here, he was behind on his chores.

Ben approached the back door. The handle had been snapped off and the door was tilting on its hinges. He edged it open and entered – more furtive now that he was trespassing in the man's home.

The air was stale. Dishes were piled high on a kitchen table, wiped clean except for one: a plate of half-eaten rotting steak and vegetables, buzzing with fat flies. In the living room were shelves of poetry books arranged in alphabetical order and an upright Pleyel piano, with a copy of Beethoven's Scottish Songs on the stand.

Ben leafed through the sheet music. It was heavily annotated with musical directions and fingering for the piano part. Folded up and tucked into the groove between the penultimate and final page was a slip of paper:

*2 p.m. 28th of September. Hagia
Sophia – Kabasakal. Black Fez.
'Did you see the Sultan's kayik?'*

Ben had received enough cryptic notes from Lennie Glass and his underlings to know a rendezvous tip-off when he saw one. Elizabeth had been photographed near the Hagia Sophia – and the 28th of September was the very next day...

A door in the hallway was open onto a narrow stairwell. Ben went to stand at the edge of the stairwell, where a kerosene lamp dangled from the ceiling, sputtering on its last oil. He peered into the gloom. The limestone walls faded into the darkness of the basement below.

For the first time since his arrival, Ben felt a tremor of fear. He was not the superstitious type, but it was as though he had chanced upon a portal to the underworld.

He descended, the wooden planks creaking under his weight. At the foot of the stairwell was a dank cellar lit by hissing electric bulbs. The cellar had been stripped bare, and Ben could see the pale outlines where paintings and furniture had once been laid. In the middle of the room was a pool of dried blood with a chalk circle traced around it.

Sitting at a table in the corner of the room was an Ottoman policeman: revolver, sabre, epaulettes and all. His head was hanging back over his chair and every few seconds he released a raspy flutter from his nostrils. He was fast asleep.

Ben knew at once what he had stumbled into: *a crime scene.* And that meant one of two things. Either Heathcote had done something unspeakable, or something unspeakable had been done to Heathcote.

He crept back to the stairs. Still the gendarme snored away.

Then a voice shattered the stillness. 'Khalil! *Uyan, seni tembel piç!*'

A second officer appeared in the doorway of a water closet, doing up his flies. He clocked Ben and stopped dead in his tracks.

'Khalil!' he barked at the sleeping officer.

Khalil jolted awake. He mumbled something drowsily to his partner. Then, seeing Ben across the room, he leapt to his feet.

'*Burada ne yapıyorsun?*' Khalil said.

Ben shook his head in panic. 'English! English!'

The two gendarmes exchanged a baffled look. Khalil took a step forward. He was a lanky junior gendarme, clearly still wet behind the ears. 'What are you doing here?'

'Tourist! Lost!' Ben said, holding up his copy of Murray's. 'I will go now!'

The gendarmes drew their guns: Devisme percussion revolvers. 'Don't you dare,' Khalil said. 'Hands. NOW.'

Ben stuck out his hands. Khalil cuffed him with iron shackles and bundled him upstairs.

'I haven't done anything!' Ben cried. '*Baksheesh! Baksheesh!*'

But the two gendarmes laughed scornfully. 'Try it on someone else! We are gendarmes – we don't take bribes.'

They hauled him out the front door of Heathcote's cottage, up Nakkaş Haydar and round the corner onto Mesnevihane, where a police carriage was stationed. Ben was shoved in the back, Khalil opposite with his gun trained on him, while the second officer took the reins. They set off, descending from the heights of Balat to the bustling heartland of the old city.

Half an hour later, they arrived at gendarmerie headquarters, next door to the Süleymaniye Mosque. Ben's belongings were confiscated and he was placed in a holding cell. He slumped against the wall with his head between his knees.

After an interminable wait, Ben was brought to his senses by a smooth baritone voice, dripping with irony:

'You English only seem to bring trouble, you know that?'

A walrus of a man stood before his cell, Khalil behind him with his cap in hand. The walrus was in full military garb, sporting a tall red fez. A curved sword was sheathed in a silver scabbard on one hip, a pistol with an ornate patterned handle holstered on the other. His fat fingers toyed lazily with the medals pinned to his chest. There was a jaded glint in his eye that Ben recognised – like the music hall actors on the skittle alleys of Drury Lane: showmen who had long ago grown weary of their performances.

'Chief Inspector Yusuf Madhat Pasha,' he said, pinching his bushy moustache. 'Now: why don't we have a little chat, Englishman?'

9

The Interrogation

Yusuf Madhat Pasha stood at the window of his second-floor office, bathed in early afternoon sunlight. He was looking down at the ancient walls around the Süleymaniye Mosque, as the sound of a growing throng echoed across the rooftops: angry chants, the stamping of feet, a slow and steady drumbeat.

He pursed his lips in disapproval.

'I was supposed to be on an outing today with my son. A day trip sailing up and down the Bosporus. We had been planning it for the better part of a month. Then came this bloody protest. Four thousand people marching the streets... Now I'm stuck here coordinating my men around it. And for what? A few loaves of bread?'

He turned. Ben was in a low wooden chair in the middle of the room. His handcuffs had been removed and Khalil was standing to attention by the door. A tumbler had been left on the Chief Inspector's oak desk, with a fat finger of whisky. He picked it up and took a comforting sip.

'Ardbeg, 1815,' he said. 'One of the very first casks commercially produced by their distillery on Islay. Would you like a taste?'

Ben said nothing. He kept his hands on his lap. Yusuf grinned.

'Are you sure? It may be the last dram you get for a while.'

Still Ben was silent. Yusuf's languid grin only grew. He sat at his desk and donned a pince-nez as he rifled through Ben's tattered papers.

'That's alright. Your documents will do the talking for you. Let's see... *Rupert... Rogers.*' His eyes flicked up, glancing over the rims of his spectacles. 'A name as bland as your cuisine.'

'You know us English,' Ben said. 'Not the most imaginative bunch.'

'I *do* know you English. Like many of my fellow Turks, I received your Western education. Mathematics at King's College London. So I know when things don't quite add up. You're a line cook, then?'

Ben nodded.

'Which ship?'

'HMS *Midas*.'

'You've missed your connection to Crimea. By approximately...' he checked his pocket-watch, 'sixteen hours! You must have lost track of time gallivanting around my city. You're liable to be terminated from your post. Where did you spend the night?'

Ben looked away. He was not about to implicate the Akbars. 'On the streets.'

'I see... And how do you know Heathcote, exactly?'

'I don't.'

Yusuf seemed surprised. 'Yet you know his address. You tracked him down. For a reason, I presume?'

Ben kept his poker face. He had sparred with enough bobbies, literally and figuratively, to know this game. Say too much and his cover would be blown – say too little and he would draw even more suspicion from the Chief Inspector.

'I came to talk to him.'

'About what?'

'A personal matter.'

Yusuf let the silence hang, sipping his Ardbeg.

'You won't get much out of him. He died last week.'

Ben's features dropped. Yusuf let out a nonchalant chuckle. 'Yes... Lynton Arabin Heathcote. Dead as a doornail. But something tells me you already knew that.'

Ben shook his head. 'I had no idea. I thought he was alive when I boarded the *Midas*. We had no contact with the outside world during our trip.'

'Playing dumb?' Yusuf said wearily. 'Come now. I have performed this rigmarole far too many times to pretend that I believe you.'

'I landed *yesterday*, Chief Inspector. Heathcote was dead by the time I arrived in Constantinople.'

'Well, before you get too carried away with this line of argument... Your documents are either real, or they are fake. I suspect the latter. And if my estimations are correct, then you could be anyone, and you could have been in Constantinople at any time. You are an *unknown quantity*. This city is awash with such people: imposters, agents, fugitives... killers. People who have one face that they wear as a mask, and another face that they hide. So, "Rupert Rogers", let's skip the foreplay and get straight to the rough-and-tumble, shall we?'

He polished off his whisky and clasped his hands together.

'Who sent you?'

It was not the question that Ben expected to hear. 'Why would anyone... send me?'

'Heathcote was what we call a *person of interest*. An attaché of the British Embassy. An information-gatherer.' He made a knowing gesture – but Ben still looked perplexed. Yusuf huffed in exasperation. 'A spy! Must I spell everything out?!'

'I got it, sir,' Khalil said from the door.

'Shut up, Khalil. So, this British spy has played an essential role as a linchpin between the gendarmerie and the British Embassy. A vital nexus of intelligence. And, well, he dies – very suddenly, might I add. And shortly thereafter, in walks a...' He waved his hands in Ben's general direction, '*A stranger*. Not too dissimilar from the late, great Heathcote, with an embarrassingly fake alias to boot. And the best explanation that you can give me for your appearance out of the blue is that you are a line cook on a military supply ship that you inexplicably jumped, who traipsed halfway across the world to talk about a personal matter with a man you claim to know nothing about. And I'm supposed to clap my hands together and say "Well done! Off you go!"'

Ben kept his lips firmly sealed. Yusuf was closing the vice around him, watching his young captive squirm.

'Or, alternatively... someone in Heathcote's line of work sent you, for an ulterior reason that might tie these strands together. I know which explanation I prefer.'

'I'm telling you the truth,' Ben forced out, trying to hide his nerves. 'Nobody sent me. It *was* a personal matter.'

'Then you better spit it out for your own sake. You're not leaving until you do.'

'You'll have to release me at some point.'

Yusuf narrowed his eyes. 'Try me. We are talking about murder.'

Ben glared at Yusuf. The Chief Inspector had him pinned and they both knew it. He reached into his jacket pocket and removed a white handkerchief, which he unwrapped to reveal the daguerreotype that he had lifted from Palmerston.

He held it before Yusuf, who squinted at it through his pince-nez. The Chief Inspector flinched – a tiny but unquestionable reaction to the person in the photograph.

'I knew this woman in London,' Ben said. 'We were... dear friends. I'd been led to believe that she died two years ago. But this image of her is dated from June of this year.'

'Where did you find it?'

'In a letter.'

'To whom?'

'What did you call it?' Ben said. '*A person of interest*. I followed the return address and it led me here.'

Something in Yusuf's mood had shifted.

'You know who she is, don't you?' Ben said quietly.

Khalil looped round to take a look for himself. He too seemed to darken as he studied her features. 'That's Prince Mavros' wife—' he blurted out.

'Khalil,' Yusuf seethed. '*Shut. Up.*'

Now it was Ben's turn to flinch. He had heard that name before. Rabbi Akbar had mentioned it in passing the previous night. Mavros: the new financier of the Ottoman war effort. Yet it was the word 'wife' that really confused him. Had Elizabeth married? Had she become some kind of Ottoman socialite?

'That makes no sense...' Ben murmured.

'No, "Rupert Rogers",' Yusuf retorted, '*you* make no sense. Am I to believe that you cavorted around London with Princess Mavros? You? A dirty little Israelite?'

There was vitriol in Yusuf's eyes. Ben knew that look all too well. It was the same look that he received whenever he strayed beyond the ghetto and the sound of Bow Bells.

'That's right,' the Chief Inspector whispered, 'I can smell the Jew in you, kid. A born troublemaker who will only understand punishment.'

'Well,' Ben said defiantly, 'this Jewish kid is a tailor's son, born and bred on Whitechapel Road – *and I know a stitch-up when I see one.*'

The Chief Inspector bared his tobacco-stained teeth. He was enjoying their sparring. 'Oh, you'll be stitched up alright. Khalil! Take him to the British Embassy and have them process his papers. Then we'll know for sure if he is who he says he is.' Yusuf turned on Ben, toying with his medals once more. 'And if you're not, the Central Porte will be contacted and the full force of the law will come crashing down on you. You're in for a world of pain. I don't envy you.'

Ben could not afford for the British to get involved. 'This is a grave mistake, Chief Inspector! I'm not involved in whatever is going on—'

'Save your breath,' Yusuf said dismissively. 'Who knows how much you have left.'

Khalil jostled Ben to the door. As he reached the threshold, something struck Ben – a name at the heart of this baffling mystery that neither party had dared to utter. One that had cast its shadow over their conversation without him even realising.

He called back to Yusuf: 'One more thing, Chief Inspector!'

Khalil hesitated in the doorway. Yusuf looked up from his files.
'Yes?'

'What is "the White Death"?'

Yusuf stared at Ben across the room for a moment too long. Then he poured himself another finger of Ardbeg 1815 and waved Ben away. 'Goodbye, Mr Rogers – and good riddance!'

Ben was taken back to the carriage that had transported him to the police station. Khalil slung his knapsack at him and they set off, weaving through the busy streets of Stamboul to the British Embassy in the north of the city.

Ben gazed helplessly out the window. He felt like an utter fool. His stay in Constantinople was supposed to have been for months, but as things stood he had lasted barely a day before everything had blown up in his face. Heathcote was dead, and having been taken into custody, Ben would miss the rendezvous at the Hagia Sophia the following day – his only lead. Now he faced one of two dire fates: either a summary trip back home, primed for a thrashing at the hands of his father – or, worse still, a Turkish jail on suspicion of a crime he did not commit.

As they approached the waterfront, the din of the food protest grew louder. The ground began to tremble from the stamping of feet and the gulls circled on high, as though sensing the chaos below. They turned onto a thoroughfare running down to the Port of Commerce on the waterfront of the Golden Horn…

They came to a halt. The carriage had inadvertently trundled into the heart of the demonstration. In the sea of angry faces, Ben could see Ottoman flags, handmade signs in Turkish, and effigies of military and political figures. Most of the crowd were young men in their early twenties: radical students from the Imperial University, chanting slogans in Turkish and French.

'You picked the wrong year to go travelling, Rogers,' Khalil snarled. 'This is the edge of the world. Take a wrong step and you might just fall off.'

Khalil tapped the window separating them from the driver's box and issued a command – but the driver could only throw his arms in the air. There was nothing to be done. The protestors had clogged up the thoroughfare and the carriage was going nowhere.

Then the carriage started to shake. Protestors were banging on the windows, kicking the wheel-spokes, grabbing the corners of the cabin and shoving it back and forth. They had recognised it as a transport of the gendarmerie.

Khalil looked agitated: this was not part of the plan. He drew his revolver and leant halfway out of the left-side window, shouting at the protestors to part: '*Çekil! Çekil!*' But the more Khalil shouted, the more the crowd fought back – pelting him with rotten figs and swarming the carriage to taunt him.

Khalil had his back turned, more concerned with the baying mob than his prisoner. Ben glanced out the right-side window. This was his chance.

As the roaring of the march reached a crescendo, he grabbed his knapsack, swung the door open, and leapt out, landing face-first on the cobbled stones. He heard a nasty *crack* – snapped cartilage, a searing pain across his face, hot blood streaming from his nose.

No time to think. He lurched to his feet and ran towards the entrance of a grand bazaar, under a stone archway off the thoroughfare. Marchers began cheering for him and clapping him on the back as he legged it. He cast a quick glance over his shoulder: Khalil had clambered out of the carriage and was tearing his way through the mob with a raised revolver, bellowing, 'STOP RIGHT THERE, RUPERT ROGERS!'

Two loud bangs: gunshots! Bullets pinged off the archway as Ben bolted into the bazaar like a dog at the races, Khalil in hot pursuit.

The bazaar was a maze. Ben barged past merchants and veiled women, through booksellers, lantern shops, coffee kiosks, leaving a trail of destruction in his wake as bullets fizzed over his head.

He turned a corner at the edge of a horse-enclosure where wild-eyed Anadolu Ponies reared up and whinnied from the commotion. There, at the end of the alley: a wall of sunlight. Ben sprinted towards it…

…and burst out onto the esplanade over the Golden Horn, just as a wagon came hurtling towards him. He threw himself out of the way and it clattered past.

Khalil staggered breathlessly from the alley, pistol trained on Ben. 'FREEZE!'

Ben backed up against the embankment. There was nowhere to run now.

'I'll shoot you!' Khalil cried.

Ben looked down at the swirling waters of the Golden Horn. The current was vicious. If he jumped from this height, he might well drown.

'Don't do it!' Khalil insisted. 'It will be a watery grave!'

Ben spotted a lone fishing trawler, passing directly below him, sailing upstream. In seconds, it would be gone.

He glanced again at Khalil – a few feet away and closing in.

'Surrender yourself!'

But Ben's mind was already made up. He took a deep breath, turned, stole one last look at the trawler – and jumped off the embankment, knapsack and all.

He dropped like a boulder, braced for impact, and landed with a crash. When he opened his eyes, he was on his back, staring up through the open roof of a storeroom in the trawler's hold. He had landed on a pile of burlap sacks filled with fine powder, which had exploded in a thick reddish mist. The view vanished as if behind the puff of a magician's smoke.

He breathed in the dust and nearly hacked up a lung. It was cinnamon – a generous helping at that.

'Still beats the *Midas*,' he rasped.

Through the haze, he caught one final glimpse of a gobsmacked Khalil, watching powerlessly from the embankment as the boat chugged upstream.

Ben clambered to his feet and hobbled from the storeroom onto deck. He was greeted by seven fishermen – brawny, bronzed, sea-battered – standing round an open stove where a pot of tea was brewing. They looked at Ben with a mixture of suspicion and perplexity.

Ben hung his head. They were the types to roll him up in a Persian rug and throw him overboard, and there was sod-all he could do about it.

The fishermen conferred among themselves. After several minutes of animated debate, one of them picked up a teacup and held it out to Ben. '*Şerefe!*' he declared in his mother tongue. The intent was clear as day: *a peace offering*.

Ben toasted him with a smile. '*Şerefe*, mate.'

The fishermen treated Ben well – clearly their mistrust of the police outweighed any annoyance at this boy having destroyed a sack of their cinnamon. The captain snapped Ben's nose back into place and stuffed his nostrils with rolls of cotton wool to stem the bleeding. They ferried him jugs of water to wash off the cinnamon, plied him with more cups of crimson tea and offered him a blue embroidered fishing jacket, a *kantha*, to keep him warm.

The fishermen dropped Ben off at a jetty in Balat. Then they bade him farewell and sailed on, bound for the grassy plains north of Constantinople. Ben turned to face Balat and breathed a sigh of relief as he retraced his steps back to Ahrida.

Dusk washed over Constantinople and the city settled into an uneasy peace. From his room at the Akbars', Ben could just about make out the sea: gas lamps wrapping the empty waterfront trading offices in an amber glow.

Next to him was a half-eaten plate of *boyoz* dumplings with onion and spinach, an afternoon snack prepared by Perla. The Akbars had kept their distance since he returned with his nose plugged, his shirt bloody, wearing a *kantha* jacket and whiffing of cinnamon. They could sense that something was off and did not want to be drawn in.

Ben was too shaken by his arrest to play the gregarious guest. He was both relieved to have escaped and in shock at his close shave. Now he was not just a foreigner, but a fugitive in Constantinople. If he put a foot wrong, his life would be over.

There came a knock at the door. It was Rabbi Akbar, fresh from the evening service in the synagogue.

'Can we talk?' he asked.

Ben welcomed him in and the rabbi pulled up a chair by the window. He seemed preoccupied.

'Perla told me that you returned in quite a state.'

'There was a frightful mix-up at the bazaar involving a bag of cinnamon…'

'Do not feed me lies, Mr Rogers. We have been exceedingly hospitable to you.'

Ben ran his hands through his hair, contemplating what to say next. 'I am from London and I am Jewish – that much is true,' he finally forced out, 'but my name isn't Rupert Rogers. It's Ben Canaan. And I was sent here by a rather nasty bloke, to go into hiding.'

Ben was expecting Shabtai to lose his temper, to boot him out on the spot for this deception. But instead, Shabtai laid a comforting hand on Ben's shoulder – a gesture of sympathy and approval that Ben was brave enough to tell the truth.

'And what really happened today?'

'There's a lead that I'm pursuing. Someone I knew, who I thought was dead, but who, as it turns out, is living in your city. The police caught me looking for her and they didn't take too kindly to it!'

'Did you tell them you were staying here?'

'No, of course not,' Ben said. 'I didn't mention you and nobody followed me. I took care.'

'That's something, I suppose…' Shabtai whispered. 'I want to help you, Mr Canaan. I feel it is my duty as a rabbi, as a fellow Jew. But I cannot afford to put my family in the firing line. You must understand.'

Ben nodded, swallowing his fear and his guilt.

'You can stay here for another couple of nights. But then you will have to make your way elsewhere. I can help you find shelter, if you'd like.'

'I'll sort it out myself... but thank you,' Ben said quietly. Then, after a pensive pause, 'There is *one* thing you could do, if it's not too much trouble.'

'Pray tell.'

'You mentioned a man last night. Prince Mavros. Is that right?'

Shabtai nodded.

'Do you know where he lives? He might be able to help me find the person I'm looking for.'

'Of course I know where he lives,' Shabtai said. 'It's hardly a secret. He's a celebrity in these parts.'

Ben produced his map from Murray's travel guide. 'Could you show me?'

Shabtai took a pencil from the writing desk and circled it on the map. 'It's a grand estate. Not far from here, but heavily guarded. You'll need an appointment.'

Perla's voice echoed across the apartment: dinner was ready. Shabtai drew Ben close. 'I will say this for your own sake, Mr Canaan, so listen closely... Constantinople is a dangerous city. Especially for the untrained traveller. Very few people are who they appear to be. Everyone from high to low has secrets, all tied together in an invisible web. The tables turn quickly, and when they do, the hunters become the hunted. Be careful. Now come and eat. And not a word of this to my family!'

That night, Ben had a strange dream. He was standing in a snowy forest. There was a woman in the distance, her back to him – Elizabeth's brown hair, but wearing Shoshanna Carmino's red dress.

He began running towards her, but no matter how fast he ran, she came no closer. He called out a name, but as the name escaped his lips, the wind carried it away and it was forgotten. Then the figure turned around…

Where a face should have been, there was a blank slate, a looking-glass into oblivion. He reached out for her in desperation as the snow thickened, the forest began to fold in on itself, and the woman disappeared into endless white.

10

The Greek Prince

The next day, Ben set off for Prince Mavros' estate. He had dressed for the occasion, borrowing one of Shabtai's suits and combing his hair to form a neat parting down the middle. He was not expecting his visit to be a success. Chances were that the Prince would not let him set foot on his property, let alone meet with Elizabeth. But nonetheless, he wanted to look presentable. And if nothing came of his visit to the Prince, he had Heathcote's rendezvous at the Hagia Sophia to follow up on.

His walk across Constantinople took him to Pera, an upscale neighbourhood situated on an elevation above the peninsula. It was traversed by the Grand Rue, a boulevard showcasing the finest luxuries of Europe: an opera house advertising a production of Verdi's *Rigoletto*, a Swiss chocolatier, Viennese café-restaurants and luxury hotels in the Parisian style.

Prince Mavros' Beaux-Arts palace lay just beyond the Grand Champs des Morts, a tranquil cemetery shaded by elms and yews. Two bodyguards were posted at the gate: hardy Greek war veterans with broad shoulders and heads like cinderblocks.

They eyeballed Ben suspiciously when he asked to see Prince Mavros. 'Name?'

Ben almost blurted out his alias – but stopped himself. If Elizabeth really was here, he would have to go by his real name. 'Ben Canaan.'

'Prince Mavros has an engagement and is not accepting visitors.'

'It's a matter concerning Princess Mavros.'

Despite the beating sun, the air between them seemed to cool. The guard closest to him placed a gloved hand on the hilt of his sword.

'Unfortunately, Princess Mavros—'

'*It's gravely urgent* – I bear important information,' Ben insisted. 'Frisk me if you need: I have no weapons.'

The guards shared a look. One of them gave Ben a curt nod and growled, 'Wait here…' before disappearing into the estate.

Ten minutes later, he returned with a servant in tow and unlatched the gate.

'His Excellency has fifteen minutes to discuss this matter with you.'

Ben was too stunned to comply. He had been fully anticipating an unceremonious boot back onto the street.

'Get a move on!' the guard barked, waving him in impatiently.

The servant accompanied Ben down a promenade through the water-gardens and into the palace. First, across a hall beneath a majestic ceiling fresco of a sun-drenched Greek island on the Ionian Sea. Then down a long corridor to the rear of the estate, lined with models of Spanish galleons and portraits of the Mavros ancestors: warlords, grand dukes, merchant tycoons. The largest was a life-sized portrait of a heroic figure carrying the flag of the Kingdom of Greece, a name engraved in gold on the frame: IOANNIS MAVROS – 'THE MARTYR'.

At every turn, he kept an eye out for Elizabeth. But for now, there was no sign of her.

He was led across the gardens, to the stables. It was here that they found Prince Mavros, dismounting a Turkoman thoroughbred. The Prince was in his mid-thirties and in his prime, with a full head of dark hair and a tanned, classically handsome face. To Ben, he looked like the swashbuckling hero of a Dumas novel. One day, there would be a bust of that head in the palace behind them.

He extended a hand, without removing his white calfskin riding gloves.

'Prince Alexander Mavros. Mr Canaan, was it?'

'Good morning, Prince Mavros.'

Prince Mavros dismissed the servant and a stableman took the thoroughbred back to its pen. Mavros guided Ben down a secluded walking path, past dark-green ponds and into a conservatory. They sat in wicker chairs, surrounded by brightly coloured tulips in full bloom.

'Beautiful flowers,' Ben said, tracing a hand along the petals.

'We have them shipped from Leiden. How about a drink? Lemonade? Cognac?'

'Too early for such poisons,' Ben said.

'Very sensible of you.' Mavros settled into a chair and slapped his thigh. 'So! All the way from London. How is the old place? I haven't been for nearly a decade.'

'I'm not sure you and I move in the same circles, Prince Mavros!'

'I've always preferred the company of working men. As hypocritical as it might sound, I find they have much more to say than any dauphin or heiress. The most devilishly fun times I had in London were in the… darker corners of the Docklands. Have you paid it a visit?'

'Once in a blue moon.'

Mavros narrowed his eyes and smirked, as if sharing in a private joke. 'Those were debauched times. Alas! Since those days, I have traded opium for mint tea. I'm older now – *creakier*.'

'You seem in rather good nick.'

Mavros swatted the air with faux humility. 'Not at all! I just have a nice house. People see how I live and they assume that I must be as grand as the premises. Far from.'

'I don't blame them,' Ben chuckled. 'Your horses have fancier digs than my whole family back in London.'

'It's a lonely existence,' Mavros sighed. 'Lots of rooms, not enough people. The monks in Scutari derive more pleasure from growing cabbage than I do commanding my acres of emptiness.'

'Looking for someone to take it off your hands?'

'You'd save me a lot of bother! I inherited it from my father, Ioannis. When I returned to Constantinople last year, it was in a state of total disrepair. It's been an all-consuming project to get it back up and running.'

Ben was trying to keep up with his host's conviviality. But beneath his charm, he was eager to redirect the conversation to the purpose of his visit. How long were pleasantries supposed to last in such elevated company?

'Where had you been?' Ben asked.

'Long story,' Mavros replied. 'I was born here – sent away as a child to be educated on the Continent – travelled far and wide… But I was drawn back. They took Mavros out of Constantinople, but they couldn't take Constantinople out of Mavros.'

Mavros smiled thinly. The pleasantries were over.

'I understand you have urgent information about my wife.'

Ben steadied himself. What he said next could determine whether or not he would ever see Elizabeth again.

'Now *this* is a long story…' he said shakily.

Mavros was unruffled. 'I'm all ears.'

'Well… I met your wife Elizabeth three years ago in London. She was visiting from her native Paris with her father George, the physician. We had what you might call – forgive me – a "romantic relationship". A brief one – it only lasted the summer. We were… *I was* deeply in love. But at the end of the summer, she disappeared without explanation. And not long after that, I received a letter from her father informing me of her… There's no other way to say it, really… of her *death*.'

The Prince was watching Ben closely – listening with great care and attentiveness – breaking off only to remove an embossed handkerchief from his pocket and polish the monocle tucked in his waistcoat.

'I spent years grieving for her, believing that she was gone forever. But just a few weeks ago, I discovered a daguerreotype of her, dated from this year – proof that she is alive and well in Constantinople. I was about to go travelling, so I decided to come here and find out the truth.'

Mavros bristled. Ben raised a conciliatory hand – worried that he had offended the Prince.

'Please believe me: I didn't know that Elizabeth was married when I came here. If she was married to you in 1851, then I can only apologise – I had no idea. But let me reassure you, I have not come to threaten the integrity of your union. I respect it entirely. All I want to know is that she is in good health. And, perhaps, if you would be so kind as to grant me an audience with her – even if just for a few minutes – then I'd be indebted to you for life.'

Mavros was looking at Ben with more sympathy now – like a doctor listening to a patient unburden himself of his worries.

'Thank you for your explanation,' Mavros said after a long pause. 'However, there is one problem… *None of what you've said in any way, shape or form describes my wife.*'

Ben's stomach hollowed out. 'I'm sorry – what are you talking about?'

'Where to begin?' Mavros said. 'Firstly, she is not French. She hailed from Greece, which was where I met her. Her father was not a physician – nor has he been alive this side of 1840 – and when he was alive, he was not called "George". She never visited Paris or London. And, last but not least, her name is not Elizabeth, but *Marta*. I hate to say it, young man, but this seems to be an unfortunate case of mistaken identity.'

Prince Mavros spoke with disarming conviction. Ben could hardly believe his ears. He reached into his jacket and removed the daguerreotype of Elizabeth on the prow of the ship. He offered it to Mavros. 'Tell me: is this not her?'

Mavros looked at the image, intrigued. 'Why, yes… I took that picture a few months ago. We went sailing on the Bosporus. It was our anniversary. I thought it was lost.' He looked at Ben, astonished. 'How on earth did you find this?'

'In the pocket of a high-ranking British government official,' Ben said. 'That's also a long story. In any case, that woman is Elizabeth de Varney – I'm sure of it.'

'Or perhaps "Elizabeth de Varney" and my wife simply look alike, Mr Canaan. Is that so hard to believe? I can show you any number of images in which Marta's aspect is completely different.'

'I know that face—'

'*And I know it better.*' Mavros' cheeks flushed: the tiniest hint of outrage that he quickly checked. 'Marta was never one for deception. I've known her, her family and her friends for years! Even the slightest lie… I would have been able to tell instantly.'

'Well, someone clearly felt this daguerreotype was important enough to steal and send to my government. Did you know that the British were keeping tabs on her?'

'Of course I did,' Mavros said icily. 'Most of the Great Powers keep us under surveillance. Perhaps it's hard for you to appreciate, but I am a very public figure. Espionage is an unfortunate but inevitable reality for me – especially in times of war.'

'If I could just talk to her – see her…' Ben pleaded. 'Five minutes—'

'Mr Canaan, you must desist with this line of questioning.'

'Two minutes. One minute!'

'You will not have one second with her.'

'Why not?'

'*Because she is dead. Because Marta took her own life.*'

At once, Mavros' anger dissolved. Ben watched the emotion well up in the man's eyes. He suddenly seemed so fragile.

'It was two months after that picture was taken, almost to the day. She threw herself into the Bosporus, with stones in her pockets. She turned up three days later, tangled in a fishing net. Because of the nature of her death, I didn't even have the dignity of burying her. She was cremated, her ashes scattered over the waters that devoured her.'

Mavros paced to the door of the conservatory and looked out onto the ponds. He had the air of a man not quite present.

'Do you know what grief is, Mr Canaan? It's when every waking moment is just a series of questions about the past that you ask yourself, that have no answer. What if I had said *x* instead of *y*? What if I had done *this* instead of *that*? What if I had... placed my wineglass in an ever-so-slightly different spot to the one that I unwittingly chose? Would even the tiniest adjustment have triggered a chain of events, rippling outwards through time and space, that might have changed the pattern of her thoughts as she stood on that bridge? Would she have hesitated for a moment – allowed a bystander to grab her? Or is everything written in stone? Are we just going through the motions of free will as life takes us on its predetermined course?'

He turned to Ben, wearing a familiar expression. A gloominess behind the 'business-as-usual' charade. Gazing with regret at the path not taken. A look that Ben had caught in the mirror every now and then – whenever he thought of Elizabeth, of university, of Sandy Rosen, of Canaan & Sons.

'I've asked myself similar questions,' Ben murmured.

'Then perhaps you and I are not so different after all. We are, in our own ways, two men haunted by the dead, because we cannot bear to let them go. Your Elizabeth, and my beloved Marta.'

Outside, a siege of herons skirted the surface of the pond. A lone frog croaked from the reeds. Ben rose to his feet. There was nothing more to be gleaned from this broken man. He had just an hour to get to the Hagia Sophia for Heathcote's rendezvous. 'I should go,' he said. 'I'm sorry for intruding, Prince Mavros.'

Mavros offered a conciliatory hand. 'It's a shame that you came all this way, and at such trouble, for nothing. But if you want my advice, Mr Canaan, the best thing for you now would be to go home. You have your whole life ahead of you. Do not spend it trapped in what's already behind you.'

Ben said nothing. Maybe Mavros was right. Maybe the face that he had seen in the daguerreotype was just the face that he wished to see. Maybe this whole expedition was simply another bad decision in a list already far too long for a boy of twenty-one.

And yet, as he was led out of the estate and wandered through Pera, he could not dispel a growing suspicion that the strands did not tie up.

What is really going on here? he asked himself.

He heard a bell toll from the Grand Champs des Morts. A single knell scattering over the treetops: *one o'clock.*

Ben looked south to the Golden Horn. Gleaming on the slopes of Seraglio Point was the great dome of the Hagia Sophia. Whomever Heathcote had been planning to meet might already be standing in her shadow, waiting.

11

Rendezvous at the Morgue

Ben arrived at the Hagia Sophia on the stroke of two. The dome of the colossal mosque was under construction and labourers were yelling orders to each other in Italian as they climbed the scaffolding. Worshippers in white cotton turbans and chiffon hijabs were pouring out after prayers, carrying with them the scent of incense, musk and sandalwood.

He checked the note once more, to remind himself of his prompt:

> *2 p.m. 28th of September. Hagia*
> *Sophia – Kabasakal. Black Fez.*
> *'Did you see the Sultan's kayik?'*

Right date, right time, right place. Ben scanned the masses...

At the entrance to the mosque, a rail-thin young man with bulbous eyes was looking around shiftily – a jumble of ticks and twitches. He was wearing a black fez.

Ben crossed the road, edging past the worshippers, and sidled up to the nervous waif. 'Did you see the Sultan's *kayik*?'

Black Fez twitched in his direction. 'I did not, although I hear it is passing by again tomorrow,' he replied.

They eyed each other up and shook hands.

'Heathcote is dead,' Ben said.

Black Fez nodded gravely. 'I know.'

'Then why are you here?'

'If I learnt one thing from Heathcote: *show up to a rendezvous, no matter what*. He always made sure there was someone to meet me. Besides, I feel that I owe it to the man – it being his last wish... Who are you supposed to be?'

'I'm a new arrival on the scene. Trying to piece this all together now that Heathcote is feeding the fish.'

'And how do I know you aren't the one who turned him into fish food?'

'Well, I can't prove that to you. So I guess you'll have to take my word for it. I found the details for the rendezvous in a copy of Beethoven and I thought I'd check it out.'

Black Fez let out a throaty chuckle. 'Beethoven. Sounds like Heathcote. But in all honesty, it doesn't really matter who you are. Heathcote was paying me for a job and now that I've done it, I expect to be paid. So, if you're good for the money, it's yours.'

'*What's* mine?'

'The dossier. It has everything you need to know. Five liras was the agreed sum.'

Ben tallied up his coins. 'I've only got two. Tell you what: I'll give you one now, and the other when I get the goods.'

Black Fez jammed the coins in his pocket. '*Gidelim*. Let's go.'

He waved down a taxi carriage, ushered Ben inside, and the carriage tore off. In fifteen minutes, they arrived at the Imperial Military Hospital: a leafy courtyard behind the city's wind-battered sea-walls. Bandaged young men sat on the lawn, convalescing and smoking in the shade of linden trees.

'If anyone asks, you're a forensic scientist from England,' Black Fez said under his breath, 'but I'll do the talking. You just walk in like you know what you're doing.'

Ben caught the eye of a pretty nurse sitting on a bench during her lunch hour, reading a book with her legs crossed.

'Place isn't too shabby!' Ben said.

'Steady on. You'd need your arms and legs blown off to get her attention.'

Black Fez whisked Ben into the hospital. Overcrowded, unventilated corridors echoed with the moans of injured soldiers. The air was stale and reeked of chemical deodoriser. Nurses and doctors rushed about, outnumbered by the invalids and stretched too thin to give a second thought to Ben's presence.

They crossed an arcade in one of the smaller courtyards, bordered by cypresses, towards a large iron door. On the other side was the hospital morgue, though it more closely resembled a haunted crypt. Gloomy offices dimly lit by gas lamps, where dieners sifted through mountains of paperwork, looking as grim and soulless as the corpses entrusted to their care. Everywhere was the oppressive stench of death.

In the darkest, dreariest recesses of the morgue was a sterile examination chamber, accessible only with a key strung to Black Fez's belt. In the middle of the room was a wooden table, and on it a colour-coordinated dossier. Along the wall was a bank of twenty metal units.

'Home sweet home!' Black Fez declared. 'First time in a dead house?'

'And last, I hope!'

'It can be rather therapeutic, you know. Death isn't quite as frightening when you see it every day. Anyway: you didn't come for small talk.'

Black Fez rolled up his sleeves and scrubbed his hands in a washbasin. He seemed much less twitchy now that he was back in his natural habitat.

'It all began in March of this year,' he said. 'Sir Lawrence Thorsbury, a British special envoy to the Ottoman Empire, was at his summer residence in Therapia. He retired at eleven o'clock, as was his habit. But the following morning, Thorsbury was found in the bathtub by his housekeeper: *stone cold dead*. His skin was drained white, like a porcelain doll. No sign of a violent struggle: not one cut or bruise. The bathtub, however, was filled with extracellular fluid. Even stranger, the body did not decompose, as though it had mummified overnight. There was a brief inquiry and the gendarmerie concluded that Thorsbury had died of a novel virus.'

'And I'm guessing,' Ben said, 'that our friend Heathcote wasn't persuaded.'

'As an attaché of the Embassy, Heathcote knew Thorsbury well. He had his suspicions – but nothing at the time to confirm them either way. That would only come in May, when a second body turned up: that of *Abraham Carmino*.'

Ben recognised the name. The father of Shoshanna Carmino – the young woman in the red dress whom he had met at Rabbi Akbar's. 'The wealthy financier who sold bullion to the Russians?'

Black Fez smirked. 'Nothing travels faster than scandal. They found him in the Bosporus. Drowned. But – and this is the important bit – the body had *the same morbidity* as that of Thorsbury. Chalk-white, unmarked, mummified. Again, the gendarmerie was quick to write it off as a killing linked to the old Jew's illicit business activities. Now Heathcote was convinced that something else was afoot – something that the authorities were stubbornly refusing to acknowledge. He gave these strange occurrences a nickname: *the White Death*.'

Ben shuddered. It was as though Black Fez had uttered a terrible curse, one that doomed any person unlucky enough to hear it.

'Then, in August, a third body was found. This time it was none other than Marta Mavros. Wife of Prince—'

'Alexander Mavros,' Ben interjected. 'I thought she committed suicide.'

'That's what her husband thinks. Another convenient story. She too was found in the Bosporus, and her corpse also carried the hallmarks of the White Death. The findings of the post-mortem were inconsistent with drowning. She was dead before she hit the water. This was when I entered the fray. After the Princess died, Heathcote approached me in secret and offered me a tidy sum to study the cadavers and write up a special coroner's report.' Black Fez smiled ruefully and took up the dossier. 'I was supposed to give this to poor Lynton today. Alas, he's ended up as its latest chapter…'

Ben leafed through the dossier. It was a work of remarkable detail: dense handwritten paragraphs describing autopsy findings and histopathology reports – illustrations of chemical compounds with long, indecipherable names – sketches of naked bodies on metal tables from a variety of angles, cut open to reveal muscle, arteries, organ, bone.

'All four victims died of the same thing: *hypovolemic shock*. Fatal dehydration caused by a catastrophic depletion of blood volume and bodily fluids. Usually, this is a very protracted death. But here's the rub: my estimates show, judging from the state of the cadavers, that they died almost instantly. Sixty seconds at most from the onset of symptoms. Which means that, in under a minute, they went from perfectly healthy specimens such as yourself, to lifeless carcasses.'

Ben was left scratching his head. He was no doctor, but Black Fez's description did not sound right. 'Is that possible?'

'Maybe through catastrophic blunt trauma – but the bodies have no wounds of any kind. Or perhaps a novel virus as the police conjectured. Then again, there's no indication of viral or bacterial infection.'

'What about poison?'

Black Fez grinned and snapped his fingers. 'Now you're thinking like a killer! I did find traces of alkaloid and glycoside compounds in the *tunica intima* – the innermost lining of the arteries – which suggests the presence of a highly toxic substance. But they're largely dissolved and I can't isolate them for analysis.'

He took Ben to the bank of steel units. He grabbed the handles of two units and looked at Ben. 'One last thing to show you. Are you ready?'

Black Fez pulled open the units – to reveal two cadavers, nametags clipped to the big toe of their right foot: HEATHCOTE, L.A. and MAVROS, M.

The bodies were white as sheets. Their eyes open, pupils clouded milky grey. Their limbs had atrophied and were lined with crude stitches from the autopsy. But despite everything, they were strangely serene. They were just empty husks – uncanny relics of the people they had once been.

Ben went over to the body of Marta Mavros. 'I thought she was cremated.'

'That's what they all think, the Prince included. But I kept her. After all, she's evidence. Too important to be smoked.'

Ben inspected her face. Was this Elizabeth? He could not tell. Those shrunken features bore no resemblance to the woman he remembered.

There was one way to be sure. He pried apart the fingers of her left hand. The flesh was stiff as leather. There, on the inside of her middle finger, was a familiar smudge. The tattooed letters: *T O*.

He waited for the tears to come, for his voice to crack and his legs to give way. But nothing of the sort happened. He just felt cold and numb.

Black Fez handed him the dossier. 'You paid for this. It's yours now.'

'Does anyone else know about this?'

'No. So, the way I see it, you have three options. One: try your luck with the police. Though I don't suspect it will make a jot of difference. If they didn't listen to Heathcote, they certainly won't listen to you. Two: hire a detective and track down whoever is responsible for the murders. Or three: get off this train before it barrels over a cliff and you end up in one of these units. I gave Heathcote the same warning, but he refused to listen to me. And look where it got him!'

Ben looked at the body of the woman he had once loved – Elizabeth, Marta, whatever her real name was. A person who once had a voice, feelings, things to laugh about, tears to shed. Now reduced to a slab of meat on a metal tray.

'I don't know if I can do that…' he whispered.

'This is beyond nature, my friend,' Black Fez hissed. 'A demon is haunting Constantinople. Everyone knows it, but cannot bear to say it. There have been legends of such creatures: *djinns* that prowl the city in times of crisis, snatching men's souls from their lips. I don't know what your motive is, but it is not worth this fate.'

The mortician was right. Elizabeth was dead. So was Heathcote. The circle was constricting. And somebody else was bound to be next. The question was: *who?*

12

The White Death

Black Fez summoned a taxi-carriage for Ben and sent him packing with the dossier tucked under his arm. It was a nervy ride back to the Akbars'. In the days following the demonstration, the streets were crawling with gendarmes. Ben kept the curtains drawn, fearing at any moment that he would be apprehended by one of Yusuf Madhat Pasha's men.

By nightfall, he was standing at the open window of his room above Ahrida, cool air on his cheeks, breathing in the scent of orange blossoms from the courtyard. Mist shrouded the rooftops, silver in the sunken moonlight. He was gripped by the feeling that some invisible enemy was gazing back at him across this no-man's-land. He waited for something, or someone, hidden in the motionless shadows to move.

But there was nothing. Just the hum of evening prayer from the synagogue below, the voices of Shabtai's grandchildren as they prepared for bed, the muezzin's call to prayer from the nearby Fethiye Mosque.

He shivered, closed the window and collapsed into a chair. The dossier lay before him. He stared at it, not daring to touch it. Finally, he dredged up the courage and turned to the chapter on Elizabeth—

He checked himself. *Marta.* Marta Mavros. He murmured the name again under his breath. It felt wrong, like an ill-fitting suit. Yet one thing was now beyond debate: *Marta Mavros and Elizabeth de Varney were the same person.* The tattoo all but confirmed it.

He studied the sketches of her corpse, trying to understand how this could be. First she was dead. Then, for a fleeting time, he had been teased with the possibility that she was alive. And now she was dead once more. Not just dead – if Black Fez and Heathcote were right, she may well have been *murdered*. And something linked her death to Heathcote's, to Sir Lawrence Thorsbury's, to Abraham Carmino's. Seemingly random acts of violence, all connected – but to what end?

Ben rubbed his brow in exhaustion. 'What on earth have I got myself into…?'

'Mister Ben?'

He snapped the dossier shut. Standing in the doorway was Duda – Shabtai's seven-year-old grandson. He was sucking his thumb and clutching a small felt elephant.

'*Buena tadrada*, Duda,' Ben grinned. 'What are you doing out of bed?'

Duda laughed and threw his arms around Ben's waist. 'Can't sleep – you tuck me in…?'

Ben carried Duda to his bedroom and lowered him into the cot next to his slumbering siblings.

'Mister Ben… are you from London?'

Ben nodded. Duda was amazed.

'What is London?'

Ben knelt by Duda's side. In the bedtime-story voice that he used with Golda, he painted Duda a picture of his home: bells at dawn – barges blaring on the Thames – palaces and cathedrals way off in the distance – the pubs and music-halls of the East End slums. 'It's a big, dirty, stinky old place! They send little boys like you up chimneys!'

Duda yawned. He was drifting off already. 'Where is your mama?'

'She's busy making dinner for when I return! She's waiting for me, with my father and brother and sisters.'

'Why did you leave them?'

It was an innocent question, and so innocently put. But it cut right through Ben. He had spent his whole life under the roof of 82 Whitechapel Road. And now it felt like a memory of some past life that he might never get back. Even if he did return, would they welcome him with open arms? Or had he broken their trust one time too many?

He pecked Duda on the forehead and the boy snuggled under his blanket. 'Go to sleep, little man.'

Ben returned to his room. He felt a draught on his face. The window was open and the shutters were rattling. The candle had been snuffed and the room had been plunged into darkness.

He went over to the windows and closed them once again. But as he did, a reflection in the glass caught his eye—

A figure right behind him – bursting from the shadows!

Ben dropped to the floor. A fist whistled past him, inches from his head, and shattered the glass pane.

A man stood over him – a full head taller, in a black greatcoat. His face was obscured by a hood-mask made of coarse flannel and covered in brown burn-patches. His breathing was distorted by an exhale valve over his mouth. Two glass circles revealed glittering grey eyes.

Ben rolled out of the way and sprang back to his feet as the man stamped down, breaking one of the floorboards.

Ben raised his fists: 'Ever heard of knocking?'

The man said nothing. He hurled himself at Ben and unleashed a flurry of devastating punches: a blow to the solar plexus – a liver shot – a piledriving hook to the side of the head. Before he knew it, Ben was on his back, gasping for air.

He hauled Ben up and slung him across the room like a ragdoll. Ben smashed headlong into a mirror. Glass shards dug into his scalp and blood ran down his forehead and into his eyes.

Fifteen seconds was all it took: Ben had been pummelled into submission.

The man grabbed him by the throat and pinned him against the wall. Ben writhed and lashed out in vain, and the man headbutted him square in the face – splitting his lip and sending white sparks across his vision.

He heard a cold, metallic rasp: 'SAY YOUR PRAYERS.'

'Sorry, mate,' Ben spluttered. 'Not the religious type…'

He whipped the mother-of-pearl penknife from his back pocket and stabbed the man in his right leg, just above the knee. The man lurched back – stunned, but without so much as a groan.

Ben vaulted over the bed and put some distance between him and his assailant. The two circled each other – a relentless predator and its wily prey. During the struggle, one of the man's gloves had come off and Ben could see his bare hand. It was mottled with burns and blisters and his fingernails were missing. He moved with preternatural speed and agility. Maybe

Black Fez was right, and a ghoul from another realm was indeed haunting this city.

Ben adopted a southpaw stance. 'Are we going to dance all night?'

Again, that mechanical voice:

'YOU SHOULD HAVE STAYED OUT OF IT.'

This could only be one person. 'The White Death...' Ben whispered.

The door swung open and Shabtai burst in, flanked by his sons and a dozen bearded rabbis wearing *tallit*. They formed a wall between Ben and his attacker.

'I don't know who you are,' Shabtai declared, 'but if you want him, you'll have to go through us.'

'Finally,' Ben said. 'A *minyan* when you need one!'

Shabtai grabbed him by the sleeve and cried: '*Stop talking and get out!* As fast as you can!'

Ben grabbed the dossier and shoved it into his knapsack. He fled with Shabtai, while the man barged his way through the melee of rabbis.

Shabtai threw open a window on the corridor outside Ben's room. Ben peered down: a fifteen-foot drop to street-level. 'Jump!' Shabtai shouted.

Ben glanced over his shoulder. The man had emerged onto the corridor and was running at him at full pelt. Ben leapt out and crash-landed in a pile of firewood. As he staggered to his feet, he heard a dull *thud* behind him. The man had landed with an agile roll on the cobbled street about ten feet away and was lumbering after him.

The fight had taken it out of Ben and his leg was injured from the fall. The man was gaining on him fast.

Then he heard a high-pitched voice: 'Psst! Beef Wellington!'

A grimy little boy of no more than fourteen was beckoning to him from an open manhole across the street.

'Now or never!' the boy shouted.

Ben limped over to the boy, who lowered him into the manhole, slammed the cover shut and locked it tight from the inside. They climbed down a metal ladder – but on the last rung, Ben slipped and fell into foul-smelling water. His new companion hauled him out and held a match to his swollen face.

'Wowee!' he whistled. 'You really got the daylights kicked out of you!'

Ben wiped the blood from his eyes. 'Thanks for saving me up there.'

'We're not out the woods yet, Englishman. That was a tenacious dog you were up against – I wouldn't put it past him to track us down here. Name's Ismail, by the way. Ismail Bilan. I've been following you all weekend.'

'On whose orders?'

Ben doubled over, hit by a sudden wave of nausea. Ismail patted his back encouragingly. 'You'll see. Now let's go. No time for mewling and puking, to borrow from the Bard.'

Ismail scurried off. Ben dragged himself after the urchin, losing his way in the pitch-black, labyrinthine tunnels of Constantinople's sewers. Yet at every turn the boy seemed to know exactly where he was going, like a rat retreating to its nest.

'You're getting quite a reputation around here,' Ismail wagged his finger. 'Only a few days and everyone wants a piece of you. You've certainly tickled Yusuf Madhat Pasha's fancy – and that lazy bastard doesn't get lathered up over anything!'

They trekked for what felt like an eternity. It was impossible to tell how much time had passed in the darkness of the sewers, but it had to have been several hours at least. Finally, they reached the end of the tunnel – the periphery of Constantinople's sewer system. A ladder led up to a manhole, guarded by a fellow urchin in an embroidered skull-cap adorned with a crescent moon.

He saluted Ismail and they exchanged a few words in an unfamiliar tongue. Ismail switched to English and gestured to Ben, 'I have the package.'

They ascended the ladder and emerged onto the shores of the Bosporus. It was the early hours of morning, the sky still black and the moon still high.

The boy looked Ben up and down. He grimaced: 'You're having a bad night, boss.'

Ben shrugged. 'Better than the alternative.'

A *kayik* was waiting for them on the water. Ismail took Ben onto the boat and they rowed across the Bosporus. A grand estate on the Asiatic shore gradually came into view. Armed guards, strapped with swords and rifles, were patrolling its stone walls. Ismail whistled as he moored the *kayik* and one of the guards opened a broad wooden gate.

Ben and Ismail were escorted into a magnificent walled garden, where magnolia trees shed their last summer blossoms and nightingales trilled from the treetops. Up ahead was a manor in the style of an English country house.

Ismail held up his hand. 'Stop there.'

He disappeared into the house and left Ben waiting on the patio with a guard. Fifteen minutes later, the French doors opened and a woman emerged. She was robed in black and was glaring at Ben with undisguised irritation.

'Shoshanna Carmino!' Ben smiled.

She scowled at him. 'If it isn't "Mr Peculiar". Wipe that gormless grin off your face. You have some explaining to do.'

13

A Risky Game

The spectre of loss hung over the Carmino estate. It was like a mausoleum, with its cold stone floors; its corridors bathed in the sombre light of waning candles; its doors half-open onto untenanted salons and studies, where shelves of books gathered dust under the watchful eye of Dutch Old Masters.

Ben leant on Ismail for support as he trailed after Shoshanna. With every step he felt dizzier, closer to passing out.

'I could really use a doctor...' he said.

Shoshanna marched on, not bothering to look back.

'Keep your voice down, you'll wake the household. Besides, I thought the British were supposed to be stoic in their suffering.'

'Stiff upper lips aren't much good when they're split down the middle,' Ben retorted. 'And I can't say I appreciate your tone.'

'And I don't appreciate you turning up unannounced and bleeding all over the floor. Does that make us even?'

Shoshanna threw open a set of double doors, into a musty parlour smelling vaguely of rose-petals. The room was lined with the finest silver Judaica that Ben had ever seen, arranged in a series of glass cabinets – though on closer inspection, it could have used a polish. Hanging over the fireplace was a stately portrait of a bearded gentleman: full-cheeked, with a proud smile, resplendent in a mink fur coat, so vividly rendered that Ben thought he might step forward to introduce himself. Etched in black at the base of the frame was a name: *Abraham Carmino*.

A heavyweight Turkish bodyguard stood in the middle of the room with a sabre tied to his belt. Shoshanna barked at him: 'Eydir!'

This giant immediately set about patting Ben down.

'I don't have any weapons,' Ben said.

Eydir produced Ben's mother-of-pearl penknife from his back pocket, still wet with blood. He raised an eyebrow.

'Well... apart from that.'

The bodyguard set the knife on a blackwood table. Shoshanna scrutinised Ben.

'You look like a ghost,' she said, with a hint of cold pleasure.

'I will be one shortly if you don't get a move on.'

'Ismail should never have brought you here,' she replied. 'But since I've got you, I may as well ask you a few questions. And if you give me straight answers, I'll send for a doctor. Does that sound fair?'

Ben was in half a mind to keep arguing. But with his head pounding and his legs feeling like jelly, he was too drained to resist. 'Delightful.'

'First things first: your name. Your *real* name. None of this "Rupert Rogers" claptrap.'

'Ben Canaan. Benjamin E. Canaan if we're being pedantic.'

'And what, *Benjamin E. Canaan*, are you up to? Because I'll tell you now, it's certainly not sight-seeing. Unless your copy of Murray's has instructions on getting arrested and diving into the Golden Horn.'

'I was looking for someone. You would know her as Princess Marta Mavros – hence my visit to her husband earlier today. I came all this way to find her, only to discover that she's dead. *Murdered.*'

'Marta Mavros took her own life.'

'No, she did not. She was killed. There's a whole string of them just like her. And guess what? *One of them was your father.* Did you know that?'

Shoshanna looked for moment as though she was ready to finish the job that Ben's attacker had started. But then outrage gave way to something else – *intrigue*.

'I guess not,' Ben added.

She took a step closer to Ben. Eydir held out a protective arm, but she shook him off. 'Who the hell are you?' she said under her breath. 'Some kind of low-rent detective?'

'I've been called many things in my life,' Ben snorted, 'but never a copper.'

'Then who do you work for? Who sent you?'

'That's the second time I've been asked that, and my answer's exactly the same. I'm a Good-for-Nothing. I work for *me*.'

Shoshanna gave Ben a scathing look. 'I see. You're a lowlife who crawled out the London gutters and fancies himself as "Inspector Bucket". Out looking for an adventure because you've got nothing better to do with yourself.'

'Do I look like I'm having a bloody adventure?' Ben cried. 'I just went toe-to-toe with a masked killer who told me that I should have "stayed out of it". He hunted me down to *silence* me because of what I know!'

Shoshanna glanced at Ismail. The urchin was listening from the sidelines.

'Is that true, Ismail?' she asked.

The boy nodded gravely.

'There is a murderer on the loose in Constantinople,' Ben said through gritted teeth. '*The White Death*. He killed your father and had him framed for a crime he more than likely never committed. He killed Princess Marta Mavros too, though everyone is convinced she threw herself off Galata Bridge. And he was *this close* to making me his next victim. So insult me all you like, but we are on the same side, and we want the same thing: *the truth*.' Ben came right up to her – their faces inches apart. 'Mademoiselle Carmino… I am not your enemy.'

Like any girl of high society, she had a fine poker face. But there was no hiding it. The tightening in her throat, the furrow in her brow – she knew that he was right.

'Now…' Ben said. 'Can you *please* get me a doctor before I keel over in your living room? Try explaining that one to Yusuf Madhat Pasha.'

Shoshanna considered Ben. Then she snapped her fingers at her bodyguard. 'Eydir: summon Dr Sarfati for Mr Canaan. But not a word of this to Mother. I'll deal with her in the morning.'

In the blink of an eye, she was gone, leaving Ben alone with Ismail and Eydir. As soon as her footsteps were out of earshot, Ismail let out a belly laugh. 'You've got something about you, Englishman! First you survive this "White Death" – then Mademoiselle Carmino's temper!'

Ben was unsteady on his feet. 'Don't speak too soon.'

Ismail eased Ben onto a settee. 'Don't you worry: you're safe here. Every inch of this place is guarded. I don't think an intruder has ever made it in on Eydir's watch!'

'It's not intruders I'm worried about,' Ben said. 'It's who's already in the house!'

Dr Sarfati arrived an hour and a half later to stitch Ben up, with a small dose of ether to ease the pain. By the time the procedure was over, Ben was swollen and bruised, with red stitches running from his nostrils to his upper lip, and another above his right ear. He looked like one of the walloped prize-fighters at Houndsditch, slumped in the corner of the ring after a brutal bout.

An attendant appeared in the doorway of the parlour and took Ben to a windowless room in the servants' quarters. They had left some food for him: lemon cake, a couple of slices of rye bread with sweet fig jam, and a glass of *raki* – a cloudy spirit made from grapes and aniseed.

Breathing alone sent a stabbing pain from Ben's chest to his head, but he forced himself to eat and the *raki* numbed his lips. He lay down on the bed and closed his eyes, letting the warmth of the alcohol rush through him and send him to sleep.

Eydir woke him early the next morning with a splash of cold water: 'Rise and shine!'

Ben groaned. It felt as though his head had been filled with hot coals and given a good old bartender's shake. 'Give me a minute, will you…?'

He was hardly given ten seconds. Eydir pulled him out of bed and ordered him to get dressed. 'Lady Leonora is waiting for you.'

Ben was led to a reception room at the front of the estate: a circular parlour with yellow wallpaper and banks of windows looking onto a sweeping front lawn. Sitting on one side of a rosewood table was Lady Leonora Carmino, once again dressed in her black mantilla, along with Shoshanna and the Rafaeli

Twins. They seemed just as dour and humourless as when Ben had first met them.

Leonora gestured for Ben to sit and tea was served, with a bowl of phyllo pastries. Gavriel removed a slip of paper from his pocket and slid it across the table to Ben.

It was a sketch of Ben's face, sandwiched between blocks of Arabic script. Below the sketch, Ben could make out a number: 200.

It was a wanted poster.

'Our errand-boy Ismail found them glued to buildings across the city. They're everywhere!' Gavriel said. 'Your face, and that name you gave us at the Akbars'...'

'A two hundred lira reward,' Shmuel added. 'Quite a hefty sum. You must be valuable to them.'

'Well, if you're turning me in, I may as well enjoy a last supper...' Ben plucked a phyllo pastry from the bowl. 'Is that spinach and feta? Delicious!'

Gavriel smiled and was about to reply, but Leonora silenced him.

'This morning,' she said, 'Shoshanna and I had a lengthy discussion about the present situation. I understand that you have been inquiring into my husband's death.'

'I have developed a theory, shall we say.'

'And I understand that you have volunteered this theory to Shoshanna.'

'I was dragged here and grilled to within an inch of my life,' Ben said. 'I wouldn't exactly call it *voluntary*.'

Shoshanna shifted uncomfortably in her seat.

'I was unaware that Shoshanna was using Ismail to follow you around Constantinople,' Leonora said. 'I must apologise for the intrusion. It was unacceptable, and I have made that clear to her.'

Ben glanced at Shoshanna. She had been crying. He could tell from the puffiness around her eyes, from the hot blush in her cheeks.

'She's a tough one, that's for sure,' Ben said. 'But she's not wrong. She suspected I knew something. She acted on her instinct. And, as it turned I out, I *did* know something. I'd say she did pretty well to find me.'

Shoshanna looked startled by the admission.

'Be that as it may,' Leonora said, 'I simply cannot permit this to persist, Mr Canaan. Abraham's passing left a gaping wound in our family. But that wound cannot heal if you, and especially Shoshanna, insist on picking at it with this hare-brained fixation on hidden plots, convoluted schemes and conspiracy…'

She seemed to soften.

'Heartbreak is not cured by flights of fancy. That is just another form of denial – a refusal to accept reality. I have seen many succumb to the scourge of grief and spiral into paranoia and madness. *I will not let that happen to my only child.*'

Ben did not protest. It was not his place to tell Leonora how to take care of her daughter. He looked again at Shoshanna, expecting her to resist her mother, but her lips were sealed. Whatever she was feeling, she kept it well hidden.

The Carminos did not hand Ben over to the police. They knew full well that placing Ben in Yusuf Madhat Pasha's clutches would be a death sentence. But Leonora left Ben with a stern caution not to inveigle himself in their affairs any longer. He would be taken back to Constantinople and from there, he would be on his own.

That afternoon, he was ushered out of the estate and into a carriage manned by Eydir, without so much as a goodbye. As the carriage trundled down the avenue at the front of the estate, passing beneath the iron gate with its armed guards, he caught one final glimpse of Shoshanna, watching him from a second-floor window.

The journey took Ben through the Beykoz countryside on the Asiatic shore of the Bosporus. Vineyards, orchards of fig trees and lonely hermitages swept by. At a cool mineral spring, young ladies dressed in the European style were picnicking in the shade of sycamore and ash-trees. Ben dozed off, lulled to sleep by the rhythmic rocking of the carriage and the fresh country air.

It was twilight when he woke. Eydir had swung the carriage-door open and motioned for him to step out. Ben emerged, expecting to be standing on the quay where he had landed several days before on the HMS *Midas*.

But instead, he found himself at the summit of a basalt cliff overlooking the Bosporus, with the Strait to his right and fields of mullein and heather to his left. Some eighty feet overhead was an ancient aqueduct, snaking south towards the Sea of Marmara.

Wherever he was, it most certainly was not Constantinople.

He turned to Eydir. 'I thought Lady Carmino was sending me back to the city.'

Eydir just smiled. '*Mademoiselle Shoshanna had other ideas.*' He tapped his nose. 'Strictly between ourselves…'

'Where am I supposed to go?'

Eydir pointed south. 'Follow the aqueduct about ten minutes that way and you'll see.'

'See *what?!*'

Eydir shrugged Ben off and took the reins. 'Good luck, Mr Canaan! I pray to God we never meet again…'

And with that, he took off up the lane, leaving Ben in the dust.

Ben slung his knapsack over his shoulder. 'Never a straightforward bloody day for you, is it, Benjy?'

He followed the aqueduct south as the sun dipped under the horizon to the west of the Bosporus. Sure enough, after about ten minutes, he saw the light of a bonfire up ahead.

Suddenly: *a gunshot!* Then a voice echoing in the darkness: *'TUKTAT!!'*

Ben raised his hands. 'Tuktat to you too! I was sent here!!'

Another gunshot, this time right between Ben's feet – throwing up a clump of dirt. *'KELME!!'*

'English!!' Ben roared, raising his hands in the air.

Silence. Then a diminutive figure came scurrying towards him. Ben squinted through the deepening shadows… It was Ismail! He was wearing traditional Crimean Tatar attire: wide trousers, a flannelled white shirt tied with a gold silk belt, and a pointed black sheepskin *kalpak* on his head.

'Beef Wellington!' he cried, clapping Ben on the back.

He shouted something in that strange tongue of his. A gang of unkempt children emerged, carrying battered muskets. As Ben's eyes adjusted to the dark, he started to make out dozens of patchwork tents clustered around the bonfire. It was a campsite at the foot of the aqueduct.

'Welcome to New Crimea!' Ismail grinned. 'Sorry for the hostile introduction. Don't want to end up as the next chapter in your dossier.'

Ben had arrived in time for dinner: a hearty stew of venison and vegetables that one of the boys, a bow-legged kid by the name of Marat Zagid, had nicked from the Sali Bazaar. Ben warmed himself by the fire as Ismail regaled him with the story of this place.

The camp was home to fifty or so street urchins, Crimean Tatars who had grown up together in the Sevastopol orphanage. They had been driven out by the Russians two years previously and ended up on a boat to Constantinople, their nearest refuge. They had banded together under the joint leadership of Ismail and Marat Zagid, and learnt to survive by working the streets of Constantinople, using this remote camp as their base. Each one of these strays had become a specialist in some sordid trade – pickpocketing, smuggling, mail-robbing, mimicry, counterfeiting – and they shared everything with unflinching loyalty, from food, to clothing, to inside information about the goings-on around Constantinople.

'It's not your conventional family,' Ismail said, skewering a hunk of venison from the pot. 'But it's the best we've got!'

Ben looked around at these Tatar refugees, hunched over wooden bowls as they dug into their hard-won meal – youngsters who, through misfortune and the sheer will to survive, seemed to have forgotten that they were still children. It reminded him of Tuvia's stories of Jewish kids who had fled the massacres in Eastern Europe. How they would hunker down at the side of the road, keep themselves going with samovars of weak coffee, tell bad jokes to while away the sleepless hours, and pray to an indifferent night-time sky when they were losing hope.

'Don't take this the wrong way,' Ben said, 'but what do the *Carminos* of all people have to do with an Artful Dodger like you?'

Ismail smirked. 'It's the old man's fault. Abraham Carmino, I mean. I did odd jobs for him every now and then, and he took pity on me. He had a good heart – gave me nice clothes, taught me Shakespeare and Dickens, wanted to take my brothers and sisters off the streets. After he died, I felt duty-bound to the ladies, and the ladies felt duty-bound to me. So I help any way I can, even if that involves chasing you across Constantinople and nearly losing my head in the process. And for my services, I get the occasional free lunch.'

'Do you believe he sold bullion to the Russians?' Ben asked.

'I doubt it. He was a crafty fellow, but honest and loyal as the day is long. Then again, do we truly know anyone, eh?'

'And what does Shoshanna want with me?'

'Beats me,' Ismail shrugged. 'She had a big old fight with Lady Leonora this morning. Her mother must have put her foot down about this whole business because Shoshanna took me to one side afterwards, all secretive, and said she was going to have you ferried here – and that Lady Leonora was to know *nothing* about it. So she clearly has a plan of some sort. But it's a risky game she's playing…'

Soon after dinner ended, as Ben and the Tatars huddled on mats by the bonfire to play blackjack, a carriage pulled up by the camp and out stepped Shoshanna, in a sweeping black coat with a hood. She cut a foreboding figure in the firelight.

As she entered the camp, the Tatars stood to attention and removed their caps out of respect. Ben remained cross-legged on the ground.

Shoshanna gestured to him. 'Come this way.'

'I'm sorry,' Ben scoffed, 'am I your lapdog now?'

Shoshanna took a deep breath and eked out a thin, '*Please?*'

Ben hopped to his feet. 'That's more like it!'

They went back to her carriage and sat facing one another – Shoshanna tense and upright, Ben leaning back across the velvet.

'So,' he said, 'what's this? Keeping me prisoner behind your mummy's back?'

'Hardly keeping you prisoner if you've got nowhere else to go.'

'I could go home.'

'We both know you're not going to do that, Mr Canaan.'

Ben could not argue with that. 'Alright then. Enlighten me.'

Shoshanna glanced out the window, searching for the words. 'You are an infuriating and impudent fellow. Your mouth should be washed out with soap – or better yet, sewn shut. Not to mention, you give off the most unpleasant odour.'

'I'm beginning to think you might be infatuated with me!'

'But like a pig sniffing for truffles, you seem to have a knack for rooting out the truth. You've cracked more of this case in a few days than I have in a few months.'

Ben locked his hands together and rested his chin on them, smiling ear to ear. 'Mademoiselle Carmino... Are you trying to be nice to me?'

'If you'll just shut up for a moment, you'll see that I'm making you an offer. *Come work for me.*'

Ben's smile faltered. Shoshanna's game had become clear. 'Work for you? Doing what, exactly?'

'I want you to unravel this mystery. I want you to find out who killed my father and why. I want to bring this house of cards crashing down.'

'And in return?'

'I will pay you a respectable fee.'

'How respectable?'

'One hundred pounds.'

Ben's heart almost leapt out of his mouth. That was a year's aggregated earnings for the entire business of Canaan & Sons. But he kept his cool.

'That is… adequate as a starting fee,' he said. 'Though if it drags on, I will require additional payment. Otherwise, frankly, it just isn't worth my while.'

'I'm sure we can work that out. More importantly, if you succeed, you will be owed a favour by one of the most powerful families on the Continent. And that, Mr Canaan, as you will no doubt come to learn, is priceless. So… do we have a deal?'

Ben mulled her proposition. It sounded dangerous. Very dangerous. Then again, whoever murdered Abraham Carmino was also responsible for Elizabeth's death. If Ben took up her offer, he could kill two birds with one stone and get paid for it. And, just maybe, if he went back to London with a hundred pounds in his pocket – enough to pay off his father's debts with change for a bottle of celebratory champagne – then his family might go easier on him.

'Tick-tock, Mr Canaan,' Shoshanna persisted. *'Do we have a deal?'*

Ben looked her dead in the eye and reached out.

They locked hands.

'Deal.'

14

The Madwoman in the Mountain

They got to work that very night. They settled on a Persian rug in Ismail's tent and Ben guided Shoshanna through the dossier compiled by Black Fez, filling her in on everything he knew about the White Death killings. Shoshanna gave Ben a notebook and he drew up a timeline of the murders:

22nd March	LAWRENCE THORSBURY
13th May	ABRAHAM CARMINO
3rd August	MARTA MAVROS
18th September	LYNTON ARABIN HEATHCOTE

Six months, four deaths, and all by the same hand – but with no trace of a murder weapon and no explanation as to why they had been killed.

The investigation into Marta's death had dried up. Ben could not go back to Prince Mavros, especially now that he was a fugitive. Nor could Shoshanna – some unspoken awkwardness in the relationship between the Mavros and Carmino clans, not helped by the fact that Prince Mavros had been gifted Abraham's seat on the Sultan's Imperial Council.

Likewise, Ben had no more clues in relation to Heathcote. He had managed to obtain the dossier, which was a valuable source of information, but Black Fez had recused himself and for now the only known suspect in Heathcote's murder was Ben himself.

And as for Abraham, Shoshanna knew next to nothing. All she could tell Ben was that, on the day of her father's death, he had seemed in a hurry to leave the old family home for a meeting in the northern district of Beshiktash. Moreover, after he died, the bullion scandal emerged seemingly from nowhere, with no indication of who or what had triggered it. It was, so Shoshanna believed, as though someone had manufactured the accusation in order to ruin them. But that was mere speculation.

So, if they were going to find a clue, it would have to be from the death of Sir Lawrence Thorsbury, the former British special envoy. As it turned out, Shoshanna had known him – he and Abraham had been good friends, and it was tradition for Sir Lawrence and his wife to attend Rosh Hashanah dinner at the Carminos'.

'It was terribly sad after Sir Lawrence died,' Shoshanna said. 'Lady Thorsbury – Antonia is her name – lost her mind. The grief must have been too much for her.'

'My contact at the morgue mentioned that,' Ben said. 'Apparently she's been committed to a convent in the mountains to recover.'

'I wondered where she'd gone. The Embassy told us nothing.'

Ben studied Shoshanna as the evening wind buffeted the tarpaulin. The urchins had taken shelter from the gale, and the once-lively camp was quiet.

'Do you know it?' Ben said.

'If it's in the mountains, it can only be one place,' Shoshanna said. 'It's at least half a day's ride.'

'Then maybe we should saddle up – pay her a visit.'

Shoshanna hesitated for a moment.

'You're right,' she said. 'Sit tight. I'll arrange transport.'

She made an abrupt farewell, eager to get home before it got too late and she drew suspicion. Ben and Ismail watched the carriage bob down a path along the aqueduct, before it disappeared into the fields under a pale moon.

Ismail nudged Ben: 'She's quite the operator, isn't she?'

'She's reckless,' Ben replied. 'A classic spoiled rich girl. Too intent on getting what she wants to think straight about the consequences.'

'Well, she got you! So if she goes down, you won't be far behind...'

Sheet lightning flashed across the night sky, followed by a thunderclap and the first sign of rain. The relentless heat was finally breaking. They retreated to their tents and wrapped up against the coming storm.

For three days and nights, the deluge hammered Constantinople. The city was subdued as news arrived from Crimea of the British advance on the Russian outposts in Sevastopol. Ben waited at the camp the entire time without word from Shoshanna.

Then, one drizzling afternoon, Ismail came running through the mud with a note for Ben written in Shoshanna's hand:

carriage waiting at crossroads outside Chibukli tomorrow at dawn

– S

Ismail reached into a haversack: 'There's more.'

He pulled out a fresh change of clothes: a cashmere frock coat, two-ply, with matching trousers, red chequered vest, white satin shirt, cravat and lapis lazuli cufflinks. It was an exquisite ensemble, worth about as much as his prospective fee.

'She said, and I quote, "If he really is a tailor's son, he ought to start dressing like one."'

'Free clothes,' Ben smirked. 'One of the perks of the job, I suppose!'

Ben set off in the early hours of the following morning. It was still dark – every now and then he would pause by the roadside and inspect the map, just to make sure that he was still on the right track. By the time dawn was creeping across the sky, and a faint sunrise in the east was burning off the mist that had enveloped the black forested hills, Ben arrived in Chibukli.

It was an impoverished village squatting on the marshy banks of the Bosporus. The waters were calmer here than in Constantinople or Scutari, deserted save for a raft of ducks paddling along and a fisherman dragging a lobster-net onto his *kayik* to survey the night's catch. Ben ambled down a lane lined with cherry trees, past a bakery where women were stoking the flames of a *tabun* oven, baking loaves of *ekmek* flatbread.

He stopped at the crossroads described in Shoshanna's note. One path led to Chibukli, the other further inland through a field of freshly reaped bulgur wheat. He looked around: no sign of the carriage yet. A bracing early morning breeze carried the aroma of hot bread and the occasional donkey-drawn wagon trundled past, loaded with boxes of apples and ears of corn.

Just when he was starting to question whether he had found the right place, he saw that familiar carriage rounding the corner towards him. The curtains were drawn, but he recognised Eydir at the reins.

He greeted Ben with a salute and a caustic smile: 'I see God did not answer my prayers.'

The door edged open and Shoshanna peeked out. She too was dressed formally, in a sombre black dress over a lace chemisette. 'Get in. Quick!'

'And a fine morning to you too...' Ben muttered as he climbed in.

Eydir whipped the reins. Ben drew back the curtains and sunlight came streaming into the carriage. Shoshanna immediately went to close them: 'We must be discreet, Mr Canaan – I cannot be seen with you—'

'Stew in the shadows in your own time, Mademoiselle Carmino. You've hired me to use my noggin and my noggin needs sun. Besides, the light brings out your natural warmth and geniality...'

'We have five hours in this compartment together,' Shoshanna interrupted him. 'Keep your quips to a minimum, please.'

They headed inland, through the steppes of the Beykoz outback – vibrant plains of oleander, studded with low-roofed cabins and tiny church steeples. Farmers breakfasted along the country lanes, dunking sesame-seeded *simit* rolls in bowls of olive oil and ewe's cheese and slaking their thirst with well-water. As the carriage pushed east, sunflowers and cicadas gave way to mountainous terrain, where river-rapids gushed and the forests were wild.

It was late morning when they heard the bells: a sharp

triple-clang floating above the treeline. Ben pulled down the window and stuck his head out for a better view.

They were skirting the edge of a ravine. About two hundred yards ahead was an almost vertical mountain-face. Built into the rock were the chapels, brick roofs and chimney-tops of the convent. A colossal statue of Christ presided over the hermitage, arms spread wide as if holding up the mountain.

'What's this place called?' Ben said.

'Gizli Ev,' Shoshanna replied. 'The Secret Home. A refuge where those who most need to escape the world can retreat, to live in isolation.'

A group of nuns stopped them at the gate and asked the purpose of their visit. Shoshanna explained that they had come to see Lady Thorsbury – old friends who had heard that she might be sequestered here. Ben was expecting to be refused entry, but the nuns were only too happy to help. Lady Thorsbury, as Shoshanna suspected, was indeed convalescing in the convent and the sisters hoped that she might be cheered by familiar faces.

One of the elders, Sister Azra, led them to the dormitories at the edge of the convent. It was a thousand-foot drop to the valley below.

'She is not in the best of states,' Sister Azra said. 'For a long time, she had lost her mind completely. Even now, she is only half-present. Do not be upset if she fails to recognise you at first – I can assure you, her soul has not deserted her. And so long as there remains a soul...' She crossed herself fervently.

'Has she had many visitors?' Shoshanna asked.

'Hardly any of late. So many friends in her old life, yet so quickly forgotten in her hour of need. Sadly, that is the way of the world these days.'

Sister Azra took them to a sparse cell in the dormitories. Particles of dust clung to the air, suspended in rays of sunlight. A metal crucifix and icons of Christ and the Apostles hung on the walls, over a single bed. A novice sat in the corner, lips moving in silent prayer. Sitting by the grated window was a gaunt elderly woman staring at her hands as she crocheted a shawl.

'Look who has come to see you, Lady Thorsbury!' Sister Azra said, tentatively approaching the woman. 'Mademoiselle Shoshanna Carmino and…'

She glanced at Ben.

'Mr Benjamin Canaan,' he said.

Lady Thorsbury did not react.

Shoshanna kneeled before her and whispered, 'Antonia…'

Lady Thorsbury drifted from her trance, like a feather floating down to earth. She was suddenly filled with great warmth and her worn features creased in a lopsided smile.

'*Paloma*,' she murmured. '*Poquita paloma.*'

The utterance made Shoshanna jolt. Until not too long ago, she had heard that name every day of her life. She had not thought that she would ever hear it again.

'How do you know that name?'

'Why, that's what your father calls you! *Poquita paloma* – little pigeon. Is it not the most charming pet-name in the whole wide world? Lawrence was telling me about it just the other day. He is lunching with darling Abraham as we speak. Goodness gracious! I daresay he spends more time with your father than with me!'

Lady Thorsbury returned to her crocheting and began humming a ditty. Ben gave Sister Azra a quizzical look.

'Sir Lawrence's death proved too much for her,' Sister Azra whispered gravely. 'To cope, she has regressed to some point in the past, before his demise, and has not left that moment since.'

'Is there any way to bring her out of it?' Ben asked.

'We have tried, but she becomes hysterical. In some ways, it is easier to play along with the fantasy and hope that, through prayer and good will, the affliction may pass.'

Ben recalled the caution that Leonora had issued at the Carmino estate: how grief drives people mad, imprisons them in an old life, and refuses to let them go. She feared that fate for Shoshanna, and here it had befallen Lady Thorsbury. How were they supposed to communicate with her when she was adrift in another time?

Ben joined Shoshanna's side. Lady Thorsbury's eyes were like sunken pearls, her nose delicate, her lips round with a hint of rosiness. Once upon a time, she must have been very beautiful.

'A colleague of my husband's?' she beamed at Ben. 'Why, I'm sure he'll be back soon – as soon as his lunch is—'

'No, Antonia,' Shoshanna said. 'This is Benjamin. He's joined me from—'

'As it happens, my lady,' Ben interrupted with his most charming smile, 'I do have some business with your husband. Sent by Whitehall, you see – on a matter of the utmost importance.'

Lady Thorsbury may have lost her mind, but she had clearly not lost her love of gossip. She set down her crocheting and leant in close, as though she and Ben were at a dinner party and had to exercise discretion. '*Utmost importance?* Then you would be wise to talk to Lawrence post-haste!'

'Actually, my lady, I would much rather talk to *you*. For behind every important man is an even more important woman.'

'You charming fibber!' she laid a hand on his arm. 'Ask away, my dear boy.'

'It concerns your husband. Has he, at any point of late, seemed out of sorts?'

Shoshanna realised Ben's game. If Lady Thorsbury could not be brought back to the present, then Ben would have to pay a visit to the past.

Lady Thorsbury frowned, pondering the question. 'Out of sorts? In what way?'

'Is he preoccupied by anything? Not behaving as his usual convivial self?'

Lady Thorsbury wracked her brain. 'There is one thing that I've noticed… Lawrence is the most unflappable man I've ever known. Nothing perturbs him! And yet, recently, he has seemed inexplicably flustered about something. He has taken to locking doors and windows before bed, which was never his habit. Day or night, he refuses to travel without an escort. And when I wish to leave the house, he asks a litany of questions and places all kinds of constraints on where I am to go, who I am to see. If he believes I have taken a lover, he is *sorely* mistaken!'

'Why do you think this is happening?'

'For a while, I was confused. But then, one evening, I was perhaps a little *cheeky*! I eavesdropped on a conversation in the study, between Lawrence and…' She looked at Shoshanna, '…darling Abraham!'

Lady Thorsbury was revelling in their little chat. But Shoshanna could not resist intervening.

'What were they talking about?' she asked.

Lady Thorsbury glanced over her shoulder to check that Sister Azra could not hear her. 'They were talking about that *poor boy's death*. They think, though they dare not say it, that they are closing in on a murderer!'

'Wait a moment – which boy?' Ben asked.

'Why, *Ahmed!* The Sultan's boy. He passed away ever so suddenly in January. Healthy as can be, and in the next moment... struck down!'

Lady Thorsbury registered Ben's shock.

'My good man! Did you not know?' she said. 'It was cholera that took him. But it seems that Lawrence and Abraham suspect foul play. What I heard them discuss that evening was the child's mother: *Mihrima* is her name. She was a witness to his death – the sole witness, I believe – and she is adamant that the boy was murdered! I gather they have been trying to establish contact with her, but it is practically impossible, as I'm sure you appreciate. She is under lock and key in the Sultan's harem, well out of bounds!'

'Have they spoken to anyone about their suspicions?' Ben asked.

'I couldn't say. They definitely took their case to the gendarmerie, but that oaf Yusuf Madhat Pasha warned them off it. Said they were on a hiding to nothing and were wasting his time.' She broke off. Her enthusiasm had waned. 'It worries me...'

Ben gripped her hand. 'Why?'

'What if they're right? I know my Lawrence – he does not lose his composure over just anything. It is as though he fears that they will be...'

She snatched her hand away. Something in her manner had changed. Her lip twisted and she bunched up the shawl and threw it across the room.

'Nothing left of him! Gone! Gone! *White as death itself!*'

She jabbed a bony finger at Shoshanna.

'BOETHIUS!' she cried. 'That was what your father's letter said – the night poor Lawrence died – just one word – BOETHIUS – I found it in the fireplace, burnt to ashes… But not from my memory!'

Lady Thorsbury stormed across the room and knelt before the icon, placing her forehead on the cold stone and pounding the floor with open palms.

'Oh Lord, my Father, my North Star – the devil himself is among us!'

As Lady Thorsbury sobbed and prayed, Sister Azra wrapped her arm around her waist, gently lifted her to her feet, and led her to bed. She issued instructions to the novice in Turkish. Then, to the two visitors: 'Leave us to calm her down.'

Ben and Shoshanna retreated to the courtyard where Eydir was waiting with the carriage. Birds scattered across the ridge hanging over the convent. That triple-clang from the bell again – a signal for the nuns to migrate to the refectory. Neither of them said anything, mulling Lady Thorsbury's strange revelations, until Shoshanna finally said: 'My father never breathed a word of a child's murder. He told me virtually everything. Why not that?'

Ben did not reply. But deep down he knew the answer: *Abraham had been trying to protect Shoshanna.* Knowledge and suspicion were what got Lawrence Thorsbury killed, and so long as Shoshanna knew and suspected nothing, she might be spared. But now Abraham was gone and the genie was out the bottle. What they had heard could not be unheard. Shoshanna's safety, for all her wealth and privilege, could no longer be guaranteed.

Sister Azra returned a few minutes later. 'She's asleep, but in no condition to talk.'

'I'm sorry for causing such a disturbance,' Shoshanna said.

'It is not your fault, my dear. Only God can save her now.'

'If she needs anything,' Shoshanna replied, 'whether money, provisions, or transport, please write to the Carmino family. We'll make whatever arrangements you require.'

Sister Azra thanked Shoshanna and blessed them. Ben watched her hurry back to the granges on the cliff-edge, where the madwoman of the mountain now spent her days. The sky had clouded over and the slate grey mountain was bearing down on the statue of Christ. Ben had just seen, up close, the real toll of the White Death – not the gruesome fate of the dead, but the endless torment of those left behind.

'Ben,' Shoshanna said. She was already in the carriage. *'Let's go.'*

On the long trip back to Beykoz, they pondered their next steps. Two things were now clear from their encounter with Lady Thorsbury. First, Abraham and Lawrence may both have been killed because they got too close to the killer. Second, there may well have been a fifth victim of the White Death, previously unconnected to the murders that had gripped Constantinople: Ahmed, son of the Sultan himself.

How and why these pieces slotted together, they did not know. But there was one way to find out. Something that Abraham and Lawrence had never been able to do: *talk to Mihrima*, the boy's mother, and figure out exactly what had happened to Ahmed that night.

By the time they reached this realisation, they had arrived at the Bosporus. Far down the Strait, washed in the golden glow of mid-afternoon and shimmering on the horizon like a mirage, was Constantinople.

'Mihrima?' Shoshanna said incredulously. 'Mr Canaan, she is a member of the Sultan's harem, one of the most secretive and heavily guarded places on earth! We don't exactly have an invitation.'

Ben looked out the window. At the summit of the hills above the Golden Horn and the Sea of Marmara was Topkapı Palace: home to the Sultan – the next step in their investigation.

'I've always thought that breaking in is more fun!'

15

The Sultan's Harem

It took two weeks to put the ruse together. First and foremost, Ben needed a way in: Topkapı was an impregnable fortress, circled by steep wooded slopes and high stone walls patrolled day and night by the guards of the Sultan's elite Mansure Army. From what Ben heard, they would have no qualms about shooting anyone bold or foolish enough to stage a break-in.

It was Ismail who came up trumps. He knew someone on the inside at Topkapı: a Tatar orphan who had stowed away with him when they first fled Crimea, now working in the palace as a *dilsiz* – one of the Sultan's deaf-mute messengers.

'Umer is his name,' Ismail explained. 'He was begging on the street one day when a secretary of the Sultan happened to pass by. The fellow noticed his pretty little face and took an instant shine to him. Umer was brought to Topkapı and presented to the Chief Eunuch. Once he had passed muster, they gave him food, shelter, employment for life… And in return? They cut out his tongue, severed the nerves in his ears and took his crown jewels for good measure!'

Ismail contacted Umer to see if he could sneak Ben into Topkapı and arrange a meeting with Mihrima. The *dilsiz* needed some convincing – he had a lot to lose if it went wrong. But for old times' sake, and in keeping with the Tatars' strict code of brotherhood, he agreed to help.

They met with Umer at a hunting lodge on the shore of a lake in Belgrad Forest, some twenty miles north of Constantinople, where there was absolutely no risk of them being seen. Umer ran through the plan, with Ismail translating the *dilsiz*'s sign language into the Queen's English.

One of the courtyards of Topkapı, known as the Divan Meydani, was built on the site of an ancient Byzantine cistern long fallen into disuse, which for centuries had served as top-secret subterranean access for the Sultan's messengers. Umer was to ferry Ben via this cistern to the Divan Meydani. From there, it was a short stroll into the harem.

Once Ben was inside, he would pose as a *dilsiz*. According to Umer, there were scores of them, dressed and coiffed to look identical. With the right clothes, Ben could quite easily blend into the background and move around Topkapı undetected.

Umer had alerted Mihrima to Ben's arrival and she had agreed to talk to him – encouraged that there was at least one person digging deeper into her son's death. While the Sultan's favoured concubines were having lunch, Ben would slip into Mihrima's chambers on the top floor of the concubines' wing, extract the information he needed and exit the way he had come. In and out, it should not take more than an hour.

Ben spent the next week studying the layout of the harem on a map provided by Umer. At the same time, he prepared his disguise according to Umer's specifications: a long green kaftan tied with a red sash, over a white shirt; an elaborate silk turban; and tall leather boots called *çizme*. He converted his tent in New

Crimea into an improvised workshop, with just a needle, thread, nimble fingers and a bucket of apple tea to keep him going. He had never been such an industrious tailor in his life. Motive aside, his father would surely have been proud.

The day before everything was to be set in motion, Ben informed Shoshanna of his plan. She would not be joining him: it was simply too risky. If Ben was apprehended, he would be on his own and at the mercy of the authorities. Ismail would report back to Shoshanna at once, but she would be able to deny any involvement in his investigation.

They made their approach from the water. Ben and Ismail stood on the deck of a hired *kayik* as it cut through the day's traffic on the Bosporus, bound for Seraglio Point, where the palace dominated the hilltop amid cypress and oak trees. It was a place steeped in myth and legend: rife with tales of debauchery, intrigue, assassination – the playground of tyrants for four hundred years – a mysterious fortress at the heart of the bustling metropolis.

The sun was at its high point – shortly before noon. They were in good time.

'Do me a favour,' Ben said. 'If they nab me, get my hundred quid from Mademoiselle Carmino and buy everyone a new tent.'

'Beef Wellington,' Ismail chortled, 'we are a civilised nation! If you're caught, I'm sure the judge will respond with a very fair punishment.'

'What do they typically do in the case of trespass in the harem?'

'Typically? A tête-à-tête with the Sultan's "Gardener" – otherwise known as his executioner. Strangulation with a steel wire!'

'No pressure then…'

They moored at a jetty and marched uphill. Umer was waiting for them in the doorway of an apothecary at the foot of the palace walls. As they entered, Umer gave a signal to the chief chemist – a hunchback grinding dried bone marrow with a mortar and pestle into some crude home remedy. The hunchback nodded and waved them down a flight of mudbrick stairs. This was a tried-and-tested manoeuvre.

Umer removed a panel from the wall of the basement to reveal a narrow tunnel, trailing into pitch-black. It was a tight squeeze, barely room to crouch, but it was not long before they reached the Byzantine cistern: a cavernous reservoir of inky water covered with a film of algal slime.

Ismail produced a sterling silver matchbox and struck a match to illuminate the way. 'The palace's old water supply,' he said. 'Built by Emperor Justinian over a thousand years ago.'

They followed the match's reddish halo to the edge of the platform, where a battered gondola was moored. Umer rowed them across the cistern, past stone columns carved with Medusa-heads and faded Arabic monograms.

Umer and Ben hopped off at the other end, by a heavy iron door. Umer swung it open onto a spiral staircase, which wound its way up to ground level.

Ben turned to Ismail. 'Two hours! If I'm not back by then, give the dossier in my knapsack to Mademoiselle Carmino.'

Ismail plopped into the prow of the gondola and gave Ben a salute. 'And if the Sultan *does* have you decapitated, it was an honour knowing you!'

Umer whisked Ben upstairs and out of sight. Ten flights up they reached a hatch in the ceiling, which Umer pushed open onto a portal of blinding-white sunlight. They hauled themselves into a cobbled passage inside Topkapı's walls.

Ben could scarcely believe his eyes. He nudged Umer: 'Hey presto! We're in!'

Umer shoved Ben up against the wall and placed a hand over his mouth. Mansure guards were pacing along the battlements above them, and at that moment their elongated shadows crossed over the two new arrivals. Umer shook his head solemnly: *no chatting*.

He led Ben down the passage, past the Sultan's stables, and into the Divan Meydani. It was a world apart from the metropolis on the other side of the palace walls – a piece of Eden disturbed only by the chirruping of swifts. The lawns were planted with Judas-trees, red heliconia and anthurium, cardinal flowers drooping into sunken ponds. Ben caught his breath as a wide-eyed gazelle loped past, staring at him with tame curiosity.

Umer and Ben crossed the Divan Meydani to its north-west corner, where two halberdiers guarded an arched wooden gate. Umer bowed his head and signed to them with his right hand – Ben copied him fluently. The guards cast a brief eye over the duo: nothing out of the ordinary. They opened the gate and, with their heads down, Umer and Ben stole into the Imperial Harem.

They were in the living quarters of the Imperial Eunuchs. Here, young men spirited from the outer regions of the Empire, from the Balkans to the North African coast, served the needs of the Sultan's concubines. Ben could see the eunuchs prostrated on carpets in prayer-rooms and instructing prepubescent princes, *şehzades* of the royal family, in French and Latin.

Umer pointed Ben towards a set of doors leading to the hammams.

'Psst, Umer! Where're you off to? Don't leave me—'

But the *dilsiz* gave Ben a final knowing smile and breezed off, his gown billowing behind him as he disappeared into one of the private apartments.

From here on, Ben was alone.

He made his way discreetly through the hammams: the steamy caldarium smelling of eucalyptus and neroli, and a cooler tepidarium where pools inlaid with Iznik tiles and nacre jewels shimmered in candlelight.

Beyond the hammams was the Imperial Hall, a magnificent reception chamber where the Sultan's twenty-five consorts were seated in groups of five, before an empty throne beneath a blue pergola. In single file along the wall were *dilsiz* pages, standing to attention with their arms folded behind their backs.

Ben glanced at the clock on the wall: twelve-thirty on the dot. Bang on time.

He joined the pages and a moment later, a door next to the throne opened. The consorts rose to their feet as two people entered: a breathtakingly beautiful woman, with pale skin and flaxen hair, accompanied by a gangly adolescent boy.

The woman sat on the throne, with the boy standing at her side. One of the eunuchs stepped forward and bellowed a phrase in Turkish, chanted back by everyone in the room. Only then did the consorts sit down again. The woman on the throne cast an imperious gaze over the gathering, clicked her fingers, and the pages filed out. Ben slipped into their ranks and exited the Imperial Hall.

So far, everything was going to plan. All he had to do was follow the pages as they passed through the *haremlik* – the concubines' quarters – en route to the kitchens, then break away from the pack to have his private audience with Mihrima.

He lingered at the back of the marching line as they crossed the courtyard of the *haremlik* – the kitchens up ahead, the entrance to the concubines' wing on his left. He darted into the concubines' wing and took cover behind an arras in the antechamber, waiting with bated breath.

No footsteps, no voices, no sounds of alarm.

The *dilsiz* procession moved on, their footsteps receding. Ben counted to ten, then climbed the stairs to the landing on the top floor, where there was a bronze door engraved with a bas-relief – the coat of arms of the Ottoman Empire.

He knocked. Footsteps shuffled on the other side, coming closer.

The door opened. He was standing face to face with a woman in mourner's black. She was younger than Ben had expected and she wore her dark hair loose to her shoulders. She seemed tired and anxious, as though she had just woken up from a troubled dream.

'Mihrima?' he whispered.

She squinted at him. A *dilsiz* with his tongue intact? And such a curious accent? That could only mean one thing.

'You must be the English detective,' she said warily.

She motioned him into her chamber and quickly shut the door. Her chamber was in disarray. Half-drunk glasses of tea cluttered a wooden table. Discarded clothing was strewn across the unmade bed and floor. The curtains were drawn against the day.

'I didn't think you would come,' she said. 'Please, sit.'

They sat side by side on the divan, almost touching, a cardinal sin in the harem. The Sultan's Gardener flashed through Ben's mind.

'They don't exactly make it easy to get in here!' Ben said.

'Getting out can be just as hard. I have barely left this room in five months. Now you are one of very few outsiders in history to see the harem with your own eyes.'

'How does one end up in a place like this?'

'Each consort has a different story. Some were impoverished rural girls captured by the Sultan's generals – the spoils of conquest. Others, like myself, were of higher birth, whose families saw an opportunity to ingratiate themselves with the Sultan by committing us to his harem, selling us off for power and influence.'

Mihrima chuckled grimly.

'But once you are here, your journey is the same. You begin as a novice – an *acemi cariye*, a glorified slave. Over years of servitude, you battle your way up the ladder until you graduate to the rank of consort. Then you bear the Sultan a child – a male child, if you're lucky. As my child was the eldest, I became the chief consort – the *bas kadin* – with my son as heir apparent. Had Ahmed succeeded to the throne, I would have assumed the position that every consort covets most: *valide sultan* – what you English would call the queen mother. At that point, your authority is supreme and inviolable. That is the mirage chased by every consort: the sacred blood of the House of Osman, blood that has coursed through the veins of Constantinople for half a millennium.'

Mihrima faltered – drawn away from herself for a moment, lost in a reverie.

'Once upon a time,' she said, 'that was my destiny. I was the *bas kadin*. My darling boy, Ahmed, was the heir apparent. But the harem, like fate, is fickle. You live and die by the fruit of your loins, and mine was to end in death – as you know.'

Ben nodded sadly. 'It was a terrible calamity, Mihrima. And I'm sorry that my presence has dredged up such awful memories.'

'Memories?' Mihrima said. 'I live it every day. Not just the loss, but the shame that they cast upon me. I have been ostracised from the harem. They claim that I carry a curse. The Sultan, who once doted on me, is too ashamed to show me his face. Now he has a new *bas kadin* – a blonde *arriviste* plucked from a Finnish village who has taken to clicking her fingers at her underlings like the Queen of Sheba.'

Ben thought back to the Imperial Hall: the sight of that woman glaring down at the other consorts. 'I think I saw her a few moments ago at lunch with the other ladies, on a throne. She looked rather… fearsome.'

'Her name is Shevkayir. And that dolt is her son, *Şehzade* Mehmet Nuremeddin. Through him, she has the Sultan wrapped around her little finger and the Empire at her feet.'

She gave a bitter, scolding laugh.

'I spent my whole life fearing the Sultan,' she said, 'vying for his approval. But now I realise that was my biggest mistake. For it is not the Sultan you should fear – it is whoever sits behind him, pulling the strings.'

They sat in an unnerving silence, as a shaft of light passed across Mihrima's face through the curtains.

'I don't think there's a curse on you, Mihrima,' Ben said softly. 'I think you've been wronged. I think Ahmed was murdered and, for whatever reason, nobody is listening to you. And if he was killed, then I want to find out who did it. I know it's painful. But please: I'm going to need you to tell me what happened.'

Mihrima began pacing about the room. She guided Ben step by step through the events surrounding Ahmed's death. It had happened on the 21st of January: the eve of Ahmed's fourteenth birthday. Mother and son were dining in his chamber to celebrate.

They were interrupted by the Imperial Guards: change of plan, they said. Ahmed was to study alone, while Mihrima was to entertain the other consorts at a ceremonial dinner. She had no choice but to go along with it. She lasted barely an hour at this tedious gathering before the desire to see Ahmed became too great. Just before dessert, she made some excuse and stole away to give her boy his birthday blessing.

'But when I returned to his chamber,' she said, 'he was lying on the floor, gasping for air. I felt a gust of wind cross the chamber from an open window. I looked up... and... *I saw her.*'

The words caught Ben off-guard. 'A woman in Ahmed's chamber? Who?'

'I don't know. She was wearing a mask. It was like a hood, and it covered her face completely – except for two glass circles over the eyes. She was standing on Ahmed's balcony, staring back at me silently. Like a *djinn*.'

'How did you know it was a woman?'

'She had an hourglass figure – her waist was too narrow, her bosom too full, for it to be a man. And what's more, Ahmed's chamber had the faint scent of a woman's perfume: Fleurs de Bulgarie, by House of Creed. It is worn only by the most fashionable European ladies of Constantinople. But I have never used it, and nobody entered Ahmed's quarters except for me and the eunuchs.'

'Did you get a good look at her?'

'No. She lingered there for a few seconds. Then she leapt off the balcony and disappeared into the night. I never saw her again.'

'And what about Ahmed? You tended to him, I presume?'

'I had never seen anything like it!' Mihrima cried. 'He was growing whiter and whiter by the second, and there was fluid seeping from his body. I thought at first he might be choking, but he wasn't. It was as though his whole body was shutting down before my very eyes, and there was nothing I could do to stop it. It took less than a minute by my estimation. And just like that… he was gone.'

Ben cast his mind back to the Akbars' – the night of his ambush. It was definitely not a woman who had attacked him, let alone one wearing a floral perfume. And yet in every other respect, Mihrima's description aligned perfectly with what he knew of the White Death: the hood-mask, the victim's white pallor, the speed of his demise.

But what could that mean? Was there more than one White Death?

'I screamed for the guards,' Mihrima continued. 'When they arrived, I told them what I had seen. But nobody believed me. Not the eunuchs, not the gendarmes, not even the Sultan. They said I was being hysterical… But it was deliberate – it was planned – it *had* to have been! Ahmed and I were separated on purpose. They wanted to get him while he was on his own. No witnesses. Nobody to protect my darling boy…'

She broke down in tears. Ben threw caution to the wind. He drew her into a hug and she buried her face in his shoulder, weeping. He soothed her, even as he felt her heart pounding and her hot tears on his cheek.

'Please save his poor soul…' Mihrima begged. 'Please… He suffers, he is not at rest, I can feel it. Give him justice!'

'I promise,' Ben said under his breath. 'I give you my word.'

Mihrima dried her eyes. Despite herself, she smiled and placed a grateful hand on Ben's cheek.

'Now, Englishman, it is time for you to leave. I tremble at the thought of what they would do to you if you were discovered.'

Ben slipped out and retraced his steps through Topkapı to get back to Ismail.

He passed the Imperial Hall, its doors open onto a sumptuous spread of macaroons and *revani* cake. He looked once more at Shevkayir, still perched on her throne sipping yarrow tea and surveying the room like a watchful hawk. For a brief moment, her eyes locked with Ben's through the doorway – before Ben hurried off.

He exited the harem and crossed the Divan Meydani. Once the coast was clear, he slid through the trapdoor behind the stables and descended to the cistern. Ismail was waiting on the gondola, feet up as he whistled a plaintive Crimean folk tune.

'Beef Wellington!' he cried. 'You made swift work of that! I'm impressed. Now let's go. To borrow from Dickens, this place is giving me "the creeps".'

Ben was taciturn, trying to process what he had learnt from Mihrima and reconcile it with what he knew. None of it made sense – and yet he could not dispel the feeling that he was closing in on *something*. Like a hunter stalking the prints left by an unseen predator: every step taking him closer to the prize – and to the danger.

They arrived back at New Crimea before sunset. Ben changed out of his disguise. Shoshanna arrived after dinner, just as she had done on his first night with the Tatars, and he told her in great detail about everything he had seen.

She was just as confused as him. Shevkayir had the most obvious motive to kill Ahmed: eliminate the competition and usurp Mihrima's place as *bas kadin*, with her own son Mehmet in pole position to become the next Sultan. If Abraham and Sir Lawrence had cottoned onto what Shevkayir had done, she would have had ample reason to silence them too.

But they had no evidence whatsoever to implicate the new *bas kadin*. And what any of this had to do with Marta Mavros or Heathcote, or how an uneducated woman of the harem could carry out such a sophisticated killing, or why there was both a male and female White Death – this all remained a mystery.

The morning after his escapade at Topkapı, Ben returned to Constantinople – to the Grande Rue of Pera, where he found a luxury perfumery that he had noticed on his first trip through the area.

He was wearing the exquisite suit that Shoshanna had lent him. The shop assistant fawned over him, assuming him to be a wealthy young gent on a spending spree for a mistress or fiancée.

'How may I help you, sir?' the shop assistant said with a bow.

'I'm looking for a perfume,' Ben replied. 'Fleurs de Bulgarie. House of Creed.'

The shop assistant gestured to a display-case. Sure enough, taking pride of place on the top shelf, was a perfume decanter filled to the brim with a pale golden liquid, engraved with the HOUSE OF CREED insignia.

'May I smell it?' Ben asked.

'Certainly, sir.'

The shop assistant sprayed a small amount on a smelling strip and held it under Ben's nose. He took a deep breath.

Bergamot. Patchouli. He knew it at once. *It was Elizabeth's scent.* The same as when she had first kissed his cheek outside the Great Exhibition. That lingered on his clothes long after every farewell. That he had not encountered once since that summer of 1851.

He breathed it in again, not wanting to believe it was her. But like that face in the daguerreotype, and the tattoo on her finger, it was unmistakeable.

'Do many women buy this perfume?' Ben asked.

'No, sir. It is one of our more… exclusive fragrances. It was created, in fact, for Queen Victoria. There have been only a handful of women with the means to afford it.'

'And, at the risk of touching on a delicate subject… Was one of those women the late Princess Mavros?'

The shop assistant was taken aback by the question. But after a measured pause, he nodded. 'I believe that she was, sir. Prices start at five thousand lira. May we interest you in a *demi-bouteille*?'

'Perhaps another time, thank you,' Ben murmured – and got out as quickly as he could.

He leant against the shop window, face turned to the sky, running his hands through his hair with a shaky sigh. The woman on the balcony – the woman in the white mask – could it really have been her?

'Mr Canaan?'

Ben nearly leapt out of his skin. Standing before him, in a crisp navy-blue suit, was none other than Prince Alexander Mavros. He was wearing his signature calfskin riding gloves, and his arms were crossed over his chest.

'What on earth are you still doing in Constantinople?' Mavros exclaimed.

'I, uh... I had some business to attend to...' Ben stammered.

Mavros glanced at the shopfront, then at Ben's suit. 'Business?'

Ben nodded stiffly. 'Yes. Business.'

'Please, Mr Canaan,' Mavros smiled at him playfully. 'Be honest with me... You're chasing some new paramour, aren't you?'

Ben gave Mavros a baffled shrug. 'I... I really don't...'

'You *are!*' Mavros grinned. 'You've met some lovely lady and now you're spending beyond your means, trying to impress her! You sweet summer child.' He laid a gloved hand on Ben's shoulder. His voice was warm, but his grip was firm. 'I must warn you, Mr Canaan: keeping up pretences can be perilous. It tends not to last very long.'

Ben cleared his throat and nodded. 'Duly noted, Prince Mavros.'

'Good show. I must be off now. I have my own "business" to attend to. Safe travels, Mr Canaan – when, or *if*, you do eventually leave Constantinople...'

Ben watched him swagger off, tightening his calfskin gloves. Not a trace of mourning about him.

Ben's nose was tingling. And it was not from the perfume.

Shoshanna was sitting in a secluded spot in the garden of the Carmino estate: a clearing surrounded by drooping willows. Before her were three headstones. The one in the middle bore the name of her father – and below his name, a couplet from his favourite Shakespeare sonnet:

> *His beauty shall in these black lines be seen,*
> *And they shall live, and he in them, still green.*

On either side of Abraham's grave were two smaller plots – one gravestone inscribed with the name EZRA CARMINO, the other with BRACHA CARMINO. Both had one thing in common: the birth and death dates spanned mere months.

There she sat, as she did almost every night, hands clasped on her lap. Usually, she would chat away – telling her father the latest news, her every thought, her hopes for the future, as if sharing them would magically make them come true. But tonight, she hardly blinked, waiting for the tomb to do the talking.

'Psst!'

She turned. Ismail was creeping through the willow-branches. In his hand was a slip of paper.

'Ismail! What is it?'

'Note for you, boss. From your new hire.'

Shoshanna unfolded the note. She was expecting a long paragraph from a boy as mouthy as Ben Canaan. But it was a single line, and it said everything she needed to know:

all roads lead to Mavros
– B

16

Portrait of a Chameleon

They started with Gavriel.

Of all the Carminos, the older of the Rafaeli Twins was the most sympathetic to Shoshanna's misgivings about her father's death. Though he had only hinted at it on occasion, he too thought that there was something dubious about the whole affair. Leonora, meanwhile, was reticent and had made her position quite clear: her beloved daughter was to stay well out of harm's way. Shmuel, for his part, was a timid man and too prudent to cross any line drawn in the sand by his rather overbearing sister.

But Shoshanna needed answers. And if anyone was going to give them to her, it would have to be Uncle Gavriel.

A few days after Ben's note arrived, Shoshanna seized her chance. Leonora was occupied in a meeting with an English barrister – a QC from Gray's Inn who had advised Abraham on setting up various trusts under English law. While he and Leonora were ensconced in the study, Shoshanna slipped out and headed a short distance up the Bosporus to Gavriel's villa.

He was overjoyed to see her, though surprised when she told him why she had come. 'I want you to tell me everything you know about Prince Alexander Mavros, and what exactly happened between our family and his all those years ago.'

'Your mother believes that sleeping dogs should be left to lie. And these are dogs with very sharp teeth!'

'If we talk quietly,' she said, 'we won't wake them up!'

Gavriel reluctantly agreed, on the condition that whatever they discussed was to remain in the strictest confidence. They sat on the terrace sipping lemonade in the afternoon sun, as he laid bare the facts.

The Mavros and Carmino families had a storied, fractious history – one which Gavriel only encountered as a young man, when Leonora and Abraham began their courtship. 'It always seemed to me to be a struggle between two epochs,' Gavriel said, 'Two tribes. Two men with the world at their fingertips.'

On one side, the House of Mavros: the old guard, a bastion of Greek princes and governors at the heart of the political elite, that reached its peak at the turn of the nineteenth century under the leadership of its patriarch Konstantinos.

'But when Konstantinos died in 1812,' Gavriel said, 'everything changed. His son Ioannis Mavros took over: father of the current Prince Alexander – chosen by default since he was the eldest son. That simple decision, one that the House of Mavros took unthinkingly, out of fidelity to tradition, would ultimately be their undoing.'

Power in Constantinople, Gavriel told her, dangled by a mere thread. The slightest disturbance could sever the cord and send everything tumbling to oblivion. To survive required skill and diplomacy.

'But Ioannis was no diplomat. He was a passionate and pugnacious romantic. Above all, an inveterate Greek nationalist. Ready to burn everything to the ground for his principles. Your father once described him as a man with a fork in a world of soup.'

The House of Carmino could not have been more different. Its history began with Abraham himself. The son of a merchant who dealt in farm tools and silver goods, who used his modest bourgeois circumstances as a gateway into the world of finance – driven by an unflinching determination to make something of himself, to attain the glory that was usually reserved for those lucky enough to be born into it.

'Abraham was of a new order,' Gavriel mused. 'No longer did you need royal blood to be powerful. Just boats, bonds and bullion. And so, by the time he was forty years old, Abraham Carmino – a lowly Jew that once would have been spat at in the street – could stand shoulder-to-shoulder with Ioannis Mavros, a man who had four hundred years on him.'

'Ioannis must have hated it,' Shoshanna smirked.

'They never fought openly. They were just... *different*. Your father was proud because he rose from the earth. Ioannis was proud because he believed that he was destined to rule over it.'

Gavriel took a pinch of snuff from a brass box.

'For a little while, the world belonged to people like us as much as it did to men like Ioannis. After two thousand years of exile, we had finally found a home.'

Initially, the families kept a fragile truce: the aristocratic grandees of the feudal age and the parvenu capitalists, edging around one another at state balls and meetings of the Imperial Divan.

Then, in 1821, the scales tipped – and everything changed.

Revolution broke out in Ioannis' native Greece. Once a vassal of the Ottoman Empire, now fighting to become an independent state. Suddenly, the House of Mavros found itself in an invidious position. Konstantinos had secured his standing in Constantinople by distancing himself from his Greek roots. But Ioannis' nationalism meant that he could not turn his back on his countrymen, even if it risked destroying the legacy that his predecessors had built.

'I heard,' Gavriel said, 'that behind closed doors Ioannis founded a secret society: the Filiki Eteria. A hidden network of Greek nationalists embedded in Constantinople, planning an insurrection that would topple the Ottoman government. And it would have worked too. They were days from mounting a rebellion. Until your father got in their way…'

As soon as Abraham caught wind of the plot, he alerted the authorities and the crisis was averted. 'In one fell swoop,' Gavriel said, 'he wiped out the entire House of Mavros. Ioannis was executed for high treason, his family exiled: wife, siblings, nephews and nieces, even his allies. And of course, his only child: *Alexander Mavros.*'

At the time, Alexander was a newborn – his life was over before he knew it. He was ferried out of the country with what remained of his family to the lonely Greek island of Antimilos, where they kept an estate. For three decades, he was not seen in Constantinople.

And then, the previous year, when the name Mavros had faded from people's lips, Alexander made his grand return. No longer was he a defenceless child. He was a man now – the spitting image of his doomed father. Carrying the knowledge of everything that had happened, of everything that had been taken away from him.

'How does it feel now, seeing Prince Mavros in Constantinople again?'

Gavriel pondered the question for some time.

'I was reminded of the night Ioannis was executed. It was the twelfth of November 1821. Six months after your parents were married. The execution was set for midnight. We were having dinner at the townhouse in Galata. After the meal, I retired with your father and Uncle Shmuel to the study. Abraham was staring out the window as the clock ticked down, pacing to and fro. You know how he'd get when the cogs were turning! Then the hour struck. Somewhere out there, in the gardens of Topkapı, a man's head was severed in the rain. At that precise moment, a letter arrived. Your father opened it to find a note in Ioannis' hand. It was as though he had sent it from beyond the grave.'

'What did it say?'

'*I set upon you the Furies.*'

Gavriel's expression dulled. The birdsong fell away.

'We never spoke about it again.'

Shoshanna returned to the Carmino estate to find Leonora still entertaining the English barrister. He was slouched like a lethargic tabby on the couch – a slightly dissolute thirty-something, with the first hint of a paunch forming around his midriff: his fondness for cigars and sherry already starting to show.

He rose with louche ease to kiss Shoshanna's hand and said with a honeyed drawl: 'Percy Trilling. As of this summer, *QC*.'

Percy regaled them with tales of his recent travels around Europe and North Africa, to celebrate having taken silk. Towards the end of the conversation, as Shoshanna was starting to tire of his superficial niceties, Percy paced to the study window to look out at the Bosporus beyond the estate's gardens.

'I say!' he exclaimed. 'To live on the shores of this magnificent Strait...' He craned his neck to peer south down the Bosporus. 'Prince Alexander Mavros also enjoys a similar view, so I've heard?'

'Why, yes,' Leonora said. 'He lives closer to Constantinople. He has one of the largest waterfront estates in the city.'

Percy kept his thoughts to himself. The pleasure had drained from his eyes and his tone was stiff. 'The man likes his luxury.'

Shoshanna was looking at him with intense curiosity. 'Do you know him?'

'Somewhat. It doesn't bear repeating at a time like this. Anyhow. I must be off. If you need anything further, Madame Carmino, you may find me at the Hôtel Pierrot in Pera. I depart for Rome next Monday but will be available at your convenience any time before then.' He bowed to Shoshanna. 'And yours too, Mademoiselle...'

Shoshanna gave a practised curtsey: 'Mr Trilling, that is music to my ears!'

By Sunday afternoon, a meeting between Percy and Ben had been covertly arranged, at the rooftop café-restaurant of the Pierrot. The two men sat face to face amid the minor diplomats and dissident aristocrats that made up the Pierrot's clientele, as a string quartet played Haydn some way off.

Percy was eyeing Ben up as he sipped his coffee: the faded bruises on the boy's face – his rumpled suit – the way his pencil hovered millimetres from his notebook.

'*You* are Mademoiselle Carmino's associate?' Percy said, baffled. 'A little far from old John Bull, aren't you?'

'That makes two of us, Mr Trilling!'

A waiter came over and placed a silver tray between them: lemon and strawberry *lokum* dusted with powdered sugar.

'Why do you have it in for Mavros?' Percy said, plucking a *lokum* from the tray.

'I'm putting together a theory,' Ben replied. 'Might not look too good for him. But I need to know everything I can about the man.'

The waiter was lingering a little too long at Ben's side. Percy gave him a withering look. '*Garçon. Vas-y, vite!*'

The waiter hurried off in a trice.

'From what Mademoiselle Shoshanna told me,' Ben continued, 'you know something "unrepeatable" about the man. Care to repeat it?'

'Mavros, my dear boy, is a scoundrel. A rogue. I'm a man of the pen, not the sword – but I swear, for him I would make an exception. I'd kill him, I tell you!'

'And why's that?'

Fourteen years previously, Percy had been with his sister on the Grand Tour: a rite of passage for wealthy young things, to travel through Europe and experience the music, art and culture of the Continent.

In July 1840, they arrived in Venice to study the works of the Renaissance at the Museo Correr. One morning, they received a knock at the door of their apartment: 'Prince Alexander Mavros himself,' Percy said, 'with a bottle of champagne and a hamper of Parisian chocolates. "The duty of any next-door neighbour!" he said in fine English. I initially thought he must be a Kensington man.'

The Trillings befriended Mavros and he quickly became a feature of their Venetian summer. Everywhere he went, Mavros possessed an air of magic and grace. At just nineteen, he was already the perfectly formed gentleman.

Yet there was also something vulnerable about him: the poor exiled prince wrested from his homeland, buffeted by the travails of a tragic life. Percy even came to pity him.

'He cultivated an air of *universality*,' Percy said. 'I saw him delight a regiment of Highlanders with tales of his exploits in Edinburgh. On another occasion, he debated the merits of Friesian horses in battle with a delegation of Russian cavalry officers. And once, he charmed a Spanish princess at a lavish party in his apartments. He was not of one place: he was a man of the world. He was anything to anyone.'

Ben huffed as he scribbled in his notebook. 'Like a good old cardsharp.'

'I eventually became weary of his games. The more I got to know him, the less I felt I knew him, if you follow.'

'And what happened exactly that was so… unpleasant?'

Percy refilled his coffee. He took a deep breath.

'*He raped my sister*, Mr Canaan. I was out gambling at the Casino di Venezia. He stayed behind because of a "fever". My sister took care of him – brought him hot toddies. They kissed: that much was mutual. Then he took it too far, despite her begging him to stop…' Percy dropped a lump of sugar in his coffee and stirred slowly. 'I found her the next morning in her bedroom, dishevelled and in tears. When I confronted him, he laughed in my face and called her a whore. He left the following week. Athens, so I was told.'

Percy put his hands behind his head, taking in the clear blue sky. 'For him… I would make an exception.'

*

Mois Navarro settled into his garden chair, Ben and Shoshanna seated opposite him. The former Chief Dragoman of the Imperial Porte may have been retired, but he had not lost an ounce of his shrewdness. As personal interpreter to the Sultan for two decades, he was used to listening closely, observing, noting every mannerism and unconscious tell.

Shoshanna smiled. She had known that kindly, unassuming face all her life. 'You're reading him, aren't you?' she said, gesturing to Ben.

'Leopards cannot change their spots, Mademoiselle...' Mois' eyes twinkled and he tickled Vidal the Abyssinian kitten, who had curled up in his lap and was pawing at his long grey beard.

'Well, now I'm really curious,' Ben said. 'What do you see?'

'Intelligence. Mischief. And a healthy dose of impatience...'

'You sound like my old man!'

Mois took a peppermint biscuit and cast crumbs to the carp mouthing at the surface of the pond a few feet away. Then he shooed Vidal off his lap – not even feline ears could be privy to their chat.

It was a year previous. After weeks of rumours, Alexander Mavros finally returned to Constantinople: an event set to end the House of Mavros' thirty-year exile. 'I've seen plenty of state visits in my time,' Mois said. 'Prussians, the British, the Chinese... But Alexander Mavros blew them all out the water. There must have been a hundred people in his retinue.'

'Why so large?' Shoshanna asked.

'A show of authority. Not as a threat – simply to send a message. "I am more powerful than you think." It had the intended effect. The awe in people's eyes as he passed... He was like Odysseus, having strung the bow, returned to Ithaca.'

The Sultan and Mavros met for the first time in the Imperial Throne Room of Topkapı Palace. On this occasion, the Sultan insisted that they speak in Turkish, with Mois acting as interpreter.

'I was struck by the affinity between these two men,' Mois said. 'They were separated by only a couple of years. Both in the prime of their lives. Both born into immense wealth, power and connections. Both with a penchant for Circassian women... Despite their history, they hit it off. It must have helped that Mavros is an inveterate charmer.'

The Prince put forward a compelling and surprisingly candid proposition. The conflict between the Sultanate and the House of Mavros belonged to another era. It concerned Alexander's father and the Sultan's father, but not Alexander and the present Sultan. Ioannis may have lost his head, but Greece had her independence. Now it was time to let bygones be bygones – to let all that came before flow like water under the bridge.

'The Sultan agreed on one condition: that Mavros pledge his allegiance to the Ottoman Empire. A vow on his life, and the lives of his future children and grandchildren, that he would support Ottoman interests and Ottoman sovereignty, come what may. Politically, financially, in public and in private.'

'And what did Mavros do?' Ben asked.

'The Prince put his hand on his heart and said, "May God strike me down if I ever betray your faith." That was all the Sultan required. In fact, as the months went by, he seemed to want to make a point of bringing Mavros back into the fold – as if to demonstrate to his Western neighbours that the Sultanate was a creature of modern times, an institution that had long since let go of the ancient code of blood. There was an air of elation around the Sublime Porte. Others, however, were more sceptical.'

Mois hesitated, as though he had caught himself saying something ill-advised. He looked coyly at Shoshanna. Without either saying a word, she knew exactly what he was referring to.

'Abraham was suspicious of Mavros from the start,' he continued. 'The world forgets, but the wise do not – and Abraham remembered well what had happened with Ioannis. He believed that the Mavros dynasty brought with it a dark cloud. In fact... he was asking me the same questions that you are asking now.'

His wizened face said it all: *tread lightly*.

The last person Ben spoke to was Clio Tavoularis: a Greek woman who, for several years until Marta's death, had been Mavros' housekeeper – first in Athens, then in Constantinople. Now she was working as a cleaner at the Church of the Holy Trinity in Pera. 'The pay is abysmal,' she was fond of saying, 'but I can give confession whenever I want!'

It was Marat Zagid, Ismail's bow-legged lieutenant, who made the introduction. He had befriended Clio not too long ago – every time he stopped by the church, she would spare him pita bread with a dollop of dandelion honey. When he found out that she had intimate knowledge of Mavros' private life – and was sure that Clio was willing to talk – they arranged a meeting at the Tatar camp.

It was another stormy night when Clio arrived. She came bustling through the rain, wrapped in a thick cloak, leather boots splattered with mud. They warmed her up by a stove in Ben's tent and gave her tea and buckwheat biscuits. She looked afraid, as though even in this dismal outpost, Mavros could hear her.

'We have to be careful,' she said as she nervously gulped down her tea. 'This is extremely sensitive information. The Prince cannot know that I came here.'

'Don't worry,' Ben replied. 'Our lips are sealed. So, if you can keep a secret…'

They began with Marta. The nature of Mavros' relationship with his wife was one of the last gaps in the picture that they were piecing together. Clio's position had not just given her a window onto that part of his life – it had also allowed her to become Marta's confidante.

'Mavros told me they met in Greece,' Ben said.

Clio gave a cynical laugh. 'That's what he told everyone. He was a bachelor in Greece. I should know. I had to clean up after his mess.'

'So where *did* they meet?'

Mavros, so Clio claimed, regularly travelled out to the Caucasus. Some place he referred to only as Z., way up in the Georgian mountains. On one occasion he was away for four months, with no word of his activity. Then, at the end of the summer, he returned to Athens with a wife in tow and his heart set on Constantinople. In one deft move, the entire course of his life had changed.

'God knows why,' Clio said. 'His motto was, as it had always been: *ask me no questions and I'll tell you no lies*. He never explained it. All very hush-hush.'

And as for the woman that he had brought back from the Caucasus? 'She was a blank slate,' Clio shrugged. 'Until she officially became Princess Mavros, she was just Marta. No friends, no relatives – I never even found out her maiden name.'

As soon as Prince Mavros and his new wife settled in Constantinople, they became the talk of the town. Every weekend there were parties held on their estate: ostentatious displays of power as the scions of the House of Mavros paraded about, as if they had retaken their old kingdom. The Prince was back in the inner circles of power, and his wife – envied and desired in equal measure – was celebrated and sought after by sycophants desperate for her husband's favour.

'It was a glittering life,' Clio said coldly, 'but all that glitters is not gold. I saw what their marriage really was: *loveless*. They kept up appearances in public, but I can't say they ever showed an ounce of affection for one another in private. Arguments filled the house. Big ones. Screamers. Other than that, they studiously avoided each other. The Prince was probably having affairs. Maybe she was as well.'

Over time, Marta's behaviour became increasingly erratic. She would sneak out at night, disappearing two or three times a week without explanation. As the months went by, her once-faultless tact gave way to indiscretion: berating her husband in front of the staff, throwing fits at public engagements, descending into paranoid and incoherent rambling. The charmed act fell apart. Marta had become a liability.

The final straw came two months before her death. Mavros had been hosting a delegation of French ministers – emissaries of Napoleon III – when Marta burst into the dining hall in nothing but a nightgown, her hair down, ranting and raving about a *dead boy*. The servants strong-armed her upstairs before she could cause any further embarrassment.

'The following day,' Clio said, wringing her hands, 'the Prince issued a command to the help. If anyone asked about *the boy*, we were to say that Marta had suffered complications in early pregnancy. A miscarriage.'

'Was that true?' Ben asked.

'Of course not. Even if they had been trying – which they most certainly were not – Marta had no ovaries. She told me so that night, drowsy from her sedatives. And when I asked her why, all she said was: *they took them.*'

The tent fell silent – just the rain lashing outside. Ben said nothing as he copied those words in his notebook. He could remember, back in the summer of 1851, seeing the faintest scars on Elizabeth's belly. He had barely noticed them – a mere passing detail – and had never bothered to ask.

Clio continued: 'Marta's mind was slipping. We hid the kitchen knives – her windows were sealed with iron grilles. The house became a prison of sorts. Soon people gave her a nickname: "The Ghost of Pera". It was only a matter of time before something dreadful happened.'

Things came to a head in July. Clio was closing up the house late one night when she overheard an argument between Mavros and Marta in her bedroom. The only thing she could make out clearly was a line from Marta: 'I'm slipping the noose…' And that seemed to push Mavros over the edge.

'I had never heard such rage from him,' Clio said. 'I was too scared to keep listening, so I ran back to my quarters. I must have lain awake the whole night.'

The next morning, Marta was missing. Mavros was distraught. He mobilised the whole estate to comb the city for her. A day went by and nothing came up. Then two days, then a week, then a month – still nothing. With each passing minute, they seemed to draw closer and closer to the inevitable.

Then came that fateful day: the 3rd of August – a blistering-hot morning. Three fishermen rowed up to the shore of the Bosporus, calling for help. The body of Marta Mavros, the Ghost of Pera, was tangled up in their nets. She was laid out on the embankment, strangers gathering round to gawp at the horrifying scene – until a tear-stricken Prince Mavros arrived in his carriage to confirm it with his own eyes.

'I suppose,' Clio said sadly, gazing into the glowing coals of Ben's stove, 'in her own way, she did slip the noose, didn't she?'

And yet, for all his outpouring of grief, Mavros swiftly moved on. Marta's portraits were taken down, the few friends she had received no further invitations, and two weeks later Clio was fired. 'He was keen to see the back of me. I had known Marta too well. He must have felt my loyalties weren't pure. She was purged from his life, and I can't say he lost any sleep over it.'

Once Clio had said her piece, she seemed in a rush to leave. Ben took her to the edge of the camp where a covered wagon was waiting. Clio threw a hood over her head: 'I don't know what you're aiming for with all this, but if I were you I would keep a low profile. When it comes to men like the Prince, you only realise how far out you've swum when it's too late to get back to shore.'

She mounted the back of the wagon, but Ben gave a signal to the driver to wait. 'One more thing: does the name Elizabeth de Varney mean anything to you?'

Clio looked surprised. 'Yes, it does! It was the alias that Marta used whenever she wanted to get around Constantinople without being recognised. She had a whole cock-and-bull story about Paris – a physician for a father – musical salons and absinthe in the Place des Vosges, can you believe! She played it off perfectly, like a good little actress.'

The driver whipped the reins.

'That's the thing about Marta that nobody really understood,' Clio called out to Ben as the wagon set off into the night. *'She was a chameleon!'*

17

Needle in a Haystack

By the following morning, the storm had passed. A chorus of birdsong echoed across the washed-out plains, as kingfishers and plovers took flight from the basalt cliffs to float over the Bosporus. The Tatar night-watchmen traipsed through the waterlogged camp back to their tents to catch up on sleep. Others were only just rising, shovelling down porridge and *ayran* – a light, foamy yogurt garnished with freshly picked mint – and throwing on sheepskin coats.

Ben was nowhere to be seen. He had headed off on his own before dawn and had followed the aqueduct south, hugging the shore of the Bosporus. Leaves were falling from the trees. The wheat had been reaped and the lavender had a pallid, silvery tint – the first indication that summer was over.

He paused at the edge of the cliff, his thoughts turning around Clio's testimony. Elizabeth de Varney – the woman whom he had believed to be his first love – was a fiction. She had played him. But why? Was it all a joke? A con, like his frolic at Claridge's with the Good-for-Nothings?

He listened to the breeze, to the tolling of a church-bell further inland. He tried to remember her voice, even something banal that she had once said, which might reveal a clue. But nothing stood out to him. She was like a good magic trick: distraction, sleight-of-hand, something inexplicable.

'Who the hell are you?' he muttered, kicking the dirt. 'And what did you want from me?'

Later that week, he met with Shoshanna in his tent at the Tatar camp to discuss their findings. All signs pointed to Marta being the culprit for Ahmed's killing – Mihrima's account, the Fleurs de Bulgarie, Marta's wild talk about a 'dead boy'.

'But that would make Marta the White Death,' Shoshanna said. 'So how did she end up as one of its victims?'

'And more to the point,' Ben replied, 'if she was the White Death, and she died in August, who killed Heathcote in September? And who attacked me at the Akbars'?'

Their suspicions fell firmly on Prince Alexander Mavros. But they had no evidence. Just Clio's oblique hearsay of marital strife, Gavriel's account of a dynastic rivalry from a bygone generation, Trilling's allegation of rape, and whispers of a vendetta against Abraham and the Sultan. Mavros' pleasure at having been freed from his marriage to Marta did not mean that he had killed her. And were they really to believe that a Greek prince and his glamorous wife were running around murdering people under cover of night?

Even if they could point to Mavros with any degree of certainty, they had no way of knowing why these killings were taking place. And with Clio's departure, they had exhausted their leads. They were at a dead end.

Shoshanna watched Ben add wood to the stove. He seemed preoccupied.

'Lira for your thoughts?'

'Not for sale. You hired me to do a job. Let's stick to the brief.'

'You know it's Sukkot tonight?' Shoshanna said. 'I take it you don't have plans.'

Ben had forgotten about the Feast of Tabernacles, a commemoration of the harvest. 'Funnily enough, it's my favourite festival.'

'Unless you plan on hotfooting it to London, why don't you come to us? We're following Carmino tradition: building a *sukkah* and hosting a dinner. It wouldn't be right to let you sit out here in a leaky tent.'

'I'm a wanted man, remember? Won't your family – at the very least, *your mother* – be suspicious?'

'I'll tell her that you stayed in Constantinople and that you would otherwise be on your own. I'm sure she'll make allowances. And if you can keep our arrangement to yourself, no one will be any the wiser!'

By the time Ben arrived that evening, the grandees of Constantinople's Jewish community had descended on the Carmino estate. There were venerable physicians to the Empire's ruling elite and prosperous businessmen of every description, from bankers to merchants to inventors with a collection of patents to their name.

These were not the Jews of the East End. They wore rings, not rags. They smoked cigarettes with gold filters, not cheap roll-ups. They stood proud and upright, not stooped over from a life of menial labour.

Ben stayed on the margins, a tumbler of whisky in his hand, and watched them schmoozing in pricey dinner suits and ermine coats. He felt ill at ease in his borrowed cashmere suit.

He was what Tuvia would call a *rachmones* guest: one invited out of pity and obligation, rather than a genuine desire to include. Leonora and the Rafaeli Twins gave him short shrift, keeping conversation to a minimum and their distance to a maximum.

He was anxious too. He could not rule out that someone might link his face to the wanted posters that Yusuf Madhat Pasha had posted around the city.

As the reception wore on, he found himself trapped in a stultifying exchange with one Amedeo Cipriani – a merchant whose monopoly over the tulip trade was matched only by his capacity to talk about it.

'Not a tulip passes through this city that does not have my fingerprints on it!' Amedeo boasted. 'The common man simply does not realise: tulips are so much more than flowers. They represent civilisation. Just as you have the Colosseum in Rome, and the Acropolis in Greece, so you have the Turkestan tulip, the Triumph tulip, the Fosteriana tulip…'

Midway through his monologue, Shoshanna appeared. She was wearing a radiant silk sapphire dress, with trimmed bretelles running from her waist to her shoulders, wide pagoda sleeves sweeping down from ruched epaulettes, and her hair had been done up in elaborate braids. Ben watched her mingle, greeting her guests with effortless poise.

When she reached Ben, she curtseyed: '*Buena tadrada*, Mr Canaan.'

'Same to you, Mademoiselle Carmino. I brought—'

Before he could finish, Amedeo threw himself between them: 'For you, Mademoiselle Carmino…'

Amedeo presented an ebony box. Shoshanna lifted the lid. Inside, three tulip bulbs were resting on a velvet bed.

'The *Semper Augustus*,' Amedeo intoned. 'The holy grail of tulips.'

She feigned amazement. 'Oh… Señor Cipriani! You shouldn't have!'

'But you must plant these beauties quickly, else they will not bloom to their full potential… as *you* have, my dear!'

As he kissed her hand, a bell summoned the guests to the *sukkah*, which had been built on the garden terrace. It had latticed wood walls lined with white sheets, decorated with framed paintings of the Holy Land and scenes from the Old Testament: Joseph and his brothers, the parting of the Red Sea, Moses bearing the Ten Commandments. Pomegranates, figs and dates hung from a roof of palm leaves and bamboo sticks.

Dinner was served: cod in sweet plum sauce, sesame-coated Jerusalem flatbreads, roasted zucchini, asparagus and artichokes drizzled with tahini on platters of red quinoa. Ben was seated with distant cousins of the Carminos and acquaintances from out of town who, like him, had nowhere else to go. Shoshanna occupied the head of the table with her mother, next to a fashionably dressed young man to whom she spent most of the evening chatting. Whenever he said something, Leonora laughed and laid an affectionate hand on his arm.

Shoshanna looked different tonight. She was lighter, freer. None of the sobriety and aloofness that Ben had come to expect of her. It felt as though, even if just for one dinner, he was being given a glimpse of what she was once like. Before the loss of her father, before grief, before the burden of her self-imposed mission.

After dessert – saffron and orange madeleines, and banana cake with rum caramel – the party dispersed. There was chess in the parlour, piano in the salon, coffee and grappa on the terrace, children playing tag on the lawn for candies and marbles.

Ben wandered down to a bench on the banks of the Bosporus. The lights of Constantinople glowed like solitary pearls on the water. The moon hung low in the sky, as though ready to drop into the Strait. A flock of geese cruised overhead. There was something elegiac in the air – a beautiful night tinged with sadness.

He heard footsteps behind him, crunching the fallen leaves. Then a voice:

'Was it that boring?'

It was Shoshanna. She hiked her dress above her ankles and joined him at the water's edge. Ben removed a packet from his jacket pocket.

'Amaretti from Yanni Tokatlia. I've been trying to give this to you all evening.'

Shoshanna's eyes lit up. 'My father's favourite! He said it reminded him of the days when Yanni's biscuits were all he could afford. But I think that was just his sweet tooth talking.'

They heard whooping and laughter from the terrace. Shoshanna sighed.

'This is what it used to be like. Family, friends, laughter, music. Good food, good wine.'

'And a beau. Seems I missed that one with my brilliant detective's eye…'

Shoshanna glanced at Ben with a chortle. 'You're not jealous, are you?'

'You just never mentioned him, that's all. It might have been relevant to our inquiry.'

'If you must know, we were introduced long before you arrived. We corresponded. Then we went for walks together – chaperoned, of course. Now we attend social functions together. And at some point, he'll propose. It's a safe, well-travelled path. Does that satisfy your curiosity?'

'I'm very happy for you – and what's-his-name.'

'Jacob. He's very decent.'

Ben studied Shoshanna's profile framed against the Bosporus. A wisp of hair fluttered on the nape of her neck.

'It started before this... *mess*,' Shoshanna said. 'Times were simpler and my priorities were set in a certain way. Now it feels like everything has changed.'

'The world is always turning,' Ben said. 'We have to turn with it.'

'But we can't let go of the memories that connect us to the past. To the things on the other side – the people we left behind.'

They gazed across the Bosporus at those flickering firelights – lonely beacons studding the sweeping black.

'Since we're trading personal information,' Shoshanna said, 'what was she like?'

'Who?'

'Oh, come on: Elizabeth, Marta. You know – *what's-her-name*.'

For a moment, Ben did not know what to say. 'I have no idea. But it felt like she saw me. Not what she expected me to be, not what she wanted to hammer me into. She just *saw* me. And I felt loved.'

'Lucky you,' Shoshanna said. 'Love is a very hard thing to find. It's like trying to spot the face of someone you've never met in an endlessly changing crowd. A needle in a haystack. And you found it.'

Ben shook his head. 'I thought I did. And then I lost it.'

'But you *must* have truly loved her, Ben – to have come all this way for her.'

Thoughts of Ben's family stirred in his mind like a thorn under the skin. They would be having dinner that night, crammed with the other congregants into the small tent in the courtyard of Bevis Marks, in rainy London. The chair next to Solly would be occupied by someone else – the insult of Ben's absence smarting despite the chatter, singing, eating and drinking.

'I didn't do it for her,' he whispered. 'The more I think about it, the more I realise: I did it for myself. Because I was afraid. Afraid of what my life was turning into. So I ran like a coward.'

He broke off and rubbed his eyes. Shoshanna placed her hand on his back – a gesture of encouragement. 'Have an amaretto. It'll cheer you up.'

Voices came drifting across the garden from the main house: '¿Onde esta Shoshanna? ¡Mademoiselle Carmino!'

'The guests are leaving,' she said. 'I should probably join them. Are you coming?'

'I'll be a minute.'

Shoshanna headed off and Ben waited on the banks for a short while longer, listening to the drunken laughter and protracted farewells. Then he rose from the bench and ambled back to the house. As he wandered through the gardens, something caught his eye: the light of a single lantern, glowing through a wreath of willow-branches.

He followed it into a small clearing, hidden behind the foliage. Arranged in a semi-circle were three tombstones, lined with pebbles in honour of the dead.

Bent over a flowerbed was a gardener. A lantern was hanging from a branch above his head to illuminate his hands as he worked.

'You must be Mr Canaan,' he said without looking up. 'I am Zoltan. Head gardener of Carmino estate.'

'Bit late for gardening, isn't it?' Ben said.

'Mr Cipriani's tulip bulbs, sir!' Zoltan replied, patting the soil. 'They need... how you say... *attention*. They only sleep right if I tuck them in nice.'

Ben looked at the graves in the middle of the clearing. 'What is this place?'

'Graves, sir. Don Abraham.' Zoltan pointed to the largest tombstone in the middle.

'And the other two?'

'Is very sad story, sir. Don Abraham and Madame Leonora, they try to have children for many years. A great struggle. Three die in the womb. And two born, but they die young. They have names, you see...' He grabbed the lantern and held it over the graves, tracing the names carved on the stone. 'The boy Ezra, the girl Bracha. Then Shoshanna come. It take ten years, but... God, He make it happen!'

Ben's eyes were drawn elsewhere. Not to the graves, but to Zoltan's hands. The skin on his fingers was red and blistered, as though doused with scalding water or shaved with sandpaper. His nails were cracked, and some had fallen out altogether.

He had seen this condition only once before: the White Death's hand, exposed during the ambush at the Akbars', when his glove had come off. The same scarring, the same blisters.

Zoltan raked the soil in broad, strong strokes. He was a good head taller than Ben and worked mechanically.

'How did your hands get like that?'

'The doctor calls it *dermatitis*. From handling tulips, yes? If you touch without gloves, this is what happens. They are beautiful, sir – but full of poison.'

Zoltan picked up the shovel and thrust it into the hard earth around the newly planted bulbs. But by that point, Ben was sprinting back to the house.

On the front terrace, where the guests were filtering to their carriages, he found Amedeo Cipriani getting into his hansom cab.

'A moment, Señor Cipriani!' Ben said. 'I have a question for you.'

'Mr Canaan!' Cipriani exclaimed, waving for his driver to wait. 'Do go on.'

'You said every tulip in this city has your name on it. Well, I was wondering: do you happen to count Prince Mavros as one of your clients?'

Cipriani gave Ben a smug smile. 'The Prince? And how! He is *mad* about the tulips – ever since he arrived last year! I cannot say there is a single client who brings me more business. The late Princess loved them too.'

'Is he still ordering them?'

'Why, yes – perhaps they remind him of her.'

'How do you ship them in?'

'From Leiden, all the way to an island off Constantinople: Büyükada. The Prince insists that I use one of his own vessels. I suppose he trusts his boat more than mine. A tad fussy of him – but it's a lovely schooner. I charter it for monthly shipments.'

'What's she called?'

'The *Boethius*. Anyway. Must be off now. Pleasure to meet you, Mr Canaan.'

Cipriani closed the door of the hansom cab and sped away, as the last partygoers mounted their broughams and buggies. Another carriage pulled up in front of Ben to take him back to the Tatar camp, Eydir at the reins.

'Ready to go?' Eydir said.

Ben climbed into the carriage. He cast a final glance back at the estate. One by one, the candles were being snuffed out, a stain of shadows slowly spreading through the house – until the only light left was Zoltan's, behind the willow trees.

He closed his eyes as the carriage barrelled into the darkness.

'*Boethius*,' he whispered. 'Not so mad after all, Antonia!'

18

The Scorpion's Kiss

It was a foggy October morning when Ben and Ismail set sail for Büyükada. According to information gleaned by Marat Zagid, Cipriani's firm was expecting a shipment of tulips dispatched from Leiden two weeks prior. If Ben's calculations were correct, the merchandise should be arriving on the *Boethius* that day.

They took the first ferry from Galata Bridge – an hour-long trip south-east across the Sea of Marmara, to an archipelago known as the Princes' Islands. Apart from Ben and Ismail, the ferry was nearly empty. 'Summer's done!' the captain bellowed over the steam engine. 'Most people are heading in the other direction!'

Büyükada, the largest of the islands, gradually took shape in the grey, rising out of Marmara like a half-sunk behemoth. Summer villas ascended from the shoreline up its forested slopes – splashes of white amid a swathe of black trees and umber-brown pebble beaches. Presiding over the island, at the summit of Yücetepe, its tallest hill, was a Byzantine abbey, marked out by a yellow dome where a bell was clanging.

They landed at a small wharf by a Naval Cadet School. Ben looked around. Donkey-drawn wagons idled outside a tumbledown hotel. Fishermen were sitting on jetties, luring fish through the gloom by dangling flaming torches over the water. No sign of the *Boethius*.

'We need a vantage point,' Ben said. 'Somewhere less exposed.'

They found a spot at the top of a grassy knoll next to the Naval Cadet School, sheltered from the drizzle under the bough of a turpentine tree. They lay there all day, taking turns to peer through a pair of theatre binoculars that Shoshanna had lent them. It was mind-numbing work: buffeted by the sea-wind, shivering from the cold, straining their eyes against the fog shrouding the harbour. Ismail picked up lunch from a café by the water – a tin of flour-cookies, a few handfuls of almonds and two strong coffees.

By the end of the day, Ben was losing hope. The fog had cleared a little to reveal the sun dipping under the horizon. The taxi-men with their donkeys were packing up shop. Even the ferries that had been coming and going every hour disappeared.

Then Ben saw it. A sleek topsail schooner, two-masted and gaff-rigged, manned by a team of four sailors – and fast approaching port. He snatched the binoculars and zeroed in on the boat. Painted on its sturdy white hull, in pristine red letters, was a name: *Boethius*.

'There she blows!' Ben whispered.

The sailors gathered at the forecastle of the *Boethius* and moored at a jetty where a wagon with two drivers was waiting for them. The sailors hefted a wooden crate down the gangway and into the back of the wagon. Once it was loaded up, the drivers gave them a hasty salute and set off at a clip.

Ben dragged Ismail to his feet. 'Let's go!'

They ran down the knoll and seized the first taxi-man they saw – a portly fellow by the name of Duman. He was initially reluctant when Ismail told him what they wanted. But a ten-piastre tip was all the convincing that Duman needed.

They tailed the wagon east, past empty summer mansions: kiosks locked up for the off-season, skeletal pine trees, squalid barns and horse-pens where Karacabey stallions grazed in eerie stillness.

Finally, as darkness set in, the wagon bearing the crates from the *Boethius* pulled up outside a derelict mansion on the water's edge, behind an iron gate.

If anyone had lived here, it must have been a very long time ago. Moss matted the boarded-up windows. Reeds ran wild in the front garden and the roots of palm trees burst from the soil to buckle the steps of the porch, where burnt-out lanterns swayed back and forth.

They ground to a halt about a hundred yards from the mansion, behind a copse of pines. They watched as the drivers carried the crate onto the property and let themselves in with a bronze key.

'What do you think they're doing in there?' Ismail asked.

'No idea,' Ben replied, 'but something tells me it's not flower-arranging. We need to find a way in. Climb the walls, maybe?'

'Easier said than done, Beef Wellington. That window at the top might be doable – but I wouldn't trust the brickwork to hold.'

The drivers re-emerged without the crate. Ben ducked out of sight so as not to be seen, but Ismail took a different tack: he jumped off the wagon and walked jauntily towards them.

'Get back here!' Ben ordered.

But Ismail ignored him. Just as the drivers were about to mount their wagon, he barged straight into them and went to ground, clutching his head, wailing in Turkish and pointing at them. But the drivers were having none of it. They knew this old trick: some street urchin plays blind, feigns an injury, then tries to make out that they were responsible, all for an easy lira.

They hauled him up by the neck like a stray kitten, slapped him on the head and booted him back the way he had come. Ismail staggered away, hurling insults at the drivers in his native Tatar as they rode off. But by the time he re-joined Ben and Duman, he was grinning ear to ear.

He slipped the bronze key into Ben's hands. *'Et voilà!'*

'Right!' Duman said, grabbing the reins. 'That's enough! Off my wagon!'

Ben offered another ten piastres in an effort to change his mind, but Duman was also having none of it. With a final curse he sped off back to the harbour, leaving Ben and Ismail alone in the middle of the road, staring up at the haunted house.

'I'm thinking, Englishman,' Ismail said, 'that one of us should stay here and keep watch – maybe the one not being paid a hundred pounds to risk his neck!'

Ben wasted no time. He crossed the garden, swatting away a swarm of gnats and climbing the steps to the front door. He slotted the key into the lock and the door opened with a heavy *clunk*.

The place was deserted. The rooms were stripped bare and had an air of decay: a broken candelabrum on the library floor, a salon with a gutted grand piano and a fireplace clogged with ash, a sitting room where the furniture had been taken apart and the wallpaper left to peel. Beneath the smell of mould and rotting wood, there was a faint chemical odour – pungent chloride salts.

Ben scoured for any sign of the crate. But it had seemingly vanished into thin air. He stopped and listened, then knelt and placed his ear to the ground. A faint hum was vibrating through the floorboards. From the front door to a room at the back, a trail had been scraped in the dust.

He followed the trail into a scullery with windows looking onto the sea. Like the other rooms, it was just another crumbling relic of what it used to be: cupboards and shelves emptied out, damp spreading across the brown walls.

Then he noticed something strange: a portion of the wall to his left that was a paler brown hue than the rest of the wallspace – and completely dry.

He tapped. It was hollow.

'Knock-knock – anybody home…?'

He dug his fingers into a tiny gap in the panels and pulled as hard as he could. The section of the wall swung open on a hinge, and behind it was a steep drop into the shadows. An intricate pulley system hung from the ceiling: two furrowed wheels tethered by thick rope to form a block and tackle, dangling in the darkness.

Ben tugged on it. It was strong. A threefold purchase, as he had been taught to use on the *Midas*. The drivers must have used this mechanism to lower the crate to a cellar below the house. And the last time he checked, he weighed a lean hundred and fifty pounds, so it would likely support his weight.

He grabbed the rope with both hands, wrapped his legs around it, and slid down into the murky underground. It was deep: a good twenty feet before his feet touched the concrete floor at the bottom of the shaft. Still the crate was nowhere to be seen, though it was near pitch-black. The only light was a thin band of white creeping through the cracks in a door to Ben's right.

He pushed it open…

First the cold hit him: a gust of bone-chilling air that burned his cheeks and made him gasp. The acrid chemical stench was even more oppressive than upstairs.

Then he saw the bodies. At least twenty of them, hanging in rows from steel hooks in a metal refrigeration chamber. All naked, drained ghostly pale, hooks impaled in their armpits to suspend them in mid-air. Their faces were serene, their eyes were clouded white and their mouths lolled open.

Their legs were pinned with yellow tags: sex, age, date, time of death. Judging by their appearance, they were homeless orphans, old beggars – the kind of people that nobody would miss, or notice missing. *Test subjects.*

Ben doubled over. He was ready to heave his guts out. If ever there was a time to leave, it was now. But at the end of the chamber, painted on a sliding glass door, were two familiar letters:

T O

The same letters tattooed on Elizabeth's finger. Ben took a deep breath and edged past the bodies. It was almost as though their eyes were following him as he approached the sliding door and eased it open.

Inside was a makeshift laboratory. An old combustion engine shuddered as it gave off immense heat, fed by a network of metal pipes running down from the ceiling. Oil drums and distillation equipment were set against the walls – pressurised steel vats connected by condensing tubes, tables lined with conical flasks bubbling with a viscous liquid. Crimson-red mist filled the laboratory, pricking Ben's tongue with the sharp taste of rust and acid.

A few feet away in the blood-red haze, a man in a black rubber apron was standing at a worktable with his back to Ben. The crate was at his side, lid removed to reveal a pile of tulip bulbs.

'Prince Mavros…' Ben said.

The man lifted his head, straightened his back, and slowly turned around.

It was the White Death: the burnt hood-mask – those lively grey eyes – gloveless to expose his scarred hands.

'Now I see why you wear those riding gloves,' Ben said.

The White Death stirred, as though ready to attack. Then he seemed to relax.

'What was it you told me?' Ben snarled. 'Pretences tend not to last too long? You had me fooled for a while, I'll give you that. Well, I see through you now.'

The White Death said nothing. He cocked his head with detached curiosity.

'You had Marta killed – your own *wife*. Why? Was she no longer useful to you? You strongarm her into killing on your behalf, then get rid of her and parade around as the poor grieving widower. And Abraham Carmino? I know revenge is a dish best served cold, but aren't you taking things a little far? Did all those people…' he pointed to the bodies in the refrigeration chamber, 'did *they* need to die as well?'

A grating, mechanical rasp emanated from behind the hood-mask, like the scraping of metal on metal. The White Death was laughing.

Ben brandished his mother-of-pearl penknife. 'I'm not afraid of you.'

'You will be,' the White Death said, his voice distorted by the hood-mask.

'That's rich, coming from a pampered prince too scared to show his own face.'

The White Death lifted the hood-mask with both hands. Ben recoiled. It most certainly was not Prince Alexander Mavros.

The man's face was riddled with burns and yellow pustules: waxen flesh punctured by those deep-set eyes. His hair was singed off, reduced to a few discoloured patches on a scalp streaked with raw-red rashes. His lips were scabbed over and twisted into a vicious smile.

'Surprise!' the White Death said mockingly.

Ben's hand was trembling. The White Death gestured nonchalantly to the laboratory.

'Impressed?' he said. 'I built this with my own two hands. It takes the toxin latent in every tulip – α-*methylene*-γ-*butyrolactone*, to use the scientific term – and distils it, concentrates it to its purest form. With a few extra ingredients thrown in, like essence of monkshood and arsenic to name but two, you have a fatal poison – the deadliest chemical weapon on earth. I call it *the Scorpion's Kiss*. And the fuel it burns can be found in every garden, greenhouse and orangery from Kabul to Amsterdam. In fact, you're breathing it in right now!'

He waved his hand through the red mist, sending a plume of gas floating towards Ben. Ben covered his mouth, but the White Death shook his head pityingly.

'Fear not: in weak doses, it does little. Over time, though, it leaves its mark. Case in point – I was not born like this. But one must suffer for one's art.'

Whoever he was, this man was mad – an utterly inhuman kind of madness. 'Who the hell are you?' Ben murmured.

'I'm whoever you want me to be. Maybe I'm George de Varney, let's say that. A beloved physician, reeling from the death of my wife, with only my dear devoted daughter Elizabeth for company. Maybe I'm a soldier. Once a handsome young man, sent by my government to a war I never chose to fight. Who broke his body and mind to serve his nation, only to be forgotten when the bells toll the hour of peace. Or maybe... *I'm the son of a tailor.* The eldest of four. Grew up in a ramshackle little place in the East End with my siblings, parents, grandparents, a foppish cousin perhaps with a penchant for tall tales. But dreaming, always dreaming, of something bigger: an education, the Bar, the intellectual life that was snuffed out in the name of family. That's the story, isn't it, Benjamin E. Canaan – son of Solomon and Ruth – of Canaan & Sons?'

Ben felt his insides hollow out in terror. The White Death knew everything about him, his family, his home, his deepest secrets. None of his loved ones were safe: they all had targets on their backs, and it was Ben's fault.

'That's the mistake people always make,' the White Death continued. 'They think that what's behind the mask is what matters. That the mask conceals the truth. But actually, Mr Canaan, *the mask is the truth*. There's nothing else there – not anymore. I am the mask, and that's why I wear it. It's the only real thing about me.'

'So you're not Prince Mavros,' Ben said. 'What does that make you? Some crony on his payroll?'

'Still stuck on Mavros!' The White Death seemed almost disappointed, like a tutor losing patience with a student. 'In the grand scheme of things, Mavros is nothing. Just one piece in the puzzle. Like Ahmed, and Sir Lawrence Thorsbury, and Abraham Carmino, and Marta Mavros, and Lynton Arabin Heathcote – and now... *you*.'

It was do or die. Ben lunged at him with the penknife. But the White Death saw it coming from a mile away. He grabbed Ben's wrist mid-thrust, twisted his arm until the knife clattered to the floor, and chopped Ben in the windpipe.

Ben was sent staggering, clutching his throat and gasping for air, while the White Death calmly turned back to his worktable.

'I was contemplating having to hunt you down – the same way I hunted down Sir Lawrence and Abraham when, like you, they cottoned onto the *Boethius*. But you did my job for me. Only Ben Canaan could be so clever and so foolish in one stroke.'

He retrieved a metal canister that was hanging on the wall. It was about six inches long, wrapped with high-tensile-steel bands, glowing with red gas, and fitted with the barrel of a pistol and a trigger.

'Though I must admit,' the White Death continued, 'you are a natural-born sleuth. Quick as a weasel. It's almost a shame that you have so carelessly signed your death sentence. It would have been interesting to see you fulfil your potential. But alas, this show must come to an end.'

Ben looked left and right. He was cornered. 'Maybe we got off on the wrong foot...' he said. 'You don't have to do this...'

'Mr Canaan, do not debase yourself with the indignity of begging. There's no talking your way out of this one. Your life was over the moment you entered the fray. Now: you either die with your eyes open, or with your back turned. Either way, *your fate is the same.*'

The White Death held up the metal canister – the barrel pointed at Ben's face.

'It's a concentrated spray,' he said. 'A short, sharp burst and it will all be over. You'll hardly feel a thing. I'll hang you up in there to dry.'

The White Death's finger curled around the trigger. Ben was rooted to the spot, bracing himself, hypnotised by the red mist in the barrel – the last thing he would see on this earth.

But the White Death did not pull the trigger. He stopped in his tracks – and those grey eyes flicked past Ben to the sliding door behind him...

The White Death flinched – took a couple of steps back – and *ran*.

Ben spun round. Three men were standing there, repeating rifles aimed over his head.

'Stay down!' one of them roared.

Ben lay face-down on the floor as the gunmen unloaded their rifles into the laboratory. Wave after wave of bullets strafed the room, ripping apart the combustion engine, pipes and distillation vats. Sparks flew through the red mist and flames began to rise from the combustion engine. Ben was deafened by the sound of gunfire and the shriek of mangled metal. In the space of fifteen seconds, the place had been obliterated.

Then the gunfire subsided. The outlines of the three men moved stealthily towards Ben through the mist. One helped him to his feet and the other two sprinted after the White Death, to a hydraulic elevator adjacent to the laboratory. The White Death was standing on a steel platform rising through the shaft from the cellar to the house above. By the time the men were raising their weapons to fire, the White Death had ascended out of sight.

The three men regrouped with Ben at the entrance to the laboratory. The shootout had breached the oil drums and the fire was quickly spreading. 'This place is going to blow up at any moment,' one of the men said. 'Let's get him out of here.'

The men frogmarched Ben out of the laboratory, up the pulley system to ground level, and onto the street outside the mansion.

Only then, in the cool moonlit air, did Ben get a proper look at them. They were a trio of bashi-bazouks: Ottoman mercenaries gaudily dressed in turbans, flared skirts, embroidered jackets and gold-studded boots. They were armed to the teeth with guns, knives and bandoliers draped across their chests.

The ringleader stepped forward: a broad-shouldered man with an elaborate moustache. 'My name is Radimir Murad,' he said gallantly. '*Enchanté*. You are coming with us.'

Two more bashi-bazouks were approaching, Ismail writhing powerlessly in their grip. They took Ben and Ismail to a jetty where a sailboat was moored, just about large enough for the five bashi-bazouks and their new captives. They set sail for Constantinople. From here, the city was a tiny cluster of glimmering lights studding the shores above the black waters.

Ben glanced back at the mansion. Smoke was climbing from the lower windows – flashes of red and igneous orange bursting from within, like firecrackers—

Then an explosion: a lithium-infused fireball mushrooming into a pillar of black smoke – and the building collapsed in on itself with a thunderous roar that echoed across Büyükada.

Radimir lit a cigarillo and took a spirited puff.

'Did you get him?' Ben asked.

Radimir laughed: 'Wishful thinking! It will take more than bullets and brimstone to bring down the White Death.'

'Who are you?'

'Think of me as a guardian angel, serving not God – but the Contessa.'

'The *what?*'

'You'll see.' He stood at the prow of the skiff and lifted his scimitar to the full moon. 'To the Pierrot!'

19

The Lost Queen of Poland

Something was troubling Countess Zofia Radozsesky. She was sitting on her Louis XIV armchair, gazing down from the gallery at the main hall of the Hôtel Pierrot. There was an arachnid quality to her: utterly still in the middle of a web that she had so assiduously spun – ready to move at the slightest tremor.

It was the usual crowd at the Pierrot: a menagerie of noble émigrés from Paris, Geneva, Heidelberg, Buenos Aires – dissolute after years roaming the political wilderness. Among them were polemical writers, anarchists and *enfants terribles* of the art world, come to gamble away their meagre income and drink themselves into a stupor. The kind who would wax lyrical about starting a revolution, then complain that the champagne was not cold enough.

'You let the inmates run the asylum, Contessa,' a voice chided affectionately behind her.

She knew that curious Baltimore-French accent only too well: it was Jerome Napoleon Bonaparte II, an American great-nephew of the original Napoleon. His Hessian boots were kicked up on a baize tabletop, where he played an idle game of

Preferans with an Astor – one of John Jacob's grandsons – and a pair of newlywed Virginian plantation heirs by the name of Horace and Arabella Clyde.

'I only let them think they're running it!' she laughed. 'Is that such a bad thing?'

'*Au contraire*, Contessa,' Jerome said, studying his cards. 'It's vastly more entertaining that way…'

She slunk over to Jerome and nestled in his lap. The young man must have been twenty years her junior – but that hardly discouraged Zofia: the younger the better.

'What's the matter with you anyway?' he said. 'Shouldn't you be swinging from the chandeliers by this hour?'

'And shouldn't you be marching on Sevastopol? Your cousin *Badinguet* would disapprove.'

'He prefers *Napoleon III, Emperor of the French*…'

Jerome reached under the table and slipped his hand inside her petticoat to stroke her thigh. 'Will you have me disciplined for my insubordination, Contessa?'

'Impatient boy!' she cried. 'The night is young. And if you must know, I have business to attend to—'

As if on cue, Radimir appeared in the doorway, flanked by his bashi-bazouks. They were sopping wet from the knee down and had left muddy footprints on the rug.

'Radimir!' Zofia leapt to her feet. 'I had Brintons ferry these carpets all the way from London.'

'And I have something else ferried from London,' Radimir retorted. 'Something much harder to find, and *infinitely* harder to replace.'

Zofia sighed in relief. How he had done it, she had no idea. But Radimir, as usual, had pulled it off. 'Ladies and lechers,' she said to her companions, 'I must be off. Do keep my seat warm, darling Jerome – and if I don't see you, send my regards to cousin *Badinguet*.'

Zofia breezed out into the corridors of the Pierrot. The bashi-bazouks flanked her in a protective formation.

'Where is he?' she asked.

'Upstairs,' Radimir replied. 'We moved the Tatar scamp to another room so that you have Canaan to yourself.'

She snatched an iced absinthe from a passing tray, knocked it back and smacked her lips. 'This should be good.'

Radimir briefed her on the events of the night as they made their way to the top floor of the hotel, where Zofia's private apartments were located. From the casino to the smoking lounges, Zofia was greeted with deferential nods. She may have been an exile from her native Poland – for reasons nobody quite knew – but in this den of decadence that she had built from nothing, she ruled the roost.

She entered her office to find Ben in a Gainsborough chair, warming himself by the fireplace and guarded by an armed bashi-bazouk. He was positively filthy: covered in sweat and dirt, reeking of smoke and the sea. But behind that feral appearance, there was an intelligence at work. His eyes were dark and bright at the same time – inquisitive and unafraid.

Zofia signalled to the bashi-bazouks and they filed out. She offered Ben a handkerchief. 'You look like a rat rescued from a drainpipe, Mr Canaan.'

Warily, Ben accepted the handkerchief and wiped the muck from his face.

'So there *is* a handsome boy under all that! I can see why Mademoiselle Carmino has taken such a shine to you…'

'Get on with it, why don't you? Who are you and how'd you find me?'

'And a sharp tongue to boot! You should be more vigilant about where you hold court, my dear boy. I have my waiters eavesdrop on nearly every conversation in the Pierrot and I found your confab with Mr Trilling most intriguing. I put a few drinks in him that evening and got the whole story. I've had Radimir tailing you ever since.'

'Seems like everyone is tailing everyone in this city.'

'That's Constantinople for you. And you've taken to it like a duck to water! So...' She plucked a cherry from a fruit bowl. 'What's your angle? Is it that you hate Mavros?'

Ben said nothing. She popped the cherry in her mouth and grinned.

'Or are you after Mademoiselle Carmino's affection? Or her dowry – what's left of it! She would never go for you, you know. Her family would have a fit if she tied the knot with an East End barrow-boy.'

'She hired me,' Ben said. 'I'm helping her with this White Death affair.'

'"The White Death Affair"!' she said sarcastically. 'I see! A young *detective*. Is this because of her father?'

Ben nodded. 'She doesn't believe the posthumous narrative about him.'

'What, Abraham Carmino selling gold bullion to the Russians? *Please*. His only peccadillo was that he loved to gamble here at the Pierrot – other than that, the man was unimpeachable. It was obviously a fix, and it paved the way for Mavros to muscle in on his trade. Which, as it happens, leads us to the here and now...'

Ben had been studying Zofia closely ever since she walked in. He had been trying to figure out whether she, like the White Death, was planning on killing him. But Zofia did not seem like the type to want to stop his clock – she was much too intrigued. She had the playfulness of someone with a much grander plan than summary execution, and she seemed to be enjoying setting up the pieces.

'You want to bring down the White Death too, don't you?' Ben said.

'Not *the* White Death, Mr Canaan. I want to bring down *all of them*.'

She let the words hang. Just the crackling of the fireplace and the muffled echoes of revelry downstairs.

'What do you mean, "all of them"?'

'I mean that the White Death is not a person – it's a *collective*. Spies, operatives, assassins, agents... whatever the term *du jour* is. Embedded in virtually every city in Europe, carrying out strategic killings on the orders of the Russian Empire. It's an organisation called the "Third Section". The *Tretoye Otdeleniye*. Run by an elusive spymaster known only as *Orlov*.'

Ben frowned. *Tretoye Otdeleniye*. 'T.O. ...' he whispered.

'Now he sees. And, alas, much like the Medusa, once you see it you are condemned to a rather sticky end.'

Ben pressed his fingers to his temple. Things began clicking into place: the male and female White Deaths – the poison – the double identities – even Heathcote, the British attaché, and the suspicions that got him killed.

'So the man Radimir sprung me from... was a Russian agent? And all these killings are their doing?'

'A plump snipe that they have been roasting in the oven for quite some time. And now the Russians are getting ready to lay the table. Most who know what's happening no longer have the luxury of breathing.'

'Then how do *you* know?'

Behind Zofia's bravado, a seriousness emerged – an awareness of the gravity and danger of their situation. 'I've been an enemy of the Third Section for a very long time. Orlov and I have a *complicated* history – a tale for another time. What I didn't know was that they were in Constantinople. That is, until a little birdie fluttered to my window…'

She looked at Ben pointedly. At first he did not catch her drift. Then he twigged.

'*Marta Mavros.*'

'A prized agent of the Third Section. Assassinations in Vienna, Stockholm, Rome, Tunis… and *London.*' She saw Ben's shock and nodded, as if to drive the point home. 'Ah, yes. The summer of 1851. Your summer of love – Britain's summer of blood, when four high-ranking civil servants met a grisly end. And you were her cover. A companion, to help her blend in. Someone who could vouch for her if things got hairy. An unwitting side dish to the main course. Did it really not strike you as odd? That a beautiful stranger would take such an immediate liking to – no offence – a lowly Jewish tailor's son?'

Ben slumped in his chair. 'It never really occurred to me. I was gullible, I suppose. Blinded.'

'It happens – don't be *too* hard on yourself. Until Marta spilled her beans, she had me fooled as well. But she had a change of heart. A life sending people down the River Styx must have lost its lustre. I suspect it was the death of the Sultan's boy. The killing of innocent children can weigh on one's conscience.'

Ben thought back to Clio Tavoularis' account of Marta's last days: the argument between Marta and Prince Mavros before her disappearance and that awful line. 'She slipped the noose…' he murmured.

'Third Section slang for *defection*. She told me everything: how she had been sent here to pose as Mavros' wife. How she had been working from the shadows, helping our mutual friend with a face like crème brûlée to set the Third Section plan in motion.'

'So Mavros is in on it, then?'

'He's not a Third Section agent, if that's what you mean. But he is a *spectacular* arse. I imagine he's set to profit somehow if their plan comes off.'

Zofia went over to the window. The streets of Pera were quiet compared to the din downstairs. Only the hooting of tawny owls pierced the calm. The shadowy outline of Prince Mavros' estate on the shore of the Bosporus was visible from here.

'She paid a heavy price for her betrayal. Not long after she came to me, our birdie was found with her wings clipped and her neck broken. The Third Section takes no prisoners – especially with their own.'

'You keep talking about a Third Section plan,' Ben said. 'What *is* it? What happens next?'

Zofia went to her desk and unlocked a drawer. Inside was a handwritten note. 'The night before Marta disappeared, I received this note from her.'

Двенадцатое ноября. Защитите Султана. Когда вы слышите Тангейзера – мат.

And below that was Zofia's translation: '12th of November. Protect the Sultan. When you hear *Tannhaüser* – checkmate.'

'They're going to kill the Sultan…' Ben whispered.

Zofia nodded solemnly. Ben re-read the note to make sure that he was not imagining things. Sure enough: the 12th of November – barely two weeks away. Hardly any time to prepare, and they were the only ones who knew.

'This is madness,' he said. 'We need to warn the authorities! Surely once they know, they can put a stop to it—'

Zofia cut him off with a bitter chuckle. 'Don't be so naive. This plot goes wider than you could possibly imagine. The authorities cannot be relied on. The Russians have their tentacles everywhere, and everyone else is too distracted by the war. I tried to inform the British through Heathcote but we got nowhere: he ended up as another victim of the White Death and the British just stood by. At this point, I don't know who to trust. And I'm inclined to follow Heathcote's motto: *trust no one.*'

'But you trust me!' Ben exclaimed. '"A lowly Jewish tailor's son"! Are you seriously suggesting we do this together?!'

'That is *precisely* what I am suggesting,' Zofia replied. 'The only ones who can stop what is about to happen are people like us. The "Great Independents", who have no state paymaster, no vested interest in the backhand dealings of geopolitics. It is *our* actions that change the course of history – even if we never asked for it, even if we remain invisible, even if, when justice is dealt, we are forgotten.'

She softened. There was no hiding it: Ben was afraid. Never before had such a burden been placed on his shoulders. He was no longer a budding detective or a two-bit English conman. He was just a boy.

'I know how it feels,' Zofia said gently. 'To be faced with insurmountable odds, saddled with a responsibility much larger than yourself. But remember, Mr Canaan: it is no curse. It is a duty. Only a special few are chosen by fate to bear it. And now, you have joined their ranks. You are, as we say in espionage, standing at the edge of the waterfall. The only way out is to put your faith in your feet... *and jump.*'

Before Ben could say anything, the door to Zofia's office swung open and Radimir burst in. 'Visitor downstairs, Contessa!'

'Who?'

'Alexander Mavros.'

'Put his cocktails on my tab and tell him to piss off when he's done.'

'He's brought friends.'

They had been rumbled. But Zofia seemed, if anything, delighted. She took Ben by the hand and led him to the door:

'Right, Mr Canaan: time for your first lesson in *brinksmanship!*'

20

Baccarat at the Pierrot

They found Mavros waiting for them in the casino. He had commandeered the baccarat table and was spinning a brass token on the felt. The place had cleared out on his arrival, leaving a still life of abandoned roulette games and half-drunk cocktails.

He was not alone. Behind him stood a dozen Greek soldiers in white sashes, armed with pistols and sabres. Languidly smoking a cigarette to his left was Yusuf Madhat Pasha, and to his right was an anxious-looking gendarme – Khalil, the deputy who had let Ben slip after his arrest.

Mavros livened up when he saw the double-doors open and Zofia enter with Ben in tow, protected by Radimir and the bashi-bazouks.

'Contessa! You look ravishing as always.'

'Prince Mavros. What an unexpected pleasure.'

'Since we're in the habit of bursting in unannounced…'

Mavros bowed courteously and kissed Zofia's gloved hand. Then his eyes turned to Ben. 'And you, Mr Canaan. The bad penny that keeps turning up. I understand you are already acquainted with Chief Inspector Yusuf Madhat Pasha and his deputy Khalil Al-Moussawi.'

'Didn't realise you were moonlighting for Prince Mavros.' Ben glared at the Chief Inspector. 'Money must be tight.'

Yusuf lumbered over to Ben as Khalil held out a pair of shackles. 'Let's begin proceedings with a demonstration of how we treat fugitives, shall we?'

Before he could so much as lay a finger on Ben, the bashi-bazouks drew their pistols. The Greek soldiers responded in kind. In a flash, both sides were engaged in a standoff: Ben, Zofia, Mavros and Yusuf caught between them, Khalil looking about as useful as a puppy in the ring with a pack of bull terriers.

'Put that piece away, you Albanian mongrel,' Yusuf sneered at Radimir, 'or it will be the last thing you do.'

'Sit your fat arse down and maybe I'll consider it.'

Mavros came between Yusuf, Radimir and Ben. 'There is no need for a shootout. I was actually fixing for a gamble. Baccarat, to be precise.'

Zofia gestured to the Greek soldiers. 'You've brought too many players.'

'So have you.'

'…Very well.'

Zofia and Mavros dismissed their men. The Greeks and the bashi-bazouks holstered their guns and left, maintaining a cautious distance. 'Play nice out there, boys!' Zofia cooed – before taking Radimir by the arm. 'Not you, dear. You shall be our dealer.'

They assumed their positions on either side of the baccarat table.

Mavros smiled maliciously at Zofia and Ben. 'Punto banco?'

'Chemin de fer,' Zofia replied. 'We're not in Macau, Prince Mavros.'

Radimir cut six packs of playing cards and slid them into a wooden shoe. Zofia rang a silver dinner bell and a waiter appeared from a service door.

'*Jean-Luc!*' Zofia called, '*Venez, venez…*'

He anxiously approached with his pencil and notepad clutched to his chest. '*L'habituel, Contesse?*'

'*Oui, Jean-Luc. Cinq verres, s'il vous plaît. Pour moi, notre cher Prince, et les compagnons.*'

Jean-Luc disappeared and returned in a hurry with a bottle of Veuve Clicquot on ice, which he meted out in five crystal flutes.

'Nobody gambles at the Pierrot on an empty stomach.' Zofia raised her glass. 'Even if it is only filled with bubbles. *Santé.*'

They raised their glasses and drank – not once taking their eyes off each other.

'Your escapade was not much appreciated, Mr Canaan,' Mavros said. 'It was a very expensive project that we had running on Büyükada.'

'I hope your man wasn't too bruised from our encounter,' Radimir sneered.

'Couldn't have happened to a lovelier chap,' Ben added.

'I wouldn't worry about him. He's a real Siberian Bloodhound. They build them differently out there. Besides, we have other locations across the city. It's good to be diversified. Spread the risk, as they say.'

Zofia placed the first wager. 'Meet me at five hundred francs, Prince Mavros.'

'How about five thousand?' Mavros laid a stack of banknotes on the table.

Zofia paid his ante without a moment's hesitation.

Radimir dealt two cards face-down. Mavros peeked at his – Zofia at hers – and they both tapped the table twice. *Hit*. Radimir slid a card to each of them, face-up: Mavros had the King of Diamonds, Zofia the Nine of Spades.

Mavros' eyes lit up and he revealed his cards. Four – Ace – plus the King: *five*.

Zofia revealed hers. Five – Queen – plus the Nine: *four*.

'One step behind. Alas, such are the rules of the game!' Mavros tutted, as he swept up his winnings. 'Orlov sends his regards, by the way. He apologises for the trouble he caused you back home.'

Zofia gave a contemptuous laugh. 'He could always say it to my face. Though I understand: that's not his style. He gets lackeys like you to handle his trifles.'

'"Trifles"? You are sorely mistaken, Contessa! This is the *prime rib*.'

Ben could not contain himself. 'That's a hell of a way to talk about the people you've killed,' he scoffed. 'The families you've torn apart. Not to mention what you've got in store for the Sultan.'

Mavros had an air of insouciance about him, but Ben could sense the fury simmering beneath the surface. 'Nothing my family has not suffered already.'

'Yes, I figured as much. That's what it comes down to in the end, doesn't it? *Revenge*. The last Sultan killed your father, left little orphan Alexander's dynasty in ruins. And now you're back: to visit the sins of the father on the present Sultan.'

'It's only fair – I had to carry the sins of mine. I was a glorified refugee, roaming Europe while this Empire fattened itself on stolen riches and slaves from North Africa. An entire family history razed to the ground in service of some arrogant generalissimo and his pampered *şehzades*. But that's all going to change – very soon.'

He refilled his Veuve Clicquot and took a self-satisfied slug.

'There is a war raging as we speak,' he continued. 'Hundreds of thousands of young men amass on a barren peninsula on the Black Sea – centuries of geopolitical struggle concentrated in a single, insignificant piece of land. A deadly whirlpool inexorably sucking in everything around it. The Ottomans are an ailing creature, as complacent as they are archaic – propped up by ambitious foreign powers. Russia is a nation that merely needs to clench its fist to strike terror into the hearts of millions. The winner of this war will have the ability to reshape Europe, Asia, the Holy Lands, Africa – their politics, economies, religions and cultures. The loser will be nothing more than a fading memory on dusty monuments to be spoken about on anniversaries as a cautionary tale. I intend to win this war – and win it imminently.'

Mavros' tone said it all: nothing could deter him. The prize of winning was too great. The price of losing was too grave to countenance.

'So you followed your greed and threw your lot in with the Russians,' Ben said. 'Allies through a common enemy. And now you play your part in having the Sultan killed. You cripple the Ottoman Empire.'

'Not just cripple – *usurp*. Take it from the inside. You see, war is messy. Expensive. It breaks morale. Brute force can only get you so far. We prefer a much more elegant approach. An iron fist in a velvet glove. One Sultan goes out…'

Ben completed the formula: 'And another goes in…'

Mavros gave an understated shrug. Ben stared at the Chief Inspector and Khalil – not quite believing that Mavros had the gall to make this confession in front of them. But Yusuf looked rather pleased with himself, and Khalil stared nervously at his feet.

Ben thought back to the infiltration of Topkapı Palace. To Mihrima's caution: *it is not the Sultan you should fear – it is whoever sits behind him, pulling the strings.*

'That's why you had Ahmed killed,' Ben said. 'Get rid of the heir apparent and replace him with a different heir, a different Queen Mother. One that's in your pocket, that will do your bidding. What was her name again – Shevkayir? And that boy of hers, Mehmet? They're just a Trojan Horse.'

For the first time that evening, Mavros had to check himself. 'So you know them by name!' he said with a bemused grin. 'Impressive. You're quite right. Through them, we will control the Sultanate – the only office in the land that nobody can question. We will use that influence to put a stop to this conflict: a truce, that ultimately paves the way for a surrender of Ottoman sovereignty and the dissolution of the Empire. Constantinople will become a passive satellite of the Great Powers. It is thus that the war ends: not by kicking down the front door – but by silently removing the hinges.'

'Good luck getting the British and French to sign up to your plan.'

'I don't think that should be a problem.'

'Liar. They're fighting tooth and nail for an Ottoman victory.'

Mavros rolled his eyes.

'Mr Canaan, you are showing your youth. They don't want to fight – nobody does! They had to be dragged kicking and screaming into this war for one reason: they were afraid that if

Russia went unchallenged, it would upset the global balance of power and close off their precious trade routes. Do you think they care remotely about sacred mosques, Persian rugs and Ottoman nationalism? At the end of the day, Russia and the West are not enemies. They are both shackled to a sick man that refuses to die – malingering, pitting them against each other – when what they could be doing is sitting down together and carving it up to everyone's satisfaction.'

For all the thousands that had died – and the hundreds of thousands more who would go on to die – to Mavros, it was just another notch on his belt, no different from the money on the baccarat table, or the bottle of champagne.

'Your own Queen met with the Tsar mere months ago,' Mavros added, 'and told him that the Ottomans being roundly beaten would be better for all concerned. But I don't suppose you would know that, would you? Your broadsheets like to pretend that Britain stands with the underdog. Meanwhile your government desperately craves a way out – praying, begging for the Ottomans' inevitable collapse. Well, I'm going to give it to them: *I'm going to put down the sick man.* And then?'

He rang Zofia's bell.

'Dinnertime! The world's empires decamp from the battlefield to the table, with the Ottomans served up as *plat principal*. Then we can get the real work done: negotiation, diplomacy, divvying up the spoils. Watch how quickly these "sworn enemies" become the best of friends as soon as it is expedient to do so. That, Mr Canaan, is the business of empire: a feeding frenzy.'

Mavros spoke with terrifying certainty. As though these war games had already been played, the conclusion foregone. History decided by an infernal machine that had been quietly turning this whole time – hiding behind the patriotic slogans, the petty partisan squabbles, the rise and fall of great men and the promises they peddled.

'And for your dutiful service,' Ben said, 'you will have bought yourself a seat at the table. Prince Mavros and his own little empire.'

'Not so little,' Mavros replied. 'The Russians will need a trustworthy pair of hands to run their new vassal state. The Prince shall become a king – or, at the very least, a viceroy.'

Zofia yawned conspicuously and emptied the rest of the Veuve Clicquot into her glass. 'You're starting to bore me with your speechifying. Have you come here just to gloat?'

'Not quite. I've come to issue a warning. A gentleman's shot. *Stay. Away*. Everyone who has died since Ahmed – Lawrence Thorsbury, Abraham Carmino, Marta, Heathcote – died because they tried to stop us. You do not want their fate to become yours. Believe me.'

'Or we go to the authorities and put an end to your sorry excuse for a *coup d'état*,' Zofia said.

'*The authorities?* Do you mean him?' Mavros pointed to Yusuf Madhat Pasha. The Chief Inspector stubbed out his cigarette and glared at Zofia. 'There is nobody you can turn to, Contessa. We have loyal servants in every station of government, from the gendarmerie to the Imperial Council.'

'I could always talk to the Sultan directly.'

'Then why haven't you already?'

Zofia had no riposte. Mavros shook his head, chastising her.

'Why do you think I had Abraham Carmino discredited? I am the most trusted man in the Sublime Porte. The Sultan eats out of my hand – quite literally, Contessa. Whenever they need bullion, they come to me. And we both know that outside the walls of this gilded cage, you are regarded as a crackpot. Nobody will believe you. And if I'm not mistaken, your only evidence was given to you by my mad wife, whose name cannot even be uttered in this city because of her sin of "suicide".'

He directed those last words at Ben. He was angling for a reaction. For a moment, Ben was inclined to give it to him – sock him in the face right then for insulting the woman he had once loved.

But he did not give Mavros the satisfaction. 'You're making the same mistake as your father,' he said.

Mavros concealed his anger behind a slick smile. 'Money is tedious,' he said to Zofia. 'Why don't we wager the boy? *Winner takes Canaan.* In a world such as ours, I'd say chance is the fairest judge.'

Ben was hoping that Zofia would roundly rebuff Mavros' idea. But far from it – the Contessa actually seemed to be considering it.

'Hmm!' she mused. 'I can't speak for Mr Canaan, but I rather fancy our luck.'

They both turned to Ben and looked at him expectantly.

'Last chance, Mr Canaan,' Mavros said darkly. 'Drop this obsession of yours and I'll let you go back to London. You can be shot of this mess and we will not trouble you. But if you pursue this path, the Third Section will hunt you down and destroy you, along with everyone you love. You have no dog in this fight – your family even less so. Think carefully before you play your next move.'

Even after all Ben had been through, it was tempting. The door was right there. He could get up, leave this behind – all this kingmaking and conspiracy, poison and high politics, bloodshed and betrayal. He could let history run its course, and slip back into obscurity, where he belonged.

But he had come too far to turn back now. And before the resolution had even formed in his head and heart, he looked at Zofia and gave her a steely nod.

'*Play*,' he said.

Zofia smiled: 'Brave man.'

Radimir dealt two cards for Mavros, two for Zofia – both face down.

Mavros rapped the table once. Zofia mirrored him. *Hold*. Radimir turned over their cards.

Mavros: Three of Diamonds and Five of Hearts. *Eight*.

Zofia: Six of Diamonds and Two of Clubs. *Eight*.

A tie.

Mavros clapped his hands in delight. 'What delicious symmetry!' he said, rising to his feet. 'Then the game must go on. And may the best man win.'

He signalled for Yusuf Madhat Pasha and Khalil to follow. The Chief Inspector flashed his revolver at Ben. The next time they crossed paths, he would not have such good fortune.

'You have left your winnings from our first round, Prince Mavros,' Zofia said.

'Keep it! I spend more on my horses.'

As soon as Mavros opened the doors, the bashi-bazouks filtered back into the casino. The Greeks circled Mavros, Yusuf Madhat Pasha and Khalil, and escorted them out of the Pierrot – leaving in their wake a crowd of unnerved guests, sobered by the violence of this intrusion.

Ben let out a sigh of relief. Zofia drained the rest of her Veuve Clicquot. 'I told you he's an arse.'

21

An Immodest Proposal

News of the explosion on Büyükada rocked Constantinople. It had started a wildfire so enormous that it could be seen fifteen miles away on the mainland. Nobody was allowed near the island other than the police and firefighters who had been arriving by boat in their droves.

When Shoshanna read about it in the papers the following morning, she knew that Ben's plan had gone awry. The last time she had spoken to him, he was preparing to sail to Büyükada with Ismail in search of the *Boethius*. All being well, they should have been in Constantinople by daybreak. But she had heard nothing.

Still, she held out hope, speculating that it might take them the day to make their way back. So she busied herself around the estate, reading and replying to her correspondence, whiling away the hours with household distractions as morning became afternoon and afternoon became evening.

Nobody turned up. She sent Eydir to the Tatar camp under cover of darkness. But he returned empty-handed: the Tatars at New Crimea had no information and were equally stumped. The police had reported no fatalities. The house in which the explosion had taken place was an abandoned property – its ownership was under investigation and that process could take months. Ben and Ismail had vanished. Which meant one of three things: either the police were covering something up; or they had escaped and were in hiding; or they had been burnt to a crisp.

Two days after the explosion, Shoshanna was driven to Kuzguncuk – a picturesque colony on the shores of the Bosporus, popular among wealthy Jews. She had been invited for lunch by her suitor Jacob, at the waterfront pavilion that his father had bought and renovated over the summer. They sat under a pergola on the terrace, shaded from the autumn sun as Jacob wittered on about his family's coal mines down south in Manisa and Mugla, pausing only to pour Shoshanna tea and offer her another slice of halvah.

Shoshanna hardly felt present. Dread gnawed at her gut – a fear that everything they had been working towards over the past month had, quite literally, gone up in smoke. That she had sent the two people she trusted most in this enterprise to their deaths. She was being slowly suffocated, with nobody to talk to and no way out.

'Strange to think,' Jacob opined, oblivious to her turmoil, 'these trinkets, the silverware, the fine clothes, the carriages, the properties – all of it comes from the most menial job in the world: *digging*. And yet, through the alchemy of commerce, it allows us to live like this. I would be lying if I said that it doesn't confound me from time to time…'

Shoshanna glanced over her shoulder to the entrance of the terrace. Their chaperone was standing in the doorway, back turned.

Jacob set down his tea.

'Might I ask you something, Shoshanna?'

'Please, Jacob.'

'Do you often think about the future?'

Shoshanna was about to brush Jacob off with a casual joke. But he raised a finger – 'It's a serious question.'

'Always,' she said.

'And what do you see?'

She tried to find something particular that she could hold up to him like the cutlery, the teapot, the ores extracted from his family mines. But nothing took shape. 'I don't know. It's like... the ocean. Vast and unpredictable. Once upon a time, I was convinced that I could chart a course through it. But that was a childish notion. None of us can. It's a force beyond our control.'

Jacob looked flummoxed. 'It doesn't *have* to be that way, you know.'

'How do you mean?'

'You don't have to look with despair at what lies ahead. I know what tragedies have befallen you and your family, and I have the utmost admiration for your resilience in the face of adversity. But I swear to you: even if the ship is sinking, the journey is not over. There is a way for us to sail this sea together.'

Jacob reached over and took her hand. It was the first time that he had ever touched her.

'You are not alone, Shoshanna. The world may disparage your father's memory, it may disdain the Carmino name. You could give them incontrovertible proof of your father's innocence and still they would disbelieve you – because they would rather blame Jews like us than countenance their own prejudice. But your future does not lie out there. It lies with our community. And, if I had the honour… with me.'

She tensed up. 'What are you trying to say, Jacob?'

'Shoshanna,' he replied, 'I should like to marry you.'

She had known this was coming from the moment Jacob offered her that last slice of halvah. But hearing the words felt unreal. She had played out this scene a thousand times in her imagination – embellished it every which way from a safe distance, until she had become the author of her own marriage proposal. But this submission by her gauche suitor fell woefully short.

'Your family is very fond of mine, and mine of yours,' Jacob pressed. 'We come from the same echelon of society, so we need not worry about the awkwardness of any financial disparity. You and I certainly like each other…'

He looked at Shoshanna expectantly. She gave him an ambivalent nod. It was enough for Jacob.

'We will be stronger together. The decline in Carmino stock can be reversed through our union. I believe, on every level, it makes perfect sense.'

'Have you spoken to my mother?'

'She gave her blessing, as did your uncles.' Then the ace up his sleeve: 'And before his passing, your father voiced his approval.'

Shoshanna was aware that whatever she said next would alter the course of her life. And yet every time she came close to replying, the words deserted her. 'Jacob… I need to think…' she said carefully.

Jacob looked momentarily dispirited but raised his hands in a gesture of appeasement. 'Of course. I wouldn't expect you to have an immediate answer. Talk to your mother and take as many hours or days as you need. We have our entire lives to be together!'

After lunch, Eydir drove Shoshanna back to the Carmino estate. She was still digesting Jacob's proposal. Even though she had known from the start what his intentions were, the timing had caught her off-guard.

She had absolutely no reason in her heart to refuse him. He was, as he had always been, a decent proposition. He was right: everything about their union made perfect sense. It was a clever match for both families. He was not even bad to look at.

And yet, every time she came close to accepting his offer, something made her shy away. As a planet orbits a star, she circled that word 'yes' – but drew no closer to it. And the further she trundled away from Kuzguncuk, the more distant Jacob became in her mind – and all she could think of as she gazed forlornly out the window was Ben. Whether he was alive, wounded, captured. Whether he needed her help. Whether he would find his way back to her.

The carriage suddenly ground to a halt. She heard Eydir calm the horses: 'Woah, easy! What are you doing there?'

In the middle of the road, blocking the path to Beykoz, was a boy on a mule. He looked no more than fifteen, and even though he was out in the sticks he was dressed like a young gent, in a wool twill suit and D'Orsay beaverkin.

As soon as Shoshanna's head emerged from the carriage window, the young dandy doffed his hat and dismounted his mule: 'Afternoon, boss!'

She squinted against the sunlight. She knew that face...

'Ismail!'

He ran to her side of the carriage. She had never seen him so coiffed and freshened up: clean as a whistle, smelling of Floris of London soap. 'Where have you been?!'

'Well, since this morning I've been following you and waiting for the right moment. It's too risky to meet at the estate for now.'

'Is Mr Canaan alright?'

'Beef Wellington? He's fine. We were well out of there by the time the mansion exploded and the island went up in flames.'

Shoshanna breathed a sigh of relief. Ismail lowered his voice.

'Listen, we have to be quick, and I can't say much. Mr Canaan and I are being held at the Hôtel Pierrot by the Contessa.'

'You mean... Zofia Radozsesky? *That* Contessa?'

'That's the one. Say what you like: that woman knows how to live! Never been so pampered in my life. Mr Canaan is not allowed to leave – too many people want him dead. So she sent me out to find you.'

'What does she want with me?'

'No idea. All I know is, something huge is in the offing. And Mr Canaan has vouched for you.' He placed a card in her pocket and whispered in her ear, 'Nine o'clock tonight at the Pierrot. Don't be late!'

And with that, he mounted his mule and took off south, in the direction of Constantinople. Shoshanna removed the item that Ismail had slipped her: it was a playing card – the Joker. And written on the back were the words: *TICK TOCK*.

Shoshanna had never met the Contessa, but the woman's reputation preceded her. An insatiable political animal who had spent years in Constantinople building a network of mysterious alliances, hobnobbing with high society by day and carousing with subversives by night. A collector of dirty secrets, which she used as ammunition on the battlefield of diplomacy and upper-class intrigue. An exile from her own nation: *the lost Queen of Poland*, as she was sometimes called. And, if that were not enough, a notorious devourer of young men.

God knew what she wanted with Ben, let alone Shoshanna. But if he was a prisoner at the Pierrot, and if Ismail was telling the truth about something momentous being on the horizon, then Shoshanna had little choice but to go and find out for herself.

She arrived at the Pierrot that night at the appointed hour and instructed Eydir to wait outside in the carriage. Dinner service was hardly over and already drunken couples were sprawled on divans around the lobby. Music echoed from the main hall – a band playing a spirited *varsovienne* based on an old Polish folk tune – accompanied by the lively stomping of dancers.

She introduced herself at reception and handed over the playing card. 'I've come to see the Contessa.'

The receptionist held the card to the lamplight and ran his index finger over a semi-translucent code printed in the corner. 'Mr Murad will be with you shortly. Please take a seat.'

A bellboy was sent hurrying upstairs. He returned a few minutes later with a bashi-bazouk, a bear of a man who came striding across the lobby towards Shoshanna.

He gave her a chivalrous bow: 'Radimir Murad,' he declared. 'Do I have the pleasure of talking to Mademoiselle Carmino?'

'You do indeed.'

'Excellent. Come with me, please.'

He led her upstairs, to the top floor: a series of interlinked suites, dressing rooms, salons and bedrooms forming the

Contessa's private apartments. They were teeming with bashi-bazouks, at least two in every room, seemingly at ease – though the sabres and guns on their hips suggested otherwise.

Radimir took her into Zofia's dining room. It was in a lavish rococo style, reminiscent of Versailles before the Revolution: paintings of exuberant *fêtes gallants* in gilded bronze frames, furniture richly ornamented with undulating curves in the shape of acanthus leaves and cherubs, and a long alder-wood dining table, shining from a fine Chinese lacquer and lined with vases of particoloured roses.

The Contessa was sitting at the head of the table, with a leatherbound file in front of her. And to Zofia's left, rising to his feet as Shoshanna entered, was Ben.

They locked eyes across the room. Shoshanna's breath caught in her throat. Like Ismail, he was well-dressed – Zofia had looked after him in that regard. But the dark circles under his eyes and his pale cheeks betrayed him. He looked exhausted, as though he had barely slept these past few days.

'Mr Canaan,' she said, with the slightest quiver in her voice.

He came right up to her and extended a hand. She gripped it tight.

'Mademoiselle Carmino.'

It was all he said. But she felt his relief – a moment of subdued tenderness, carefully disguised as Zofia scrutinised them from her perch at the head of the table.

'I take care of my guests, Mademoiselle Carmino,' Zofia said.

Shoshanna looked askance at her. 'That's an odd way to describe someone who isn't permitted to leave. Isn't the word "hostage"?'

'I don't think Mr Canaan would be too desirous of leaving if he had the choice. Constantinople has become a firing alley, with his pretty head as the target.'

'Come,' Ben said to Shoshanna. 'We have a lot to discuss…'

He sat her down and walked her through everything that had happened – from his excursion to Büyükada and the discovery of the laboratory, to his escape from the White Death with Radimir's help, to their confrontation with Mavros at the baccarat table. At last, he laid bare the truth:

'We've cracked the case of the White Death murders. It's a coup. An attempt by the Russian Empire to bring down the Sultanate and destroy the Ottoman Empire from within. The killings were carried out by assassins working for the intelligence arm of the Russians, known as the Third Section. The man we've been pursuing and Marta Mavros were both Third Section operatives, and Prince Mavros has been collaborating with them all along.

'The first victim, Ahmed, was murdered so that he could be replaced by Mehmet and his mother Shevkayir, who would serve as regent in the event of the Sultan's death as puppets of the Russians. When your father became suspicious and threatened to reveal the plot, they killed him too. Mavros took his place as the Sultan's right-hand man and, with the help of Yusuf Madhat Pasha, he has been keeping the Sultan in the dark about the conspiracy. Sir Lawrence Thorsbury and Heathcote were killed because they knew too much, and Marta because she became disillusioned with the Third Section and shared government intelligence with the Contessa. Now the Russians are about to play their hand: *kill the Sultan – win the war.*'

Shoshanna remained tight-lipped all the while. It was a strange feeling, listening to him talk – so different from how she felt listening to Jacob's proposal. He was giving her the one thing that she had been hankering after, ever since her father died: *the truth*. She had long imagined the vindication, the satisfaction, of knowing for sure that he was innocent.

But there was no pleasure in it. Only regret. A sad sense of what might have been – gazing at the untravelled road of a different life, where he was still alive and things were so much simpler. Now the future of the Empire lay in their hands. And yet, however high the stakes, it did nothing to diminish the heartbreak and cruelty of her father's death. He was a pawn sacrificed in a game of chess that none of them had ever asked to play.

She sat in silence as they finished their account. Ben laid a sympathetic hand on her arm.

'I'm sorry, Shoshanna.'

'Why are you sorry?' she murmured. 'You did your job. A hundred pounds well earned.'

'Except,' Zofia said, 'it is far from over. The Russians launch their coup on the twelfth of November. A mere ten days from now. And if they pull it off, we lose our last buffer against their conquest of Asia Minor. Who knows what they would seize next – the Holy Lands, the Arabian Peninsula, North Africa, the Balkans…'

'And I suppose you have a plan to stop them, do you?'

Shoshanna was being sarcastic. But neither Zofia nor Ben was laughing. Zofia held up the leatherbound file and raised an eyebrow.

'As a matter of fact… I do. And I must say, I think it's rather ingenious – with just the right amount of cunning.'

Shoshanna looked at Ben. His hands were interlocked on the tabletop and he was avoiding eye contact.

Shoshanna turned on Zofia furiously.

'You've already roped him into this, haven't you?'

Ben held his tongue. Zofia was about to respond, but Shoshanna cut her off.

'How dare you! This isn't his battle. He never signed up for whatever nefarious scheme you're planning!'

'I haven't even told you what it *is* yet!'

'*Let him go.* None of this is his fault – if anything I put him up to it, I persuaded him to investigate the White Death—'

'I agreed of my own volition,' Ben said firmly.

He was wearing an expression that she had never seen before: grave and resolute.

'I've spent my whole life running from my responsibilities,' Ben continued, 'lost in distractions and deceptions. Lying to the people who trusted me, and trusting people who didn't care for me. I was selfish. I let people suffer so that I could have an easy time. I can't do that anymore, Shoshanna. There were dozens of bodies in that laboratory – human beings reduced to test subjects. For what? To perfect a poison? And then there was Ahmed, and Thorsbury, and Marta, and Heathcote, and your father… If I run for the hills to save my own skin like a good-for-nothing, they'll have died in vain. And in the fullness of time, countless others will join them – every Ottoman subject that the Russians want to erase in the name of their church, their Tsar, their grand designs. Everything around us will crumble to the ground and nothing will be left – nothing but rubble and roubles. Countess Radozsesky is right: this is my fight. Not because I have something to lose, but because *they need me* and I'm in a position to do something about it. I'm not shutting my eyes and ears to this one. It's not a question of choice – it's a question of duty.'

There was no quipping, no mockery, no disguise. The world seemed to stop turning as he spoke.

Zofia, for all her cynicism, was stirred. 'Bravo! I couldn't have put it better myself.'

She turned to Shoshanna and slid the file across the table, into her hands.

'Allow me to make an *immodest* proposal. I didn't conscript Mr Canaan into my little enterprise because I'm a sadist. Sure, I have a small army of wild bandits at my disposal, but none of them will quite do for the task at hand. I need someone of Mr Canaan's age, disposition, description, profile, skill set and, most importantly, motivation. But there is a fly in the ointment. For the operation to be a success, he will need a companion – a female companion, to be exact. Someone we can trust. Someone of a similar age and… *motivation*. Someone who is aware of the Russian plot and might be invested in bringing them down…'

Shoshanna had been through too many proposals today to be any under any illusion as to what Zofia was driving at.

'You want me,' Shoshanna said.

'Well, that depends,' Zofia replied, snapping her fingers at one of the bashi-bazouks, who hurried out. 'Do you want to save the Empire? To redeem your father's name and reputation? To take back what has been stolen from your family?'

The bashi-bazouk returned with a bottle of Château Lafite and popped the cork, three glasses at the ready.

'If I say no?' Shoshanna asked.

'Mr Canaan will have to go it alone.'

Ben shook his head adamantly. 'You don't have to say yes, Shoshanna.'

Zofia poured wine into each of the three glasses. She placed one in front of Ben, one in front of Shoshanna, and reclined like a feline Venus.

Shoshanna made to open the file, but Zofia stopped her with a tut. 'If you open that file, I will take it as an irrevocable agreement. And I mean *irrevocable*.'

Ben had taken the base of his wineglass and was twirling it restlessly.

'Is it dangerous?' Shoshanna asked.

'Reasonably,' Zofia replied, her smile slowly broadening. 'Covert, of course: if we go in all guns blazing, the Russians will retreat into the shadows and strike when we least expect it. But if we come away with it, we can reverse everything that the White Death has done. An end to the murders. Mavros exposed for the backstabbing traitor that he is. The Sultan's favour regained. The tide of the Crimean War turned. In a word: *victory*. But you must decide quickly, Mademoiselle Carmino – time is running short.'

Shoshanna thought back to Jacob's words under the pergola that afternoon. It seemed like a lifetime ago. A proposal that offered safety and superficial comfort. A set of blinkers for her to wear like a horse on parade, blinding her to the nasty truths of the world that lay on the periphery of her life. A proposal that would shackle her to tradition and routine. A decent life with a decent boy. Always wondering about that untravelled road – a road that Ben would be travelling alone.

Without hesitation, Shoshanna opened the file.

Zofia held out her glass to clink with Ben and Shoshanna.

'Let's get started, shall we?'

22

The Tannhaüser Overture

'What in hell do they call this confounded affair anyway?!'

Arabella Clyde was not listening to her husband. She was mesmerised by her own reflection in the mirror of her jewellery cabinet. Her dark hair was moulded with pomade into pompadour waves. *Crème celeste* lent a ruddy glow to her ivory complexion. Draped around her neck was a distinctive bright-yellow, teardrop-shaped gem: the Kapstad Diamond – a prized family heirloom.

Horace Clyde huffed as he buttoned up his dinner suit. He was standing by the window of their Imperial Suite in the Hôtel Pierrot, one hand tucked into his jacket like an ersatz Napoleon. He could see the waterfront of the Bosporus from up here: Dolmabahçe Palace – the Sultan's newest seraglio and tonight's destination – shimmering in the early evening light of the setting sun.

'I said,' he fumed, 'what do they *call* this confounded affair?!'

Arabella sighed. Horace was beginning to irritate her. 'It's called a *bay-ram*.'

'A *bay-ram*?' he scoffed.

'Y'aint old enough to be acting deaf, sugar plum! It's just their word for a *ball*.'

'I ain't deaf, I just don't like it. If I'm to be cavorting and canoodling through the night, I should prefer to do it on Virginia soil.'

'There will be no cavorting or canoodling with yours truly if you keep on with this bellyaching!' Arabella sashayed past him to retrieve her Venetian Carnival mask from the bedside table: a *Gnaga* cat-mask dappled black and gold.

'Ain't the tune you sang when we were courtin',' Horace said gruffly.

'We're *married* now, Horace, did you not receive the memorandum?'

'Yes, as of about a month. But when did you decide to turn into Captain-goddamn-Ahab?'

'Ever since you started behavin' like a Moby-goddamn-Dick! And that ain't no way to speak to your beloved! My daddy has paid top dollar for this honeymoon. So *bee-have* and tell me I'm pretty.'

Horace looked like he was chewing a wasp. 'My, ain't you pretty.'

'And did I happen to mention,' she purred, donning her mask and curling her arms round his neck, 'that my daddy hired one of the private boxes in the Sultan's palace just for me and you?'

'No, you did not…'

She slipped Horace's mask over his face – leaving only their cheeks and lips exposed – and kissed him full on the mouth. He shuddered, unsure whether to be annoyed or aroused.

'Perks of marrying an heiress!' Arabella giggled.

They were interrupted by four heavy thuds at the door. Horace reluctantly pulled himself away from Arabella. 'And here I was about to be harpooned!'

He opened the door and came face to face with two tall turbaned men. One of them seemed familiar, with a tobacco-stained moustache, a bronze complexion, and bright blue eyes. It was the Contessa's bruiser. What was his name again?

'Ah, it's you... Radley!' Horace said impatiently. 'Time for our carriage to Dolmabahçe, is it, boy?'

The bruiser grabbed Horace by his necktie. 'Change of plan.'

Arabella screamed as the other bruiser picked her up and carried her out the suite. 'You're ruining my cosmetics, you raggedy band of backward savages!'

Horace kicked out in vain. 'Just wait until my father-in-law *the venerable Mr Jedediah Kapstad* hears about this, Radley—'

The bruiser silenced him with a boot to the seat of his trousers. 'It's Radimir, *boy*.'

They dragged the newlyweds upstairs to Zofia's apartments. The Contessa was waiting for them in her study, knocking back a shot of neat vodka. Standing to one side, watching in silence, was a swarthy Israelite and his female companion of about the same age.

'Countess Radozsesky!' Horace bellowed, glaring at Radimir, 'I demand an explanation – and satisfaction!'

'You'll be getting neither,' Zofia said. 'I'm sure you were very excited to be attending the Sultan's annual *bayram*. It is one of the world's most exclusive parties, after all, and nothing could possibly deter our dear Emperor from hosting it – not even war. But I'm afraid your tickets are being put to much better use.'

Arabella's despair at her wrecked makeup turned to fury. 'Do you realise what my daddy had to do in order to secure an invitation—'

'I am well aware, Mrs Clyde. Even I could not obtain one. However, I can assure you that this is for the greater good. Besides, what your "daddy" doesn't know can't hurt him. Ah! That reminds me...'

She approached Arabella and removed the Kapstad Diamond. Arabella let out a gasp as Zofia went over to the other young woman and clipped the jewel around her neck.

'Evil hellspawn!' Arabella wailed. 'The value of that gem is incalculable—'

'If you so much as scratch that diamond,' Horace interjected, 'I swear I'll gut this whole place!'

'Fear not: you'll get it back perfectly unscathed! Radimir, show them to their seats for tonight's entertainment. Good evening, Mr and Mrs Clyde!'

Radimir escorted the couple out the study and into the living room, where they were held at gunpoint on one of Zofia's divans. Zofia turned with a mischievous grin to the pair standing at her side: 'And a very good evening to you, Mr and Mrs Clyde...'

Ben had been staring for most of their exchange at the Kapstad Diamond. One fragment of it would make him the richest fellow in Whitechapel.

'That's a lot of carats...' he murmured.

Even Shoshanna, who had seen her fair share of jewellery, was astonished. 'Is it really wise to be flashing this thing about?'

'It is *essential*, my dear,' Zofia replied. 'Nobody will question you when they see that monstrosity on display. Just try not to lose it, will you? I wouldn't put it past her old man to sue me over that rock. And to be honest, they probably *could* gut this place…'

Radimir handed them the assets for their infiltration. The Clydes' international pass-cards, complete with Christian names, dates of birth, residence (Ithaca Plantation, Virginia), and their reason for travelling to Constantinople. Their masks, per the ball's dress code. A wax-sealed invitation to the *bayram* – a honeymoon gift from the bride's father.

'That covers the "bureaucracy",' Zofia said. 'What about the rest?'

Shoshanna patted her broad hoop-skirt crinoline: 'The gun is hidden in here.'

'Good. They may pat Mr Canaan down, but they'll never risk offending you. Much too prudish.'

Ben reached into his jacket pocket and removed a soft-cased brown rubber ball, about the size of an orange. 'And this… What did you call it? *White phosphorous?*'

'Indeed! An inspired invention by a rather clever countryman of yours, Mr Canaan. Throw it as hard as you can against a solid surface and – *poof!* A smoke bomb, he calls it. May come in handy if you need to beat a hasty retreat.'

They took the manual elevator down to the ground floor of the Pierrot and mounted the carriage waiting outside. It was a nervy trip to Dolmabahçe. Ben and Shoshanna barely exchanged a word. They preferred instead to look out the window at the city as it passed by, girding themselves for the task ahead. All around them, the hard-working subjects of the Sultan were going about their lives as they would on any late autumn evening, in blissful ignorance of the catastrophe that was looming.

Ben could see himself among these people. Like them, he used to gaze up at nameless luminaries in their carriages, speeding past him as he toiled in the dust. Yet the East End now seemed to belong to another world, and his family felt so far away – like figures painted on the canvas of a dream.

They joined a queue of carriages winding up to the entrance of Dolmabahçe Palace, the *Saltanat Kapısı*. Mansure Guards stood at the gate, vetting entry to the palace. Ben produced their identity papers.

'Right,' he said. 'Let's hope my American accent is convincing!'

Shoshanna leant across and held Ben's hand.

'What are you doing?' Ben said.

'Keeping up appearances,' Shoshanna said matter-of-factly. 'We are husband and wife, after all.'

It came their turn. They rolled down the window and Ben handed over their papers, along with the invitation. As the Mansures waved them through, he glanced up at the clocktower that loomed over the *Saltanat Kapısı*: almost six-thirty.

Sultan Abdulmejid stood alone in the Imperial Box, staring at the pocket-watch in his white-gloved right hand, as the seconds ticked down. The curtains were drawn and the box was filled with shadow. On the other side of the curtains, orchestral strings hurtled through a fast-paced *galop*. The chandelier above him vibrated with the groundswell of three hundred dancers.

Six-thirty. He nodded to his two bodyguards at the back of the box. They tugged a pair of velvet cords and the curtains were thrust open. Light flooded into the box, illuminating the

Sultan's vulpine face and reddish beard. He straightened his back, held his chin high and strode to the balcony.

As he came into view, the Great Hall of Dolmabahçe Palace erupted in deafening applause. He extended a hand, as though holding the audience in his palm – as he had done so many times since he first assumed the throne at the tender age of sixteen. Now he was a more sober man, thirty-one years old, and a father. His conscience weighed more heavily on him these days. Only recently he had returned from a state visit to the Danubian Principalities – won back from the Russians, but left in a state of ruin, the region decimated by disease and famine. Yet he had never tired of this exhilarating rush of power, and for a few tantalising moments, the war was forgotten.

He slowly closed his hand into a fist and the crowd fell silent.

He picked up a mask from the balustrade and placed it over his face. Then he turned. Dismissed the guards. Settled into his throne. And only when he was seated did the conductor raise his baton and the orchestra resumed the *galop*.

Abdulmejid watched from on high as the dancers span in concentric circles, and quietly took note. The number of guests weighed against the number of attendants. The canapés being carried to and fro. The tempo of the *galop* – a hundred and twenty beats per minute, to his ear: a well-judged allegro.

Everything, and everyone, was in its perfect place.

He faltered. Not quite everything. Next to him were two empty thrones: one for his chief consort, the other for his favoured *şehzade* – his chosen heir. The spot where Ahmed used to sit – the child that was always bursting with questions and observations, equally as comfortable in French and English as he was in Turkish and Arabic. A little vessel of life and light from the moment he was born to the moment he was taken. And now, for the first *bayram* in thirteen years, the Sultan sat on his own, without his true heir at his side.

'*Bonsoir, Seigneur.*'

Shevkayir was standing at the door to the box. Mehmet was with her – awkwardly toeing the ground and looking ungainly in his military tunic with its oversized epaulettes.

'Mehmet,' Abdulmejid said sternly, '*remets ton masque.*'

Mehmet put his mask back on as Shevkayir led him over to Abdulmejid. He bowed before his father. Abdulmejid only half-acknowledged him, gesturing with a cold nod for Mehmet to sit in the throne next to him.

Shevkayir laid a hand on Abdulmejid's shoulder, but he ignored it. 'Not in public,' he said.

Shevkayir took the throne next to Mehmet. Father, mother and son sitting in silence, faces hidden from the world and from each other.

'What do you think, Mehmet,' Abdulmejid finally said, 'of the conductor's chosen tempo?'

'Tempo?' Mehmet sounded confused.

Abdulmejid rolled his eyes at Shevkayir. 'What are they teaching him all day?'

Shevkayir held her tongue. It was no secret that Abdulmejid did not approve of Mehmet – that he had only agreed to his selection as heir because of the unanimous recommendation of the Chief Eunuch and the harem advisers. Abdulmejid, after all, hardly knew his own offspring – he was too busy exercising his divine right to rule. So he was wont to follow the guidance of others more familiar with the *şehzades*. But Ahmed had been his favourite: 'My greatest piece of poetry,' he would often say.

God, she was sick of hearing about that boy. Ahmed the musician. Ahmed the archer. Ahmed the natural leader. And now Mehmet: treated by his own father like a block of wood, a sorry disappointment. Still, it would soon be over. And all Shevkayir needed to do was keep her mouth shut.

Abdulmejid studied Mehmet more closely. The boy was white as a sheet. 'What's the matter with him?'

'He must be tired,' Shevkayir said.

'If he's that tired, he should go to bed.'

'Don't worry – I'll take him when it's time.'

There was a knock at the door to the Imperial Box. The bodyguards entered with a visitor: Prince Alexander Mavros. The Greek prince was dressed in his finest tails, polished Hessian boots to the knees, the eagle-crest of the Mavros dynasty pinned to his chest. '*Bonsoir, Seigneur!*' he said deferentially.

Abdulmejid offered a royal hand. Mavros bowed to kiss the Sultan's ring. 'I wanted to pay my respects and wish you a splendid *bayram*, Your Imperial Highness – and a triumphant year ahead.'

'You are much too kind, Prince Mavros,' Abdulmejid replied cordially. 'How have you been coping?'

'Surviving,' Mavros said. 'Keeping busy! Is there ever rest for the wicked?'

'It has been a stressful time for all of us – especially with this war in Crimea. The uncertainty takes its toll.'

'How is our military campaign? I heard about the debacle at Balaklava.'

The Prince was overstepping the mark. 'That is a matter for my generals, Prince Mavros,' Abdulmejid said. 'But I thank you for your concern – and your steadfast support.'

Mavros concealed his displeasure with a ready smile. 'Well, this is an opportunity for Your Imperial Highness to have some respite! The war will still be there in the morning. Of that I am most certain.'

He glanced at Shevkayir. She had turned in her chair to look directly at him.

'*Bas kadin*,' he said with a bow.

Shevkayir looked to the floor and said nothing.

Mavros made his goodbyes and exited, flanked by the Sultan's bodyguards. He was greeted in the corridor by none other than Yusuf Madhat Pasha.

'Good evening, Chief Inspector.'

'Good evening, Prince Mavros. Is everything to your liking?'

'That remains to be seen!' Mavros said. 'After all, we have a long night ahead of us.'

Yusuf pulled the bodyguards close. 'When you hear *Tannhaüser*,' he whispered, 'you leave. Understood?'

The bodyguards nodded. Disobeying Yusuf was risky enough. But disobeying Yusuf *and* Prince Mavros? That was suicide.

Yusuf and Mavros descended the staircase to the floor below: a gallery circling the Great Hall, with doors at regular intervals leading into private boxes reserved for the wealthiest guests.

'Any sign of those foxes scurrying about the chicken-coop?' Mavros asked.

'Not yet. I'll keep my eyes peeled.'

They stopped outside Mavros' box. Mavros extended a hand. 'Well done, Chief Inspector. We'll be in the clear within the hour.'

'It's been a long time coming!' Yusuf said as he trudged off.

Mavros entered his box and went straight for the drinking cabinet, pouring himself a Napoleon cognac. Bottled thirty-three years ago in Rouillac, so the label swore, on the very day of Mavros' birth – procured by his father as a gift for the young Alexander to savour on a truly special occasion in later life. He could not have imagined a more appropriate evening for this tipple.

He looked out across the hall – at the dancers and the orchestra below – at the Sultan's box one storey above – and took a sip. Maybe it was the air, maybe it was the adrenaline, maybe it was the soil from which this amber nectar came. Whatever the reason, it was the best damn cognac he had ever tasted.

He raised his glass and looked over his shoulder: 'Chin-chin!'

At the back of his box, obscured by the shadows, was a man standing to attention with his hands behind his back. He was tall, dressed in black, and was wearing the hood-mask of the White Death.

'Ready for the fireworks?' Mavros asked.

The White Death did not respond.

Down below, the Chief Inspector was moseying his way through the crowd, towards the entrance of the Great Hall, where the Master of Ceremonies was admitting guests with pronouncements from a scroll.

'*Monsieur et Madame Horace Clyde, de Virginie!*'

Ben and Shoshanna entered to a smattering of applause from the partygoers hanging about the entrance. They were arm in arm, masked up and deep in conversation to ward off any overly inquisitive strangers.

Yusuf waddled past. His gaze briefly alighted on them, drawn to the stupendous diamond around Shoshanna's neck. She ignored him and sure enough, the Chief Inspector lumbered on, prowling the crowd.

They could see the Sultan from here: untouchable in the Imperial Box fifty feet up, with Shevkayir and Mehmet by his side.

'If I'm not mistaken,' Shoshanna said, 'I believe we have a box waiting for us up there. With a somewhat closer view of His Imperial Highness.'

'Indeed you're right! First things first…' Ben snatched two glasses of champagne from a passing waiter. 'Shall we? Nothing like a bit of Dutch courage.'

They downed the champagne – final confirmation that they were in this together and there was no turning back. They weaved across the dancefloor towards a private staircase leading out of the Great Hall, where an usher was waiting to guide them upstairs.

'Mr and Mrs Clyde,' he said as they entered the box. 'You are welcome to order any refreshments that you wish from the menu. May I recommend the oysters in cherry vinegar.'

Ben took his best stab at a Southern twang: 'Why, thank you very much, bucko! But my beautiful wife and I wish to remain undisturbed.'

'Of course, sir. And, permit me to say, your accent is most delightful!'

He bowed and closed the door. Once he was gone, Shoshanna snorted.

'"Bucko"?'

'Well, he fell for it, didn't he?'

They scanned the boxes. As Zofia had predicted, Mavros was in the box directly opposite, separated from them by the dancefloor. He was not alone. A waiter entered with a tray of oysters. In the shaft of light from the corridor outside, Ben caught sight of a man standing in the corner of Mavros' box – wearing that familiar hood-mask.

'He's right there…' Ben whispered.

'Hiding in plain sight,' Shoshanna murmured. 'The audacity!'

They took their seats. There was nothing to do now but wait. Shoshanna watched the dancers through her opera glasses. Ben slouched on the balustrade. The party rumbled on. And Mavros just sat there: one leg crossed over the other, sipping his cognac and slurping oysters. He had the air of a falcon that had already caught its prey and was playing with it before the feast.

As the *galop* reached an exuberant climax and the orchestra took a bow to the cheers of the crowd, the White Death silently exited Mavros' box.

It was time. 'I'll follow him,' Ben said. 'You keep an eye on Mavros.'

He made for the door.

'Aren't you forgetting something?' Shoshanna tutted.

He turned. She was gesturing to her crinoline. 'I don't exactly have the best mobility in this thing,' she said. 'You might need to…'

Ben knelt down before her. 'Didn't think I'd be getting down on one knee tonight, did you?'

With the utmost care, he reached under her skirt, tracing his fingertips up her leg until he reached the Webley Longspur, which was strapped to the inside of her thigh. He removed the gun and pocketed it. 'Let it not be said I don't know my way around a crinoline!'

Shoshanna turned bright red. 'You certainly do! Off you go. And… try not to die, will you, Mr Canaan?'

'Can't make any promises! But think of it this way: you'll be a hundred pounds richer if I do.'

Before Shoshanna could draw breath, Ben was out the door.

The conductor gave a final bow to his audience and turned to face his players with a smile. He raised his baton.

Clarinets, bassoons, French horns. A stately chorale. So heroic, yet so tender, that it hushed the hall at once. It was the noble refrain from Wagner's *Tannhaüser* overture – a call to the soul from a distant land.

Sultan Abdulmejid closed his eyes and allowed himself to be lifted up and swept away by it. The strings entered: rich cellos and warm violas in aching minor harmonies.

Shevkayir stirred: 'I'm taking Mehmet to bed. He's ready to collapse.'

Abdulmejid did not even open his eyes. 'If it pleases you.'

Shevkayir took Mehmet by the wrist. The boy barely had time to say 'Goodnight, Father—' before he was ferried away.

The corridor outside the Imperial Box was empty. Mehmet frowned. 'Where are the guards, Mama?'

'Hush!' Shevkayir said.

She led Mehmet to the west wing of the palace – a set of private chambers reserved exclusively for the *bas kadin* and the favourite *şehzade*. She ordered the attendants out and soon she was alone with her son.

'Listen to me very carefully, Mehmet,' Shevkayir said, taking him by the shoulders. 'You are to go to bed right now, do you understand?'

'What do you mean, Mama? I'm not even tired—'

'Mehmet! Listen to me. *Go to bed*. Shut your eyes and ears. You do not leave your chamber until the morning. I'm not asking you – I'm *telling* you.'

Mehmet looked at his mother in perplexity. 'Is something wrong?'

'On the contrary, my son. Everything will be fine. I made a vow that I would do anything to protect you. And this is the only way. Show no fear. Doubt does not befit a sultan.'

She looked up at the clock. It was nearly seven o'clock. *Any minute now…*

Out on the corridors of Dolmabahçe, Ben was tailing the White Death. He could hear the rich melody of *Tannhaüser* reverberating from the Great Hall. The Third Section's 'checkmate' was at hand.

He kept his distance, hugging the shadows as the White Death moved stealthily through the inner recesses of the palace, until they arrived in a library bathed in yellow moonlight.

The White Death came to a halt before an antique globe. What was he up to? Ben edged towards him and raised his Webley Longspur.

'Turn around!' he barked. 'I brought a gun this time.'

The White Death did not oblige.

'I said turn around!'

The White Death removed the hood-mask and turned to face Ben.

Standing before him was not the scarred man whom Ben had confronted in the laboratory on Büyükada – but Yusuf Madhat Pasha's deputy, Khalil Al-Moussawi.

Then came the cock of a hammer. And not from Ben's gun.

'Drop it, boy.'

It was the baritone drawl of the Chief Inspector.

Ben hung his head. They had smoked him out. He lowered the Webley Longspur to the floor and Khalil snatched it away.

'That wasn't so hard, was it?' Yusuf said. 'Now how about *you* turn around.'

Ben complied. Yusuf pressed the barrel of his gun to Ben's temple – the Chief Inspector's bloated face, his smug grin, sallow in the moonlight.

'So this is it,' Ben said. 'Killed by the fat man. Why waste a bullet when you could just sit on me?'

'No, Mr Canaan,' Yusuf chuckled. He came in close to get a good look at the boy – so close that Ben could see the pupils of his murky brown eyes contract. 'I'm going to do *much* worse than that.'

23

Death at Dolmabahçe

The crowd in the Great Hall was transfixed by the *Tannhaüser* overture. Its racing strings and thundering timpani resounded through the palace. The Sultan was swaying in time with the music. Mavros had polished off his oysters and was enjoying a cigarette as he watched patiently. Shoshanna was still in the Clydes' private box, looking from Mavros to the Sultan – alert to any sign of the Sultan's impending fate.

But nothing happened. Neither Ben nor the White Death was anywhere to be seen.

In the library, Yusuf was listening to the muffled reverberations of the orchestra with a smile. The Chief Inspector needed no watch – the music was his timer.

'Four and a half minutes until we cross the Rubicon, by my calculation,' he said to Ben, sucking through his teeth. 'Here's how it's going to work. Soon that pretentious racket will be over and Abdulmejid will be dispatched. But we will need a culprit for such a brutal killing. Perhaps a disgruntled Briton? A young hot-headed radical who resents the Ottomans for dragging his countrymen into war? A known fugitive, no less – already suspected of killing a high-ranking British attaché and absconding from the police when they caught him red-handed at the crime scene!'

'You might have some trouble selling that cock-and-bull story to the world,' Ben said. 'I've got my own people who can vouch for me.'

'You mean your new squeeze? Or the Tatar alley-rat? Or perhaps that saucy Polish hag who's taken you under her wing? They'll be brought down with you. And as for Mehmet, he's sufficiently dim and weak-willed to do exactly as he's told. So the great irony of all this, Mr Canaan, is that *you* will be remembered as the White Death – a serial killer whose legacy to the world will be a string of senseless murders. And the only fair punishment for taking the eye is, naturally, *the eye*. Death for death. Good luck arguing your case from six feet under. Meanwhile, I can take an early retirement – relax on a two-hundred-acre plot in Cappadocia bought with my not-so-humble winnings from this enterprise, toasting the sunset with a grappa and a roast dinner.'

'You're cheap,' Ben snorted. 'Is that all it took for you to sell your own people down the river?'

'You don't understand, do you, Mr Canaan? You're fighting the flood. The decline and fall of this decrepit Empire is inevitable. Someone will benefit. So it may as well be me and my faithful deputy. And do you know something?'

He grabbed Ben by the hair and drew him in.

'When you wear nice clothes, eat good food, live in a big house, dole out money to your friends and family, and say the things that people want to hear… you realise, nobody actually cares about the "truth". Just about who's doing the talking. That's history, boy. And you are an irrelevant footnote. I admit, you were wilier than most. But every pest is caught at some point. And when your time is up, in the end, *you never see it coming.*'

Ben lowered his hand into his jacket pocket.

'You know what, Chief Inspector?' Ben replied. 'For once, I completely agree with you.'

He closed his thumb and finger around the smoke bomb, drew it from his pocket and threw it to the ground as hard as he could. A shockwave rippled through the room: a pulse of hot air blowing them off their feet – sending books flying off shelves – filling the library with hot white mist.

Ben saw the shadow of the Chief Inspector, fumbling in the fog for his gun. He charged at him, tackled him to the ground, pinned him on his back and pummelled him with all his might. It was a blur: Ben's fists flying through the swirl of white phosphorous – blood dashing his knuckles – the Chief Inspector dropping his gun. Ben let go of him and he slumped to the ground, out cold.

The smoke was beginning to clear. He could see the door of the library straight ahead – a way back to the Great Hall – to the Sultan, before it was too late—

'Freeze!'

Ben spun round. It was Khalil, taking aim with Ben's Webley Longspur. Ben raised his hands. 'Khalil… Haven't we been here before?'

'Quiet. There's nowhere to jump this time.'

Ben could see that Khalil was scared. He had been the same once, when he did his first job for Lennie Glass. A sheep in wolf's clothing.

'You know full well this is wrong,' Ben said.

'Are you deaf?!' Khalil shouted.

Ben could hear the orchestra building and building. The sand in the hourglass was running out.

'I know why you're doing this,' Ben said. 'An easy payday, right? The good favour of the powers that be. It's probably worth more than any salary you'll ever make. But it's not worth what you're giving up by letting this happen. If you're caught, it's your head that will roll. If you get away with it, it's everyone else's.'

Khalil was shaking.

'You didn't become a gendarme for this,' Ben said, taking a step closer to the deputy. 'To betray your nation? You're no good to the Russians. They'll probably kill you as soon as this is over. One less loose end to worry about. They're using you – just like they used Mavros, Shevkayir, Mehmet, Marta…'

'It's too late.'

'It's not, I swear. Give me the gun. Let me stop this madness. And if we make it out alive, I promise I'll defend you.'

'I have to follow orders,' Khalil whispered.

'That's just an excuse for cowards. You have a choice, one that will define you forever, for better or for worse. But we're out of time. You have to make it now.'

The next moment felt like an eternity. *Tannhaüser* approaching its grand finale. Ben trapped before the barrel of a gun – Khalil trapped by the magnitude of his decision.

Finally, Khalil let out a tortured sigh and handed the Webley Longspur to Ben. His face was burning with shame.

Ben pocketed the weapon. 'You're a good man, Khalil.'

Khalil went over to the unconscious body of the Chief Inspector and cuffed him to the grille of a nearby fireplace. 'Not sure how well you know Wagner,' Khalil said grimly, 'but the coda has begun. It's two minutes long, and on the last note, the Sultan will meet his end.'

It was a splendid view from the rooftop of Dolmabahçe Palace. Galata Tower, about a mile south, rose from the alleys and warehouses by the Golden Horn – marked out in the night by flaming torches at its summit. A full moon hung in a cloudless sky, nightjars and sparrows swooping by. At the mouth of the Bosporus, where it met the Sea of Marmara, the Maiden's Tower was flashing at regular intervals – a distant lodestar on the dark surging waters. Pinpricks of firelight dotted the forested hinterlands to the north of Constantinople.

But the White Death was not interested in the view. After nearly a year in this city, he had grown weary of it. Its filthy lodging-houses, its incessant calls to prayer, its stray cats loitering in the nooks and crannies of mosques and palaces, left him indifferent. For him, there was no beauty here. Even their tongue, which he had learnt to speak as well as any native, gave him no pleasure.

He looked down through the glass roof of the Great Hall, at the crowds mesmerised by the orchestra and the conductor, who was waving his arms like a furious marionette. The echoes of the *Tannhaüser* overture surged up to him. It was loud enough to reach the streets of Beshiktash, to grace the ears of the lowly Ottoman subjects who had assembled to stare in awe at Dolmabahçe's impenetrable walls.

It was a majestic cue for this final job in Constantinople. The Sultan's favourite piece of music, so he was told. The last thing that Abdulmejid would ever hear.

He followed the harmonies closely, anticipating every modulation, suspension, the long arc of each phrase, waiting for the right moment.

There it was. Dignified horns marking the return of the *leitmotif*. The start of the coda. The beginning of the end.

He donned his mask, tightened his gloves and removed a glass panel. He slid one leg in, then the other, feet dangling over a ten-foot drop to the roof space below. From there, it was a clean run to the Sultan's box.

Just as he was about to make his move, he hesitated. A small dappled-brown sparrow had come to perch on the glass next to him.

It blinked at him curiously. He stared back. Neither of them dared move. It was almost as though that little bird had recognised him from the air and had picked him out from the multitude. He slowly reached out to touch it.

Then a blast from the brass sent vibrations through the glass – and the sparrow darted off into the night.

The White Death levered himself over the edge and dropped down to the gallery. He descended the stairs, onto the deserted corridor leading to the Sultan's private box. As planned, the coast was clear: the bodyguards had been relieved of their duties.

He approached the door of the Imperial Box. It was decorated with an ornate Arabic monogram – the *tughra* of Abdulmejid's father Mahmud II – proclaiming the legend, *Forever Victorious*.

The door was unlocked. He pushed it open to find Abdulmejid sitting on his throne, facing the Great Hall. The emperor was exposed, like a tortoise on its back. *Tannhaüser*'s fortissimo finale had him enraptured.

The White Death pulled at the velvet cord and the curtains snapped shut. The Great Hall disappeared from view. Abdulmejid spun round and locked eyes with the apparition silhouetted in the doorway.

'Who are you?' he asked in French. 'What are you doing here?'

The White Death closed the door. 'Don't you know who I am, *Seigneur*?'

'Remove your mask and I shall tell you.'

The White Death was silent.

Abdulmejid strode towards the White Death. 'How dare you! Guards!'

But his voice was drowned out by the music. The White Death grabbed him by the throat and shoved him back into his throne. 'Now, now,' he said. 'Let's not be rash.'

The Sultan tried to get up. This time the White Death slapped him hard in the face: a sharp *crack* with the back of his hand. The Sultan looked at the White Death, stupefied.

'If it's money you want…'

'I have no use for money.'

'A title then?'

'Baubles for the grave? No… There's nothing you can bargain with.' He removed a metal canister from the inside of his jacket – glowing with the red gas of the Scorpion's Kiss. 'Make your peace.'

The Sultan raised a conciliatory hand: 'Whichever government you work for…'

'This is no time for diplomacy,' the White Death said as he released the safety catch. 'You have precious little time left to live and an eternity to be dead. Life is a capricious maiden, *Seigneur*. She will desert you at the flick of a switch.'

'I am immortal,' Abdulmejid replied. 'Even after I am dead, people will remember my name. And you? You don't even have the courage to show your face.'

The White Death seemed amused by the Sultan's rejoinder. He removed his hood-mask. The Sultan recoiled at the sight of that hideous, scarred vision.

'I have ended the lives of all manner of people,' the White Death said, 'and they all die in precisely the same way: *in vain*. From hardened soldiers, to beautiful women... to innocent children, *Seigneur*.'

The shadow of doubt that had nagged the Sultan for months suddenly took shape. 'It was you...' he said. 'You killed my Ahmed.'

The White Death held the barrel over the Sultan's face. 'Don't worry: you'll see him soon enough.'

Tannhaüser soared to its celestial climax—

They were interrupted by a crash as the door to the Imperial Box was kicked open. Ben was standing in the open doorway. He raised the Webley Longspur, cocked back the hammer, and on the final ecstatic chord of the overture – *he pulled the trigger*.

The gunshot rang out across the Great Hall. The orchestra was abruptly cut short. Confused murmurs rippled through the crowds on the other side of the curtain – followed by cries of alarm.

The barrel of the Webley Longspur was smoking. Ben's ears were ringing from the discharge and he hardly felt his own breathing, as though in the act of pulling the trigger, he had left his own body.

The White Death was rooted to the spot. A slow trickle of blood crept from a wound in his belly, staining his shirt and dripping down to his boots. The canister slipped from his grasp and fell to the carpet. 'Oh…' he murmured with a strange banality, before collapsing to the floor.

The Sultan leapt to his feet. He was looking at Ben in utter bewilderment, his mouth hanging open. Ben collected himself and gestured to the door.

'Quickly, go! Get to safety.'

The Sultan did not need to be told twice. He bustled past Ben, only to stop in the doorway. 'Who are you?'

With all the adrenaline in his system, Ben almost forgot he was talking to a man who commanded thirty-five million subjects. 'My friends call me Benjy. Now go!'

The Sultan turned and ran off.

'You're welcome…' Ben muttered.

The White Death was lying still on his back. Blinking slowly. His breathing ragged. Ben stood right over him, the gun trembling in his hands.

He heard a *click*, then saw a flicker of movement below him. Before he could react, two explosions: a quickfire double-bang and a blow to the torso that knocked him back, as though struck by a gale-force wind.

At first, he felt nothing. Then a burning sensation spread from his chest up to his head. His shirt began to dampen, clinging to his skin as the blood came out in dark rivulets. He tried to move his arms and legs, but they refused to obey. He tried to take a deep breath, but his lungs would not let him. The next thing he knew, he was staring at the ceiling.

The White Death lugged himself to his feet, stooped and grimacing from the excruciating pain. 'I told you that you should have walked away,' he growled, dropping his pistol.

Ben coughed up a mouthful of blood. As the shock wore off, the numbness turned to searing heat and his heart felt like a balloon that was about to burst.

'It doesn't matter,' Ben said in a faint voice, 'I stopped you.'

From the Imperial Box, they could hear the trampling of feet: Mansures rushing upstairs from the Great Hall to apprehend the Sultan's attacker.

Ben smiled through the pain. 'Better think fast…'

The White Death looked around the box. The Sultan had escaped and would already be under the protection of his guards. Canaan was right. He had failed.

He knelt and retrieved the metal canister. Then he walked over to the curtains at the front of the box and yanked them apart. The Great Hall lay before him: the light shining on his scarred face as gasps erupted from the crowd.

He saw Mavros standing at the edge of his own box – white as a sheet, too stunned to move. A woman wearing a cat-mask, with a large diamond around her neck, was watching from the other side of the hall – one hand over her mouth in horror.

The White Death turned to look at Ben, his back to the Great Hall. He was smiling vacantly, as though this was one great relief.

'*Dl'ya Rodiny!*' he said in Russian.

He raised the canister, spinning the barrel round on his own face – and pulled the trigger. A spray of red gas shot from the barrel and shrouded his features. He took a deep breath, staring all the while at Ben.

The Scorpion's Kiss took effect instantly. His muscles contracted in a violent seizure. His breathing was cut short by an ugly choke. The colour rapidly drained from his flesh – his jaw locked – and the last hint of humanity was snuffed out as his eyes clouded a lifeless milky-grey.

The White Death toppled backwards, over the edge of the box, and crashed three storeys to the dancefloor. The guests dispersed as fluid began seeping from his corpse. Gasps turned to screams and several women fainted on the spot.

Ben dragged himself to his feet with his last ounce of energy and hauled himself to the balustrade. 'There's been an attempt on the Sultan's life!' he roared, pointing across the Great Hall, 'AND ALEXANDER MAVROS IS RESPONSIBLE!'

Every single person in the Great Hall turned to look up at the solitary figure of the Prince. Still he did not move. The man with the silver tongue, who had kept up an impeccable performance – who, in the words of an English barrister, was *anything to anyone* – was at a total loss for words.

It was the last thing Ben saw. A wave of exhaustion washed over him and he slumped onto the Sultan's throne, dipping in and out of consciousness. At that very moment, the Mansures burst into the Imperial Box and surrounded him. He closed his eyes and sank into a deep well. High above him, he could hear shouts for a doctor and pleas in broken English for him to stay awake.

He took a shallow breath – and everything fell away.

24

Ms Nightingale's Patient

It was a dazzling, clear-skied winter's day in early December, a month after the foiling of the Dolmabahçe Plot. A rumour was doing the rounds in the Selimiye Barracks, concerning a highly sensitive matter of national security, never spoken about in more than a whisper.

It could be heard among the bandaged soldiers recuperating in the courtyard: chain-smoking amputees recently returned from Crimea to recover from their battle-wounds. Nurses mouthed it to each other in the laundry as they folded fresh linen. Even the bed-bound patients still groggy from ether had cottoned onto the rumblings.

Nobody knew his name. Only his personal nurse – Ms Nightingale, recently arrived from London to run the military hospital – and the occasional well-to-do visitor whisked in under tight security had seen his face. Mansures had been guarding his door around the clock for the length of his stay.

But by noon the same line was on everyone's lips: *the Jew who had saved the Sultan's bacon was going home.*

Ben could not have cared less about all that tittle-tattle. He was in a deckchair on the private balcony of his top-floor room, wearing a dressing gown and slippers and enjoying one last hospital breakfast: a steaming feta omelette, rye toast, an almond croissant and a large cafetière of sweet black coffee.

There was a knock at the door. 'Busy!' he shouted between mouthfuls.

The door opened and he heard a female voice behind him: 'Is Detective Ben Canaan accepting visitors?'

It was Shoshanna. She was dressed for an occasion, in a white and blue floral blouse and a chiffon stole. Her hair was parted down the middle in elegant barley curls, topped with a silk capote bonnet.

'Afraid you'll have to come back later,' Ben replied. 'I'm convalescing after a frightful brush with death and I will need every available second to recover.' He popped the last of his croissant in his mouth. 'The doctors were very concerned.'

'Concerned you were never going to leave! Anyway, today you re-join the real world. What's more, I come bearing good news.' She took the deckchair next to him and held out a newspaper: the English edition of *Takvim-i Vekayi* – Constantinople's premier weekly.

DISGRACED PRINCE TO BE EXECUTED FOR TREASON

'Like father like son,' Ben said.

Alexander Mavros had finally met his comeuppance. Complicity in five 'White Death Murders' and one attempted assassination was, to quote a bobby from Ben's past, 'quite the charge sheet'. His pleas had little effect: the Imperial Tribunal was quick to give him the maximum penalty. Now the Prince was locked up in a military garrison on the outskirts of the city, in solitary confinement, as the fatal date neared. Not even his wealth could save him from having his head pruned by the Sultan's Gardener.

Yusuf Madhat Pasha was gone too. Life imprisonment in a penal colony on the plains below Mount Ararat. He tried to curry sympathy at the tribunal, showing up on crutches and claiming that he was suffering from pneumonia. It did little good: his associates were left desperately selling off his newly acquired two hundred acres in Cappadocia, his horses, his wine collection. But people in those parts were superstitious, and the auction was largely unattended. Now the Chief Inspector's early retirement was to be enjoyed in the company of the very men he had spent his life putting away. So much for that grappa in the sunset.

And with Yusuf's departure went numerous Mansures and halberdiers in the Sultan's retinue – the Chief Eunuch shipped back to Alexandria – and half the gendarmerie sacked. Overhaul was the word of the hour. A Russian infestation of this scale required a thorough spring clean.

Deputy Khalil Al-Moussawi was the only co-conspirator to make it out with both his head and livelihood intact. For his change of heart at the eleventh hour, his punishment was commuted to a hefty fine and demotion from the Chief Inspector's deputy to another run-of-the-mill gendarme waving carriages down Galata Bridge. But Khalil was the last to complain. After flirting with treason, he was thankful for a more mundane existence.

'And our delightful Contessa?' Ben asked.

Shoshanna turned over the page for him. 'Staying out of the limelight, as usual!'

There was a double-spread on Zofia Radozsesky: a conference that she headed up with reporters from *The New York Times*, *The Times* of London, and *Le Siècle* of Paris. Zofia had spun them all a convincing story – how she and her bashi-bazouks gathered intelligence on the impending assassination, infiltrated Dolmabahçe, and singlehandedly averted the plot. Zofia was doing what she loved most: lapping up attention like a cat with its head in a pail of milk. Meanwhile, Ben and Shoshanna's names had been scrubbed from the narrative.

Ben poured himself another coffee. Shoshanna noticed a shiny pink scar running five inches down his chest, just visible beneath his dressing gown and still raw from the extractive surgery.

'Does it hurt?' she asked.

'Not really,' he said. 'Besides, I got a good story out of it. Was your mother angry when she found out what we did?'

'At first, very much so. But I was able to talk her round, with some help from Uncle Gavriel – especially when it became clear what we had achieved.' Shoshanna paused, watching Ben as he sipped his coffee. 'She wanted to you to come over for a Friday night dinner.'

Ben gave her a puzzled look. 'I thought I wasn't strictly speaking welcome.'

'Things have changed. Think of it as a gesture of appreciation. After all, you did save the day – even if your methods were rather unorthodox!'

'What about your suitor? Word has it he proposed.'

'Who told you that?'

'Ismail said he heard something. He's been visiting me a few times a week. Brings me baklava and keeps me up to date.'

'That rascal! He can be so indiscreet.' Shoshanna shrugged. 'Well, to tell the truth… I'm still thinking about it. I daresay Jacob is not going anywhere.'

They caught each other's gaze for a moment.

'Right!' Shoshanna said abruptly, lifting Ben's breakfast tray off his lap. 'Time for the boot. We have a meeting to attend.'

Ben gulped down the dregs of his coffee, had a quick shave, changed into a suit, and strolled out with all his worldly belongings in his trusty knapsack. He was waved off by a group of adoring nurses and envious patients. Ben Canaan was back in business.

Eydir was waiting for them outside the Selimiye Barracks, at the helm of the Carminos' *kayik*. 'Where are we going?' Ben asked as they climbed aboard.

'Let's just say, it's one of your old haunts!'

An hour later, they arrived at Topkapı Palace: the same fortress that Ben had broken into with Ismail and Umer's help. Only now, he was waltzing through the front door – receiving a salute, no less, from the halberdiers at the Imperial Gate.

'Somewhat easier than last time!' he said.

They were met in the first courtyard by a phalanx of eunuchs, who waited obediently behind the Grand Vizier, the head of the Sultan's government. He was a solemn fifty-something bearded man in funereal attire, by the name of Mustafa Reshid.

'Mademoiselle Carmino,' he bowed, 'Mr Canaan. Welcome to Topkapı Palace. We are most grateful for your decision to accept the Sultan's invitation.'

'It is our privilege and our pleasure, Mustafa Reshid,' Shoshanna said. 'And we thank the Sultan for his generosity.'

Mustafa Reshid led them to the *Sofa-i Hümayun*, the innermost courtyard of Topkapı, past a grove of orange and lemon trees and across a bridge over a stream.

'I never tire of seeing someone step into Topkapı for the first time,' Mustafa Reshid said to Ben with a twinkle in his eye.

'Oh yes!' Ben replied, feigning wonderment. 'I never imagined I'd set foot in a place like this…'

They were taken to the doors of a pavilion in the middle of the gardens, surrounded by freshwater ponds. Dragonflies flitted across the surface of the water and hummingbirds hovered between the fig trees.

Mustafa Reshid pushed open the door to the pavilion.

'Avert your eyes,' he whispered.

They were ushered into a large octagonal reception hall, the walls patterned with turquoise Iznik tiles. They looked down at their feet.

Suddenly, a measured voice: 'Do raise your heads, please.'

The Sultan stood before them, in an impressive red brocade kaftan. He had risen from his throne on a dais in the middle of the hall and stood before them with his hands clasped. His head was held high. He was expecting a bow.

Shoshanna obliged with a well-practised curtsey and Ben gave a nervous bow. 'Your Imperial Highness,' Shoshanna added.

Abdulmejid nodded in approval. 'Mustafa Reshid: you may leave us.'

The Grand Vizier shuffled out while facing the Sultan, so as not to pay his ruler the disrespect of showing his back. The doors shut with a soft *click*. The Sultan beckoned for Ben and Shoshanna to join him in a seating area by the windows overlooking the gardens, where cushions had been laid around a low writing table.

'First of all,' Abdulmejid said, 'I owe you both a sincere thanks. Without you, I would be dead and the war effort in tatters.'

'We were happy to be of service, Your Highness,' Shoshanna said.

The Sultan looked questioningly at Ben.

'What's a few broken ribs between friends?' Ben said, smiling.

The emperor narrowed his eyes at Ben. Despite his naturally sombre demeanour, he seemed oddly charmed.

'Second of all,' he continued, 'you are both owed an unreserved apology. Mr Canaan, for being labelled a fugitive by our former Chief Inspector – whose motives, I understand, were severely compromised. Rest assured, in the new order of things, you are as free in the eyes of the Sultanate, and by extension the Empire, as any citizen.'

Then he turned to Shoshanna.

'Mademoiselle Carmino. It has been a difficult and tumultuous year. We have both lost people close to our hearts – your parent, my child. Though we have not seen each other in that intervening time, we have both been on the same journey as we contend with grief. You, however, have suffered something unique: the injustice of a false accusation against your father's name and your family as a whole. Not just any accusation, but one of treason. It is clear now that it was a fabrication, designed to cover up your father's murder, to disgrace the Carminos and to elevate the status of Prince Mavros. The bait was thrown and, I am ashamed to confess, I took it. Blinded by my sorrow, I allowed this unforgiveable calumny to take root. For that, I can only offer a profound apology and an exhortation for your indulgence.'

Shoshanna listened to every word of Abdulmejid's eloquent apology with a look both of sadness for what had happened, and of hope for what that extraordinary gesture might mean for her. When he was finished, she nodded with conviction, holding back a wellspring of feeling.

'I forgive you absolutely, Your Highness. It is not my place to judge, especially when you have suffered so greatly. Know that I look upon your suffering with the deepest sympathy, and always shall. I pray you may find peace.'

Abdulmejid seemed to withdraw into himself. 'It is no excuse. But it has been exceedingly hard to come to terms with Ahmed's passing. And knowing all the while that I nearly handed my throne to his killers. I failed him.'

'Where are they?' Shoshanna asked.

'Shevkayir and Mehmet?' The Sultan gave a careless shrug. 'They have been separated. Shevkayir is imprisoned, for now. Mehmet will be kept under close watch, though it seems he knew nothing of the plot. He will be sent somewhere far away. A military academy. Shevkayir will never see him again.'

'Did she confess?'

'She is not a Russian agent, if that is what you mean. Her motive, so she said, was "survival". Harem politics. The *kadins* jostle for supremacy. The winner takes the spoils, the loser is destroyed. That makes people desperate, and the Russians capitalised on it. They exploited her precarious position by offering her a way out – a lifeline for Mehmet that would take him to the very summit of power in this Empire.'

The Sultan shook his head bitterly.

'In my world,' he continued, 'this behaviour is to be expected. The promise of power tends to bring out the worst in people. They fight to the death to usurp me, thinking that once you become the Sultan, all your problems will be solved. But they are wrong.' The Sultan trailed off, not wanting to reveal any more.

Ben had always thought that men in positions of power – from the Sultan, to the Home Secretary, to the entitled son of the Earl of Northbridge – were free from the stresses and strains of the working man. But it was clear that for all his concubines and riches, servants and subjects, the Sultan did not know if he had one true friend in the world. The wider the circle of influence, the narrower the circle of trust.

'In any case,' the Sultan said, perking up, 'today marks a new beginning. And one must look forward, not back. So, thirdly, as a token of my gratitude, I offer you each a gift.'

He picked up a varnished wooden box that had been left next to his cushion, and placed it on the writing table between them.

'For you, Mr Canaan,' he said. He opened the box to reveal a gold pocket-watch, with two perfectly shaped diamond studs on either side of the clock-face. 'Since you saved me in the nick of time. The makers are very skilled – Messrs Patek and Philippe of Geneva.'

Ben could recall only one occasion when he had seen a Patek-Philippe up close. All those years ago at the Great Exhibition, of all places: a model just like this one. Back then, it was separated from him by a pane of glass. Now he held it in his hands as its new owner.

'Thank you, Your Highness.'

'Do take care of it,' the Sultan said, 'there are only five such models in the world. I believe your monarch owns one of them! And for you, Mademoiselle Carmino…'

He reached under the writing table and removed an illuminated Arabic scroll, which he carefully unfurled and presented to her.

'Written on this scroll is an edict from the Sublime Porte: an order of total restitution. Compensation for the property seized after your father's posthumous conviction, along with every asset that was claimed from your family that still subsists. The Carmino Family Bank may be no longer, but you will have the funds, the assets and most importantly the freedom to start afresh.' He slid the quill and inkpot over to her. 'Sign it, and tomorrow I will have it promulgated.'

Shoshanna took up the quill. She had nerves of steel, but the prospect of emancipation at her fingertips made even her tremble.

She was ready to sign. The quill was millimetres from the papyrus.

But something stopped her.

'I will sign this,' Shoshanna said, 'I promise. But may it be on one condition?'

Abdulmejid faltered. Nobody imposed conditions on this man, let alone when he was bestowing a favour.

'Pray tell,' he said.

'Show mercy on Shevkayir and Mehmet.'

Shoshanna could have knocked the Sultan over with the very feather she was holding. If she had been anyone else, Abdulmejid might well have torn up the order on the spot. But he was indebted to her, and it was enough to stay his hand – at least for the moment.

'They do not have to live in the harem,' Shoshanna continued. 'You never have to see them again. But if she sought merely to protect Mehmet – your son too, might I add – then please: *let them go*. Give them a small stipend. A roof over their heads, somewhere safe, where they can be together.'

Abdulmejid put his foot down. 'Grant beneficence to a woman complicit in Ahmed's murder? Who plotted my downfall under my very nose and threatened my dynasty and this great nation? Out of the question. I must make an example of them.'

'She turned on you because, even in your fold, she was not safe.'

'Do you honestly believe that the House of Osman is ever truly safe?'

Shoshanna spoke with total respect – but without fear, subservience or flattery. 'I know full well of the perils that come with a life such as yours. I am no royal, but my life is not completely dissimilar. The fact of the matter is this: your own wife, under your own roof, was driven to a heinous crime. She was not malicious, she was *desperate*. And the Russians exploited her desperation, because of their mistaken belief that you are nothing more than a barbarian. Prove them wrong, Your Highness. Be a husband, be a father, be a truly great leader – and, instead of pushing them down, lift them up. Give them the dignity that our times demand.'

Abdulmejid was astounded by Shoshanna's mettle. To talk so candidly to this king of kings – to risk her own freedom for what she believed to be right.

'Power is fickle, Mademoiselle Carmino,' Abdulmejid said. 'Only the strong survive. It is cruel, but it is life. I never had a choice in the matter.'

Shoshanna gave up. There was no convincing the man. Perhaps it would be best to simply sign the document and move on.

But it was Ben who intervened, with the care and incisiveness of a seasoned diplomat.

'Your Highness. Permit me if you will. I grew up in the East End ghetto of London. My father is a tailor. My grandfather is a refugee, who fled the massacres of the Jews when he was fourteen. Often we lament to have been born into this life of persecution. But the truth is, if my grandfather did not have a choice, he would have stayed in the *shtetl* and been slaughtered by Cossacks. If I did not have a choice, at this very moment I would be at Houndsditch boxing club, trading jabs with my friend Leo Pereira. And I definitely would not have been at the *bayram* of Dolmabahçe Palace to save your life. Every one of us, high and low, is trapped by the circumstances of our birth. But whether you are an emperor like yourself, or a Good-for-Nothing like me – *we can all choose.* Our lives are built on the choices that we make, not on that which was chosen for us.'

The Sultan considered Ben's words. This impudent boy who had no right to be here – and yet, here he was. A plot that had a snowball's chance in hell of being foiled – and yet, it was. Ultimatums that had no right to be issued – and yet, they were.

For a moment, it was as though the cage that Ben described, the one that had hemmed Abdulmejid in all his life, seemed to vanish – and the man long-buried beneath the accoutrements of power stepped forth.

'Very well,' he conceded. 'I will show mercy on Shevkayir and Mehmet. I give you my word.'

With this oath, Shoshanna signed the promulgation. Then Mustafa Reshid returned to ferry Ben and Shoshanna out of Topkapı. Before they left, the Sultan reached out to shake their hands – a gesture not typically made, let alone with a pair of commoners.

'Welcome back, Mademoiselle Carmino,' he said with a nod of appreciation.

As Ben and Shoshanna ventured across the garden, in the footsteps of the black-robed figure of Mustafa Reshid, Shoshanna breathed in the sweet smell of hyacinths, felt the crisp air on her cheeks, and reached out to squeeze Ben's hand.

'Thank you, Ben,' she whispered.

25

The British Ambassador

A week after Ben's meeting with the Sultan, he was summoned to the police station. The gendarmerie had a new Chief Inspector: Hasan Izzet, an old rival of Yusuf Madhat Pasha. During Yusuf's tenure, Hasan had been cast out to minor posts on the coast of Ottoman Tripolitania, far removed from Constantinople. But now Yusuf was disgraced and Hasan Izzet had been called in to replace him, in large part thanks to his reputation for being a strait-laced and conscientious inspector.

Ben arrived at Hasan's office at noon. He had taken over Yusuf's former ground-floor chambers. The room had an air of calm, orderly professionalism. A framed diploma from military college hung above his desk. Jars of tobacco leaves lined a shelf by the window. One of the walls was taken up with a large map of Tripolitania and the Eyalet of Tunis, where Hasan Izzet had lived for the best part of a decade.

Hasan had company. He was talking to a patrician-looking gentleman with a thin white combover, a bored expression on his face and the cross of the Order of the Garter pinned to his lapel. Hasan greeted Ben cordially, while his companion glowered with barely disguised contempt.

'Back in the land of the living, Mr Canaan,' Hasan said.

'Hell was fully booked, as it turned out.'

They shook hands. Hasan nodded in approval. 'Good firm grip. You've healed up nicely. As they say, whatever doesn't kill you…'

'…is still a bloody drag!' Ben grinned.

Hasan gestured to his companion. 'Mr Canaan, allow me to introduce to you to the British Ambassador.'

'Stratford de Redcliffe,' the Ambassador said sharply. 'How do you do, Mr Canaan? Or should I say, *Rupert Rogers?*'

Ben had been expecting the British to give him a telling-off at some point. He had always had a prickly relationship with authority figures, and the British establishment was no exception. He did not trust Redcliffe as far as he could see him.

'Mr Canaan will do.'

They sat around the table as coffee and marzipan were served. Hasan studied Ben through his round spectacles. The boy had the look of those journeymen confidence tricksters who would roam the plains of the Sahara: affable, but always scanning for an opening. They were on the same side – for now.

'How's your war going?' Ben asked the Ambassador.

'The war rages on,' Redcliffe replied. 'Seventy thousand of our men have circled the Russians in Sevastopol and dug in for the siege. A long winter lies ahead.'

'I thought they were coming back by Christmas.'

'If they were told otherwise, they would never have gone.'

Hasan seemed eager to change the subject. 'Congratulations are in order,' he said. 'If not for you, the plot against the Sultan would certainly have succeeded.'

Redcliffe was implacable. 'Though you acted without our authorisation.'

'I suppose Her Majesty's government had it all under control, did it?' Ben shot back.

'We had an excellent man in Heathcote—'

'*Had* being the operative word. He was looking less than excellent when I clapped eyes on him at the morgue.'

Redcliffe's nostrils flared. The insolence of this upstart! Hasan nudged him and the Ambassador reluctantly conceded the point. 'Very well,' he sighed. 'You did it, Canaan. Albeit by the skin of your teeth. But I have not come here to flatter your ego. I am on a tight schedule, so let us attack the matter head-on.'

Ben folded his arms over his chest. 'Go on then.'

'My personal view, as the representative of British interests in the Ottoman Empire, is that you should be locked up for your antics and the key thrown into the North Sea. However, the Cabinet does not share my opinion and, despite this messy affair, an executive order has been issued from the Earl of Aberdeen—'

'The Earl of who?'

'*The Prime Minister*, Mr Canaan. According to his executive order, you are to be pardoned and offered a ticket home at Her Majesty's expense. Post-haste.'

Ben frowned. Of course: home. The tenement on Whitechapel Road. The kitchen filled with steam. The stuffy workshop. The watercolours on the stairwell. The lonely attic-room. A place that now seemed to belong to another life.

'Does my family know where I am? Or what's happened?'

'Absolutely not,' Redcliffe said. 'This is a matter of international security. The only people who know of your involvement are the Cabinet, the Chief Inspector, the most senior members of the Sublime Porte, and myself. It is a condition of your return that you do not breathe a word to your family of what has gone on these past months.'

'They'll have questions.'

'Then you will have to conjure up answers, won't you? Unless you would prefer to try your luck with the Turks.'

Ben looked to Hasan for support. Hasan gave a sympathetic smile. 'Given all that Mr Canaan has done,' he said, 'I'm sure we Ottomans would be honoured to count him among our own.'

Redcliffe huffed in frustration. Why Ben was not leaping at the opportunity to travel *gratis* back to London was simply baffling to him. 'Then you must make up your mind, Mr Canaan – but I urge you not to tarry. Our offer stands for now, but politics is a fickle business, and the longer you leave it, the harder it will be to justify the olive branch that the Cabinet is extending to you.'

The Ambassador was out of time and patience. He checked his pocket-watch, abruptly rose to his feet and shook Hasan's hand, but did not bother with Ben. He was about to leave when Ben stopped him with a question:

'What about the Third Section, Ambassador?'

The mood shifted. Suddenly Redcliffe was no longer in such a hurry. He turned to Ben, keeping one hand on the doorknob.

'Like I said, Mr Canaan: *the war rages on*. What happens in respect of the Third Section is no longer your concern. Go back to London, stick to your own kind – and, most of all, do not blab. Your life shall depend on it.'

The door slammed shut behind him and Ben was left alone with a vaguely apologetic Hasan.

'I beg your pardon for Viscount de Redcliffe's bedside manner.'

'Trust me,' Ben said, 'I've been subjected to worse.'

Hasan went over to the shelf and unscrewed the lid of his tobacco jar. 'Fancy a smoke? These leaves are from the Syrian port of Latakia.'

'Why not?' Ben shrugged.

Hasan laid two meerschaum pipes and a box of matches on the table, packed the leaves into the first pipe, struck a match and circled the flame over the bowl. He took a few contented puffs and handed the pipe to Ben. Ben rolled the smoke in his mouth – spicy, resinous, a hint of vanilla.

'You're really not a detective?' Hasan mused.

'Not by training.'

'Remarkable! I must say: you are a natural. If you're content risking your life like this on a regular basis, you could have a luminous career. Then again, only those with a few loose screws would enjoy making a living from making enemies!'

Ben puffed on the meerschaum pipe and poured himself another coffee. 'It seems I'm good for something after all...'

The Carminos delivered on the Friday night dinner that Shoshanna had promised Ben. He arrived at the estate in a brougham buggy hired with six shillings of the hundred pounds that Shoshanna had paid him for his service. The place was transformed, all vestiges of neglect and gloom swept away. The rich aroma of *hamin* – a stew of slow-cooked beef, roast vegetables, garlic and smoked paprika – filled the house.

It was a smaller affair than Sukkot: just Leonora, Shoshanna, the Rafaeli Twins and Rabbi Akbar, with his wife and family. Despite what had happened when they last crossed paths, Shabtai embraced Ben like an old friend.

'You don't look so lost now, Mr Canaan! On the contrary, you seem to have slotted right in.'

'I'm sorry for the trouble I caused you,' Ben said, bowing his head.

'Not at all!' Shabtai winked. 'I'm relieved that everything worked itself out in the end. Besides, a little excitement is not such a terrible thing for an old bookworm like me!'

They gathered around the table in the reception room – the very spot where, all those months ago, Leonora had instructed Ben never to return to the Carmino estate. Shabtai filled a silver goblet to the brim with wine, ready to make Kiddush. But before he began, Leonora drew Shoshanna in close and placed her hands on her cheeks. In a loving voice, full of tenderness and pride, she murmured a familiar blessing in Hebrew:

'May God make you like Sarah, Rebecca, Rachel and Leah. May God bless you and safeguard you. May God illuminate his face for you and be gracious unto you. May God turn his face unto you and give you peace.'

By the end of the blessing, tears were rolling down her cheeks. Not of sadness, like the tears that had flowed in the months since Abraham's passing, but of joy. It was the joy of knowing that justice had been delivered, that all would be well despite their travails, and that she had her child to thank for this change in fortune.

Ben watched in silence. He knew that blessing all too well. Every Sabbath eve, Solly would say it over him, Judit, Max and Golda – one version for the girls and the other for the boys. Somewhere on the thoroughfare of Whitechapel Road, he was saying it now, his prayers winging their way across the world in search of his eldest son.

Ben could see Solly's face now, inches from his own. He could feel his coarse hands brushing his cheeks. For a moment, Ben even thought that he could hear his old man's voice.

After the blessings over the wine and the challah, they sat down for a convivial dinner. As the *hamin* was ladled out with spicy matbucha, baba ghanoush and thick slices of poppy-seeded bread, Ben felt strangely at home. No mention was made of London or his exploits. He was simply accepted as a peer and a friend – discussing the latest community gossip, showing off the few phrases in Judeo-Spanish that he had picked up during his stay.

After dinner, they decamped to the parlour to while away the evening. Shabtai and the Rafaeli Twins discussed *Vaychi*, that week's chapter from Genesis. Shoshanna taught Ben a new card game: Sixty-six, a favourite of her father's that he had learnt on a business trip to Westphalia and brought back with him to Constantinople.

At the end of the night, Ben said his goodbyes and Shoshanna offered to see him out. They ambled onto the front terrace, wrapped up against the chill and a little tipsy from the wine.

Shoshanna took Ben in: his flannel winter suit – the brougham waiting for him on the cobbled stones – the air of a suave gentleman whose star was on the rise.

'You're like a cat,' she mused. 'You always seem to land on your feet.'

'Well, I had to fall from a great height to find that out!'

'I heard you met with Hasan Izzet and the British Ambassador this week,' Shoshanna said. 'What did you discuss?'

'Nothing unexpected. A few outstanding matters. A very begrudging thank you.' Ben stuffed his hands into his pockets. 'And a ticket back home.'

'London?'

Ben nodded. 'Queen and Country calls.'

For a moment, Shoshanna did not reply. She was looking at that brougham. At the horses shaking their heads and kicking the ground – ready to go.

'That's good,' she said. 'Your family must be missing you. They'll be relieved to have you back.'

'Yes, I think so. I hope so. Either that, or they've changed the locks!'

'When will you be leaving us?'

'I believe the word the Ambassador used was "post-haste".'

Ben checked his pocket-watch: nearly midnight.

'I should head off. It's a long ride to Constantinople.'

He turned to face Shoshanna. The lanterns dappled her light-brown skin with faint amber. She was smiling. Her eyes were glowing and her lips were parted.

'Goodnight, Mademoiselle Carmino,' Ben said, extending a hand.

Shoshanna ignored his hand and drew him into a hug.

'Goodnight, Ben.'

They held their embrace for a few seconds longer – then she let go and Ben hopped into the brougham. Shoshanna watched him pull away into the darkness. She stayed an impulse to call after him, took a breath of cold air, and headed back inside.

It was two in the morning by the time Ben returned to Pera. The streets were deserted. Gas-lamps lit his way back to the Pierrot, where Zofia had arranged to put him up free of charge.

His only company as he gazed out the window of the brougham was the occasional vagrant, slumped in the recess of a shuttered shopfront.

He entered the Pierrot to find it as raucous as ever. On Friday nights, the parties tended to wrap up at dawn. He had become a familiar face to the more permanent guests – among them, Zofia's friend Jerome Bonaparte, who tried to lure Ben into a round of absinthe and blackjack. But Ben was not in the mood for a binge and instead went upstairs to his room to sleep off the wine.

He went straight for the basin to wash his face, patting some cold water on his cheeks and brushing his teeth. He paused in the mirror and studied his reflection, wondering, when he finally did appear at the door of 82 Whitechapel Road, whether his family would even recognise him. He walked to bed, ready to collapse – but then he caught sight of something that made him stop dead in his tracks.

A shadowy figure was sitting in an armchair in the corner of the room.

Ben's blood ran cold.

'What the hell?!' he blurted out.

The figure struck a match. In the flame, Ben saw his face: it was Radimir – lighting up a cigarillo and looking rather pleased with himself.

'God Almighty, Radimir! You gave me the fright of my life. What are you doing here?'

'What do you think? The Contessa sent me. She wants to talk to you.'

'I think I've had my fair share of intrigue thanks to Zofia. I'd rather get some much-needed sleep.'

'Of course you can go to bed, young man!' Radimir rose to his feet and gestured to the door. 'Right after you talk to the Contessa…'

Ben knew that tone: Radimir was not asking.

26

The Third Section

Ben found Zofia in the drawing room. She was wearing a silk dressing gown and leaning over a Pembroke table, where an old tattered flag had been laid. It was white, with a red crucifix in the middle and Polish words in big black print on either side. She tugged on the corners and smoothed out the wrinkles with great care.

'*Za naszą i waszą wolność,*' she intoned, reading the words on the flag. '*For our freedom and yours.*'

She looked up at Ben, who was standing in the open doorway. Radimir closed the door behind him and the two were left alone. Zofia beckoned him in. A fire was burning in the hearth and candles had been lit around the room.

'The motto of my homeland. Just over twenty-four years ago, it was the slogan of an uprising to liberate us from the Russians. And this was its banner.' She carried the flag to Ben and sat next to him. 'My father planted it atop the Warsaw Arsenal when it was taken by the rebels. It flew over our capital for one miraculous year, as he led the revolutionary ranks in a war against the Russian Imperial Army. We were on a mission to create something that our people had dreamed of for centuries, that had been denied to us by the long arm of tyranny: *an independent Poland.*'

She folded the flag and placed it on the sideboard. She looked forlorn.

'He sounds like a brave man,' Ben said.

'He was. But the Third Section took him from me. Six faceless assassins, not unlike the people who terrorised this city. They lured him to an isolated spot in Kabacki Forest, under the pretence that he was to meet with Lithuanian partisans – only to ambush him. They emerged from the trees with daggers and stabbed him eighty times – then left him to bleed out in the snow, as a warning to his Polish compatriots. And it did not stop with him. By the time the uprising was crushed, they had delivered the same fate to my mother, my two sisters, my nephew, my last surviving grandparent. They would have killed me too, were it not for a colleague of my father – one General Umiński – who saved my life and spirited me away from Warsaw. Since then, our nation has been reduced to a Russian garrison, and I must spend the rest of my days as an exile.'

Ben did not know exactly what to make of this new side to Zofia. Her customary irony and humour had been stripped away. Behind it was a wound that had never healed.

'The tragedy of my story,' Zofia said, 'is that it is common. How many people have been hounded from their native land and chased across the seas? How many houses of wisdom have been sacked and burned? How many millions have been tortured and killed in the name of conquest? Is it even possible to number them?'

With each question, Ben felt himself drawn back into his own history. One that he had set aside like a book in the Harleian stacks. The Canaans who had come before him – speaking another language, in a world that he had never seen and which, for the most part, no longer existed.

He shook his head solemnly.

'What did you tell the police were the White Death's last words?' Zofia said with venom in her voice, *'Dl'ya Rodiny*? Do you know what that means?'

'Yes,' Ben murmured. 'I was told it means: *For the Motherland.*'

Zofia laughed scornfully. 'And that, Mr Canaan, is the great sickness of our age. The relentless pursuit of land, wealth and resources at the cost of human dignity. People reduced to tallies on a death toll. Countries reduced to lines on a map drawn by a handful of men without a care for those who live in them. Now a functionary can sign a piece of paper and hellfire will rain down on countless innocents that he will never meet. And what makes this sickness so uniquely evil is its capacity to seduce us with the riches that it siphons from this chaos. We have built palaces, banks and courts of justice on its foundations. The tea you drink, the tobacco you smoke, the sugar in your coffee, every strand of cotton in your evening suit – facilitated by the exploitation and destruction of people like you and me.'

Zofia opened the drawer of the sideboard and removed a stained leather case folder. She handed it to Ben.

'This is the enemy that we are fighting. Go on. Read.'

Ben unclipped the case folder. It was packed with documents.

The first thing he saw was a photograph. A sepia-toned calotype of a dozen uniformed men and women in a magnificent reception hall. It was titled: *Winter Palace, St Petersburg – Tretoye Otdeleniye Initiation – 1st January 1845*. He squinted at their faces. They were all so young, some in their early twenties but most looking even younger than him. Their hands were held behind their backs, their postures were upright – honed by military discipline.

Then a print of a man's portrait. He was middle-aged, seated against a plain black background. He had the sallow, unremarkable face of a bureaucrat and he presented an air of cool equanimity. Only his eyes gave away the menace: small dark points that pulled in the light. The title of this one was simply: *ORLOV*.

There were profiles of Third Section agents. The White Death himself was among them: forties, birth-name redacted, Status One – the highest rank. Lists of 'completed targets' in London, Vienna, Stockholm, Budapest, Constantinople. Blueprints and sketches of a military complex in a barren mountain range.

The last item in the case folder was a handcrafted bronze locket. On the front was an engraving of a howling wolf and a crescent moon. He opened the locket to find a miniature portrait inside. It was a girl of no more than five or six years old, with a white semi-transparent shawl covering her head and a black dress decorated with silver coins.

'Who is this?' he said, holding the locket up to Zofia.

'Don't you recognise her?'

Ben looked again at the locket. There was something familiar about that face. It seemed to speak to him across time.

'That, Mr Canaan, is the woman you now know as Marta Mavros. Whom you once knew as Elizabeth de Varney. But her real name was Zoya Sa'id. She was born in Dagestan – an inhospitable wilderness east of the Caucasus Mountains. It is a region that, for a half a century, has been embroiled in a brutal war against the Russians, who seek to conquer the land and subjugate its people. She was the daughter of a lieutenant in the

Avar Tribe: Islamic warriors beating back the Russian advance. And, like hundreds of children from this tribe, the Russians kidnapped her – raised her as a Russian subject – trained her to be an agent of the Third Section – and sent her out to do Orlov's bidding. To kill on his command. Almost every Third Section agent was recruited in this way: through systematic abduction and indoctrination. The gradual erasure of an entire race of people. So you see: even Marta was a victim of this conflict – her life snatched away for reasons beyond her control.'

Ben looked again at her portrait. Ever since that summer, he had wondered who she really was. Questioned whether anything they had shared was real. Blamed her first for abandoning him, then for lying to him, and finally for her crimes. But now it was as though he had peeled back the layers of the enigma, one by one, to reveal a kernel of truth beneath a thousand lies. That is all she was in the end: a once-innocent child crushed by the slow march of empire.

He closed the locket, put it back in the case folder and handed the folder to Zofia. 'How did you get these documents?'

'When Marta slipped the noose, she gave them to me. It was all the intelligence that she could amass on her employers. I would have shown you earlier, but I wasn't sure how you'd react – and we had more pressing matters to attend to at the time.'

Ben rubbed his eyes. He was so tired. He had shot his bolt foiling the White Death. But it felt as though, in the grand scheme of things, he had done nothing at all. The war, as Redcliffe had put it, raged on. The violence and the injustice continued unpunished. And there was nothing he could do to stop it.

'What happens now?' he asked.

'As far as Orlov and the Third Section are concerned,' Zofia said, 'I have my own plans. Orlov is based in the Caucasus, conducting Third Section operations from Mount Elbrus, in the north. The Avars are waging a campaign against them – to end their incursion into the Caucasus and take back the Avar children who have been kidnapped. I have been corresponding with their leader, a rather fearsome general by the name of Imam Shamil. He has spent many years trying to drum up support for their cause among the Great Powers, to no avail. But I intend to join the fight by ferrying him all the intelligence and support that I can. It's the best chance we have of bringing an end to the Third Section. And as for you... You are to go home and live your life. Take solace in the fact that, in some small way, you changed the course of history.'

Zofia clasped her hands around his and pulled him in close.

'And who knows? Maybe, one day, you'll be called up again by fate to do the same.'

Ben could picture it now: Zofia on horseback, in a keffiyeh, flanked by mountain-warriors in the snowy wilds of Georgia – a romantic heroine drawn from the pages of books that he had read as a child.

But for him, this was the end of the line. The adventure would continue, but he had reached his stop. And what waited for him as he stepped onto the platform was precisely what he had left behind: Saturday tea – Bevis Marks – Canaan & Sons.

He felt the tiniest pang of regret. The inexplicable desire to take up arms with Zofia and fight back against the evil that she had described.

'It's funny,' he chuckled. 'When Radimir dragged me up here, I thought you were going to seduce me!'

Zofia laughed pityingly and brushed a lock of hair from his brow.

'What you need, my dear, is an education. But you won't find it at university. Only life can teach you such things. You must simply have the courage to go out and find it.'

She rose to her feet. 'Now, Mr Canaan, you may go to bed!'

The sombre spell that Zofia cast was abruptly broken. Ben made for the door. But before he left, he turned back to Zofia, who had taken the flag that her father had flown over a land that she would never see again, and placed it in a drawer.

'It's a powerless feeling, Contessa,' he said. 'To know that no matter what we do, there will always be some greater evil waiting in the wings. It's like cutting the head off the Hydra.'

Zofia could only shrug. 'Well, someone must do the cutting!'

Ben made his way back to bed. 'Touché!'

27

A Brush with History

It was the second day of the new year of 1855. Journalists had gathered in the rain on the Bankalar Caddesi in Galata – the financial heartland of Constantinople. They huddled under black umbrellas, some of them peering through box-cameras on tripods, outside a grand four-storey building with a banner draped across the front:

BANQUE FAMILIALE CARMINO

Standing under an awning by the door were Shoshanna, Leonora and the Rafaeli Twins. The Minister of Finance, a recent appointee by the name of Ali Sefik, was consulting with them in an undertone. He offered Shoshanna a ceremonial gavel and wooden anvil. She placed the anvil on the doorframe at the entrance to the bank and raised the gavel.

Ali Sefik turned to the crowd and proclaimed in Turkish:

'I hereby declare the re-establishment of the Carmino Family Bank!'

Shoshanna banged the gavel: three sharp *cracks* that echoed down the Bankalar Caddesi. And just like that, the institution that had brought the Carminos fame and fortune – that for a short time had been consigned to the dust-heap of history – was reborn.

Ben watched proceedings unfold from the ranks of journalists. He had received a letter from Shoshanna the previous week, inviting him to the unveiling. It had been a busy period over Christmas and New Year. He had not seen or spoken to her once, so he had cleared out the day for this occasion. As the doors were thrown open and Shoshanna was escorted inside, she glimpsed Ben across the Bankalar Caddesi. Amid the pomp and circumstance, she gave him a little wave.

After the unveiling, there was a reception in the bank. It was, as expected, a crowd of investors, ministers of the Sublime Porte and well-to-do friends from Constantinople's elite circles. They gathered in the foyer, where a marble statue of Abraham Carmino had been erected. There was an almost casual air about him, as though caught in the middle of a spontaneous conversation, standing with one hand in his pocket and the other splaying open a copy of Shakespeare's Sonnets. Engraved on the plinth was his name and a Hebrew word: *Abba – Father*.

The Rafaeli Twins, now joint chairmen of the bank, opened the reception by introducing their new directors. Chief among them was Edouard Pradervand – Abraham's Swiss protégé who, after running Lombard Odier in Geneva, had relocated to Constantinople to continue his mentor's legacy. 'This is the greatest honour of my life,' he addressed his audience in French. 'To follow in the footsteps of a man who now numbers among the great scions of business. He had a brilliant mind, he was deeply principled, and above all he was a righteous man. I am proud to have been called his friend.'

Several figures from the political set who were in attendance, including Ali Sefik, vaguely recognised Ben. Like so many, he had heard the rumours about this mysterious young Englishman who, though it could not be spoken about openly, had won the favour not just of the Carminos, but of the Sultan himself.

'And what is it you *do*, exactly, Mr Canaan?' Ali Sefik asked slyly, as he sipped his coffee.

'I'm a tailor by training,' Ben replied.

His answer seemed to confound Ali Sefik. 'Well, do you have a card? I am on the hunt for a new suit.'

'Not on me,' Ben smiled.

Ali Sefik wagged a finger. 'You should always keep a card on your person, young man! How else will you drum up business here in Constantinople?'

Ben entertained the Finance Minister's overtures with superficial charm. But his focus was on Shoshanna, who was standing by Abraham's statue, in conversation with Jacob. The earnest suitor was talking at great length, and she was nodding politely. Her arms were folded, her gaze was steady and assured, and she radiated confidence. She was truly in her element, right where she belonged among the great and the good.

Ali Sefik's chatter seemed to fade into the background. Ben had not come to socialise. His boat to London had been arranged for the following afternoon, and he had wanted to take one last chance to say goodbye to Shoshanna – not by letter, not via Ismail, but in person.

For the briefest moment, Ben saw another life. Wandering into an old café in Stamboul for coffee and fried *lokma*. Services at the Ahrida on Friday nights. Elderflower cordial on balmy summer afternoons. Picnicking at the mineral springs of Beykoz. The occasional night of debauchery at the Pierrot, nursed the morning after with a hot, peppery shakshuka and *tursu suyu*, the local pickle juice. The view of Constantinople from the prow of a *kayik* as it passed beneath Galata Bridge.

Time passing. Growing old.

'I should be off,' he murmured, shaking hands with Ali Sefik, 'Lovely to meet you.'

'And you, Mr Canaan. I hope to see you around Constantinople.'

Ben turned away and slipped unseen out of the Carmino Family Bank.

The harbour on the shores of Galata, where Ben had first set foot on Turkish soil, was as busy as ever. The beggars were washing their feet at the embankment, still crying 'English Johnny' and 'Dis-Donc' at the passing soldiers. Shirtless ruffians gathered on the decks of trawlers moored along the waterfront and were cannonballing into the Golden Horn. Even now, after so many months of war, military steamships were docking – bringing the most gravely injured troops for treatment that was not available on the battlefield. The warbling cry of the *Dhuhr* came echoing from on high, as muezzins called the city to prayer.

Ben sat on the terrace of Yanni Tokatlia, his favourite waterfront coffeehouse. He was in a suit and silk tie, complete with a gold chain for his pocket-watch. A leather suitcase lay at his feet on the pavement. He had shaved and his hair was combed down the middle, smoothed with a drop of Macassar oil.

Suddenly the light was blotted out. A silhouetted figure stood over him.

Ben shielded his eyes to get a better view. 'I don't recall asking for a parasol!' he joked.

'Apologies,' the man stepped aside. 'I was just wondering: is this seat taken?'

He gestured to the chair on the other side of the table, where Ben had left his knapsack. 'By all means,' Ben said, retrieving it. 'Try the cardamom coffee. It's the house speciality.'

The man sat down. He was a few years older than Ben, dressed in austere navy blue, with a broad face, high cheekbones, somewhat large ears and wavy black hair. He was darkly handsome, his youth hardened by experience.

He ordered a coffee, opened his journal and began writing. Ben studied him: the pencil frayed from chewing, the jumble of heavily edited prose filling each page to the margins. The man was writing in Russian. Ben raised his guard.

'Hard at work?' he asked.

'Oh, yes!' the man replied. 'These are my "sketches".'

Ben saw black marks under the man's nails. Not ink – that would have stained a darker shade. It was gunpowder residue, impacted from repeated exposure.

'A Russian officer so far behind enemy lines?' Ben remarked. 'Paint me intrigued.'

The man looked at Ben askance. He laid down his pencil and closed his journal. 'I have protected status. Just passing through.'

'As am I,' Ben replied – then, after an awkward pause, 'Don't worry: I'm not an informant. You were in Sevastopol?'

'Indeed I was. That's what I'm writing about.'

'Siege still going on, I take it?'

'We're in for the long haul now. It's not as pretty or noble as the politicians would have us believe. No prancing horses, no streaming banners, no beating drums. Just blood, suffering and death. Committed by otherwise decent men who, this time last year, were leading otherwise decent lives. Compelled by the institutions of government to partake in an evil as old as time itself.'

'And,' Ben added, 'against people with whom they have no quarrel. I mean, look at them…' He gestured to the British, French and Ottoman soldiers walking jauntily down the waterfront. 'What does a chap from Yorkshire have against another chap from Siberia? Neither wants to die on the icy plain of a foreign land. In any other circumstance, they might just as easily have been chums.'

As Ben spoke, the Russian watched the soldiers – then turned a keenly observant eye on Ben.

'Crimea has taught me a special kind of pain,' he said. 'Day in, day out, you watch your friends die with an abruptness, an arbitrariness, that shakes the soul. As grief overwhelms you, an image forms in your mind of the monsters who took them. But then, in fleeting moments, you catch glimpses of the other side. You see those men shed the same tears for their own fallen brothers. And you realise in your shame that they are not monsters. They are as helpless and confused as you are.'

He and Ben shared a look of mutual understanding.

'Every last one of us,' the Russian continued, 'East and West, is at the mercy of history. Dragged about in the river of time – until, at some point, it deposits us on its banks and flows swiftly on.'

A bell clanged from a steamer on the harbour.

'That's me!' Ben declared. He dropped a few lira on the table. 'That was a stimulating little chat. Let me cover your coffee.'

'That won't be necessary,' the man replied.

'Please – I insist.'

The man reluctantly accepted Ben's gesture. 'Thank you.'

'What is your name?' Ben asked as he scooped up his bags.

The man extended a hand: 'Lev. Lev Tolstoy. And yours?'

'Ben. Ben Canaan.'

'Well, Ben Canaan – safe travels.'

They shook hands. Lev returned to his journal and Ben marched off to the steamer. The other passengers were climbing up the ramp, showing their tickets to the attendants and handing their luggage to the stewards. He was about to join them, when he heard a voice yelling across the harbour:

'Oi! Not so fast!'

He spun round and saw the Carminos' carriage barrelling down the esplanade and onto the quay. Eydir was at the reins and Ismail was leaning out the window, cupping his hands around his mouth as he hollered at Ben. Behind Ismail, sitting with her hands on her lap, was Shoshanna – in the red dress that she had been wearing the night Ben first laid eyes on her.

They descended from the carriage and approached Ben.

'Did you think you could escape without a proper goodbye?' Shoshanna said.

'How did you know I was here?'

'I found out from the embassy that you were travelling today. And when I paid a visit to the Pierrot, they informed me that you had checked out.'

Ismail slipped an arm round Ben's shoulder. 'Well, Beef Wellington: you did it. I was convinced you'd be oven-roasted within a week trying to survive this city. But you passed with flying colours. And now, much as I hate to admit it: it's a little sad to see you go.' He handed Ben his silver matchbox. 'A parting gift. Next time you're smoking a gold-leaf cigarette, spare a thought for poor Ismail Bilan!'

'Don't feel too sorry for him,' Shoshanna laughed. 'This one has found gainful employment as an assistant in the family bank. I suspect he'll be just fine.'

'Then congratulations are in order!' Ben exclaimed. 'You'll be wrapped in gold leaf by the time you're finished!' He ruffled Ismail's hair and raised an eyebrow at Shoshanna. 'And I suppose congratulations are in order for you too…'

'What do you mean?' Shoshanna frowned.

'I saw you and Jacob at the reception yesterday. I assume…'

But Shoshanna shook her head. 'I rejected his proposal. He had come to convince me, in a last-ditch effort, to reconsider. But my mind is made up.'

'I'm sorry to hear that. Your mother can't be too pleased.'

'As it happens,' Shoshanna replied, 'she's not as upset as I thought she'd be. The truth is, I can't wake up every morning to someone I simply don't love.' She glanced quickly at Ben, and then away again. 'I have to follow my heart. I need someone who is a little more…'

'Peculiar?'

Shoshanna smiled and reached into her purse, producing her own parting gift. It was a circular object about the size of Ben's palm. He opened the front-piece: it was a compass. And engraved on the inside was a phrase – *May the wind be always at your back.*

'In case you get lost as you go through life,' Shoshanna said, 'hold onto this and it will guide you home.'

Ben pocketed the compass. 'Thank you, Shoshanna.'

'No: thank *you*, Ben. You did something extraordinarily brave, for someone you barely knew, in circumstances that were fraught with danger. I don't know what waits for you in London, or what kind of life you will lead, but I do know that you are a good man. And I am deeply grateful for everything you have done. Not just for me – but for my family, for my father's legacy and for our nation.'

It was the first time in Ben's life that anyone had thanked him so passionately for anything. And the feeling it inspired made the thrill of being a Good-for-Nothing pale in comparison.

She took his hand.

'If ever you need help, call on me. I'll be here.'

Ben nodded.

'I won't forget you,' was all he said.

They were interrupted by the bell: the last call before setting sail. Shoshanna let go of Ben's hand, he slung his knapsack on his back and he ascended the ramp to the deck. He had a first-class ticket, and as soon as he was on board a steward carried his bags to the executive suite, hoping for a generous tip from this well-dressed gent.

Ben went over to the guard-rail and looked down at Shoshanna and Ismail, who were still standing on the pier. As the boat detached from the harbour, and Shoshanna and Ismail mounted their carriage, it suddenly struck Ben that he had no photograph of her. His only image of her was now in his memory.

As the ship picked up pace, Eydir whipped the reins. The carriage wheeled round and vanished in the afternoon hubbub of markets, ministries and mosques.

Constantinople floated by. A city of killers, a city of secrets. The jewel at the centre of the world. A city which, now that he was leaving, already seemed to have forgotten him. He had arrived a stranger, and was departing a stranger.

Soon there was nothing around him but the cold blue expanse of the Sea of Marmara. Constantinople had fallen below the horizon.

28

An Interview at No. 10

It was a Saturday morning like any other: eight o'clock and Whitechapel was still half-asleep. A boy glued posters for a Yiddish comedy to the stone columns of the Pavilion Theatre. Now and then, a barge on the Thames let out a sluggish boom and flocks of pigeons fluttered from the rooftops. The biting February cold was softened by the sweet aroma of Mrs Adler's beigels and cinnamon rolls.

Ben strolled up Whitechapel Road. He saw the sign for Canaan & Sons take shape not fifty yards ahead. He was feeling apprehensive. He had returned, just as unexpectedly as he had disappeared, and he had no idea how his family would react.

He glanced up to the top floor: the curtains of his attic-room were drawn. He strained his ears, listening for any sign of life on the other side. But he heard nothing. No clatter of plates, no loud arguments. Had they moved out?

He knocked – two firm raps – and braced himself.

The floorboards creaked. The lock unlatched. The door edged open...

His mother was standing before him. She was exactly as he remembered: hands red from cooking and scrubbing, hair tied up in a bun, an apron round her waist. The instant she saw him, she let out an involuntary cry. '*BENJY!*'

Ben spread his arms and cracked a vintage smile. 'What did I miss?'

She practically threw herself at him. Months of anxiety came pouring out in tears, kisses and reprimands. 'Why, you broke your nose! What happened to you?'

Max and Golda came tearing down the entrance hallway.

'Surprised to see me?' Ben laughed.

'Not in the slightest!' Max declared. 'I was quite confident that you would return in due course! I even theorised with Papa where your peregrinations may have taken you—'

Ben silenced Max with Ismail's matchbox, surreptitiously dropped into the boy's hands. 'A box of lucifers for the aspiring gentleman and his cigar collection…'

Ruth bustled after him, hands on her head. 'Solly, come quickly! He's back!! Broken his nose – the *meshugeneh!*'

As Ben approached the kitchen, two more people blocked his path: Judit and his pal 'Hurricane' Jack Hauser.

'Benjamin E. Canaan!' Judit grinned, running into his arms. 'You're in for a world of pain!'

'What the hell are you doing here?' Jack exclaimed.

'What the hell are *you* doing here?!' Ben shot back.

Judit held up her left hand: a simple gold band on her ring finger.

Now it was Ben's turn to process the shock. 'You're marrying a Good-for-Nothing? I hope you know what you're getting into—!'

Jack laid a reassuring hand on Ben's shoulder. 'Benjy, Benjy… Those days are long gone. I've finished my apprenticeship and I'm a junior hand now!'

'Well, Mazal Tov to you both,' Ben kissed them heartily on the cheeks. 'We'll talk about this later!'

He found Herschel at the kitchen table, still in his pyjamas and buried in *News of the World*. 'Morning, Benjamin,' he stifled a yawn. 'What's all this commotion?'

'*Uncle Herschy.*'

'What *is* it, Benjy—' Herschel folded up his paper – and nearly fell off his chair. 'Benjy! Where in the Lord's name have you been?! You're dressed awfully fancy,' Herschel fingered the lapel of Ben's suit. 'Look at those brogues! Is that a *gold* watch-chain? And since when do you wear silk ties?! Pull up a pew, confess!'

'Let me say hello to *Bubbe* and *Zeyde* first!' Ben dropped his knapsack on the kitchen table and bounded into the living room.

Hesya was sitting in her rocking chair, knitting a shawl. But Tuvia's fireside throne was empty. An unread copy of the JC was folded neatly on the side-table, next to the old man's glasses and an empty tumbler.

'I couldn't bring myself to cancel his subscription,' Hesya said.

Ben sat in Tuvia's chair and laid his hands on the armrests. He could feel the heat of the fireplace and could see through the kitchen onto a narrow view of Whitechapel Road.

'It was quick, Benjele. He didn't suffer – *Gottze Dank!*'

At that moment, his father appeared in the doorway, in his familiar grey suit, with that sober expression. Subtle details gave away the passage of time and the agony that he had endured in Ben's absence: his facial hair speckled with grey – the tiniest hint of crow's feet in the corners of his eyes.

Ben rose and Solly pulled him into a warm embrace.

'Boychik,' he whispered. 'I missed you.'

'I did too,' Ben said.

They gathered round the breakfast table to fill Ben in on all that had happened since his departure. After he fled from Sergeant O'Connor, the police mounted a manhunt, turning over the boxing clubs, pubs and music-halls of Whitechapel and keeping an eye on the Canaan family should he return. But after a fortnight, they moved on. Trouble came thick and fast in the East End, and there were bigger fish to fry than Benjy Canaan.

The Canaans conducted their own search, questioning every Jewish kid in Whitechapel with even the slightest connection to Ben. Jack and Leo even paid a visit to the Docklands, but Yanky gave them short shrift: 'If you do find him, tell him to get lost!' It was as though Ben had dropped off the face of the earth.

For the first month, they took turns keeping vigil at the window. All they could talk about were the circumstances of his disappearance and the mystery of his whereabouts. The days got shorter. The nights got colder. As time went by, they started to come round to the possibility that their eldest son was not missing, but dead.

Judit and Jack announced their engagement in early December. When Jack asked Solly for Judit's hand, Solly granted it on one condition: that Jack commit himself fully to the workshop and behave like a *mensch*. So Jack forswore all drinking, thuggery, finagling and brawling, and the nuptials were set for the end of May.

On the cusp of the new year, their *simcha* was overshadowed by tragedy: Tuvia's passing. He was taken ill with a serious bout of pneumonia and collapsed at the dinner table on the last night of Hanukkah. A physician was called in and they discovered that what they had thought were gallstones was in fact prostate cancer. The disease had metastasised and was inoperable. Tuvia had weeks left with nothing to do but prepare for his final voyage.

Hesya did not leave his bedside. The morning he died, a few days shy of the New Year, he asked her to look out the window and describe the view of London. She talked of the seagulls over the Thames, the chimney-divers darting across the rooftops, the itinerant costermongers pouring through Whitechapel.

When she turned back to check on him, he had slipped away.

It did not take long for the conversation to shift its focus to Ben. 'Where *did* you disappear to, Benjy?' Herschel probed, on the edge of his seat, 'Tangiers? You know, I had a business venture there – many moons ago…'

'It wasn't Tangiers, Uncle Herschy!' Ben said. He was about to mention Constantinople, when he remembered Redcliffe's warning: that there were some things not even his nearest and dearest should be privy to. 'But it was far away,' Ben added. 'And there was, I admit, an element of danger.'

'*Danger?!*' Ruth exclaimed. 'What kind of danger?'

But Ben gave an evasive shrug. 'I just can't say. I'm sorry.'

'War?' Max squeaked from the end of the table. He struck a match and smiled knowingly at Ben.

'Max,' Ben replied. '*Don't play with fire at the dinner table.*'

They sat talking for almost the entire day. As darkness set in, the fatigue caught up with Ben and he retreated to his old attic-room. It was a comforting sight. Ruth and Judit had left fresh sheets and a warm face-towel. The window where he had so often stood, dreaming of escape, was open onto a view of the East End, echoing with the sound of Bow Bells. Ben collapsed into bed. He was sound asleep the moment his head hit the pillow.

*

Not long after Ben's return to London, the Canaans received another letter from Her Majesty's Executive – yet again, an invitation from Viscount Palmerston. Except this time, Palmerston had left the Home Office. As of the previous week, he was Britain's new Prime Minister. Moreover, only Ben was invited – and he was instructed in no uncertain terms to bring back the letter and daguerreotype that he had lifted from Palmerston's jacket.

That Wednesday at nine o'clock sharp, Ben arrived at 10 Downing Street. It was a miserable enclave of decrepit terraced flats reeking of sewage – scarcely easier on the eye than the Whitechapel ghetto.

The solitary doorman outside No. 10 brusquely waved him in. It was even worse on the inside. The walls were cracked and the corridors stank of coal-smoke and bleach. Everything seemed slightly lopsided, as though the building was sinking at an angle into the subsoil. A grubby locale appropriate for the grubby underhand dealings of high politics.

He met with Palmerston in the Pillared Drawing Room. The Prime Minister seemed worn out. Was it the last six months, or had one week of leadership already taken its toll?

'Mr Canaan,' Palmerston said drily. He was as supercilious as ever, though Ben could sense a begrudging respect as they shook hands.

The PM was wearing a beautifully crafted suit. A black woollen double-breasted frock coat, cut into tails. A high collar, with large silk lapels. Dyed ivory buttons. Sleek pantaloons held up by silver-buckled braces.

'Prime Minister,' Ben said. 'A very fine suit, if I may say so.'

'Your father's handiwork.'

'How fitting!'

'It was an excellent job. Your tribe has a knack. Fast minds, faster fingers. Which reminds me...' He beckoned with a curled digit. 'Hand it over.'

Ben gave the letter and daguerreotype to Palmerston. He pocketed the contents. 'Matters of national security must remain under lock and key.'

They sat at Palmerston's partners desk and the Prime Minister lit a cigar.

'Congratulations on your new appointment, Prime Minister,' Ben said.

Palmerston gave a vicious grin. 'Aberdeen lost the confidence of the House. The lily-livered do not last long in politics – let alone in times of war. We need a more forceful approach to policy. But I did not summon you here to discuss party matters.'

Ben could not tell whether he was about to receive a medal or a jail sentence.

'I know *everything* that transpired,' Palmerston continued. 'Whether or not you intended it, you performed a vital role for the Turks and the Russians have suffered a calamitous setback. According to our intelligence, the Third Section has been recalling its agents from the Continent and their backers – industrialists and plutocrats of the Tsar's court – have been withdrawing their support for the organisation. The Russians are divided, their casualties mounting, and they have been left to lick their wounds.'

'What about Count Orlov?'

'Orlov, or someone like him, will crawl out of the woodwork with yet another dastardly scheme. Such is espionage – such is war – and such, I am afraid, is life. The world is full of battles we cannot win on our own. Mysteries that, every now and then, can only be solved with *bespoke* methods.'

Ben nestled into his chair. Palmerston's agenda was coming into focus. 'Is this a job interview, Prime Minister? If I had known, I would have worn my lucky cufflinks.'

'Consider the last few months an extended audition.'

Ben mulled Palmerston's proposition. 'Does this job have a title?'

'Not officially,' Palmerston mused. 'More of a special arrangement. Think of yourself as a globetrotting detective of sorts. Providing an invisible but invaluable service. And if you accept our offer, you and your family will enjoy the protection of Her Majesty's government. You may look forward and we will handle the sordid business of looking over your shoulder.'

'Unless I cross you?' Ben countered.

'Of course,' Palmerston clamped his teeth around the cigar. 'But you would not be so foolish as to do that, would you?'

The same sensation shivered through Ben as when he had looked at Prince Mavros across the baccarat table – at the Sultan in the Imperial Throne Room of Topkapı Palace. The allure of power and the threat that lay behind it.

Palmerston was staring at Ben, as inscrutable as a lizard baking in the sun. Ben's next words hovered on the tip of his tongue.

Epilogue

In the months following Ben's return to London, normal life resumed. Ben worked hand-in-glove with his father and Jack at Canaan & Sons. All the humdrum tasks that he had once spurned – picking up fabrics from the Ganguly brothers in Spitalfields, preparing bastes for first fittings, tapering trouser legs – brought him an unexpected pleasure. Canaan & Sons chugged along, though now with added prestige thanks to its association with Palmerston. There was none of the 'scale' that Max dreamt of, but business was good.

The Canaans' financial troubles were alleviated by the hundred pounds that Ben had brought back with him. One evening after dinner, when everyone else had gone to bed, Ben sat his parents down at the kitchen table and placed the money before them. It was theirs to pay off their debts and invest in the business. But it came with two conditions. Firstly, they were not to tell a soul, not even his siblings. And secondly, they were not to ask him how he had acquired the money – the most he could give them was an assurance that he had come by it honestly. Ben gave them every penny he had left, save for a single gold sovereign.

When he was not working, Ben spent less time with the Good-for-Nothings and at the boxing club, and more time with his family. He accompanied his father to Bevis Marks on the Sabbath, as he had done when he was a child. He was on time for

Friday night dinner. He stayed for the entirety of Saturday tea. He chatted to Max about what the boy was reading and gave him recommendations – particularly the books by Schopenhauer and Spinoza that he had loved so much as a schoolboy.

For the first few weeks, the Canaans were worried that Sergeant O'Connor might show up again. But Ben seemed unconcerned. It was never discussed explicitly, but Solly was convinced that it had something to do with Ben's meeting with Palmerston.

There was one last loose end for Ben to tie up. At the beginning of April, he crept under cover of night to the Isle of Dogs. Yanky escorted him to Lennie's office at Ah Jiang's. Lennie had heard that Ben was back in London, earlier than he would have liked – but he had also heard rumours of a clandestine visit to 10 Downing Street. From Lennie's perspective, this was either a golden opportunity to have one of his boys within earshot of the executive, or it presented a risk that Ben would sell him out.

Usually, there were only two ways to leave the Dogs: death by natural causes – or death by unnatural causes. But Ben wanted to call it quits on his own terms. Lennie would need to find some other East End no-goodnik to smuggle his Webley Longspurs. And, if Lennie let him be, Ben would keep *shtum* about his operations. Not friends, but definitely not enemies.

Lennie was not accustomed to being put in a corner. But he decided not to look a gift horse in the mouth. Before he swept out of Lennie's office, Ben dropped the gold sovereign on the desk: compensation for the expense of his Disappearing Act. And with that, Ben and London's most notorious gangster were even.

In May, Judit and Jack were married under the *chuppah* in the courtyard of Bevis Marks, followed by lunch for the Canaans and their closest friends. Ben sat at a long table surrounded by familiar faces – mates from his *cheder* days, now married with children of their own. Young professionals in small family businesses, one or two already balding, a little plump, looking ever more like their fathers. The world had moved on in Ben's absence. He was unsure who had changed more.

After the main course, Solly stood up and clinked his glass with a teaspoon. He placed his hat against his chest and looked out at his small audience – the dutiful servant, for once, was master of proceedings.

'Nearly two thousand years ago, the Second Temple in Jerusalem – the *Beyt ha-Mikdash* – was destroyed by the Romans. In the wake of this catastrophe, a period of exile began that has continued to this day. Now we are a diaspora, dispersed across the world. A nation that does not know what it feels like to have a land that is truly our own. Denied the most basic dignities by powers that either hate us or simply do not care for us.'

The gathering had fallen quiet. It was a moment of solemnity amid the celebration.

'And yet…' Solly continued, 'here we are. By the grace of God, I sit at a table, in a *shul*, at my daughter's wedding, surrounded by family, friends and colleagues. This land may not be our own, but we are not *on* our own. Why? Because, though the Land of Israel is no more, we carry its promise in our hearts – and by sharing that promise, we make a home in one another. That is what makes us Jews: not who we are as individuals, but who we are as a people.'

He placed one hand on Judit's shoulder, the other on Jack's – but he was looking straight at Ben.

'What is a Jew without his tribe? What are we without each other?'

He raised his glass.

'God bless us all.'

The guests too raised their glasses and cried: *Sh'koyach!*

They returned to work that Monday: up at six, a quick breakfast, then an hour to prepare the shop. By the time Solly came downstairs from the main house, Ben and Jack had swept the floors, hung the ready-to-wear garments on the racks and thrown open the blinds. Ben and Solly worked front-of-house, while Jack was on cutting duty in the workshop at the back. Ben was alert to Solly's needs as they tended to clients – fathers of brides-to-be, bar-mitzvah boys, a cantor looking for a new frock coat.

At the end of the morning, as Ben was folding up a pile of dress shirts, he caught Solly looking at him from the shop counter. His father was leaning forward, studying him with a contented smile.

'I dreamed of this my whole life,' Solly said suddenly.

Ben folded the last shirt and placed it on the shelf. 'But I made you wait for it, didn't I?'

Solly nodded, lost in thought.

'You know, Max has really taken to the business side of things!' he piped up again. 'The stitching and the sewing, not so much. He says it's "menial". That it's a waste of time if you want to build "equity".'

'The way he talks…' Ben muttered.

'He's got bigger ideas in his head than needles and threads. It took me a while to realise that that's not such a bad thing. You want your children to be better than you are.'

Ben came over to the counter. He had never seen that look from his father. The love was there, kept in check as always.

But it was shot through with something else. Was it pride? Or regret? He could not tell.

'I'm sorry for pulling you out of school, Benjy,' Solly said gently. 'I know it hurt you. I know you too dreamed of bigger things. I should have listened to you.'

Ben felt his chest tighten at those words.

'I also know,' Solly added, 'that you have… *other plans*. I don't need to know the details. But I want to make something clear to you.' He placed a hand on Ben's arm. 'I trust you, Benjy. To make the right decisions. To do well for yourself.'

Ben bowed his head. 'Thank you, Papa.'

'Whatever you choose, let the choice be yours. Go down that path with your head held high. Your mother and I will always love you.'

He patted Ben affectionately on the cheek.

Then the bell at the door tinkled. A rather short, slender gentleman entered. He had a pencil moustache and was wearing a pinstripe suit with a pair of polished gold-buckled Oxfords, a pince-nez and a top hat. He smiled politely.

'Welcome to Canaan & Sons, sir,' Solly said. 'How may we assist you?'

'Please do not mind me,' he said, 'I am just browsing.'

His accent was central European, difficult to pinpoint. Without waiting for a reply, he turned to a rack of cravats.

'I'll check on Jack in the workshop,' Solly whispered to Ben. 'You take care of the gentleman.'

Solly left Ben and this well-heeled client alone. Ben watched the man idly flicking through the cravats. Only when he heard the muffled thud of the workshop door closing did he address the stranger.

'Palmerston sent you?' he asked.

The man's gaze settled on Ben.

'What gave it away?'

'Call it a hunch. A man who can afford those shoes doesn't need to wander around Whitechapel on a Monday morning looking for a cravat. Let alone a *second-hand* cravat on sale.'

'You are as quick on your feet as they claim,' the man said. 'My name is Gustav Bruckner. My superiors have been liaising with Viscount Palmerston concerning a matter of some importance.'

He handed a letter to Ben. It was sealed with red wax and stamped with a heraldic crest.

'What kind of matter?'

'Read the letter,' Gustav replied. 'No doubt it will be of interest. Your tickets are enclosed.'

No sooner had Ben taken the letter than Gustav made for the door. As he pulled it open and the bell rang once more, he looked back at Ben.

'Welcome aboard, Mr Canaan.'

'Happy to be of service.'

Gustav nodded approvingly and walked off.

Ben stared at the letter in his hands. His father was still in the workshop.

As he broke the seal and read the contents, he was struck by the same feeling that had gripped him when he had first set foot in Constantinople: the irresistible thrill of the unknown.

'Right!' he said under his breath. 'Königsberg, Prussia…'

But first, he had a suit to finish.

THE SERIES CONTINUES IN

DEATH ON THE PEARL RIVER

COMING 2026

AVAILABLE AND COMING SOON FROM PUSHKIN VERTIGO

Jonathan Ames

You Were Never Really Here
A Man Named Doll
The Wheel of Doll

Simone Campos

Nothing Can Hurt You Now

Zijin Chen

Bad Kids

Maxine Mei-Fung Chung

The Eighth Girl

Candas Jane Dorsey

The Adventures of Isabel
What's the Matter with Mary Jane?

Margot Douaihy

Scorched Grace

Joey Hartstone

The Local

Seraina Kobler

Deep Dark Blue

Elizabeth Little

Pretty as a Picture

Jack Lutz

London in Black

Steven Maxwell

All Was Lost

Callum McSorley

Squeaky Clean

Louise Mey

The Second Woman

John Kåre Raake

The Ice

RV Raman

A Will to Kill
Grave Intentions
Praying Mantis

Paula Rodríguez

Urgent Matters

Nilanjana Roy

Black River

John Vercher

Three-Fifths
After the Lights Go Out

Emma Viskic

Resurrection Bay
And Fire Came Down
Darkness for Light
Those Who Perish

Yulia Yakovleva

Punishment of a Hunter
Death of the Red Rider